EMPIRE TRILOGY

J. G. Farrell was born in Liverpool in 1935 and spent a good deal of his life abroad, including periods in France, America and the Far East. Among his novels, *Troubles* won the Faber Memorial Prize in 1970 and *The Siege of Krishnapur* won the Booker Prize in 1973. In April 1979 he went to live in County Cork, where, only four months later, he was drowned in a fishing accident.

BY J. G. FARRELL

Troubles

J. G. FARRELL

PHOENIX

A PHOENIX PAPERBACK

First published in Great Britain in 1970
by Jonathan Cape
This paperback edition published in 1993 by Phoenix,
an imprint of Orion Books Ltd,
Orion House, 5 Upper St Martin's Lane,
London WC2H 9EA

An Hachette UK company

Reissued 2007

Printed in Great Britain by Clays Ltd, St Ives plc

The Orion Publishing Group's policy is to use papers that
are natural, renewable and recyclable products and
made from wood grown in sustainable forests. The logging
and manufacturing processes are expected to conform to
the environmental regulations of the country of origin.

www.orionbooks.co.uk

Part 1

A MEMBER OF THE QUALITY

In those days the Majestic was still standing in Kilnalough at the very end of a slim peninsula covered with dead pines leaning here and there at odd angles. At that time there were probably yachts there too during the summer since the hotel held a regatta every July. These yachts would have been beached on one or other of the sandy crescents that curved out towards the hotel on each side of the peninsula. But now both pines and yachts have floated away and one day the high tide may very well meet over the narrowest part of the peninsula, made narrower by erosion. As for the regatta, for some reason it was discontinued years ago, before the Spencers took over the management of the place. And a few years later still the Majestic itself followed the boats and preceded the pines into oblivion by burning to the ground—but by that time, of course, the place was in such a state of disrepair that it hardly mattered.

Curiously, in spite of the corrosive effect of the sea air the charred remains of the enormous main building are still to be seen; for some reason — the poor quality of the soil or the proximity of the sea — vegetation has only made a token attempt to possess them. Here and there among the foundations one might still find evidence of the Majestic's former splendour: the great number of cast-iron bathtubs, for instance, which had tumbled from one blazing floor to another until they hit the earth; twisted bed-frames also, some of them not yet altogether rusted away; and a simply prodigious number of basins and lavatory bowls. At intervals along the outer walls there is testimony to the stupendous heat of the fire: one can disinter small pools of crystal formed in layers like the drips of wax from a candle, which gathered there, of course, from the melting of the windows. Pick them up and they separate in your hand into the cloudy drops that formed them.

Another curious thing: one comes across a large number of tiny white skeletons scattered round about. The bones are very delicate and must have belonged, one would have thought, to small quadrupeds ... ('But no, not rabbits,' says my grandfather with a smile.)

It had once been a fashionable place. It had once even been considered an honour to be granted accommodation there during the summer season. By the time Edward Spencer bought it on his return from India, however, it retained little or nothing of its former glory, even if it did retain some of its faithful guests of the year-by-year variety, maiden ladies for the most part. The only explanation for their continued patronage (since under Edward's management the hotel went swiftly and decisively to the dogs) is that as the hotel declined in splendour the maiden ladies became steadily more impoverished. In any event they could keep on saying: 'Oh, the Majestic in Kilnalough? I've been going there every year since 1880 ... ' and the man who sold the place to Edward could claim that he had, at least, his few faithful customers who kept coming every year without fail. In the end these faithful customers became something of a millstone for Edward (and later for the Major)—worse than no customers at all, since they had their habits of twenty years or more; the rooms they had been staying in for twenty years were dotted here and there over that immense building and, though whole wings and corners of it might be dead and decaying, there would still be a throbbing cell of life on this floor or that which had to be maintained. Slowly, though, as the years went by and the blood-pressure dropped, one by one they died away.

From the *London Gazette*, General List:

The undermentioned relinquishes his commission on completion of service, Temporary Major B. de S. Archer, and retains the rank of Major.

In the summer of 1919, not long before the great Victory Parade marched up Whitehall, the Major left hospital and went to Ireland to claim his bride, Angela Spencer. At least he fancied that the claiming of her as a bride might come into it. But nothing definite had been settled.

Home on leave in 1916 the Major had met Angela in Brighton where she had been staying with relations. He now only retained a dim recollection of that time, dazed as he was by the incessant, titanic thunder of artillery that cushioned it thickly, before and after. They had been somewhat hysterical —Angela perhaps feeling amid all the patriotism that she too should have something personal to lose, the Major that he should have at least one reason for surviving. He remembered declaring that he would come back to her, but not very much else. Indeed, the only other thing he recalled quite distinctly was saying goodbye to her at an afternoon *thé dansant* in a Brighton hotel. They had kissed behind a screen of leaves and, reaching out to steady himself, he had put his hand down firmly on a cactus, which had rendered many of his parting words insincere. The strain had been so great that he had been glad to get away from her. Perhaps, however, this suppressed agony had given the wrong impression of his feelings.

Although he was sure that he had never actually proposed to Angela during the few days of their acquaintance, it was beyond doubt that they were engaged: a certainty fostered by the fact that from the very beginning she had signed her letters 'Your loving fiancée, Angela'. This had surprised him at first. But, with the odour of death drifting into the dug-out in which he scratched out his replies by the light of a candle, it would have been trivial and discourteous beyond words to split hairs about such purely social distinctions.

Angela was no good at writing letters. In them it would have been impossible to find any trace of the feeling there had been between them during his home leave of 1916. She had certain ritual expressions such as 'Every day I miss you more and more—' and 'I am praying for your safe return, Brendan' which she used in every letter, combined with entirely factual descriptions of domestic matters: the buying of skirts for the twins in Switzers of Dublin, for example, or the installation of a 'Do More' generator for electric light, the first of its kind in Ireland and destined (they were sure) to restore the Majestic's reputation for luxury. Any personal comment, any emotion was efficiently masked out by this method. The Major did not particularly mind. He was wary of sentiment and had always had a relish for facts—of which, these days, his badly rattled memory was in short supply (in hospital he had been recovering from shell-shock). So on the whole he was glad to learn the size and colour of the twins' new skirts or the name, breed, age and condition of health of Edward Spencer's many dogs. He also learned a great deal about Angela's friends and acquaintances in Kilnalough, though sometimes, of course, his defective memory would cause whole blocks of facts to submerge for a while, only to reappear somewhere else later on, rather like certain volcanic islands are reputed to do in the South Seas.

After he had been receiving a letter a week for a number of months he acquired a remarkable skill for reading these letters and totting up the new facts, even sometimes peering past them into the lower depths where the shadow of an emotion occasionally stirred like a pike. There would be a list of Edward's dogs again, for example: Rover, Toby, Fritz, Haig, Woof, Puppy, Bran, Flash, Laddie, Foch and Collie. But where, he would wonder, is Spot? Where are you, Spot? Why have you failed to answer the roll-call? And then he would remember, half amused and half concerned, that in an earlier letter the vet had been called because Spot had had 'a touch of distemper' but had pronounced it 'nothing serious'. In this way, thread by thread, he embroidered for himself a colourful tapestry of Angela's life at the Majestic. Soon he knew the place so well that when he went there at the beginning of July he almost felt as if he were going home. And this was fortunate because by this time, except for an elderly aunt in Bayswater, he had no family of his own to go to.

On leaving hospital he had paid a visit to this aunt. She was a meek and kindly old lady and he was fond of her, having grown up in her house. She hugged him tightly with tears in her eyes, dismayed at how much he had changed, how thin and pale he had become, but afraid to say anything for fear of annoying him. She had invited some of her friends to tea to welcome him home, feeling no doubt that a young man returning from the war deserved more of a welcome than a solitary old lady was able to provide. At first the Major appeared put out to discover her house full of guests holding teacups, but then, to the old lady's relief, he became very cheerful and talkative, talked gaily with everyone, leaped around with plates of cakes and sandwiches and laughed a great deal. Her guests, alarmed at first by this gaiety, soon became enchanted with him and for a while everything went splendidly. Presently, however, she missed him and after looking for him everywhere finally came upon him sitting by himself in a deserted drawing-room. There was a bitter, weary expression in his eyes that she had never seen before. But what else could one expect? she wondered. He must have been through horrors that peaceful old ladies (such as herself) might not even begin to comprehend. But he was alive, thank heaven, and he would get better. Tactfully she withdrew and left him to his thoughts. And in a little while he returned to the tea-party once more and seemed perfectly cheerful, his moment of bitterness amid the silent, hooded furniture forgotten.

The Major, of course, was aware that he was distressing his aunt by his odd behaviour. He was annoyed with himself, but for a while found improvement difficult. When on another occasion, hoping to divert him, she invited some young ladies to tea he dismayed everyone by the hungry attention with which he stared at their heads, their legs, their arms. He was thinking: 'How firm and solid they look, but how easily they come away from the body!' And the tea in his cup tasted like bile.

And there was yet another thing that disturbed his aunt: he declined to visit any of his former friends. The company of people he knew had become abhorrent to him. These days he was only at ease in the company of strangers—which made the thought of a visit to his 'fiancée' doubly welcome. It was true, of course, that he was slightly uneasy as he set off for Ireland. He was about to be plunged into a circle of complete strangers. What if Angela turned out to be insufferable but insisted on marrying him? Moreover, his nerves were in a poor state. What if the family turned out to be objectionable? However, it's hard to be intimidated by people when one knows, for instance, the nature and amount of the dental work in their upper and lower jaws, where they buy their outer clothes (Angela had delicately omitted to mention underwear) and many more things besides.

The situation in Petrograd is desperate. According to a manifesto issued by the Soviet, the evacuation of the city is going on with nervous eagerness. Trotsky has ordered that Kronstadt shall be blown up before it is surrendered. .

It was the early afternoon of July 1st, 1919, and the Major was comfortably seated in a train travelling south from Kingstown along the coast of Wicklow. He had folded his newspaper in such a way as to reveal that in Boston Mr De Valera, speaking about the peace treaty signed the day before yesterday, had said that it made twenty new wars in the place of one nominally ended. The Major, however, merely yawned at this dire prediction and looked at his watch. They would shortly be arriving in Kilnalough. In Kingstown Theda Bara was appearing as Cleopatra, he noted, Tom Mix was at the Grafton Picture House, while at the Tivoli there was a juggler 'of almost unique legerdemain'. Another headline caught his eye: SATURDAY NIGHT'S SCENES IN DUBLIN. IRISH GIRLS SPAT UPON AND BEATEN. A party of twenty or thirty Irish girls, assistants of the Women's Royal Air Force at Gormanstown, had been attacked by a hostile crowd ... jostled, maltreated, slapped all along the street. Whatever for? wondered the Major. But he had dozed off before finding the answer.

'As a matter of fact, it is,' the Major was now saying to his fellow-passengers, 'though I'm sure it won't be my last. To tell the truth, I'm going to be married to a ... an Irish girl.' He wondered whether Angela would be pleased to be described as 'an Irish girl'.

Ah, sure, they smiled back at him. So that was it. Indeed now one might have known, they beamed, there was more to it than a holiday, sure there was. And God bless now and a long life and a happy one ...

The Major stood up, delighted with their friendliness, and the gentlemen stood up too to help him wrestle his heavy pigskin suitcase out of the luggage net, patting him on the back and repeating their good wishes while the ladies grinned shyly at the thought of a wedding.

The train rattled over a bridge. Below the Major glimpsed smoothly running water, the amber tea colour of so many streams in Ireland. On each side mounted banks of wild flowers woven into the long gleaming grass. They slowed to a crawl and jolted over some points. The banks dived steeply and they were running along beside a platform. The Major looked round expectantly, but there was nobody there to meet him. Angela's letter had said without fuss, factual as ever, that he would be met. And the train (he looked at his watch again) was even a few minutes late. There was something about Angela's neat, regular handwriting that made what she wrote impossible to disbelieve.

A few minutes passed and he had almost given up hope of anyone coming when a young man appeared diffidently on the platform. He had a plump, round face and the way he carried his head on one side gave him a sly air. After some hesitation he approached, holding out his hand to the Major.

'You must be Angela's chap? I'm dreadfully sorry I'm late. I was supposed to meet you and so on.' Having shaken the Major's hand, he retrieved his own and scratched his head with it. 'By the way, I'm Ripon. I expect you've heard about me.'

'As a matter of fact I haven't.'

'Oh? Well, I'm Angela's brother.'

Angela, who recorded her life in detail, had never mentioned having a brother. Disconcerted, the Major followed Ripon out of the station and threw his suitcase, which Ripon had not offered to carry, on to the back of the waiting trap before climbing up after it. Ripon took the reins, shook them, and they lurched off down a winding unpaved street. He was wearing, the Major noted, a well-cut tweed suit that needed pressing; he could also have done with a clean collar.

'This is Kilnalough,' Ripon announced awkwardly after they had ridden in silence for a while. 'A wonderful little town. A splendid place, really.'

'I suppose you've lived here some time,' the Major said, trying to account for Ripon's absence from his sister's letters. 'I mean, you haven't recently returned from abroad?'

'Abroad?' Ripon glanced at him suspiciously. 'Not really, no. I'm afraid I haven't.' He cleared his throat. 'I suppose the smell of the place seems strange to you, turf-smoke and cows and so on.' He added: 'I know Angela's looking forward to seeing you. I mean, we all are ... jolly pleased.'

The Major looked round at the whitewashed walls and slate roofs of Kilnalough; here and there, silent men and women stood in doorways or sat on doorsteps watching them pass. One or two of the older men touched their caps.

'It's a splendid town,' repeated Ripon. 'You'll soon get used to it. On the right a little farther down is the Munster and Leinster Bank ... on the left O'Meara's grocery and then the fish shop, we're near the sea, you know ... beyond, where the street bends, is the chapel of Our Lady Queen of Heaven, fish-eater, of course ... and then there's O'Connell's, the second best pork-butcher's ... ' Curiously, however, they passed none of these places. The Major, at least, could see no trace of them.

They were now on the outskirts of Kilnalough; here there was little to see except a few wretched stone cottages with ragged, barefoot children playing in front of them, hens picking among the refuse, an odour of decaying vegetation in the air. Reaching the top of an incline they saw the dull sparkle of the sea above a quilt of meadows and hedges. The smell of brine hung heavily in the air.

Abruptly Ripon was in good spirits, almost jubilant (perhaps even a little drunk? wondered the Major) and kept recognizing landmarks of his childhood. Pointing at the middle of a flat, empty field he told the Major that that was where he had flown his first kite; in a hawthorn hedge he had once shot a rabbit

as big as a bulldog; in the barn over there he had had a reward-
ing experience with the peasant girl who in those days used
to be cast in the role of the Virgin Mary every year for the
Christmas pageant mounted by Finnegan's Drapery Limited
... and yes, in the copse that lay on the other side of the barn
young Master Ripon, watched by all the servants and all 'the
quality' from miles around, had been daubed with the blood
of the fox (a not dissimilar experience, he added cryptically)...
and on this very road ...

Not far away the two massive, weatherworn gateposts of
the Majestic rose out of the impenetrable foliage that lined
the sea side of the road. As they passed between them (the
gates themselves had vanished, leaving only the skeletons of
the enormous iron hinges that had once held them) the Major
took a closer look: each one was surmounted by a great stone
ball on which a rain-polished stone crown was perched
slightly askew, lending the gateposts a drunken, ridiculous air,
like solemn men in paper hats. To the right of the drive stood
what had once no doubt been a porter's lodge, now so thickly
bearded in ivy that only the two dark oblongs of smashed
windows revealed that this leafy mass was hollow. The thick
congregation of deciduous trees, behind which one could hear
the sea slapping faintly, thinned progressively into pines as
they made their way over the narrowest part of the peninsula
and then returned again as they reached the park over which
loomed the dark mass of the hotel. The size of the place
astonished the Major. As they approached he looked up at the
great turreted wall hanging over them and tried to count the
balconies and windows (behind one of which his 'fiancée' was
perhaps watching for his approach).

Ripon brought the trap to a halt and, when the Major had
alighted, kicked his suitcase off the back on to the gravel
(causing the Major to wince at the thought of the fragile
bottles of cologne and macassar that it contained). Then without getting down himself he shook the reins and moved away,
calling that he had to take the pony round to the stable but

that the Major should go ahead without him, up those steps and in through the front door. So the Major picked up his suitcase and started towards the flight of stone steps, pausing on his way to inspect a life-size statue of a plump lady on horseback, stained green by the weather. This lady and her discreetly prancing horse were familiar to him from Angela's letters. It was Queen Victoria, and she, at least, was exactly as he had expected.

The Major had considered it possible that his 'fiancée' would be waiting to embrace him inside the front door, a massive affair of carved oak which was so heavy that it was by no means easy to drag open. There was no sign of her, however.

In the foyer at the foot of the vast flowing staircase there stood another statue, this time of Venus; a dark shading of dust had collected on her head and shoulders and on the upper slopes of marble breasts and buttocks. The Major screwed up his eyes in a weary, nervous manner and looked round at the shabby magnificence of the foyer, at the dusty gilt cherubs, red plush sofas and grimy mirrors.

'Where can everyone be?' he wondered. Nobody appeared, so he sat down on one of the sofas with his suitcase between his knees. A fine cloud of dust rose around him.

After a while he got to his feet and found a bell on the reception desk which he rang. The sound echoed over the dusty tiled floor and down gloomy carpeted corridors and away through open double-leafed doors into lounges and bars and smoking-rooms and upwards into spiral after spiral of the broad staircase (from which a number of brass stair-rods had disappeared, causing the carpet to bulge dangerously in places) until it reached the maids' quarters and rang in the vault high above his head (so high that he could scarcely make out the elegant gilt tracery that webbed it); from this vault there was suspended on an immensely long chain, back down the middle of the many spirals from one floor to another to within a few inches of his head, a great glass chandelier studded with dead electric bulbs. One of the glass tassels chimed faintly for a brief moment beside his ear. Then all was silent again except for the steady tick-tock of an ancient pendulum clock over the reception desk showing the wrong time.

'I suppose I'd better give this gong a clout,' he told himself. And he did so. A thunderous boom filled the silence. It grew, he could feel it growing throughout the house like a hugely swelling fruit that would burst out of all the windows. He shuddered and thought of the first moments of a heavy barrage before a 'show'. 'I'm tired,' he thought. 'Why don't they come?'

But presently a plump, rosy-cheeked maid appeared and asked if he would be the Major Archer? Miss Spencer was expecting him in the Palm Court. The Major abandoned his suitcase and followed her down a dark corridor, vaguely apprehensive of this long-delayed reunion with his 'fiancée'. 'Oh, she won't bite!' he told himself cheerfully. 'At least, one supposes she won't ... ' But his heart continued to thump nevertheless.

The Palm Court proved to be a vast, shadowy cavern in which dusty white chairs stood in silent, empty groups, just visible here and there amid the gloomy foliage. For the palms had completely run riot, shooting out of their wooden tubs (some of which had cracked open to trickle little cones of black soil on to the tiled floor) towards the distant murky skylight, hammering and interweaving themselves against the greenish glass that sullenly glowed overhead. Here and there between the tables beds of oozing mould supported banana and rubber plants, hairy ferns, elephant grass and creepers that dangled from above like emerald intestines. In places there was a hollow ring to the tiles—there must be some underground irrigation system, the Major reasoned, to provide water for all this vegetation. But now, here he was.

At one of the tables Angela was waiting to greet him with a wan smile and the hope that he had had a good journey.

His first impression was one of disappointment. The gloom here was so thick that it was difficult for the Major to see quite what she looked like, but (whatever she looked like) he was somewhat taken aback by the formality of her greeting. He might have been nothing more than a casual guest for bridge. Of course it was true, as he hastened to point out to himself, that their meeting had been both brief and a long time ago. As far as he could make out she was older then he had expected and wore a fatigued air. Though apparently too exhausted to rise she held out a thin hand to be squeezed. The Major, however, not yet having had time to adjust himself to this real Angela, seized it eagerly and brushed it with his shaggy blond moustache, causing her to flinch a little. Then he was introduced to the other guests: an extremely old gentleman called Dr Ryan who was fast asleep in an enormous padded armchair (and consequently failed to acknowledge his presence), a solicitor whose name was Boy O'Neill, his wife, a rather grim lady, and their daughter Viola.

The foliage, the Major continued to notice as he took his seat, was really amazingly thick; there were creepers not only dangling from above but also running in profusion over the floor, leaping out to seize any unwary object that remained in one place for too long. A standard lamp at his elbow, for instance, had been throttled by a snake of greenery that had circled up its slender metal stem as far as the black bulb that crowned it like a bulging eyeball. It had no shade and the bulb he assumed to be dead until, to his astonishment, Angela fumbled among the dusty leaves and switched it on, presumably so that she could take a good look at him. Whether or not she was dismayed by what she saw she switched it off again with a sigh after a moment and the gloom returned. Meanwhile the Major was thinking: 'So *that* was what she looked like in Brighton three years ago, of course, now I remember'; but to tell the truth he only half remembered her; she was half herself and half some stranger, but neither half belonged to the image he had had of her while reading her weekly letter (an image he had been thinking of marrying, incidentally—better not forget that this fatigued lady was his 'fiancée').

'Did you have a good crossing, Brendan?' she was inquiring. 'That boat can be so tiresome when it's rough.'

'Yes, thank you, though I can't deny I was glad when we got into Kingstown. Have you been well, Angela?'

'Ah, I've been dying'—a fit of weary coughing interrupted her— 'of boredom,' she added peevishly.

Meanwhile, without taking her eyes off the Major's face she had stretched out a leg under the table and begun a curious exercise with it, grunting slightly with the effort, as if trying to tread some slow-moving but resilient beetle into the tiled floor. 'Is she trying to find my foot?' wondered the Major, perplexed. Then at last, after this curious spasm had continued for a few moments (the O'Neills were either accustomed to it or pretended not to notice), a distant bell rang somewhere away in the jungle of palms. Angela's leg relaxed, an expression of satisfaction appeared on her pallid, fretful features, and an aged and uncouth manservant (whom the Major for a moment mistook for his prospective father-in-law) shambled out of the jungle breathing hard through his mouth as if he had just had some frightful experience in the scullery.

'Tea, Murphy.'

'Yes, Mum.'

Angela switched on the lamp long enough for Murphy to collect some empty cups in his trembling hands, then turned it off again. The Major noticed that old Dr Ryan was not asleep as he had supposed. Beneath the drooping lids his eyes were bright with interest and intelligence.

'I wish we could trust *ours*,' Mrs O'Neill was saying.

'It is a problem,' agreed Angela. 'What do you think, Doctor?'

Dr Ryan ignored her question, however, and silence descended once more.

'In a lot of ways they're like children,' Boy O'Neill said at length and his wife assented. 'What an extraordinarily inert tea-party!' thought the Major, who had become aware of a keen hunger and looked up hopefully at the sound of a step. But it was only Ripon, sliding apologetically into a chair beside Mrs O'Neill.

'Did you wash your hands, Ripon?' asked Angela. 'After that horse.'

'Yes, yes, yes,' replied Ripon, smiling furtively across at the Major and lounging back in a self-consciously casual manner. A moment later he threw a leg over the arm of his chair, narrowly missing Mrs O'Neill's face with his shoe (which had the wandering contours of a hole worn in the sole). 'Where are the twins?'

'They've gone to spend a week in Tipperary with friends from school. But one wonders whether the roads are really safe these days.'

'Trees have been felled on the road to Wexford. It really can't go on. Three policemen killed in Kilcatherine. The *Irish Times* said this morning that a levy of six shillings in the pound has been put on the whole electoral division. That should make them think twice.' Mr O'Neill spoke with the fluted vowels of an Ulsterman; his drawn, yellowish face had reminded the Major of the fact (recorded in Angela's letters) that the Spencer family solicitor was thought to be ill with cancer, had been up to Dublin to see specialists, had even travelled to London to see doctors there. Though the verdict had been omitted from Angela's letters to the Major, this omission was eloquent. Death. The man was dying here in the Palm Court as he nervously discussed the abomination of Sinn Fein.

'Those who live by the sword ... ' said Mrs O'Neill.

'Ah, more tea,' exclaimed Angela as Murphy once more appeared out of the jungle like some weary, breathless gorilla, pushing the tea-trolley. Mustard-and-cress sandwiches. The Major took one and cut it in half with a small, scimitar-shaped tea-knife. Weak with hunger, he put one half in his mouth, then the other. They both vanished almost before his teeth had had time to close on them. His hunger increased as he took another sandwich from the plate, ate it, and then took another. It was all he could do to restrain himself from taking two at a time. Fortunately it was now getting quite dark in the Palm Court (though still only mid-afternoon) and perhaps nobody noticed.

Meanwhile Angela (who had once, so she said, sat on the lap of the Viceroy) had begun to talk languidly about her childhood in Ireland and India, then with a little more energy about the glories of her youth in London society. Soon she became quite animated and the tea grew cold in the cups of her guests. Ripon, while champagne was being quaffed out of his sister's slippers, kept catching the Major's eye and winking as if to say: Here she goes again! But Angela either failed to notice or paid no attention.

Handsome young rowing Blues in full evening dress plunged into the Isis or the Cam at a word from her. Chandeliers were swung from. Her hand was kissed by distinguished statesmen and steady-eyed explorers and ancient pre-Raphaelite poets and God only knew who else, while Boy O'Neill sucked his moustache and grunted in surprise and alarm at each fresh act of immoderation and his wife took on a primly disbelieving look, rather hard about the mouth, as if to say that not everyone can be taken in by all the nonsense they hear; while Ripon smirked and winked and Dr Ryan appeared to doze, motionless with age. The Major listened with amazement; never would he have suspected that this was the same person (part girl, part old maid) who had written him so many precise and factual letters, filled as they were with an invincible reality as hard as granite. Angela talked on and on excitedly while the Major pondered this new facet of his 'fiancée's' character. At the same time, with the gloom thickening into a mysterious, tropical night, he guiltily wolfed the entire plate of sandwiches. At last it was so dark that the light had to be switched on, which brought everyone back to earth with a bump. The sparkle slowly faded from Angela's eyes. She looked tired, harassed and ordinary once more.

'Ah, things were different before the war. You could buy a good bottle of whiskey for four and sixpence,' Mr O'Neill said. 'It was those beastly women that started the rot.'

'They took advantage of their sex,' his wife agreed. 'They blew up a house that Lloyd George was going to move into. They damaged the Coronation Chair. They dug up the greens of many lovely golf-courses and burned people's letters. Is that a way for a woman to behave? It never pays to give in to such people. If it hadn't been for the war ... '

' ... In which the women of England jolly well pulled their weight in the boat, more than their weight, I take my hat off to them. They deserved the vote. But the British public doesn't give in to violence. They didn't then and they won't now. Take that Derby in which the woman killed herself. The King's horse was lying fifth and was probably out of the running ... but if Craiganour had fallen the anger of England would have been terrible to behold.'

Abruptly the Major noticed that Viola O'Neill, whose long hair was plaited into childish pigtails, who wore some kind of grey tweed school uniform, and who could scarcely have been more than sixteen years of age (plump and pretty though she was), was nevertheless looking him straight in the eye in a meaningful way. Embarrassed, he dropped his gaze to the empty plate in front of him.

As for Ripon, he was plainly bored. He had resumed a more orthodox sitting position and, with legs crossed, was tapping experimentally at his knee reflex with a teaspoon. The Major watched him drowsily. Now that he had eaten he was finding it an agony to stay awake and at the same time was painfully aware of being hunted by Miss O'Neill's importunate eyes. Fortunately, just as he was feeling unable to resist for a moment longer some overpoweringly sedative remarks that Boy O'Neill was making about his schooldays, there was a diversion. A large, fierce-looking man in white flannels stepped from behind a luxuriant fern at which the Major had happened to be looking with drugged eyes. He said: 'Quick, you chaps! Some unsavoury characters have been spotted lurking in the grounds. Probably Shinners.'

The tea-drinkers goggled at him.

'Quick!' he repeated, twitching a tennis racket in his right hand. 'They're probably looking for guns. Ripon, Boy, arm yourselves and follow me. You too, Major, delighted to make your acquaintance, I know you'll want to be in on this. Come on, Boy, you're not too old for a scrap!'

In the semi-darkness the old doctor stirred imperceptibly. 'Damn fool!' he muttered.

The fierce man in flannels was Angela's father Edward, of course. There was no mistaking that stiff, craggy face with its accurately clipped moustache and broken nose (at least not for the Major, who had studied his daughter's letters so assiduously). The broken nose, for example, was the result of having boxed for Trinity in a bout against the notorious Kevin Clinch, a Roman Catholic and a Gaelic speaker whose merciless fists had been a byword in those days (so Angela said, anyway). The savage Clinch (the Major remembered with a chuckle), mouthing incomprehensible oaths through his bleeding lips, had got as good as he gave, until he had finally succeeded in flattening 'Father' with a lucky punch. Time and again the elder Spencer had been battered to the canvas, time and again he had risen to demonstrate English pluck and tenacity against the superior might of his Celtic adversary. The Major imagined him stretched out at last, his fists still twitching automatically like the limbs of a decapitated chicken. What difference had it made that Edward had ended the contest horizontal and motionless in spite of all his efforts? Why, none at all. He had proved his point. Besides, the game's the thing, it doesn't matter who wins. Besides, Clinch was a stone heavier.

As he followed the others down a corridor the Major

noticed Edward's ears, which he also knew about—that is, he knew why they were so remarkably flattened against his skull, the reason being his mother's horror of ears which stuck out. They had been taped back against his skull throughout his childhood, an intervention which the Major considered to have been a happy one. The rugged forehead, the heavy brows, the stony set of the jaw would have been too harsh if they had not been countered by those winsomely folded ears. But Edward turned at this moment and glanced back at the Major, who saw in his eyes a mildness and intelligence, even a hint of mockery, that did not go at all with his leonine features. For a moment he even suspected that Edward had divined his thoughts ... but now they had reached Edward's study, a room smelling strongly of dogs, leather and tobacco. It turned out to contain a staggering amount of sporting equipment piled haphazardly on an ancient chaise-longue scarred with bulging horsehair wounds. Shotguns and cricket stumps were stacked indiscriminately with fishing-rods, squash and tennis rackets (excellent ones made by Gray, Russell's of Portarlington), odd tennis shoes and mildewed cricket bats.

'Take your pick. More in the gun room if those won't do. You'll find the ammo over there.' Edward pointed at a drawer which had been removed from a sideboard and was lying on the floor beside the empty, blackened grate. A huge and shaggy Persian cat was asleep on the pile of scarlet cartridges it contained, scarcely bothering to open its yellow eyes as it was lifted away and deposited on a brass-mounted elephant's foot.

By now they had been joined by two or three other men in white flannels who were also rummaging for ammunition to suit their respective firearms; evidently a tennis match had been in progress. The Major, who had no intention of shooting anyone on his first day in Ireland if he could possibly avoid it, tugged dubiously at a ·22 rifle which had become entangled with a waterproof wader, a warped tennis racket and hopelessly tangled coils of fishing-line. Ripon, meanwhile, had discovered a plumed cocked hat on the mantelpiece and having shaken a cloud of dust from it was adjusting it in front of a mirror. He then removed one of a pair of crossed rapiers from the wall and stuck it through the buttoned arch of his braces. This done, he picked up a javelin he found standing in the corner behind the door and began to tease the cat with it.

'Oh, for God's sake, Ripon!' muttered Edward testily. And then: 'If everyone's ready we'll sally forth.'

'How incredibly Irish it all is!' thought the Major wonderingly. 'The family seems to be completely mad.'

A tall, stout man in a dark-green uniform with a shiny black leather belt was standing in the foyer, picking his nose and looking abstractedly at the white marble bottom of the Venus figure. He stared in surprise at Edward, who was still holding the tennis racket in one hand but now brandished a service revolver in the other, as if about to take part in some complicated gladiatorial combat. He shifted his gaze from Edward to the men in white flannels with shotguns broken over their arms. Nor did he seem reassured by the appearance of Ripon with his javelin and plumed hat.

'All right, Sergeant. Just show us where you think the blighters may be lurking.' The sergeant indicated respectfully that all he wanted to do was use the telephone; the men might be dangerous.

'All the better. We're more than a match for them. Now, tell me what makes you think they're hanging around here ... ' And Edward put a paternal hand on the sergeant's shoulder and steered him out on to the sunlit drive.

As the makeshift white-flannelled army straggled chuckling towards the trees someone drawled: 'I suppose we should be asking if the womenfolk are safe.'

'They're safe when you aren't around, anyway,' came the reply and everyone laughed cheerfully. Ripon had attached himself to the Major and had begun to tell him about a curious incident that had occurred at a tennis party not far away at Valebridge a few days earlier. A heavily armed bicycle patrol had surprised two suspicious individuals (no doubt Sinn Feiners) tampering with the canal bridge. One of them had fled across the fields and made good his escape. The other, who had a bicycle and was disinclined to leave it, had been confident that he could outpedal the Royal Irish Constabulary. Although for the first fifty yards the fugitive, pedalling desperately, had swerved to and fro in front of the peelers almost within grabbing range, he had then slowly pulled away. By the time they had slowed their pursuit to draw their revolvers the Sinn Feiner had increased his lead to almost a hundred yards. He slowed too, however, when the first shots began to whistle round his ears and had possibly even decided to give himself up when disaster struck the pursuers. One of the constables had removed both hands from the handlebars in order to take a steady, two-handed aim at the cyclist ahead. Unfortunately, just as he was squeezing the trigger he had veered wildly, colliding with his companions. The result was that all three had taken a nasty fall. As they had painfully got to their feet and dusted themselves off, expecting to see their quarry vanishing over the brow of the hill, they saw to their surprise that he too was slowing down. They hurriedly straightened their handlebars and, standing on the pedals to accelerate, sped towards the Sinn Feiner; the chain had come off his bicycle. Instead of awaiting capture he had abandoned his bicycle and fled into the drive of the house where the tennis party was going on. What a shock the tennis players and spectators had got when all of a sudden a shabbily dressed young man had sped out of the shrubbery and across the court to gallop full tilt into the wire netting (which he evidently hadn't seen)! Under the impact he had crumpled to his knees. But though he seemed stunned, almost immediately he began to pull himself up by gripping the wire links with his fingers. Then someone had hurled a tennis ball at him. He had turned round as if surprised to see so many faces watching him. Then another tennis ball had been thrown, and another. At this the man had come to his senses and veered along the netting in search of an opening. Not finding one he had leaped up and clung to the netting to drag himself upwards. But by now everyone was on their feet hurling tennis balls. Then one of the women had joined in, throwing an empty glass but he still managed to pull himself up. Someone (Ripon thought it might have been old Dr Ryan, the 'senile old codger' they had been having tea with) had shouted for them to stop. But nobody paid any attention. A tennis racket went revolving through the air and only missed by inches. Someone tore off his tennis shoes and threw them, one of them hitting the fugitive in the small of the back. He had paused now to gather strength. Then he was climbing again. A beer bottle shattered against one of the steel supports beside his head and a heavy walking-shoe struck him on the arm. Then, at last, a racket press had gone spinning through the air to hit him on the back of the head. He had dropped like a sack of potatoes and lay there unconscious. But when the breathless, red-faced peelers had finally arrived panting to arrest their suspect it was to find the tennis players and their wives still hurling whatever they could find at the prone and motionless Sinn Feiner ...

'Good heavens!' exclaimed the Major. 'What an incredible story! Frankly, I find it a bit hard to believe that people would throw things at an unconscious man. Did you see all this happen yourself?'

'Well, no, I wasn't actually present. But I've spoken to a lot of people who were there and ... but what I wanted to say ... '

'I must ask Dr Ryan, the "senile old codger" as you call him.'

'But I haven't finished,' cried Ripon. 'The thing is, it turned out later that this fellow wasn't a Shinner at all. He was just repairing the bridge with another workman.'

'Ah, but that's absurd,' the Major began. 'Why should they be running away if they weren't ... ?' But Ripon's attention had been diverted and he was no longer listening. With a contemptuous smile he was watching his father lead the way into the cedar grove, beyond which the 'unsavoury characters' were thought to have been seen (though by whom was still unclear to the Major).

Revolver and tennis racket at the ready, Edward had now reached the broken wall of loose stones that separated the cedar grove from the orchard. The orchard was a large one (there was an even bigger one on the other side of the road and in better condition, the breathless and yellow-faced O'Neill had just informed the Major), thickly planted and stretching over almost three acres from the kitchen garden to the road; at one time this orchard alone must have provided a great harvest of fruit, but for some years the trees had gone without pruning; consequently the apples were left for the most part sunless, shrivelled and bitter on trees that had grown as thick as hedges.

Edward was looking around cautiously. He stepped over the wall. There was a rustle in the undergrowth. He fired two deafening shots. A rabbit flew away, careering wildly through the trees. A man in flannels at Edward's side snapped shut his shotgun and fired both barrels. The noise made the Major's stomach lurch. It was the first time in months that he had heard gun-fire.

The sergeant was looking dismayed but helpless as Edward stepped back over the wall, smiling.

'Both missed. No shifty individuals in the undergrowth. Perhaps we'd better have a look through the out-houses just to make sure, though.' He led the way through the orchard and into the kitchen garden which was protected from the north-easterly wind by a high wall. A number of cabbage whites fluttered peacefully here and there in the late afternoon sunlight, but there was no other sign of life. One by one they trailed through potting-sheds, a laundry house, a small conservatory glowing with ripe red tomatoes, the apple house (in which great mounds of green apples had been piled almost to the ceiling without any apparent thought for their preservation), an empty barn, the garages which housed a Daimler and a

31

Standard, empty stables with feed-boxes still stuffed with dusty straw ... and then they straggled back again into the sunshine.

'Let's finish that set,' one of the men in flannels said. 'I think the whole thing was just a bally ruse of Edward's to avoid facing my deadly serve.'

The party disintegrated. While the tennis players strolled back to the courts, unloading their guns, the policeman continued, though somewhat resentfully, to poke through the buildings that had already been searched. The Major was uncertain what to do: should he return to his 'fiancée's' side? Perhaps by now the tea-party would be over and a tête-à-tête would be possible. He lingered with Ripon, however, and accompanied him to retrieve the javelin which he had just hurled at a mudstained plaster nymph arising incongruously from a bed of cabbages. It had missed the nymph's plump stomach by a few inches and transfixed a giant cabbage a few feet farther on.

'I say, Edward,' a voice floated back to them. 'I don't think much of your local sleuths.' The sergeant, who had just emerged from a second inspection of the barn, avoided the Major's eye.

Coming to the edge of the orchard at a point where the drive touched it at a tangent, the Major saw a girl in a wheel-chair. She was holding up two heavy walking-sticks and trying to use them as pincers to grasp a large green apple that hung out of her reach. Ripon hesitated when he saw her and whispered 'Oh Lord, she's seen us. She's absolutely poisonous.'

'Don't go away,' the girl called. As they approached she added: 'My name is Sarah. I know who you are: you're Angela's Major and you've just arrived from England for a holiday.' 'Ah, for a holiday?' wondered the Major.

'You see, I know everything that goes on ... including everything about Ripon, don't I, Ripon? Everything about what young Ripon has been up to in Kilnalough recently. He's like an evil little cherub, don't you think so, Major, with those round cheeks and curly hair.'

'You're cruel,' the Major said lightly. And though her eyes were clear and grey and the backs of her hands sunburned (which suggested that she might be rather modern) and her hair dark, shining and very long, dividing round her nape and falling over her chest, and though she was quite beautiful, all things considered, the Major thought that perhaps Ripon was right and she was, as he had said, poisonous.

'One of the things I know about Ripon is that he constantly tells lies, isn't that so, Ripon? He even tells lies to innocent young girls who don't know any better than to believe him, that's true, isn't it, Ripon? No, Major, don't look so startled, I'm not talking about myself. Young Ripon would have to get up early in the morning before he caught me believing one of his yarns. So now you know why Ripon has to be nice to me (though I'm sure he says spiteful things behind my back). I know everything. Are you going to be nice to me, Ripon?'

'Yes, yes,' mumbled Ripon, who, with his head on one side, did in fact look somewhat discomfited. 'You always make such a fuss when you know very well that we all dote on you.'

'Well,' said the Major. 'I know one or two things about *you*, Sarah. Your father is the manager of the only bank in Kilnalough and you give piano lessons to private pupils in your father's home behind the bank. I hope I haven't got you mixed up. No? You've had a grand piano brought down from Pigott's in Dublin. In order to get it into the house you had to remove the legs and then replace them, I understand ... What else do I know? Let me see, your name is Devlin, isn't it? I'm sure I know some other things but my memory is terrible these days.'

'Angela told you all that, of course. But you've forgotten the most important thing.'

'What's that?'

'The fact that I'm a Catholic. Yes, I can see that she told you but that you regard it as a fact too shameful to mention. Or perhaps you regard it as good manners not to mention such an affliction.'

'What absolute nonsense!'

'Pay no attention, Sarah got out of bed the wrong side as usual.'

'Be quiet, Ripon! It's not nonsense at all. Ripon's father calls us "fish-eaters" and "Holy Romans" and so on. So does Ripon. So will you, Major, when you're among the "quality". In fact, you'll become a member of the "quality" yourself, high and mighty, too good for the rest of us.'

'I hope not to be so bigoted,' said the Major smiling. 'Surely there's no need to abandon one's reason simply because one is in Ireland.'

'In Ireland you must choose your tribe. Reason has nothing to do with it. But let's talk about something else, Major. Is it true what they say (because, of course, I hear all the gossip), is it true that Angela's Major had to stay in hospital so long because he wasn't quite himself, so to speak, in the head?'

'Ah,' thought the Major, nettled, 'she's cruel ... cruel ... but then life in a wheelchair must be terrible.' He tried to picture himself in a wheelchair for the rest of his life and it did indeed seem terrible. All at once he felt extremely tired remembering the breathless, swaying cabin on board the mail boat, remembering also an interminable conversation he had got into with some army chap on his way to Dublin Castle, drinking brandy and soda in the bar, on the subject of cricket, and the afternoon seemed endless, endless.

'I was looking at the flowers which have run wild over by the summerhouse,' Sarah was saying, 'and I heard the shots. Were you hunting that policeman? How peculiar! And then what was I doing? Yes, I was going to steal an apple and you caught me in the act.'

'Let me help you steal it,' the Major said. 'I'm sure it will give you indigestion though.' He reached up to detach the apple and it fell with a flurry of leaves into Sarah's lap.

'Thank you, thank you,' she exclaimed, sinking her pretty white teeth into the apple and making a face because it was so tart. 'As a reward, Major, and you too, Ripon, I shall allow you

to wheel me back to watch all those fat men playing tennis ...
or rather, no, the Major shall have the honour of wheeling me
because I hurt his feelings just now by saying he wasn't
quite himself, and I want to make amends and, besides, he
won't think me so nasty if he wheels me.'

'Ah, she's cruel,' thought the Major, his feelings hurt
afresh. Nevertheless he took hold of the wheelchair and began
to push her. And, curiously enough, he did feel a little better
as he pushed her up the drive and thought that perhaps she
was not quite as nasty as he had supposed.

'Actually,' Ripon said, 'it was one of the appalling Shinners
we were hunting, not the policeman.'

'Ah, a Shinner,' Sarah replied absently. 'That's a different
matter altogether.' And she fell silent as they made their way
slowly up the drive and round past the garages to where they
could hear the ping of tennis rackets and the sound of voices
in the still evening.

The Majestic's grounds were laid out on such an expansive
scale that the Major was surprised to find that Edward's game
of tennis was taking place on a rather cramped and grassless
court tucked in the right angle formed by the dining-rooms and
another wing of lighter and less weatherworn stone, evidently
an addition to the main building to cope with the hotel's
former popularity. This court had an advantage for spectators,
however: outside the French windows there was a terrace
with comfortable deck-chairs which the Major, who was
exhausted, eyed hopefully. Sarah had changed her mind about
watching the tennis and had dismissed Ripon and himself
before reaching their destination. No sooner was she out of
earshot when Ripon had said: 'She can walk perfectly well, of
course, without that wheelchair. That's just to get sympathy.'
Seeing the Major's disbelief, he added: 'I've seen her walking
perfectly well when she thought no one was looking. I know
you don't believe me but you'll see, you'll see.'

'What an odious young man,' thought the Major. 'No

wonder Angela didn't mention him in her letters.' But nobody else was taking an interest in his arrival at the hotel, so for the moment he was obliged to remain in Ripon's company. Besides, Ripon had at last made up his mind to head in the direction of the deck-chairs that stood invitingly unoccupied on the terrace and the Major was aching to sit down.

Before he could reach them, however, he was intercepted by a maid with the news that the ladies wanted to speak to him. Looking round, he saw that a number of elderly ladies were gathered round a table at the far end of the terrace in a corner sheltered from the breeze. They waved and beckoned eagerly as he looked in their direction; they had evidently been in considerable trepidation lest he pass by without seeing them. As he walked over to introduce himself their anticipation increased visibly.

'Yes, yes, Major,' one of the ladies said with a smile. 'We already know who you are, we've heard such a lot about you from dear Angela and we do hope you're better. It must have been very alarming for you.'

'Much better, thank you,' replied the Major and as he was introduced to Miss Johnston, Miss Bagley, Mrs Rice, Miss Porteous, Mrs Herbert, and Miss Staveley (without, however, being able to identify clearly who was who) he wondered just how Angela had described the prolonged attack of 'nerves' which had accompanied his convalescence. But the ladies were becoming impatient with the long introductions and with the little speech of welcome to the Majestic which followed, delivered by the only lady whose name and face had remained firmly cemented together, Miss Johnston. 'Ask him, ask him!' they murmured, clutching their shawls and stoles around their shoulders, for by now the westering sun had all but left the terrace, blotted out by the great mass of the Majestic, and presently they would have to go indoors.

'We should like to know', began Miss Johnston impressively, 'whether you had tea this afternoon in the Palm Court.'

'Tea? Why, yes, thank you, I did,' replied the Major,

staring at them in surprise. The ladies were exchanging significant glances.

'Thank you, Major. That was all we wanted to know,' Miss Johnston said in clipped tones and the Major felt himself to be dismissed.

In the meantime, to the Major's relief, Ripon had sloped off somewhere and there was a prospect of being able to relax undisturbed in one of the deck-chairs by the tennis court. Hardly had he sat down, however, when Ripon reappeared with a glass of beer in his hand and sat down beside him. Without offering the Major a drink he began to make comments in a confidential tone about anyone who happened to stray within his field of vision. The old ladies? Permanent residents 'battening on the poor old Majestic like leeches, impossible to get rid of, most of them won't even pay their wretched bills unless one gets a bit sticky with them ... ' That poor old blighter sitting by himself near the summerhouse, the chap with the drop on the end of his nose? 'Used to be a friend of Parnell and a man of great influence with the Parliamentary Party. These days no one speaks to him, he's a dreadful old bore ... ' That young fellow with the pale face lurking on the steps down to the next terrace? 'The twins' tutor ... but since they don't need a tutor (or refuse to have one, it comes to the same thing) the chap never does a stroke, always lurking around and toadying to Father. I can hardly bear to look at his neck, his collar always looks like a dirty, bloodstained bandage. Frightful fellow. Another thing, I have it on reliable authority that he has a cloven hoof; he has been observed bathing.'

Ripon fell silent. Sarah was approaching with Angela, who wanted to know if the Major had met her 'best friend in the world' ... the person without whom she didn't know what she would do in Kilnalough, where life was so dull and the people, although kindness itself, so uncultured that one hardly knew what to say. Did the Major know that, apart from the one in the vestry at St Michael's and perhaps one at the chapel (she didn't know about that) and two or three broken-down old things here at the Majestic, Sarah was the only person in Kilnalough who owned a piano and that this piano had been brought down from Pigotts of Dublin? The Major, as he listened and nodded politely, began to wonder, not for the first time, whether Angela was conscious of having written him so many letters. Could it be, he wondered as Angela explained how the beast's legs had been sawn off and re-attached, that this was a case of automatic writing, that one night in every week she would throw back the bedclothes and with staring eyes and arms outstretched, clad only in a shimmering nightdress, walk mechanically to her writing-desk and set to work?

Sarah said: 'Angela, how are you these days? I see so little of you.'

'Much the same,' Angela murmured. 'Much the same.' And there was silence for a moment except for the sound of scuffling feet and hard breathing from the near-by tennis court. Brightening, however, she added: 'But how are *you*, Sarah? Life must be such a trial for you—yes, I know it must be—the things all the rest of us take for granted and yet you're like a perfect angel, never a word of complaint!'

'Oh no, that's not true at all. I'm evil and bad-tempered and always complaining but you're so good yourself that you don't even notice it.'

'Well,' said Angela, 'I'm sure that's not true but, anyway, it's so nice to be having a conversation that's not about Home Rule and Nationalism and so forth, which is all we ever seem to talk about these days. I'm sure London's not what it used to be before the war (everyone says it's not) but at least there's still conversation. Brendan, you must tell us all about it, we're becoming hopelessly provincial although even in Kilnalough we hear the most tantalizing rumours.'

But the Major was at a loss to find anything to tell them. The few chats he had had with his aunt, pleasant though they had been, would certainly not qualify as conversation in Angela's eyes. And as to what the tantalizing rumours might refer to he had no idea. In any case before he had time to reveal his ignorance Edward Spencer called up from the tennis court: 'See that the Major gets himself a room, Ripon, will you? Show him the ropes and·... ' He was interrupted by a flurry of agile volleying at the net ... 'and all that sort of thing,' he added lamely, picking up the ball, which had ended in the net at his feet. And then Angela had wandered away absently and was helping a very old lady, whom the Major provisionally identified as Miss Bagley, to wind her wool.

'If I were you, Major,' Ripon said gesturing up to the left, 'I should aim for a room up there somewhere around the third floor ... that part of the place is in reasonable condition by the look of it.' He must have noticed the Major's look of astonishment because he added: 'A lot depends on how the roof is. We're not as watertight as we might be ... though the weather does seem fairly settled at the moment.'

Could it be that Ripon was actually suggesting that he should go and forage for a room by himself while he remained slumped in a deck-chair? A moment later and there was no doubt of it. Ripon said: 'In my experience it's usually best to have a look before the sun goes down because sometimes, you know, one finds that not all the lights are working.'

'How incredibly ... well, *Irish!*' thought the Major bitterly. The fellow might at least have collared a servant and told him to show him up to a room. And was one expected to draw one's own bath? However, he would no doubt have accustomed himself to the idea since the quickest way to find a bed and a bath was plainly by not depending on the Spencers, had not the wretched, cruel (though crippled) girl Sarah not immediately divined his suffering and said: 'Ripon, you can't possibly let the Major who looks so pink and exhausted and offended wander all over the hotel by himself trying to find a pillow on which to lay his head. Major, you mustn't let the thoughtless and inconsiderate Ripon treat you this way.' A surge of anger took hold of the Major. He would gladly have strangled her.

As he stood up Ripon said: 'Oh, the Major doesn't mind fending for himself, do you?' Then, possibly concluding that the Major did, after all, mind, he added: 'I'm going upstairs anyway so I may as well give you a hand.'

Ripon got to his feet and led the way out, but not before Sarah had caught the Major's sleeve and said: 'I'm sorry ... I'm always saying stupid things that come into my head.'

She must have known, of course, that that would only make things worse—but no, perhaps she really wanted, in spite of everything, to be forgiven.

The room he found, though dusty, was a pleasant one on the third floor facing the sea. He had chosen it after looking at only three or four others. Ripon had disappeared immediately, but arrangements, he hoped, had been made for someone to clean it and make up the bed later on. In the meantime he had unpacked his suitcase and was glad to find that his bottles of cologne and macassar were unbroken after all; for some time he had been intending to achieve a smarter appearance, hoping that this might dissipate the notion that he was unstable and suffered from 'nerves'. Having arranged the bottles on the dressing-table beside his silver hairbrushes he investigated the adjoining bathroom. A great gush of rust-coloured water came out of the taps at first, but then gradually it cleared to a pale amber and though it never became quite warm enough for comfort he endured it and felt better afterwards.

It was true that there was a curious smell in the room, a sweetish and disturbing smell which lingered even when he opened wide the French window on to the balcony. But he decided to forget about it and enjoy the splendid view over the series of terraces descending to the sea, until at last he heard the distant boom of the gong and made his way downstairs in search of the dining-room.

He found the Spencers waiting for him around a dimly lit table above which a faint aura of exasperation seemed to hang. He assumed that they were displeased at being made to wait for him. As soon as he made his appearance Edward picked up a heavy hand-bell and rang it vigorously. This done, he went to a small concealed door in the oak panelling (which the Major took to be a broom cupboard) and whisked it open. An elderly lady stepped out. She was dressed entirely in black except for a white lace cap pinned haphazardly to her faded bundle of grey hair. She was evidently blind, for Edward led her to the table and sat her down before instructing her in deafening tones that Brendan, that was to say the Major, Angela's Major, had come home, home from the war ...

'Angela's Major,' she murmured. 'Where is he?'

And the Major was apologized to and led forward to kneel beside the chair while the old lady ran a withered hand over his features. Suddenly she cried petulantly: 'That's not him! That's someone else!' and there was confusion for a moment while old Mrs Rappaport (for the Major had identified her as Angela's widowed grandmother) was shifted into a position suitable for addressing the steaming plate of brown soup in front of her. A silver spoon was put in her hand, a napkin was tied round her neck and, still protesting feebly, she began to siphon up her soup with great rapidity.

Thereafter the meal became lugubrious and interminable, even to the Major who thought that in hospital he had explored the very depths of boredom. Edward and Ripon were annoyed with each other for some reason and disinclined for conversation. The tutor apparently did not eat with the family; at any rate he was nowhere to be seen. The food was entirely tasteless except for a dish of very salty steamed bacon and cabbage that gave off a vague, wispy odour of humanity. But the Major did not really mind. He was hungry once more and chewed away with a weary ferocity. Indeed, he was light-headed with fatigue and as he chewed his thoughts kept wandering to the bed that awaited him, as a bridegroom throughout a long wedding-feast might contemplate his bride.

In the farthest shadowy reaches of the dining-room a hand-ful of guests dotted here and there at small tables occasionally revealed their presence by a cleared throat or a rattle of silver. But silence collected between the tables in layers like drifts of snow. Once in the course of the meal a brief, querulous argument broke out at the other end of the room; someone complained that his private jar of pickles had been used without his consent (it seemed to be the old man Ripon had described as a 'friend of Parnell' but the Major could not be sure); but then silence returned, and once again the clinking of cutlery. Why are we all sitting here in shadowy silence clinking our chains like souls in perdition? Even in Kilnalough, he felt sure, in the wretched whitewashed cottages he had seen or in the parlours behind the straggling shop-fronts there would be identical shadowy figures clinking in silence as they ate their meals around a hearth. And it was too much for him, tired as he was, to endure. For this was the Major's first night in Ireland and, like a man struggling to retain his consciousness as he inhales the first fumes of chloroform, he had not yet allowed himself to surrender to the country's vast and narcotic inertia. He would leave the Majestic tomorrow, he told himself, or the day after, at latest. He would settle his business with Angela and go. After all, he had never really believed that they would get married. At most it had never been more than a remote possibility.

The meal progressed to some form of apple pudding which the Major, gorged on bacon and cabbage, declined politely. Edward and Ripon maintained their sullen feud. (What the devil was it all about?) Old Mrs Rappaport ate noisily and voraciously. As for Angela, his erstwhile 'fiancée', she seemed to have exhausted herself completely with her afternoon's evocation of the splendours of her youth. Pale and listless, oblivious of her Major's return from the war or of her ritual 'every day I miss you more and more', she toyed with her napkin ring and kept her eyes, unfocused and unseeing, on the sparkling silver crown of the cut-glass salt-cellar in front of her.

When at last it was over (no question of the women retiring

while the men drank port; at the Majestic everyone retired together, 'like a platoon under fire', thought the Major sourly), and in the pitch-black corridor of the third floor he felt his hand close over the handle of the door to his room the Major was assailed by an immense sensation of relief and surrender. With a sigh he opened the door.

Inside, however, he received a truly terrible shock. Either he was in the wrong room or his bed had not been made up! But he *was* in the right room: his suitcase was there, his bottles of cologne and macassar were standing on the dressing-table.

He had no sheets to sleep in.

Now this was really too much! He picked up a china pitcher and dashed it savagely against the wall. It made a terrible crash as it splintered. But then silence descended, the all-absorbing silence of the mild Irish night. A squadron of fat brown moths zoomed clumsily in through the open window, attracted by the light. He closed it and sat disconsolately on the bed. The house was dark and silent now. He could hardly rouse the Spencers and demand sheets. He would simply have to sleep here as best he could, wrapped in dusty blankets. (It was true, of course, that he had slept in worse circumstances, but all the same ... !)

Then he noticed again, more strongly than before, the sweetish, nauseating odour he had decided to forget about earlier. It was an awful smell. He could not stand it. But the thought of opening the window to more moths made his skin crawl. He took a slipper from his suitcase and stalked the fluttering moths. But after he had splattered one or two against the wall he stopped, his nerves jangled by remorse, and wished he had left them alive. So while the others continued to whiz and circle around the electric light he started to search for the source of the smell, looking in cupboards, sniffing the washbasin, peering under the bed (none of these things, as it happened, smelled very savoury).

A small cupboard stood beside the bed. He wrenched open the door. On the top shelf there was nothing. On the bottom shelf was a chamber-pot and in the chamber-pot was a decaying object crawling with white maggots. From the middle of this object a large eye, bluish and corrupt, gazed up at the Major, who scarcely had time to reach the bathroom before he began to vomit brown soup and steamed bacon and cabbage. Little by little the smell of the object stole into the bathroom and enveloped him.

'Let us pray. Let us thank the Lord for all His mercies, let us thank Him for His Justice enshrined in the peace treaty signed in Versailles last week in which the Prussian tyranny is accorded punishment ... For the righteous shall triumph, saith the Lord; and in this world we are all subject, great and small, to God's Justice and to His Order. For there *is* an order in the universe ... there *is* an order. Everything is ordained for a purpose in this life, from the lowest to the highest, for God's universe is like a pyramid reaching from the most lowly amongst us up to Heaven. Without this purpose our life here below would be nothing more than a random collection of desperate acts ... I repeat, a random collection of desperate acts. Ripon, would you have the common decency to put that cigarette out and wait until I've finished?'

'What?' said Ripon, looking surprised. 'Oh, sorry.'

Edward waited impressively while his son dropped his cigarette into the murky water of a vase containing a few pale-yellow roses.

'Now,' Edward went on with a frown, his concentration disturbed, 'let us ... let us never forget our position, the part each one of us must play in the Divine Purpose. We must not shirk. For there *is* an order. Without it our lives would be meaningless. So let us thank Him for the duties that accompany our privileges and pray that we may always discharge them as His faithful servants ... Now let us thank the Lord for all His other mercies to us, for the reunion of families, for the produce of the land which comes to our table ... '

Edward, inspiration gone, eye flitting round the room in

search of reasons for giving thanks, was obliged to pause every now and then to collect and review fresh evidence of the divine magnanimity. In this way, among the more commonly acknowledged gifts of heaven he came to give thanks for some curious things: 'the chairs on which we rest our tired bodies', for example, 'the faithful dogs' of Kilnalough, or, most curious of all, 'the splendid century made by Hobbs against Lancashire yesterday'. It seemed to the Major that there might possibly be no end to this list: after all, if one was going to give thanks for chairs, dogs, and cricketers, why should one ever stop?

As it happened, however, Edward did stop, after a particularly long and distressing pause, by giving thanks for all those present who had come safely through 'the dark watches of the night'. 'Amen to that, anyway,' thought the Major peevishly.

But Edward had not quite finished. He still had to commemorate the Fallen. The Major, who was hungry again (either because the country air was giving him an appetite or because he had vomited up the only solid meal he had consumed in the last twenty-four hours) and who had been entertaining disabused thoughts about Edward's prayers, now felt displeased with himself. With his eye distractedly on a giant silver dish bearing a domed lid surmounted by an ornamental spike (strangely reminiscent of a Boche helmet) beneath which he believed eggs, bacon and kidneys to be cooling, he did his best to reverse his thoughts into a more pious direction.

The breakfast room, though small by comparison with the dining-room, was spacious, airy, and on sunny days presumably sunny since it faced south and was lit by immense windows, the upper part of which (beyond where a man with his feet planted on the low sill might be able to reach) was opaque with grime. The Spencer family and a number of the hotel guests were grouped round the largest table, hands on the backs of chairs and chins on chests (with the exception of Ripon who with his head on one side was staring up at a generous cobweb billowing near the ceiling). Behind them, grouped at random in an attitude of devotion or subjection (rather as if they had

45

been left chairless in a frantic game of Musical Chairs) stood Murphy, three or four maids in uniform, a hugely fat lady in an apron and Evans, the tutor, his face pitted and pale as death. The servants, the Major assumed, were not taking part in this alien act of worship but mereley waiting for it to be over so that they could serve breakfast. But Edward was still going through his ritual.

To the wall behind the table was attached a carved wooden memorial in the shape of a gigantic book with open pages; from behind them rose the head of a unicorn. Book and unicorn together made up the Spencer family crest; all Angela's letters had been embossed with it. In this case the varnished, elaborately curling pages had recently had two long lists of names chiselled into them, startling in their newness, the white wood beneath the varnish exposed like wounds.

Who were these poor chaps? the Major wondered distantly, without pity. On what basis had selection been made? Young men from Kilnalough? But recruiting had been poor in Ireland. Connolly, the Sinn Feiners, Nationalists of every hue had declared that Irishmen should not fight in the British Army. But if not from Kilnalough from Trinity, perhaps, or from some heroic cricket club or old school. There were so many ways in which the vast army of the dead could be drilled, classified, inspected, and made to present their ghostly arms. No end to the institutions, civilian and military, busy drawing up their sombre balance-sheet and recording it in wood, stone or metal. But if there was no end to the institutions there was no end to the dead men either. In truth, there were more than enough to go round several times over. 'Greater love hath no man than this,' the Major thought mechanically. Bacon and eggs ... the saliva rinsed shamefully around his teeth.

Long ranks of tiny eyes were now staring at the Major as if accusing him of being both alive and about to eat breakfast. With a dignified gesture Edward had grasped each page of the book and folded it outward and back on concealed hinges, revealing row after row of photographs of young men, most of them in uniform. The photographs were not very good, some of them. Fuzzy or beginning to fade, ill-assorted; one or two of the young men were laughing unsuitably or, dazzled by the sun, looked to be already in agony. For the most part, though, they were meticulously uniformed and the Major could imagine them sitting there, grim and composed, as if for a portrait in oils. As often as not this long exposure to the unblinking eye had so completely steamed the life out of them that now one was difficult to tell from another.

Edward said in somewhat sepulchral tones: 'They gave their lives for their King, their country and for us. Let us remain silent for a moment in their name.' Silence descended. The only sounds to be heard were Murphy's regular, whistling breath and a faint gurgle of gastric juices.

Meanwhile the Major was trying once again to delve into the past with the paralysed fingers of his memory, hoping to grasp some warmth or emotion, the name perhaps of a dead friend that might mean the beginning of grief, the beginning of an end to grief. But now, as he stood at the breakfast table, even the dead faces that nightly appeared in his dreams remained absent. There was only the cold and constant surprise that would come, say, from dreaming of home and waking among strangers. He ground his teeth at the accusing, many-eyed memorial and thought: 'Hypocrisy.'

As Edward said grace his eye met the Major's for an instant and perhaps he noticed the Major's bitterness, for a shadow of concern crossed his face. Turning, he closed the memorial and took his seat.

Now that the domed lid was being lifted from the silver dish the Major's spirits improved and he thought that today, after breakfast, he must have a talk with Angela and clear up her misconceptions. Then he would leave. After all, if he did not leave promptly his presence might well foster more misconceptions. If she could nominate herself his 'fiancée' on the strength of a few meetings in Brighton she might well be capable of arranging the wedding without consulting him. All the same, it was difficult to bring the matter up while Angela continued to treat him as a casual acquaintance. It seemed indelicate to recall that time they had kissed with the cactus in Brighton.

'Did you sleep well, Brendan?' Angela wanted to know ... and looking at her pale and frigid face he wondered whether the kiss might have taken place only in his imagination.

'Yes,' the Major replied curtly, hoping to indicate the contrary.

'That's good,' Edward said with satisfaction, spearing the fat rump of a kidney and a few leaves of bacon (all stone-cold by now and remarkably greasy). 'Don't pay any heed to what those bally guide-books say. It may not be quite what it was in the old days but it's still a comfortable old place. Anyway, they're all written by Liberals and Socialists and so forth ... They envy us, if you want my opinion, it's as simple as that.'

This was too much for the Major. 'There was a sheep's head in the cupboard by my bed.'

'Good heavens,' exclaimed Angela, though without surprise.

'That's what we give the dogs. Boil 'em down. Very nourishing and they cost nothing at all. The butcher would probably throw them away if it wasn't for us, though I've heard the country people sometimes eat them too. You should see the healthy coats they have on them. Come along with me afterwards and see for yourself.'

The Major, who hoped never in his life to see another sheep's head, could only nod mutely and trust to luck that Edward would forget.

He didn't, however. Just as the Major was preparing to slope off after breakfast (and perhaps corner Angela to drop a few hints about not wanting to marry her) Edward abruptly materialized at his elbow and steered him firmly down unfamiliar corridors, through a yard festooned with damp sheets bulging in the wind and into a smaller yard walled by outhouses. Here a dozen or so dogs of varying ages, shapes and sizes (whose names the Major already knew by heart) were dozing on piles of straw or empty sacks.

'My dogs,' Edward said with simplicity. 'Aren't they beauties? Mind where you walk.'

'They certainly are,' the Major replied insincerely.

The dogs brightened up at the sight of Edward and crowded round him excitedly, snapping at his fingers and trying to land their paws on his chest, barging, quarrelling and getting in the way to such an extent that the two men had trouble wading through them to reach a gate on the far side. This led into yet another yard, empty this time except for a three-sided fireplace sprouting black smoke and orange flames. Over the fire hung the round black belly of an iron cauldron, steaming and bubbling. The dogs sprang towards it in a frenzy of excitement.

Evans, the tutor, was standing beside the cauldron stirring it, his pale, unhealthy face completely expressionless. 'What a strange fellow!' thought the Major. Stirring the cauldron with the flames leaping about his ears made him look positively sinister.

'Thank you, Tutor. A good brew today, is it?' Edward turned to the Major. 'Evans does the cooking, I do the feeding. Dogs know who feeds them, believe you me. It's not the same thing if you tell your servants to do it ... they don't know who's master (I mean, the *dogs* don't). Now take a look at that. Rich and juicy!'

The Major peered with distaste at the simmering liquid. Fortunately the surface was covered with an oily grey froth which masked the pot's macabre contents.

'Very nourishing, I shouldn't be surprised,' observed the Major drily. But Edward was not yet satisfied. Picking up a couple of charred sticks, he fished with them until he had located something beneath the surface. A moment later the Major was face to face with a long, narrow skull, eyeless and tipped with grinning teeth.

'Well, thanks a lot for showing me. I think I'll take a stroll

49

round while the weather holds.' The Major stared up at the overcast sky and then, backing away a couple of paces, almost fell over a massive sheepdog that had moved up behind him. Edward grasped him firmly by the upper arm — whether to help him keep his balance or to prevent him from leaving was not immediately clear.

'Look here, Major,' he said in a conciliatory tone. 'We don't want to be too hard on the boy, do we?'

The Major stared at him and Edward, taking his silence for disagreement, continued: 'A lot of it's my own fault, I realize that. He was sacked from school, d'you see, and I had him sent to a crammer. Shouldn't have done that ... turned him agin the government. I was angry, you know, and thought I wouldn't let him get away with it ... not scot free, anyway.'

'You mean Ripon?'

'Yes, yes, Ripon. I know you've been wondering why he didn't volunteer and so forth. It's only natural after what you've been through.'

'Really, Mr Spencer, I can assure you ... ' But Edward was patting his arm soothingly and saying: 'Only natural. Anyone would feel the same in your position. Those who go and those who stay at home ... white feathers and all that rot. He's not a coward, though, and neither am I. Take a look at this!' Dropping the charred sticks, he unbuttoned his waistcoat and began pulling his shirt out until he had uncovered a patch of pale skin at his waist. In the middle of the patch was a round white scar as big as a halfpenny.

'In the service of the King-Emperor. Didn't think I'd get back from that little affair. Somehow or other it missed the intestines or I wouldn't be here to tell the tale. Get down, sir!' A spaniel was attempting to lick the exposed patch of skin.

While Edward adjusted his clothing the Major repeated his innocence of any critical thoughts about Ripon. 'Lot of fuss about nothing, was it?' Edward hastened to agree. 'Well, that's all right then. Still, I wouldn't have wanted you to think we were a family of milksops. Ripon told Angela that the first thing you asked him was whether he'd been abroad. He was angry with Angela, d'you see, because he thought she'd been telling tales.'

There was silence for a moment. Edward had retrieved one of the sticks and was stirring the pot, with the dogs milling and woofing round him. His rugged face with its clipped moustache and flattened ears was still scowling with anxiety in spite of the Major's reassurance.

'He's not a bad boy at heart, you know. It's true he was sacked from school (though not for anything unhealthy, mind) ... and I suppose that rather set him agin the government. I lose my temper with him at times and that doesn't help ... Get down! I'll tell you when it's ready,' he added to a large Alsatian puppy that from behind had forced its head under his arm. 'All the same, he should have volunteered when he was needed, coward or no coward. He may never have another chance as good as the one he missed.'

A chance to do what? wondered the Major. To have his name carved into the dark wood of Edward's war memorial, a dead servant of His Majesty? But a nation must require all its people to participate. A just cause must be defended by everyone. There's no room for young men who are 'agin the government'. Believing, as the Major did, that the cause *had* been a just one and that throughout the world the great civilizing power of the British Empire had been at stake, it was right that Ripon should be held in contempt. Besides, Ripon was perhaps alive in the place of one of those destroyed men who came at night to plead with him in the agony of his dreams.

The Major glanced at Edward. What a man to have such a son! How stiff and military he looked! When he moved, one half expected to hear the clinking of medals. The sort of man who in peacetime looks rather out of place, like a heavy fur coat on a hot summer's day. But again he noticed that mild and disabused expression of the eyes which contrasted so strongly with Edward's military appearance, that trace of self-mockery so firmly restrained that perhaps even Edward himself refused to acknowledge it except in his most private thoughts.

'No you don't,' Edward said, aiming a kick at a tall and rickety Afghan hound that was poking its long nose into one of the Major's trouser pockets. 'Come on then,' he added, addressing the multitude of dogs. He unhooked the cauldron and at the centre of a whirlpool of barking, yelping animals dragged it over to a shallow trough, saying over his shoulder to the Major: 'You know, it smells so good I shouldn't mind eating it myself.'

The Major spent the rest of the morning trying to corner Angela. For a while he wandered the hotel aimlessly, meeting no one at all. He walked down corridors, through deserted rooms in twilight, often as not curtains still drawn from the evening before (perhaps even from many, many evenings before), up a staircase here, down a staircase there. Shortly before eleven o'clock, attracted by a smell of coffee, he found his way to the kitchens, which were chilly and cavernous, the whitewashed walls hung with an armoury of giant pots and pans (some of them big enough to braise an entire sheep, legs and all) which for the most part were rusted beyond recognition, so that they looked more like huge reddish-brown growths sprouting from the walls. In the middle of the table a tortoiseshell cat lay in a veined meat-dish, dozing.

Here in the kitchens the Major was given a cup of tea (the coffee had been an olfactory illusion) stewed black and bitter by numerous reheatings, served to him by the extremely fat lady he had noticed at breakfast. She was the cook, he gathered, but though she appeared garrulous her accent was such that he could understand little of what she said. He did believe her to say, however, that 'the mistress' might be found arranging flowers in the dining-room above.

'The mistress?' he repeated, wanting to make sure (he had

been trailing long enough through empty rooms). He pointed up at the ceiling. The cook nodded vigorously and began to speak again, rapidly and with considerable urgency. Evidently what she was saying was important. Her face was working with emotion; between volleys of words there were shuddering intakes of breath; her shoulders shook, causing the gelatinous layers of flesh on her arms to shiver. 'Good heavens!' thought the Major with concern. 'What can it all be about?' Here and there he recognized a word: 'heaven' … and 'poor creature' … and 'gone to the angels'; but to capture the sense of what she was saying was impossible. Presumably the good lady was referring to Angela's mother who also, come to that, might be described as 'the mistress' — dead of an embolism, he remembered, on St Swithin's Day, 1910. But the cook obviously thought that he had understood her tirade, so to show sympathy he nodded glumly as she stopped speaking and began to chop away with extraordinary speed and ferocity, using a kitchen knife as big as a bayonet. And then, to make things worse, he noticed that her eyes were streaming with tears. She was weeping without restraint! And it was all his fault. He swallowed his tea (making a face, it was as bitter as wormwood) and stole out of the kitchen. But a little later, as he felt his way along the damp, stone corridor to the stairs, it occurred to him that the cook had been chopping onions — a fact which might have contributed to her display of emotion.

It took him a little time to find the right stairway to make the ascent to the dining-room. This was because he did not fathom immediately that it was necessary to go on down a few steps before joining the main staircase, from where one could go on up or down as the case might be (though God only knew where 'down' might lead to). In other words, the kitchens were situated, for a reason that the architect alone could have explained, on a tributary staircase. Other similar staircases branched off here and there, but though he was curious to see where they led the Major was now hastening upwards to find Angela.

53

He was not surprised, however, to find that there was no sign of Angela in the dining-room. He stood there for a moment looking round. It was very silent. Some of the tables, it was true, were decorated with fresh flowers. On one of the tables a bunch of carnations and feathery green leaves lay on a newspaper waiting to be arranged in vases. A pair of scissors lay beside them, giving the impression that they had perhaps been abandoned a moment before he had stepped into the room. It was, he presumed, out of the question that Angela was deliberately avoiding him, so, in theory at least, all he had to do was to station himself beside these cut flowers which she certainly would not leave for long before putting into water.

A ponderous creaking began on the far side of the room. Ah, it was the dumb-waiter rising from the kitchen, he could see the ropes shivering as it rose. He walked over to have a look at it. Abruptly he had an intuition that there was something strange or terrifying on it: a decaying sheep's head, for example, or something even stranger, perhaps the cook's weeping head on a platter surrounded by chopped onions. The dumb-waiter stopped for a moment and then started again. When it reached the top he smiled at what it contained. It was the tortoiseshell cat he had seen in the kitchen, still sitting on the meat-dish. When the conveyance had come to a halt it jumped off and wound through his legs. The dumb-waiter started down again empty.

A few moments later, with the cat cradled in his arms, he spotted Angela. She was on the next terrace below the tennis court carrying a spray of beech leaves and walking swiftly towards a flight of steps some distance away. Thinking that if he could find the entrance she was making for he might be able to intercept her, he set off rapidly, taking the cat with him for company. The cat did not like the idea, however, leapt out of his arms and vanished back the way they had come. The Major pressed on down the corridor he was following, relatively certain this time that he was going in the right direction. On his way he passed one of the old ladies he had been introduced to the evening before. She was leaning on a stick, arrested half-way between two sharp bends in a long section of the corridor without doors or windows. As he passed she murmured something indignantly but he merely nodded cheerfully, pretending not to hear. He was in a hurry. Excited, he turned another corner at the end of which, by his calculations of the exterior of the building and the distance he had walked, there should be a glass door through which Angela would enter at any moment. But there wasn't. At the end of the corridor there was merely a blank wall and a musty, dilapidated sitting-room. 'This is absurd', he thought, half irritated and half amused. 'To hell with her. I'll see her at lunch.'

But Angela failed to appear at lunch. The Major sat beside Edward, who was by turns morose and indignant about the state of the country. Another R.I.C. barracks had been attacked and stripped of arms; the young hooligans had nothing better to do these days, it seemed. They preferred shooting people in the back to doing an honest day's work. But for all that, he hadn't noticed many of them coming forward when Sir Henry Wilson had called for volunteers to join in a fair fight. At this the 'friend of Parnell', who was sitting at the next table, stirred uncomfortably and muttered something.

'What's that you say?' demanded Edward.

'Thousands of Nationalists fought against Germany,' the old man murmured, his voice still scarcely above a whisper. 'Constitutional Nationalists who fought not only for France's and Belgium's freedom but for Ireland's too. Not all Nationalists belong to Sinn Fein, you know ... '

'But they're all tarred with the same brush. Sinn Fein demands a republic. Why? Because they hate England and sided with Germany during the war. Would they change their tune if Ireland was given Dominion Home Rule? Of course they wouldn't! It would merely whet their appetites for more.

There's no middle of the road in Ireland, for the simple reason that the Home Rulers are playing right into the hands of Sinn Fein. Perhaps they mean well. Maybe they're just fools. But the result is the same.'

'They're *not* fools!' cried the old man, raising his voice. A faint flush had crept over his gaunt cheeks and water slopped on to the table-cloth from the trembling glass he had been in the process of lifting to his lips. 'Irishmen fought in the British Army in defence of the Empire. Those men have a right to a voice in the settlement of their country's future.'

'Exactly so,' agreed Edward with a contemptuous smile. 'And you know as well as I do that the bulk of those who served and died came from the Unionist families of the south and west. Who have a better right to a voice than the survivors of the men who fought at Thiepval, their fathers, sons and brothers? And yet everyone seems to take it for granted that they can be suppressed or coerced just for the sake of a temporary peace or because a rabble of Irish immigrants in America have been kicking up a fuss. My dear fellow, it simply won't wash. No British Government, not even one with a tremendous victory under its belt, could get away with being so rash and unjust. If you simple-minded Dominion-Home-Rulers got your way and tried to coerce Ulster we'd end up with a bloodbath and the Empire in ruins. I repeat, there are only two sides in Ireland. Either you are a Unionist or you support Sinn Fein, which means endorsing their mad and criminal rebellion in 1916, not to mention their friend the Kaiser ...'

'Who will shortly be tried and hanged in London,' spoke up a gentleman in heavy tweeds. 'Lloyd George said so in the House yesterday.' There was a moment of approving silence and then the gentleman in tweeds went on to say that he'd met a man who knew personally one of the constables killed at Soloheadbeg quarry, a fine young man, 'as straight as the day', who had only been doing his job. If that wasn't murder what was?

The Major had listened to all this with detachment. After all, it was hardly any of his business (and would be even less of his business once he had managed to have a talk with Angela). Although he felt sorry for the 'friend of Parnell' who, whitefaced and evidently upset, had pushed his plate aside, unable to swallow another mouthful, it seemed to him that Edward was undoubtedly right. The Irish, as far as he knew, had always had a habit of making trouble. That was in the nature of things. As for the aim of their unruly behaviour, self-government for Ireland, that seemed quite absurd. What would be the advantage to the Irish themselves? They were so ill-educated that they could not possibly hope to gain anything from it. The English undoubtedly knew more about running the country. The priests would presumably take over if the English were not there to see fair play. He was inclined to agree with Edward that the Republican movement was merely an excuse for trouble-makers moved more by self-interest than by patriotism. For the important fact was this: the presence of the British signified a *moral* authority, not just an administrative one, here in Ireland as in India, Africa and elsewhere. It would have to be matched by the natives themselves before self-government became an acceptable proposition. So thought the Major, anyway.

But by now he had had more than enough of politics, so he decided against joining Edward and the others for coffee. Other considerations apart, the coffee at the Majestic was execrable, brewed as it was by the manservant Murphy according to some recipe of his own. Instead, he went to his room for some tobacco, passing on his way the fat cook he had reduced to tears earlier in the day. She was coming heavily down the stairs, panting slightly with the effort of negotiating the dangerously bulging carpet with a tray held in front of her. The Major peered at this tray: on it there was an entire lunch (cottage pie and stewed apple), hardly touched, pushed aside, one might suppose, by a person without appetite. The thought occurred to him that perhaps Angela was ill and this was her lunch. However, since she had been up and about during the morning it could hardly be anything serious. The cook nodded to him somewhat nervously and then stumbled on a loose stair-rod. For an instant it seemed that she must plunge headlong to the foot of the stairs. But she righted herself somehow with a rattle of plates and a slopping of water and continued on her way, leaving the Major to wonder in which room lay his pallid 'fiancée'.

Later in the afternoon, restless but with nothing to do, he walked into Kilnalough with the intention of finding out at the railway station at what time the trains left for Kingstown and Dublin. On his way there, however, he encountered Sarah, who was being wheeled by a very plump, voluptuous girl with dark hair and rosy cheeks ('All Irish girls are as fat as butter,' thought the Major). Hardly had this person been introduced (as 'Máire') when she whispered something urgently into Sarah's ear and hurried away, leaving Sarah to wheel herself.

'Well, am I as terrifying as all that?'

'She's shy. Also I expect she had some idea that I might ... well, never mind. Shall I tell you who she is? After all, the sooner I tell you all the gossip the sooner you'll find Kilnalough as dull as the rest of us.'

'By all means.'

'She's the daughter of the wealthiest man in Kilnalough — yes, even wealthier than your friend Mr Spencer (not that I should think *he's* all that wealthy, mind you, by the look of the Majestic) — the owner of the flour mill to be precise. You didn't know that we had a flour mill here? How ignorant you are! On every single bag of Noonan's flour sold in Ireland you'll find a picture of Máire dressed up as Little Red Riding Hood carrying a basket. Isn't that charming?'

'I was hoping to hear something more scandalous.'

'Very well then. Can I rely on you to be discreet?'

'Of course.'

'She and your friend Ripon have an understanding.'

'An understanding? You mean a ... sentimental under-standing?'

'On her part it's sentimental. On Ripon's I have the feeling it's more commercial than sentimental, but as you know I have a habit of thinking the worst of people. In any case, there's little chance of it coming to anything since their respective families can't abide each other.'

'Romeo and Juliet.'

'It would be more true to say, let me see ... Iago and Juliet. What's more, Juliet is a snob.' The Major laughed and Sarah turned to him with a sweet smile. Her malice amused him and, really, it was quite harmless, intended to entertain rather than hurt.

Sarah had declared her intention of buying some material at Finnegan's and they were progressing slowly up the main street in that direction, the Major pushing and Sarah chatter-ing, teasing him by turns about his 'Englishness', his 'respect-ability', his 'ramrod posture' and anything else that came into her head. The Major was only half listening, absorbed in looking round at the men in cloth caps idling on doorsteps (so few of them appeared to have any work to do), at the women in black shawls with shopping baskets, at the barefoot children playing in the gutter. How very foreign, after all, Ireland was!

Their progress up the street was now considerably impeded by a herd of cows ('How delightful, how typical!' thought the Major) which strayed not only over the road but on to the rudimentary pavement as well. Presently a motor car came up behind them with the driver sounding his horn, which did very little good since cows are inclined to panic; one of them almost charged straight back into the motor's radiator but was diverted at the last moment by a lad in a ragged overcoat who was herding the animals with a stick. Sitting beside the driver the Major recognized the burly figure of old Dr Ryan wrapped in a trench coat and numerous mufflers though the day was mild. He saw them and waved, telling the driver to pull in to the kerb to give the cattle time to move on. When they came

level with him he said sternly: 'Always in that chair, Sarah.
You should be walking. You never do as you're told.'

'Yes, yes, I know. You're always telling me,' Sarah replied
petulantly and glanced helplessly at the Major.

'You know, I think you like being in that chair.'

'Oh you know *everything*, Doctor!' Sarah retorted, and for
an instant the Major glimpsed a bitter, sly expression on her
face.

'Don't be impertinent,' Dr Ryan said sharply. 'And let me
see you get out of that chair and walk over to me. Take hold of
your young man's arm.'

Sarah made a face and for a moment remained seated.

'Come on, we can't wait all day,' snapped the doctor.

Looking confused and miserable, Sarah pulled herself up
and, leaning heavily on the Major's arm and one of her sticks,
she began to move forward. He was immediately surprised
by how well she could walk. She was unsteady, it was true,
but her legs seemed firm and strong. Dr Ryan, his aged head
looking small and infirm on top of his great pile of clothing,
watched as she reached the car and started back to her chair,
her slender fingers gripping the Major's forearm with a
strength which surprised him.

'If you weren't so spoiled you'd be out of that chair the whole
time. You could walk perfectly well if you took the trouble.
And as for you, Major, perhaps you'd be kind enough to tell
Edward Spencer from me to stop aggravating his tenants or
there'll be trouble.' With that the doctor waved to his chauffeur
to drive on.

'What a dreadful old man,' the Major said. 'He's as sour as
vinegar.'

Sarah had changed her mind and no longer wanted to go to
Finnegan's Drapery. She wanted to be taken home, off this
hateful street; it wasn't far, the Major needn't worry, she
wouldn't detain him long even though he obviously thought
her company intolerable and was dying to get away ...

'But I don't think anything of the kind,' protested the Major, amazed. 'Wherever did you get that idea?'

Ah, it was as plain as anything from the way he kept looking round him all the time, particularly when a pretty girl (one with two sound legs) passed by, dragging her skirts so prettily through the cowpats. The Major, with his 'ramrod posture', obviously had far better things he could be doing and, besides, he must be simply dying to get back to his dear Angela by now and, in any case, he had been in a great old hurry off somewhere when they had first bumped into each other ...

'That's true. I was going to make some inquiries at the railway station. I'd forgotten completely.'

'What? Are you leaving Kilnalough so soon? Have you and Angela had a quarrel?'

'Not only have we not had a quarrel; we haven't even spoken to each other—at least, privately. There was never really an understanding between us, you know—at least, I don't think there was; nothing serious—except that we wrote to each other regularly, of course.'

'I *didn't* know that. In fact, I thought ... but never mind what I thought. Why did you come here, then?'

'Oh, to get it straightened out, I suppose. I hardly know why myself. In any case I never seem able to find Angela alone. You don't think she might be deliberately avoiding me, do you?'

But Sarah made no reply. They had now turned into a street of small but well-kept buildings of red brick, in one of which was housed the bank, behind and above which Sarah lived with her parents. Would the Major care to come in and have some tea?

They went in by a side gate and followed a path between trellises of climbing roses to where a shallow wooden ramp made for Sarah's wheelchair led up to the back door. Of course, she explained, the house was not nearly as grand as the sort of place he was no doubt used to, but it would do him no harm to be in a 'miserable hovel' for a change. Indeed it would do him good. She pointed out the door of a room and said she would join him there in a minute, he was to make himself at home as best he could. The Major went into the room and sat down on a blue velvet sofa to wait. An oil-painting of a cow and some trees hung over the mantelpiece. There were a few books in the bookcase, for the most part fishing and travel reminiscences. There was the piano, too, no different from other pianos except for the iron clamps which held its broken legs together. In this neat, clean room, so utterly without character, it was only these broken legs which provided a touch of comfort.

The *Irish Times* lay neatly folded on a table. He picked it up and scanned it idly. Officers' families in abject poverty. Good luck to the R34. A new era in transatlantic travel was about to begin. The Bolshevists were advancing—British seaplanes had been in action on the Finnish border. At Wimbledon Lieutenant-Colonel A. R. F. Kingscote, M.C., R.G.A., had gratifyingly beaten a young American. Dr King's Liver Pills (Dandelion and Quinine), guaranteed without mercury. Absolutely cure the symptoms of the TORPID LIVER ... combat Depressed Spirits, etc. The Major folded the paper carefully and replaced it with a sigh. He was ill at ease, wondering whether it had been disloyal of him to discuss Angela with Sarah.

'I hope you won't mention our conversation to Angela,' he said when Sarah at last appeared. 'As you know, I haven't yet had a chance to talk to her properly.'

'Of course not,' Sarah said with indifference. 'It's none of my business. Besides, I never see her.'

'But I thought you were great friends.'

'We used to be friends, but not any longer. I'm surprised you're so unobservant. Didn't you notice how coldly they treated me at the Majestic? Edward hardly speaks to me any longer. The only reason he invites me to his absurd tennis parties is because Angela is sorry for me. Yes, that's right, sorry for me! It's as clear as day. I expect you're sorry for me too if the truth be known, but I don't care. I shouldn't go to the Majestic, it would be much better not to, but I get so bored sitting here all day like a miserable cripple ... '

'But Angela was so pleased to see you; and you're so pretty and amusing. Really, I'm sure you must be imagining all this,' exclaimed the Major in surprise. 'What possible reason could they have for not liking you?'

'They think I've been encouraging Máire (you remember that fat, ugly girl who was pushing my chair), they think I've been helping her to "trap" their darling Ripon. They're quite wrong, of course. The last thing I'd do for a friend of mine (and she is a friend of sorts, that part is true) is to help her to "trap" someone as odious as Ripon.'

'But what do they have against her, anyway? I mean, if she's so rich and so on. The Spencers live in that huge hotel, but they don't appear to be all that well off. Ripon could surely do a lot worse.'

Sarah shook her head sadly. 'I can't believe that you're such an innocent, Major. D'you really mean to tell me that you don't see why the Spencers wouldn't want Ripon married to that rich, ugly creature? Well, I shall tell you, though I refuse to believe that you don't know. The reason is that Máire is a Catholic. Now do you understand?'

But before the Major had a chance to reply there was a polite knock on the door and a small dapper man dressed in a grey flannel suit of dubious cut made his appearance. He advanced holding out his hand nervously. He was, he said, Sarah's father (Sarah made no comment but looked annoyed) and he hadn't been able to resist taking a moment off to say hello to the Major, about whom he'd already heard a great deal, both from his old friend Mr Spencer and, of course, from Sarah herself (here he smiled fondly but Sarah looked more exasperated than ever) ...

'I hope what you heard was complimentary.'

Oh, most complimentary, of course, and it was really very

kind of the Major to wheel Sarah home ... getting about was something of a difficulty for her, as he could imagine, but she did very well, all things considered, she had so many kind friends who helped to lighten her load. He hoped too that the weather would be less changeable than it had been recently, particularly while the Major was visiting, it made such a difference, especially if the Major was, as he expected, a sporting man ... And this was Mrs Devlin ...

A heavy-set lady had entered wheeling a tea-trolley on which (the Major noticed with relief) there were only two cups, saucers, plates and cake-knives (and a splendid-looking cherry cake). Mrs Devlin nodded at the Major without speaking, hesitated for a moment and then withdrew. Mr Devlin patted his hair which was oiled flat and neat against his skull, smiled, and said that he would have to be getting his nose back to the grindstone but that it had been a pleasure and that he hoped the Major would often come again to visit them. He backed out of the room smiling and the door closed softly.

Sarah's mood had changed. To the Major's attempts at conversation she answered only in peevish monosyllables, all the time glancing round the room as if she were seeing it for the first time. Abruptly she interrupted a laborious compliment that the Major was paying to the cherry cake and said: 'What an appalling room this is. You'd think some awful English person lived here.' And with that she wheeled herself quickly to the door, opened it deftly and disappeared, almost before the Major had time to realize what was happening. He sat there, a half-eaten piece of cake in his fingers, wondering what she had meant by 'some awful English person' and whether she intended to come back. Presently he heard the sound of a muffled argument from some other room, a woman's voice raised in protest. But then a door slammed and a moment later Sarah reappeared, her face so dark that the Major asked her what was the matter.

'Nothing at all.'

As she wheeled her chair forward the Major saw that in her

lap lay a number of religious ornaments. Two plaster saints, painted in bright colours, she arranged on the piano within a few inches of his head. A wooden crucifix was propped on the mantelpiece while a crudely coloured and alarming picture of the Sacred Heart was placed on the bookcase backed by a pile of books removed from the shelf. That left another wooden crucifix which she put on the tea-table itself. The Major watched all this in amazement but said nothing, allowing himself to be given more tea and more cherry cake (which really was delicious). He munched it cautiously under the eye of the saints.

'I lease them the land at a price that's so cheap they laugh at me behind my back. I mend their roofs for them and give them seed corn and potatoes in return for a miserable percentage of their crop. I send them the vet when their cows get sick. I help them make ends meet when they spend all their money in the pub. Am I entitled to some loyalty, Major? Answer me that.'

The Major had come upon Edward with a hoe in his hand, standing motionless beside a rose-bed sunk in thought. With the hoe he was now poking at the horizon to the south where a cluster of grey farm buildings stood on a ridge in the distance. Shading his eyes against the sun which for the first time that day had just appeared from beneath smooth carpets of grey cloud, the Major agreed that someone who did such things was indubitably entitled to loyalty.

'You know what I did to "aggravate my tenants", as old Ryan says? I asked them to sign a piece of paper saying they were loyal not to me, mind you, not to me but to the King ... and that they wouldn't get mixed up in any of these Sinn Fein goings-on. Is that so terrible? Is it aggravating them to ask them to abide by the law? Well, I'll be damned if the blighters don't refuse point-blank to sign. It's Donnelly that's put them up to it, an old fellow with no teeth ... "What's the meaning of this, Donnelly?" I ask him. "Ah ture," says he, "we'd be in danger." "In danger from who?" He can't tell me the answer to that one. "You'd never know," he says. "Well, Donnelly, I can tell you," I said to him, "if you don't sign it quick sharp you'll be in danger from me!" ' Massive and imposing, Edward punctuated his explanation with sharp jabs of the hoe.

There was silence for a moment. The Major was surprised to see that Edward, who had been scowling angrily, now had a rueful smile on his face. He threw down his hoe with a sigh and fell into step beside the Major, who had decided to take a stroll round the southern corner of the hotel. 'The joke is that I don't really give a damn about all that. I only lease them the land because I have to; they'd starve if I didn't. But I have no interest in it and it only causes me endless trouble. I'm not a farmer, never have been. I'd sell them the land in a trice but they couldn't even pay me the half of what it's worth. I'm not as young as I was but I often think I'd like to do something with my life. Yes, do something completely different ... go back to the university, maybe, and do some research (I still take one or two scientific journals, you know, but in Kilnalough it's impossible to keep up). Have you ever thought, Brendan, how many completely different lives there are to be lived if only one could choose? I can tell you one thing, I certainly wouldn't choose to be a landlord in Ireland. One gets no thanks for it. However, that's the job I've been called to, so I suppose I must make the best of it.'

As they walked they were joined by a shabby spaniel that appeared out of a clump of rhododendrons and trotted along behind Edward.

'Does old Ryan even know his doctoring? Frankly I doubt it. He must have been in the College of Surgeons when all they knew was leeches and bloodletting. And yet he's the only doctor in Kilnalough, so everyone treats him as if he's God Almighty.' Edward was scowling again. He halted suddenly at a diamond-shaped bed of lavender and his scowl faded.

'Planted by my dear wife.' After a moment, as if to clear up a possible misunderstanding, he added: 'Before she died.'

The spaniel mutely lifted a leg against an acute angle of the diamond and they set off again. The Major looked up at the great turreted wall that hung over them. They were so close to it at this point that it was impossible to gauge its size. A few yards farther on, however, they made another turn and this allowed him to see the back of the hotel which was really, in fact, the front, since the building had been designed to relate entirely to the sea. It was into the Irish Sea (and not into Ireland) that the most magnificent flight of steps led, and they were in the middle of the crescent whose curving arms spread out to embrace the distant coast of Wales across the vast expanse of windswept water. The Major was staggered to see for the first time just what this side of the crescent looked like: the extraordinary proliferation of turrets and battlements and crenellated cat-walks that hung from the building amid rusting iron balconies and French windows with drooping shutters. In the very heart of the crescent above the staircase of white stone and running from the slate roofs on one side to the slate roofs on the other was a great construction of glass which at this moment caught a stray gleam of sunlight and flared gold for a few seconds.

This, Edward was explaining, was the ballroom the Major might already have seen from the inside, a place impossible to keep warm in winter because of its glass roof. This glass roof, he went on with his eyes on his shoes, could be a bit of a problem in summer too. However (he brightened a little), in the old days it must have been really magnificent: the great Hunt Balls, the carnivals, the regattas (think of the lanterns glimmering on the yachts that bobbed at the landing-stage) ... the dancing would go on until the rising sun dimmed the chandeliers and the waiters carried in silver trays steaming with bacon and kidneys and fried eggs gleaming in the sunlight and silver coffee-pots breathing wisps of steam like ... like old men talking in winter, ah, but the marvellous part was that the whole thing would have been visible from above because of the glass roof, almost as if it were taking place in the open air ... the nannies and the children crowding on to the balconies to watch and to listen to the violins until they, the children, became sleepy and even maybe fell asleep completely and were carried in and put to bed, not even waking up when the grey, exhausted but content grown-ups came in to kiss them good night in the early hours of the morning before themselves retiring to sleep till the afternoon, undisturbed except for memories of violins and glinting chandeliers and silk dresses and an occasional cry of a peacock (because there had been peacocks too, still were, come to that) settling on their sleeping minds as soft as rose-petals ...

'Eh? Good heavens!' said the Major, astonished by this flight of fancy.

'Hm ... actually, one of our guests wrote a sort of poem, you know, about how the place probably used to look in the old days. Lovely bit of work. Angela embroidered some of it for me on a cushion. I'll show it to you later on. I think you'll appreciate it.'

'I'm sure I shall,' agreed the Major.

The dog barked, doubtfully.

'What is it, Seán?'

A handsome, grinning young man had appeared on the steps that led up from one of the lower terraces. In his hand he swung a white feathered object which turned out to be a dead hen.

'Oh, he hasn't killed another, has he?' Edward grabbed the mutinous spaniel by the collar and thrust the chicken under its nose. The dog whined unhappily, averting its eyes. 'I know the way to cure him of this. Get some twine, Seán, and tie the hen round his neck.'

A few moments later the hen's neck had been tied to its legs and the dog, whose name was Rover, was shaking himself violently in an effort to rid himself of his heavy white boa. Then they walked on, the Major somewhat disturbed by this administration of justice.

Dinner that night closely resembled the lugubrious meal of

68

the previous evening (old Mrs Rappaport once again stepping out of the broom-cupboard on the given signal) with, however, the important difference that Angela again failed to appear. Edward and Ripon faded away into the shadows after the meal, leaving the Major to play whist in the comparative comfort of the residents' lounge, in the company of Miss Porteous, Miss Archer and Mrs Rice. The ladies, though well muffled in shawls and cardigans, were nevertheless skewered at intervals by the invisible daggers of draughts leaking into the room from the many enormous windows. Whist continued until at length the Major's partner failed to respond to suggestions that it was her turn to play (he had been shuffling and dealing for each of them in turn). She had fallen asleep. Her companions interpreted this as a sign that it was time for bed and so they packed up swiftly, wishing the Major good night and leaving him with three unplayed aces.

Since it was early and he still felt wide awake he set off for a stroll, hands in pockets and whistling mournfully, through the deserted hotel rooms (he had taken to roaming about the house at will by now, no longer caring whether the Spencers might suppose that he was spying on them). Presently, on the first floor, he stumbled upon the Imperial Bar: curtains drawn and in total darkness, it was to all appearances just another empty room. Having felt his way cautiously inside, embracing on the way a slender lampstand which slipped between his outstretched arms to bump against his chest, he drew the curtains. Outside, a fortress of black clouds towered towards the Majestic from the west.

There was a faint mewing sound. A dark shadow slipped off the bar and approached him. It was the tortoiseshell cat, arching her back and rubbing herself against his ankle.

'So this is where you live, is it?'

On the bar he discovered an oil lamp which still contained a trace of oil. He turned up the wick and lit it. Behind the bar, ranks of bottles picked up the glimmer. Having vigorously dusted a brandy glass with his handkerchief he searched among the array of bottles until he found some cognac, poured himself a drink and went to stand by the window.

The light was poor by now. It had been raining heavily for some time. Nothing moved except for the occasional flutter of a bird, almost invisible against the background of leaves trembling under the downpour. The cat leaped up on to the sill and sat there looking out, its tail neatly curled around its feet.

Presently Edward materialized out of the rainy dusk that lay beyond the statue of Queen Victoria, followed at some distance by a whitish object that might have been a newspaper blown in the wind, rolling a few feet, halting, rolling forward again. The white object was Rover, still wearing the chicken round his neck. The Major sighed and took a sip of cognac.

Edward was clad in a streaming hat and sodden overcoat and seemed oblivious of the rain. The Major was appalled by his unexpected air of abandonment: it was as if he had received some terrible shock and no longer knew what he was doing. What on earth could be the matter? Rapping sharply on the window-pane, he shouted for Edward to come in out of the rain. But Edward failed to hear him. He continued his sightless walk, sloshing through pools that lay here and there on the grass, then crunching his way over the gravel in the direction of the clump of lavender planted by his wife 'before she died'. At the lavender he froze into an attitude of despair. A little later Rover struggled up and under the impression that something was being hunted did his best to align himself and the dead chicken in a pointing position. The master, the dog and the dead chicken remained there motionless as the rain pelted down on them in the gathering darkness.

The Major drank off the rest of his cognac, shuddered, and picked up the oil lamp to light his way to bed. In a day or two the Spencers would no longer be his affair. It was only when he was half-way up the stairs that he realized that he still had no sheets on his bed. And once again it was too late to do anything about it.

*

But a day or two passed and the Major was still at the Majestic. By now he had succeeded in doing something about the most obvious sources of misery (finding sheets, avoiding morning prayers by having breakfast in his room), but there was a sadness hanging in the empty rooms and corridors like an invisible gas which one could not help breathing.

Angela remained behind a closed door (it was impossible to tell which, there were so many) and was quite certainly ill, though nobody said so. Indeed, nobody made any reference to her at all in his presence. Perhaps they thought he would 'understand'; perhaps they thought he had not even noticed that she was not there; perhaps this was the Spencers' method of dealing with unhappiness, by simply failing to mention it, as, in one of Angela's letters, a reference to the dog called Spot (who had presumably been carried off by distemper) had been omitted. At this moment, for all the Major knew, Edward was compiling lists of the living beings at the Majestic which failed to mention his daughter Angela.

One day, passing through the Palm Court on his way to the Imperial Bar, which he had taken to sharing with the tortoise-shell cat, he heard an elderly lady, a new arrival, asking in a ringing whisper if that was poor Angela's unfortunate young man. Turning involuntarily, he had been met by a battery of pitying, interested glances.

Once or twice again (in truth, several times), before or after meals, he had met the cook on the stairs carrying the invalid's tray. Whether she was struggling up or down the stairs it seemed to make very little difference, he noticed, to the amount of food on the plate. Only, coming down, the meat and vege-tables might be somewhat disarranged, mixed up together, one might suppose, by a listless hand. And a fork might be lying on the plate, though the knife was rarely touched; most often, on the way down, it lay beside the plate, clean and shining as it had been on the way up. Similarly, the apple on the tray usually made the return journey with its skin unflawed; if baked, though, with custard, it might be squashed a little or the meat dug out of the skin and spattered with the yellow, viscous fluid; if stewed and sprinkled with brown sugar as much as half of it might disappear. Apples—after all, there was a mountain of them in the apple house which had to be eaten—played a significant part in the diet of those living at the Majestic. One day, however, he noticed a raw apple travelling upstairs that looked so fresh and shining that it might even have been an early arrival of the new season's crop. On the way down it was still there on the tray but one despairing bite had been taken out of it. He could see the marks of small teeth that had clipped a shallow oval furrow from its side, the exposed white flesh already beginning to oxidize and turn brown, like an old photograph or love-letter. He was extremely moved by this single bite and wanted to say something. He paused and almost spoke, but the cook, as if in fear, was already hastening clumsily down the stairs away from him. Every time they met on the stairs now she would nervously avoid his eye and once or twice she even blushed deeply, as if she had caught him doing something indecent. And it was true that he had become fascinated with this tray and often tried to be on the stairs when it was going up or down. Usually, though, he tried to limit himself to one casual, greedy glance that would note everything.

Most afternoons, he would take a walk with Edward here or there in the Majestic's immense grounds accompanied by four or five of the dogs, freed for the occasion and ecstatic, leaping and bounding, chasing birds or butterflies over the meadows or through the trees, delirious with their sudden freedom. Very often the dog Rover would struggle along obstinately behind them, stopping and starting like a blown newspaper, the no-longer-white hen swinging from his neck, scarcely able to keep up, he and the hen getting caught in a hedge from time to time or having to be helped over a stone wall.

Edward was unpredictable. Sometimes he would say nothing at all for the duration of the walk. At other times he delivered ringing speeches on a general topic, usually to do with Ireland, the state of the country, the impossibility of making progress in a country ridden with priests, superstitions and laziness, the 'blighter Redmond' who had put ideas into people's heads, the cynical indifference of Westminster to the Unionist predicament, the splendid example of Sir Edward Carson and his militia in the north ... Did the people of Ireland want to govern themselves? They most certainly did not. They knew on which side their bread was buttered. Ask any decent Irishman what he thinks and he'll answer the same thing. It was only criminals, fanatics, and certain people with a grudge who were interested in starting trouble. I ask you, is Murphy capable of governing himself? He couldn't even govern his Aunt Fanny! The 'decent' Irish (they were ninety-nine per cent according to Edward) were still friendly to the British and as appalled as anyone by the outrages that occurred every now and again.

But on the day after Edward made this claim the Major read in the *Irish Times*:

Exciting scenes in which baton and bayonet charges were a feature took place at Newtownbarry, Co. Wexford, following the arrest shortly after midnight of John Mahon, a small farmer, living at Gurteen, about a mile outside the town. When the police arrived at the barracks with the prisoner they were hissed and booed by a crowd of over three hundred people, accompanied by the members of the local brass band who started to play ... Some of the civilians ran away but the majority remained and a struggle between the crowd and the police ensued. The latter used their batons freely while the members of the band employed their instruments with which to beat the police.

The Major smiled when he had read this and thought:

73

'How splendidly Irish! The brass band fighting the police with their instruments! I wish I'd been there.' All the same, it was hard to avoid the conclusion that Edward was exaggerating the number of 'decent' Irish. And since Newtownbarry was hardly any distance from Kilnalough surely there was cause for concern here too? But the Major was not concerned, at least not for the time being. For the moment he was merely diverted by the spectacle of the Irish behaving as Irishmen are supposed to behave.

The Major laughed aloud. But a day or two later there was a more sombre description of how the crowd had jeered at District Inspector Hunt as he lay dying on the street in Thurles, having been shot from behind. The Major was busy however, and hardly glanced at it. He had made up his mind to tackle Edward about Angela.

Though she was certainly ill, perhaps it was nothing too serious. On the other hand, she was eating so little that at this rate she might starve herself to death. He must know the truth. He was on the point of asking a direct question when Edward said gruffly: 'Look here, Brendan, I'd like to thank you for all you're doing in these ... well, trying circumstances. No, no, don't say a word ... I know how it is. I just want to say that I appreciate it, that's all.'

The Major stared at him in astonishment. *What* was he doing? And *what* were the 'trying circumstances'? Once again he was about to ask, bluntly, make an end of the mystery and get down to brass tacks ... But Edward was visibly moved; the harsh lines of his face had softened, reminding the Major of how he had looked the other evening standing under the downpour in an attitude of despair. How defenceless one is when one is beginning to get old in a country where they are killing the policemen, with a son agin the government, with a daughter ill in bed! Later he realized that he really should have spoken up (by that time it was too late, naturally) because his position had become more delicate than ever. Supposing that, without realizing it, he should stop doing 'all that he was doing' (whatever it was), or just as bad, once the 'trying circumstances' were over, should continue doing it, thereby revealing that he had not been doing it deliberately. He shook his head sadly (but could not help smiling) over this absurd situation.

BUY VICTORY LOAN!

'We have won the fight, but we have gone into debt in buying the "gloves". It was a glorious fight for humanity, but the creditors call regularly for interest on the loan nevertheless. They are about to demand the whole amount ... hundreds of millions of pounds fall due for payment within the next few years.'

HELP YOUR COUNTRY OUT!

❧

Two or three of the elderly ladies who resided permanently at the Majestic had approached the Major to ask his advice on the Victory Loan, alarmed at the thought that England had got herself into debt (although, of course, in a perfectly respectable way). But the Major disappointed them. He listened politely, of course, but his indifference was plainly visible. He contented himself with murmuring: 'Afraid I don't know much about that sort of thing. Perhaps Edward or, let me see, that bank-manager fellow Devlin might be able to give you some tips.' To tell the truth, the ladies were somewhat distressed by his attitude; after all, in a manner of speaking the 'gloves' had been bought expressly for his use. They retired with tight lips and the ill-defined but somehow distinct impression that the Major, in spite of all the evidence to the contrary, suffered from a lack of patriotism.

This impression was reinforced when, with glistening eyes, Miss Johnston read aloud to Miss Devere, Mrs Rice, and Miss

Staveley an account of the Great Victory Parade. 'The faultless alignment, perfect unison of step, the smartness with which salutes were given and eyes righted, was a matter of general comment. Demobilized men in 'civvies' were plentiful, and, in spite of orders to the contrary, they could not refrain in the majority of instances from lifting their hats in homage to the King.' But the Major, slumped in an armchair, was observed to have a dazed and listless expression on his face as he listened (there was no option) to Miss Johnston's ringing tones echoing through the resident's lounge.

'On they marched, through the Mall, Admiralty Arch, Fleet Street, Ludgate Circus, St Paul's Churchyard, Cannon Street and Queen Victoria Street to the Mansion House where the crowd was densest. A pandemonium of cheering greeted every detachment ... '

A thick blue cloud of tobacco smoke was to be seen swirling around the Major's armchair when Miss Johnston next glanced up. The ladies exchanged significant glances when it had cleared. The Major had vanished.

As it happened, the Major had vanished on an important mission. He really *had* to find out what was wrong with Angela, otherwise he might find himself here for weeks! He had resolved to cultivate the cook, spend sufficient time with her to get to understand her dialect, accent, or speech-infirmity, whichever it was (he suspected that there might be something wrong with her palate), and then find out how things stood.

But this plan was a failure. He made a sudden appearance in the kitchen and began the sort of cheerful, slightly roguish banter which he expected would be irresistible to a fat Irish cook, ignoring her unintelligible (though clearly embarrassed) replies. He had somehow seen himself sitting on the edge of the table and swinging a leg as he chatted, winking a great deal, chaffing the cook about her boy-friends, stealing strawberries — or, at any rate, apples, of which there was a better supply — dipping his finger into bowls of sugar-icing and being chased laughing out of the kitchen with a rolling-pin. It soon became clear, however, that the cook was paralysed with embarrassment in his presence, flushing horribly and looking round for some place of escape. Anyone might have thought he was some kind of sexual deviate the way she behaved! It was simply no use at all. He was obliged to give up almost as soon as he had begun, afraid that the stupid woman might give notice or tell Edward that he had been molesting her. In future he thought it best not to nod to her when they passed on the stairs (though he could not prevent himself from glancing greedily at the tray as usual).

There were two other ways in which he could find out about Angela: one was to ask Ripon, the other was to ask the doctor. But Ripon was plainly avoiding him (the Major's brusque manner had evidently offended him) and, besides, he spent a great deal of time away from the Majestic. The doctor was another matter. He had taken to visiting every day now, usually in the morning or afternoon but sometimes even quite late at night. Long after the great building had been steeped for hours in darkness and silence and he had assumed everyone to be fast asleep the Major, sitting in the Imperial Bar with the tortoiseshell cat on his lap and reading a book with the oil lamp at his elbow, would hear the deep chug of the doctor's motor as it swept up the drive spraying gravel. At the window he would see Edward leaving the porch with short, anxious steps, carrying a lantern to light the old man's laborious progress from motor car to door.

These visits normally took a long time. The reason was that Dr Ryan, however alert his mind, had to cope with a body so old and worn out as to be scarcely animate. Watching him climb the stairs towards his patient was like watching the hands of a clock: he moved so slowly that he might not have been moving at all. One day the Major saw him on his way upstairs, clinging to the banister as a snail clings to the bark of a tree. After he had smoked a cigarette and glanced through the newspaper he happened to pass through the foyer again and there was the doctor, still clinging to the banister and still apparently not moving, but nevertheless much nearer to the top. The Major shook his head and hoped that it was not an emergency.

After his visit to Angela (though no one admitted that this was the purpose of his ascent) the same process of clinging to the banister would be gone through in reverse. Afterwards he would doze in an armchair in the Palm Court or the residents' lounge and around him would gather a group of chattering old ladies who looked, by contrast to his immense age, as sprightly and exuberant as young girls. And maybe, reflected the Major, in Dr Ryan's presence they did become a little intoxicated with their youth again. He found it touching, this recovery of youth, and enjoyed hearing them chatter in this girlish and charming way and thought that, after all, there is not so very much difference between an old lady and a young girl, only a few years diluting the exuberance with weariness, sadness, and a great sensitivity to draughts.

However, the presence of the old ladies made it a little difficult for the Major to bring up the subject of Angela. And perhaps, too, the doctor resented their enjoyment of his extreme old age, because one day, after his usual ascent of the stairs, he was to be found in none of his usual haunts. Disconsolate, petulant and elderly, the ladies took their knitting from one room to another and back again ... but in vain. The old man had disappeared.

The Major, however, soon came upon him (though by accident) while searching for the place where the tortoiseshell cat, who had grown suddenly and eloquently thinner, was hiding her kittens. He was dozing in a wicker chair in the breakfast room behind a great oriental screen inlaid with mother-of-pearl dragons, pagodas and sampans. Seizing his chance the Major said: 'How is she, Doctor?'

'Eh?' The old man started guiltily. 'Ah, it's you.' Reaching out with a blue-veined, freckled hand, he dragged the Major down into another wicker chair at his side. 'It's nothing.

Nothing serious. A chill. Touch of fever. But that's nothing ... It's her future here in this town that I'm worried about. Her father has no guts. She's a fine girl but what will become of her? She's of a different metal from the rest.'

'I'm glad to hear it's not serious,' replied the Major, surprised to hear the doctor say that Edward had no guts. There was a silence, broken at length by the doctor saying with a sigh: 'Why are you young men so stupid? You'd marry her if you had any sense. What's your name, did you say?'

'Brendan Archer.'

'He's as spineless as jelly. What'll become of the girl? Ireland is no place for a girl like her with a bit of spirit ... '

The doctor's eyelids stole down over his eyeballs and he slept, or seemed to sleep. The Major told himself that this was the news he had been waiting for, that he was liberated, that since Angela was only suffering from a chill she would surely be up and about again in a day or two so that everything could be settled. He got to his feet quietly so as not to disturb Dr Ryan, but the old man was awake and watching him.

'Don't tell them where I am, Mr Archer. Ach! Old women!' And he chuckled faintly, with disgust. 'She's the only one worth a farthing in the whole of County Wexford,' he muttered, half to himself. 'What fools!' He paused and sighed heavily once more. 'The English are fools; they'll lose Ireland if they go on like this. Do they even want it? Do they even know what they want? Ach, the Protestants will die of fright in their beds and serve them right!'

One afternoon, tired of sitting in the Imperial Bar reading the newspaper while the kittens played with his shoelaces and romped on the carpet, the Major set out for a walk in the company of Haig, a red setter. On his way across the fields he passed the grey stone buildings that before he had only seen from a distance, pointed out to him by Edward as the home of his ungrateful tenants. There was no sign of life: a dilapidated farmhouse built of loosely matched grey stones rising out of a yard of dried mud, once grass perhaps but long since worn into deep ruts. For a moment he considered having a look round, but as he climbed over a stile and made his way along the edge of a cornfield (the corn was still as green as grass) a dog started barking angrily; then another took up the cry, and another, and he imagined he could see a grim face staring at him from a window, and then, all around him, dragging on chains somewhere out of sight behind walls, beyond hedges, inside closed doors, a whole pack of dogs was fiendishly barking.

After he had crossed two more fields and a stream a gravel road came into sight which the Major judged would take him into Kilnalough. The day had turned chilly now that the sun was declining. The thin grey smoke of turf-fires rose from one or two of the chimneys of Kilnalough, very faint against the opal sky to the west where there were no clouds; the horizon looked very cold and clear, as if it were already winter. He shivered. Winter 1919. A peacetime winter: skating on frozen ponds, roasted chestnuts? He had forgotten what winter in peacetime was like and through the unbroken bubble of bitterness in his mind, inches thick like plate glass, he tried to visualize it. But the war was still there. He had not yet finished with it. Although he no longer attended morning prayers to be confronted by the photographs from Edward's memorial, there were other photographs, smudged and accusing, that still continued even now to appear on the front page of the *Weekly Irish Times*. The harvest was not yet complete. And what about the survivors? The pathetic letters inquiring about pensions and employment printed in 'Our Servicemen's Bureau' and signed WHIZZ BANG, DUBLIN TOMMY, DELVILLE WOOD, 1916, IMPERIAL RULE, DUBLIN and suchlike? When would it all be finished and forgotten?

On his way down the main street he was hailed by a man whom he at first did not recognize. Nearer at hand, though, he recalled the dapper appearance and the obsequious smile: it was Mr Devlin, Sarah's father. He had been spotted by

Sarah from her bedroom window. She was bored and had nothing to do, confined to bed by a slight chill, it was nothing really, the doctor said, but the Major knew how young people were ... they were inclined to be fretful. She was over the worst, of course, thanks very much, but she was so highly strung ... In short, she had asked him to ask the Major, if it wouldn't be too much of an imposition (he needn't stay more than a minute—it was more for the sake of variety than anything else) if he wouldn't mind stopping by for a chat ... just to say 'Hello'.

'I'd be delighted. I'm afraid the dog is rather muddy, though.'

'Well, we could shut him up somewhere,' replied Mr Devlin, looking at the dog with distaste. He led the way through a side door of the bank.

'Careful he doesn't gobble up all your bank-notes,' laughed the Major as the dog shook itself and frisked cheerfully about the room. Mr Devlin did not appear to find this funny, however; indeed, he looked quite upset. The dog was shut in the kitchen and the Major was shown upstairs to the room where, propped against pillows, her eyes shining, her cheeks flushed and looking, as her father had said, fretful, Sarah was waiting for him.

'I'll be downstairs,' Mr Devlin said, adding with a cough: 'I'll leave this door open in case you need anything.' And he withdrew. They could hear his footsteps descending the stairs.

'Well, what's this I hear about you being sick? You've had a chill, I understand, but you're better now. I must say you look as if you're sparkling with health.'

'Major, do stop talking nonsense and come and sit down. Here on the bed ... don't worry, I won't bite you. And where's the lovely dog you were with? It was really the dog I wanted to see, not you. And now I suppose you'll be thinking it was for yourself. Men are so conceited, young as I am that's one thing I've found out. And you needn't bother to contradict me, Major, because I *know* it's true, and I'm perfectly sure that you're more conceited than anyone, I can tell instantly by that absurd moustache you have on your lip, it's written all over your face, not to mention your ridiculous 'ramrod posture' which is the most arrogant thing I ever saw in my life. Why can't you let yourself droop a bit like a normal person? Well, it's none of my business, thank heaven. And you needn't smile like that either in that condescending way you have, as if I know nothing at all because I'm a country girl. I'm sure you think I'm a complete fool who knows nothing at all; I expect you're used to these young women they have in England who paint their faces and stay out all night—the magazines are full of talk of such creatures—smearing paint on one's skin, I must say it sounds disgusting!' And she laughed, a trifle hysterically.

'Dogs? Painted women? Really, what nonsense you talk. I think you must be more ill than I supposed.'

'When I saw you walking down the street (look, from the window I can just see people passing by) I said to myself: "There goes that absurd English person with a beautiful dog. How nice it would be to have a chat with him ... " But now you're here I can't think of a single thing to say and I can't imagine for the life of me why a few moments ago I wanted to talk to you ... But never mind, I shall make the best of it and surely think of something. And there you sit looking uncomfortable and really it almost looks as if your hand is sitting beside you, it hardly looks like a hand at all; it looks like some big leathery creature, like a toad or something, and it looks so rough and dry, is the other one the same? Yes, I can see that it is. They look as if they're made of leather dried out in the sun ... You know, Brendan (I shall call you Brendan since I no longer recognize the British Army which is a force of occupation in Ireland against the wishes of the people, you don't mind, do you?), when I was a child I used to dream that I was lying in bed with a toad sitting on my chest and although that sounds rather frightful it was really a pleasant, warm feeling. This toad used to be a particular friend of mine, I wish I could have dreams like that now. But tell me (I mustn't bore you with my childhood or else you'll make some excuse and hurry away), tell me why you were looking so miserable when you were walking along. Has Angela been making you miserable? But no, don't tell me, because I really don't want to know anything about your private affairs. They're of no concern to me, you'd simply be wasting my time. Instead I shall tell you something about Ireland since you clearly know nothing. Have you even heard of the Easter Rebellion in Dublin?'

Of course he had heard of it, he assured her smiling. That was the treacherous attack by Irish hooligans on the British Army so busily engaged in defending Ireland against the Kaiser.

'Did Ireland ask to be defended?'

Whether they asked for it or not they obviously wanted it, since so many Irishmen were fighting in the army.'

'Obviously? Nothing was less obvious! The Irish people weren't even consulted. No one asked them anything. Why should it make any difference to them whether they were invaded by the Germans or by the British? It might even be better to be subject to the Germans; at least it would make a change ... ' And the Major was quite wrong in saying that the heroes of the Easter Rising were hooligans. On the contrary, there were many gentlemen among these patriots. Did he know nothing at all? How ignorant the English (only politeness, she laughed, prevented her from saying 'the enemy'), how ignorant the English were. Had he even heard of the débutante Countess Markievicz who with a pistol in her belt defended the College of Surgeons and was sentenced to death for shooting at a gentleman looking out of the window of the Unionist Club (even though the shot missed)? Or did he think that Joseph Plunkett, jewels flaring on his fingers like a Renaissance prince and who *was*, in fact, the son of a papal count, did he think that this man was a hooligan? Already doomed with T.B., he had got up out of his bed to fight; did that make him sound like a treacherous criminal? Did the Major know that Joseph Plunkett got married to Grace Gifford (a beautiful young aristocrat whose Protestant family disowned her, naturally, the pigs) by the light of a candle held by a British soldier in the chapel of Kilmainham gaol in the early hours of the morning shortly before he faced a firing-squad? Did *that* sound like the behaviour of a hooligan?

'Indeed, no,' said the Major smiling. 'It sounds more like the last act of an opera composed by a drunken Italian librettist.'

'Ah, it's impossible to argue with someone so cynical!'

'But you ask me to believe in these operatic characters when one reads entirely different things in the newspaper. Just the other day I was reading about a woman who had pig rings put in her buttocks for supplying milk to the police ... and then there was the brass band that started a rough house with the police, using their instruments as clubs ... and a donkey stabbed to death for carrying turf to the R.I.C. barracks and labelled as a traitor to Ireland!'

'Such things are invented by the British to discredit us. We've no way of knowing whether the newspapers tell the truth. Everything belongs to the British in Ireland. Everything.'

There was silence for a moment. Sarah's flush had faded but she still looked rather fretful. She said abruptly: 'Did you know that Edward thinks you a cold person, Brendan?'

'No, I didn't know that,' said the Major, surprised.

'I think it's because you're always so very polite and distant.' She smiled at the Major's look of concern and shook her head. 'However, I told him I thought quite the opposite ... in fact, I told him I thought you were probably as soft as a steamed pudding.'

'That doesn't sound very complimentary, I must say. But how do you know what Edward thinks of me? You said he was always unfriendly to you. I thought you never saw him.'

'Oh, in Kilnalough one meets everyone,' Sarah said vaguely.

'One couldn't avoid people even if one wanted to. Now do stop looking so uneasy. Close the door and come and sit here on the bed. Don't be silly, you don't have to be paying any attention to *him* (my father, I mean) ... What, you're off already? Don't say I've offended you *again*!' And she broke into peals of laughter that rang pleasantly in the Major's ears all the way home.

But before he reached the Majestic a disturbing thought occurred to him. Could it be that Dr Ryan had been talking about Sarah and not about Angela with his 'chill' and his 'touch of fever' and his 'father as spineless as jelly'? If that were so, poor Angela might be gravely ill after all. And the more he thought about it the more likely it seemed.

'Well,' said Ripon, who was drunk. 'It was the most farcical business I've ever seen in my life. It happened right after the Soloheadbeg affair, which was the first of many attacks on the peelers, and, as you might expect, indignation and patriotism were running high. There we are, all sitting at the dinner table munching peacefully when suddenly Himself stands up and says in ringing tones: "I intend to go into Kilnalough this evening to have a drink and show the flag. Any of you men who care to join me will be most welcome." Well, a hush falls, nobody says a word ... "Ripon, how about you?" Needless to say, I had no appetite for such a reckless venture. Himself puts on a contemptuous expression and says: "Very well, if no one cares to join me I shall go by myself." We're all looking rather sheepish —at least I was— but inwardly heaving a sigh of relief (lucky for you, Major, that you weren't staying here at the time; you don't look to me like a man who could resist a call on his patriotism) when lo and behold, from a shadowy table at the other end of the dining-room a voice pipes up, thin, quavering, but determined. It's Miss Johnston. "I shall accompany you, Mr Spencer!" Everyone is dumb-founded. "And I shall come too!" cries Miss Staveley. And soon everyone is clamouring and even Mr Porter, whose wife had volunteered, is carried away by the general enthusiasm and changes his mind. And so Himself rather reluctantly found himself at the head of a party of old ladies—there must have been a good half-dozen of them—plus the doddering old Porter and plus, finally, having scented a splendid fiasco on the wind, myself.

'By the time we arrived, of course, everyone including me was practically fainting with terror (too bad you weren't there, Major, since you're obviously abnormally brave when it comes to a rough house). Byrne's pub isn't such a bad place, though nobody, mind you, would think of going there unless for the purpose of harassing the natives, nobody from the Majestic anyway. A bit ramshackle, perhaps, with its thatched roof and stone walls. There was a rank, beery smell from the open door which made the ladies wrinkle their noses.

'I hadn't ever been in there before so I had a look round (looking for the safest place in case there was a scrap, you know, Major, not being a brave and manly fellow like you). Dark, low ceiling, shabby, sawdust on the floor, chairs and tables all wooden, a bit of stench coming from the old *ghuslkhana* (as Father insists on calling it), a long mirror over the bar badly in need of silvering, and propped against it, beside a plaster statue of Johnny Walker with cane and monocle, a calender or something with one of those frightfully gruesome Sacred Hearts on it. I think there were probably some wilted tulips in a jam jar in front of it.

'Oh, look! I've forgotten that there was another man in our party, that frightful tutor fellow Evans, who's always lurking in the shadows. Actually, on this occasion he was as keen as mustard. As soon as he heard what Himself was planning he volunteered right away, could hardly restrain the chappie from leaping at the first native we saw. Anyway, there he was looking around keenly, frightfully belligerent (you'd have been delighted with him, Major, I'm sure; no white feathers for old Evans), but fortunately none of the locals seemed anxious to let him fracture their jaws.

'In fact, everything was quite peaceful. Surprising number of people there, sitting around or leaning on the bar, men for the most part. A couple of haggard and blowsy women at one of the tables, some men playing cards at another, an old crone by the fire with a big glass of porter beside her. Everyone had obviously been having a jolly good time until we showed up. But now there was Himself, standing there like that terrifying stone statue that turns up at the feast at the end of *Don Giovanni* to deal with the rotter who's been tampering with everyone's daughters! It was most alarming, Major, I can assure you (though naturally it wouldn't have been alarming for a man of your moral fibre). So Himself goes clanking across the room to a big table in the very middle at which there was nobody except a toothless, wrinkled old man. This old codger had his white head lowered over an immense mug from which he was supping liquid with a faint whistling noise. As he came up for breath he inhaled his shaggy brown moustache and sucked it white and dry before lowering his head again. This fellow took to his heels when he saw the stone statue approaching. Can't say I blame him, actually.

'Chairs were found and we all sat down. "Could we have some service please," demanded the Man of Stone in a voice from Beyond the Tomb. A perspiring red-faced chap in an apron scurried out from behind the bar wiping his hands.

'Silence still gripped the room, Major, like a heavy frost. Everyone at our table was wondering why "they" didn't start talking again, in respectful undertones, of course. Suddenly one of the men at the bar snorted into his glass, sending a great brown spray over his neighbours, hanging on helplessly to the brass rail, barking again and again with uncontrollable laughter, gasping so desperately for air that for a while it wasn't clear that it was laughter and not some dreadful epileptic fit he was having. Little by little, though, his need for air strangled his merriment and he was led outside, half drowned, by one of his companions, who then returned alone. After this some of the other men were obviously having trouble keeping their faces straight; on every side faces were long and solemn, tight as violin strings. (It was awful, Major, you've no idea). The restrained laughter bulged like an abscess in the room. At any moment one had the feeling that the wretched thing might burst with a loud report and drench us all with the yellow pus of laughter (sorry about some of these metaphors, Major, I'm doing m'best). One could feel it coming, that terrible, cataclysmic burst of laughter ...

'At this point Himself, alone in the silence, stood up and began to sing:

"GodSaveourGraciousKing
LongliveourNobleKing
GodSavetheKing."

The other members of the Majestic party were now on their feet. Two or three of the ladies, their voices reedy and defiant, joined in here and fluted:

"Sendhimvictor-rious
Happyandglor-rious
LongtoreignOh!-verus
Go-od sa-ave the King."

(Oh, Major, you can't imagine what it was like! Your hackles would have bristled with pride at that dear uplifting sound!)

'Well, an instant of silence followed. Then it came: a great rolling storm of applause, of laughter, of clapping and crying and cheering. The noise was positively deafening. The skin that covered that straining, bulging tension in the room had broken and the relief was divine, Major. Even I was applauding.

'The Man of Stone and the ladies, however, looked far from pleased at this favourable reception. Their faces darkened, the Man of Stone grimly licked his granite lips while the ladies elevated their rheumy eyes to a more noble, uncompromising angle than ever. What was to be done? Hardly had the cascade of applause begun to subside when the Man of Stone, marble nostrils quivering, launched once more into the National Anthem, singing the same verse as before (I suppose there *are* others, you're the sort of chap, Major, who'd be likely to know about that sort of thing, but never mind for the moment.)

'This time not only the contingent from the Majestic but also some throaty tenors from the bar joined in, raising their foaming tankards and showing a tendency, common to many Irishmen when singing, to warble sentimentally and allow their eyes to fill with tears. In our party at that moment, Major, muscles were tensing, necks were growing red, veins were bulging, fists were being clenched. Evans, the appalling tutor-wallah, in particular, looked as if he were about to swoon in an ecstasy of hate and violence if he didn't get to bash someone up pretty quickly.

'Now everyone was singing, not just a few drunken tenors at the bar. It was wonderful, the way everyone was singing together. And, not content with singing, a young fellow wearing a cap much too big for him and baggy trousers that looked as if they'd been made out of potato sacks jumped up on a stool and began to conduct, now the Man of Stone, now the chorus at the bar.

'The applause once again was deafening. The Man of Stone was by now looking a tiny bit defeated. He stood perfectly still for a moment, head just a little bowed. Then he fumbled in his pocket and dropped a handful of silver on the table beside his untouched glass of stout. After that he turned and clanked stiffly towards the open door, with his dignified platoon of elderly ladies trailing behind him.

'Well, we all trooped back to where we'd left the motors and for a while nobody said a word. We just stood there waiting for everyone to get in the motor cars until one of the ladies said: "You know, I think they were making fun of us." Well, nobody had anything to say to that, so I said (hoping to make things better, Major, you realize): "Couldn't it be that they just enjoyed singing and that was the only song we all knew?" But that didn't seem to help at all.

'It was then we realized that there was a bit of a scuffle going on. Evans had hung back looking for someone to punch in order to avenge the slight on Himself's honour. But in a moment or two he was bundled out by two or three grinning natives with his jacket pulled over his head like a strait-jacket. And that was that. He wasn't thanked for this splendid bit of loyalty. Himself told him angrily to get in the motor and stop playing the fool. Himself and I were the last to climb in, watched by all the drinkers who'd come pouring out of the pub and stood watching us from the door. Himself looked back at them, you know, and just for a moment it occurred to me—there was something about the expression on his face— that he was afraid of them, and I felt a bit sorry for him. But now, Major, I'm afraid you'll have to pardon me a for moment while I go and vomit—I should think probably into yonder pot of ferns would be the best idea. I realize it's a rotten show, mind you (particularly to a man like yourself who's frightfully good at holding his drink) ... '

GRAFTON PICTURE HOUSE

The principal film exhibited in the Grafton Picture House was one in which Charles Ray and Frank Keenan appear, 'The Coward', a dramatic episode of the American Civil War. It is a story of a man who was a coward, but who, when the test came, proved himself as ready to fight and die for his country as the most hardened soldier, and it possessed those essentials which make a picture interesting.

❧

At a meeting in Belfast on July 12th (the anniversary of the Battle of the Boyne) Sir Edward Carson said: 'And now there are only two policies before the country ... One is the maintenance of the Union and loyalty to the King and the other is (God bless the mark!) an Irish Republic. An Irish Republic with your hats off to the President, Mr De Valera (laughter), who is now working against you in America, with the help of the Catholic Hierarchy in that country, backed up by the Catholic Hierarchy in this and all other countries, and who imagines, in his vanity, that one day or the other, he is going to march through Belfast and Ulster (cries of 'Never!') and you will all willingly take off your hats ('No!') and bow the knee to the head of the organization which, in the darkest hour of the war of the world's freedom, shot His Majesty's soldiers in the streets of Dublin. I invite Mr De Valera to come to Ulster and I undertake that he will get a proper Ulster welcome. An Irish Republic! What is the good of the British Empire as compared with an Irish Republic? Just imagine how small the British Empire will look when the Irish Republic is established, and just imagine how the British Navy will bow their heads in shame when they see two canal boats with the Irish Sinn Fein flag (laughter) and Admiral Devlin (laughter) bringing them into action at Scapa Flow. Yes, but there is more than that. I talk of the men sleeping their last sleep on the plains of Flanders and France, in Mesopotamia and Palestine, in the Balkans and elsewhere—the men who have done their share, not for the Irish Republic, but for the great British Empire ... and, forsooth, the reward we are to have is that we are to give up all that we have won, and we are to be false and untrue to all that they suffered, in order that these rebels, prompted by ambitions of trampling upon the Protestants of the North of Ireland, may have a dot on the map which might be represented by a pinprick ... I tell the British people from this platform here, in your presence today— and I say it now with all solemnity—I tell them that if there is any attempt made to take away one jot or tittle of your rights as British citizens, and the advantages which have been won in this war of freedom, I tell them, at all consequences, once more I will call out the Ulster Volunteers (cheers). I call an Ulsterman, an Ulsterman. I call a Sinn Feiner, a rebel. I call Dominion Home Rule the *camouflage* of an Irish Republic ... '

❧

It was now the middle of July and the Major had decided to leave Kilnalough. Enough, after all, was enough. It was his intention to tell Edward that he would not be coming back, that he had been called away on some rather permanent business and would be leaving for England (if not somewhere more remote). But Edward looked so upset when he mentioned his departure, running his fingers through his hair and saying: 'Of course, I'm afraid it's not much fun for you being here ... ' deaf to his protestations that that wasn't the reason he was going (although of course, it *was*), that in the event he found himself hurriedly revising his prepared speech, saying that he was merely going to Dublin for a week and that the reason he was going ... He paused in desperation, unable to think of a reason. But at this point a miracle occurred. Edward's face brightened. Patting the Major on the back he said: 'Of course, of course, my dear fellow, I know perfectly well. You want to see the Peace Day parade on the nineteenth; I only wish I could come with you. Love to see it myself, but I'm afraid I can't leave my post. Will you be marching yourself? No? I hear that French is going to take the salute. He was asked to march with Haig in London but turned them down. That's the spirit. But look here, I must see if I can wangle you a room in Jury's. You should get a good view from there. Otherwise you won't be able to see a thing ... ' The result was that the Major was thoroughly dissatisfied with himself as he boarded the train that stood hissing in Kilnalough station; he had left himself the cowardly task of explaining by letter that his temporary visit to Dublin had become permanent. Just before the train pulled out there was a commotion on the platform as a late-arriving passenger scurried out of the ticket office laden with a brief-case and bulging packages, and attended by the station master and a porter. The Major just caught a glimpse of some battered suitcases and the gaunt, wild-eyed face of 'the friend of Parnell' as he struggled past the window. But the old fellow clambered into a third-class compartment and the Major saw no more of him. He remembered however, having heard the distant rumble of a violent argument the previous evening as he sat with a lapful of kittens in the Imperial Bar—Edward's harsh and angry tones filtering through walls and floorboards in the hush of evening. No doubt that was the reason for his departure.

All afternoon the sun shone steadily on lettuce-green leaves. The Major sat beside the open window in a pleasant daze, allowing the wind to ruffle his hair, catching now and then a breath of warm grass or the cool moisture from some bubbling stream. Soon the warmth made him drowsy and his thoughts slipped away into the heart of this golden afternoon. Half asleep, with the sunlight swilling like molten gold on the floor of the compartment, with blue smoke from his pipe swirling here and there in the breeze, he at last allowed himself to relax and felt himself at peace. Presently he knocked out his pipe, put it in his pocket and fell asleep. Slowly the feeling of peace dissolved. Beneath the shadows of his lowered eyelids tattered figures crawled towards him, pallid and speechless, through a desolate countryside.

On Saturday, the day reserved for the celebration of 'Peace' throughout the Empire, the streets of Dublin were crowded from an early hour. Over the past three days the Major had seen the grey buildings of the city gradually blossoming into colour as flags were hung from windows and arches of bunting-were stretched across the main thorough-fares. Now, in Sackville Street, the Union Jack, the Stars and Stripes, and the Italian flag floated from the ruined walls of the General Post Office; another immense Union Jack flew from the top of Trinity College while from the banks and brokerage houses lining College Green fluttered a thick tapestry of banners. It was here in front of the Bank of Ireland (a number of soldiers were already on duty guarding its roof) that the Viceregal Stand had been set up beneath a red-and-white canopy surrounded by gold-tipped staves. On this platform the Lord Lieutenant, his staff, and various Government officials would presently make their appearance; on the other side of the railings, in the courtyard of the bank, two more wooden platforms had been constructed for the wounded, to allow them an unimpeded view of this historic pageant. Beside them massed bands had been assembled, their instruments winking in the sunshine.

Although Edward, as good as his word, had procured a room for the Major with a window overlooking Dame Street (affording him a splendid view of the route that the parade would take), shortly after eleven o'clock he became restless and made his way out to the street. Above him the windows and balconies of College Green were packed with eager faces. Ladies and gentlemen had crowded on to the roof of Trinity College. People clung to parapets or precariously embraced chimney-pots. The statue of King William, horse and rider, was festooned with patriots. Red, white and blue rosettes or miniature Union Jacks glowed in every lapel as the Major forced his way through the excited throng.

By now only the most important places in the Viceregal Stand remained empty. At any moment the pageant would begin, the triumphant apotheosis of the Empire's struggle for Peace. A boy had climbed one of the tramway poles on the pavement and was shouting hysterically, signalling the approach of four motor cars from the direction of Westmoreland Street. An open motor with a grim-looking cargo of police dashed past. Then the Major just managed to catch a glimpse of a second motor as a tremendous roar broke out. He had arrived!

Standing on tiptoe (luckily he was taller than anyone around him) the Major craned forward to see through the waving forest of hats and caps. The dense crowd by the railings of the Bank of Ireland was stirring violently. A number of tall policemen were to be seen fraying a passage for the new arrival who still remained invisible. Very faintly, beneath the continuous cheering, the Major could make out the thud of drums; the bands were playing 'God Save the King'. And still he had not come into view. So thick was the crowd, so great their enthusiasm to catch a glimpse of the celebrity who was making his slow and dignified way through the tunnel of their waving, clutching hands, that a way had to be brutally forced through them. For he must not be touched: that much was clear. An assassin might have positioned himself in the great man's path. A suddenly drawn revolver, a hastily pulled trigger ... what a blow struck for Sinn Fein! But now the violently stirring whirlpool of heads had almost reached the steps up to the Viceregal Stand. Any second now and he would climb into view ...

Abruptly, he was there! The cheering increased to a thunderous cascade. Tiny and plump, fierce and dignified in his gleaming cavalry boots, swagger-stick under his arm, Lord French of Ypres scurried to the centre of the Viceregal Stand a pace or two ahead of the tall and languidly strolling officers of his staff. For a moment, while he sternly acknowledged the delirious cheering of the crowd, his thick, pale moustache flared in the sunshine (surely that head, the Major was thinking, is too big for the rounded shoulders and dapper little body). Then, having greeted the representatives of the Government, he made ready to take the salute. Meanwhile the Major had turned and was forcing his way back through the crowd towards Jury's Hotel.

Already the leading contingents had turned the corner from the Castle Yard and were moving up Dame Street beneath the tossing, brilliant roof of flags and bunting. First came the Mounted Police, men with granite faces on superb, caracoling horses; as the Major made his way through the crowded entrance to Jury's a great cheer was sent up to welcome their arrival at the Viceregal Stand. The hotel foyer was deserted.

Everybody was either on the street or at some vantage-point on one of the upper storeys. But as the Major, without impatience, was climbing the stairs to his own room, he almost collided with a gentleman coming down in great haste. He glanced at the Major and then cried: 'Man, what a stroke of luck! I've been looking for you everywhere.' It was Boy O'Neill, wild-eyed and in a great state of excitement.

'Edward told me you had a room with a view. You don't mind, do you? Can't see a blessed thing from the street. Left the ladies up on the landing above. Quick, we'll miss it all.'

Mrs O'Neill and Viola, looking tired and rather cross, were standing near a window entirely blocked by a group of very fat and ecstatic ladies. They brightened up when they saw the Major.

The Major opened the door of his room and stood aside for the ladies. Boy O'Neill thrust them aside, however, sped across the room and threw the window up with a crash. The skirl of pipes filled the room, diminishing gradually as they passed on towards College Green.

'The Irish Guards,' groaned O'Neill. 'We missed the pipers.' He craned out over the street. 'Here come the demobbed lads.'

While her father and mother gazed hungrily down at the passing troops and recited the names of regiments (the Royal Irish, the 'Skins', the Royal Irish Rifles, the Connaught Rangers, the Leinster, the Munster Fusiliers), Viola O'Neill, who had stationed herself at another window with the Major, kept turning to bestow smiles and lingering glances on him.

'Will there be tanks, Major?' she inquired, opening her eyes very wide.

'I expect so,' replied the Major gloomily.

'I'm sure I shall be frightened if there are,' Viola went on, running the tip of her tongue around her parted lips. 'I mean, just the sight of them.'

'Wait! Is it them?' barked O'Neill from outside the other window. 'Is it them or is it not?'

With feigned interest Viola leaned out to see what her father was looking at. 'I've no head for heights,' she assured the Major. 'I'm afraid I'll fall if I lean any farther.' And her small hand slipped into the Major's large paw, gripping it tightly. Frozen with alarm, the Major stared down at the grinning, jauntily striding Munster Fusiliers. The child was flirting with him! And she was certainly no more than fifteen years old. Although today her hair had been released from its pigtails and hung in thick shining tresses, she looked if anything younger than she had on their previous meeting in the Palm Court of the Majestic. What if the O'Neills should suddenly look back into the room and see him holding hands with their daughter?

'It is!' roared O'Neill from outside. 'It's them! It's the Dubs! I can see them.'

The volume of cheering below in the street increased to a deafening roar as the Dublin Fusiliers swung into sight. Viola withdrew a little from the window, making a face at the noise, and the Major took the opportunity of relinquishing her hand. But under the pretext of looking at something in the street she changed her position so that her perfumed tresses brushed against his chin. A scent of warm skin rose from her bare neck. The Major stepped back hurriedly and busied himself with lighting his pipe. And not a moment too soon. The O'Neills, hoarse with cheering, had just decided to restore their heads to the room.

The parade dragged on for another hour—an eternity it seemed to the Major, who presently retired to sit in an armchair with a newspaper. When at last the O'Neills had been granted their first view of armoured cars and tanks (Viola had gasped with emotion at the sight of the monsters creeping along Dame Street and silently besought the Major for comfort with her lovely grey eyes) and the parade had come to an end, Boy stepped back satiated from the window and remarked cryptically: 'That should give the blighters something to think about.'

His face appeared less drawn and yellow than when the Major had seen him at the Majestic and his listless manner had been replaced by a disquieting nervous energy. He'd never felt better, he assured the Major. Found a new doctor who'd done him the world of good ... indeed, he felt a new man. He wouldn't give a farthing for your Harley Street specialists. 'I feel a new man,' he repeated categorically. Saying this, he looked angrily round the room, as if expecting the Major to disagree with him.

The O'Neills were going to spend the afternoon and evening in Kingstown. There were two ships in Kingstown harbour, H.M.S. *Umpire* and H.M.S. *Parker*, which were to be illuminated that evening to supplement the bonfires and fireworks. It should be a splendid sight. Would the Major not care to come along? The Major, whose patriotic zest had lapsed once again into apathy, declined. He said vaguely that he had to go and visit an acquaintance. When the O'Neills had gone the Major had lunch and went for a stroll. The streets were still packed with rowdy, enthusiastic men and women of all classes, many of them still wearing rosettes or Union Jacks. But now (or so it seemed to the Major, who was out of sorts) their enthusiasm had already begun to wear an aimless air. Peace had been celebrated; now there was the future to think about. The pubs were doing a thriving business, full of shouting and good cheer. As he passed their open doors he kept hearing the same song: 'Tipperary' and other songs from the first year of the war. To the Major they sounded incongruous and pathetic. Dublin was still living in the heroic past. But how many of these revellers had voted for Sinn Fein in the elections?

On Monday morning the Major read in the *Irish Times* that Peace Day had been a splendid success: 'The section of demobbed soldiers and sailors revealed the spirit of camaraderie that prevails in their ranks and the democratic side of army life. Men with top-hats walked beside men in their working clothes. Spats moved in time with hobnailed boots.' There was also an account of how an ex-Dublin-Fusilier had marched over the whole route from the Castle to St Stephen's Green on crutches. By the time he reached the Green his palms were bleeding from the friction. When asked why he did not fall out he replied: 'No, I knew it was my last march and I wouldn't fall out while I had a breath left in my body.'

Only towards evening had a rowdy element manifested itself. Young men carrying Sinn Fein flags and singing 'The Soldier's Song' had gathered outside the Post Office in Sackville Street. There had been a few scuffles before the police arrived to disperse them. Later in the evening a large crowd had threatened to throw a soldier into the Liffey at Ormond Quay. A police sergeant coming to his rescue had been shot at close range and was now lying gravely ill in hospital. But when one considered the magnificence of the occasion, the nobility of the marching troops, the enthusiasm of the cheering crowds, perhaps these incidents might represent only the tiniest flaw in the smooth and majestic edifice of Peace Day—a flaw that was scarcely visible to a man of broad vision.

The Major was now faced with the alternative of abandoning Angela and crossing to England or returning to Kilnalough to assume his heavy but nebulous responsiblities as her fiancé. Unable to make up his mind to do the one thing he was equally unable to make up his mind to do the other. The result was that for the time being he remained irresolutely in Dublin.

One day, while on a tram returning from Kingstown where he had spent the afternoon looking at the yachts and sitting in tea-shops, he suddenly found himself in the middle of a disturbance. The tram had come to a halt at the end of Northumberland Road just short of the canal bridge. A dense crowd had formed and motor cars had stopped on each side of the bridge. All the passengers were on their feet trying to see what was going on. Impatient with the delay, the Major decided to walk and forced his way through the crowd as far as the bridge. Abruptly shots rang out from close at hand and the crowd convulsed, forcing him back against the parapet. He almost fell but somehow managed to cling to the brickwork and pull himself up. On the far side of the canal two men in trench coats sprinted away in the direction of the quays. A tall, strongly built man lumbered after them, his movements impeded by a sandwich-board that hung to his knees; in his right hand he carried a revolver. Behind the southern wall of the canal the Major glimpsed the khaki uniforms of British soldiers. There was a volley of rifle shots and the man in the sandwich-board was buffeted by an invisible wind. A few yards farther on he paused, raised his revolver and fired back across the canal at the soldiers; then he hastened on again. More rifle shots. Once more the big man was buffeted, then ran on clumsily a few yards. He was shouting something. His companions had vanished by now. Abruptly he collapsed inside the sandwich-board, subsided slowly to his knees and hung there, head lolling, arms trailing, still supported by the boards, like an abandoned puppet.

Slowly the crowd began to move again, stunned and cautious, releasing the Major. He moved forward a few steps until he could see what had stopped the traffic on the bridge. An old man—white moustache, grey face spattered with scarlet— lay on his back, eyes rolled up beneath the lids so that only the whites were visible. A gold watch, linked by a chain to the top buttonhole of his waistcoat, still lay in the palm of his right hand encircled by long ivory fingernails.

Shaken, the Major shoved his way through the crowd in the direction of Mount Street. The big man still hung like a rag doll strapped into the sandwich-board. The Major was close enough now to read in black letters HOLY MARY MOTHER OF GOD PRAY FOR US SINNERS! The sandwich-board was made not of wood but of iron; the metal, deeply scored by bullets, gleamed through the torn paper. The big man had been using it as a suit of armour.

The Major began to stride rapidly up Mount Street. On each side the windows of grey, shabby houses glared down at him. The pavement before his eyes was spattered with scarlet drops. Such a bright scarlet! How new the blood of an old man looked! Not at all faded, weary, desiccated like the man himself. In no time at all he found himself in Leinster Street and turned into College Park. Here everything was suddenly peaceful; one could hardly hear the motor cars and drays that went spinning along on the other side of the high wall. Here there was no cloth-capped pedestrian who might step out from among the passers-by and ask you the time. Look, he thought, how does one recognize them? They wear no uniform. They're like spies. They should be shot like spies. They look like anyone at all. It was absurd, he thought, walking beside the tranquil green field scarred here and there by the brown patches of abandoned cricket pitches ... it was absurd that in Ireland an old man consulting his watch should be killed. In wartime innocent old people were killed—but Ireland was a peaceful country.

The next day he read an account of the incident. The old man was an Englishman, of course, a retired army officer who worked in the Intelligence Department in Dublin Castle. He was a widower and lived near by in Northumberland Road. He had been coming home from his office after work when a man carrying a sandwich-board had stepped out of the crowd and asked him the time. And someone had heard the man say: 'Ah then, your time has come!' and with that he had raised a revolver to the old man's head and pulled the trigger. But the assassin had been unlucky. A party of British soldiers had just finished searching a house beside the church on the corner and they had been ready for trouble. The man in the sandwich-board had died without giving his name. Who was he? Nobody knew. The unknown murderer had been carrying a sandwich-board with a religious message (the Major overheard someone in Jury's say with a laugh) because it was thought that Englishmen, Protestants, would turn their eyes away from the name of Our Lady, and these days so many people were being stopped and searched for arms ...

The Major read this newspaper account and the next day found one or two more. But although it was mentioned in passing once or twice, the murder of the old man had been classified and accepted. It was odd, he thought. An old man is gunned down in the street and within a couple of days this senseless act is both normal and inevitable. It was as if these newspaper articles were poultices placed on sudden inflammations of violence. In a day or two all the poison had been drawn out of them. They became random events of the year 1919, inevitable, without malice, part of history. The old man lying on the bridge with his watch in his hand was a part of history. And thus, the Major reflected —looking out of his window at the bustling traffic of Dame Street, at the gentlemen in bowler hats, at the fine ladies in their billowing dresses, at the flower and fruit sellers, at the ragged women with babies and barefoot children clinging to their skirts begging in the street below 'For the Mercy of God' ... 'For the Holy Vargin!' ... at the gleaming motor cars, at the friendly faces, at the jaunting-cars with their nodding horses and at all the other things which would not be recorded—a particle of the history of this year is formed. A raid on a barracks, the murder of a policeman on a lonely country road, an airship crossing the Atlantic, a speech by a man on a platform, or any of the other random acts, mostly violent, that one reads about every day: this was the history of the time. The rest was merely the 'being alive' that every age has to do.

This thought must have displeased him, for he said to himself: 'I'll leave tonight and go back to London. And then perhaps I'll go abroad and spend the winter in Italy.' The boat train left Westland Row at ten past seven. He would get into Euston at half past five tomorrow morning. 'I have plenty of time. I'll ring for someone to pack my bags.'

But at this moment there was a knock on the door. It was the chambermaid in her black uniform and white apron and cap. She had a telegram for him. It was from Edward to say that Angela had died the night before and would he return to Kilnalough as soon as possible.

Gone to the angels. The Major thought about her on the train back to Kilnalough. He thought about the tea-party the day he had arrived in Kilnalough a few weeks earlier; indeed, it was his only memory of her. He had no other. And somehow he could not help smiling sadly when he remembered her fierce nostalgia in the tropical gloom of the Palm Court.

And now Angela had gone to join the ancient pre-Raphaelite poets and the steady-eyed explorers who had shed their earthly envelopes (as the saying goes). She had gone to join the dead rowing blues (they were most probably among those blurred chaps on Edward's War Memorial) who had quaffed pre-war champagne out of her slippers. She had gone to the place where all the famous people go, and the obscure ones too for that matter.

'I'm dying', she had said to him, 'of boredom', and even that remembered statement seemed to lack pathos or tragedy. It was almost as if one might expect to find 'of boredom' written on her death certificate. 'Well,' he thought, 'I don't mean to laugh at her, poor girl. She must have been ill even then.' Indeed, it made him feel sad to think of her now, sitting there in that pseudo-tropical clearing in Kilnalough and dying 'of boredom', if not of something that reminded her more painfully of the harshness of reality, of the transience of youth, and of her own mortality.

The Major did not arrive at the Majestic until after dark and it would not have surprised him to find nobody there to greet him. However, as he climbed the stone steps and dragged open the massive front door he saw that there was a glimmer of light in the foyer. The electric light appeared not to be functioning but an oil lamp was burning dimly on the reception desk and beside it, asleep on a wooden chair, was the old man-servant, Murphy. He started violently as the Major touched

his arm and gave a gasp of terror; it was true that there was
something eerie about this vast shadowy cavern and the Major
himself felt a shiver of apprehension as his eyes tried to probe
beyond the circle of light into the darker shadows where the
white figure of Venus flickered like a wraith. He bent an ear;
Murphy was wheezing some information.

Edward had retired early on Dr Ryan's instructions, worn
out. He would see the Major in the morning. The twins,
Miss Faith and Miss Charity, had returned from their holidays
earlier that same evening for their sister's funeral which would
be held tomorrow at eleven. If the Major required anything
to eat he would find sandwiches in the dining-room.

Murphy took the oil lamp and led the way to the dining-
room without volunteering to carry the Major's suitcase. But
the Major was by now an old hand at the Majestic, so he
picked it up without a murmur and plunged down the corridor
in the wake of the dancing lamp. Soon he was wearily masticating soda-bread sandwiches which contained some sort of
fish; he supposed it to be salmon. There was no sound except
for the creaking of the wind outside and an occasional flash
of rain against the window-panes. Murphy had gone away
with the oil lamp and the only illumination was provided by
the two-branched silver candlesticks that flanked his plate
of sandwiches.

A great melancholy stole over him. He sat there at the table
in his mackintosh (which he had not bothered to remove) and
thought of Angela and felt sorry for her, and he felt sorry for
Edward too. And presently, thinking of the old man dead on
the canal bridge, he felt sorry not only for the dead but for
the mortal living too ... it made so little difference. Having
eaten, he drank a glass of beer and climbed the creaking,
treacherous stairs to the room he had used before. It was
exactly as he had left it. The sheets had not been removed
(thank heaven!) and the bed had not been made. He undressed
and cràwled beneath a generous pile of damp blankets.

The sun shone brilliantly on the day of Angela's funeral.

The Major woke very late and by the time he had gone downstairs to breakfast dressed in a dark suit and black tie for the sombre occasion Edward had already left for the church. So had the twins, apparently. There was no sign of them. Only Ripon was left, looking pale and wretched, unable to find anything to say. He looked relieved when the Major refused his offer of a lift to the church, saying that he would prefer to walk.

'Angela had leukaemia,' Ripon told him in reply to his question. 'We thought you knew.'

'Well, no, actually, I didn't,' replied the Major, sounding rather cross. How typical of the Spencers to leave him to find out for himself!

He entered the churchyard by a side gate of wrought iron which at some time in the distant past had been left open so long that it had rusted that way and was now immovable, embroidered by thick green threads of grass into the bank behind it. In earlier days it had borne an inscription in Gothic letters so ornate that one could hardly read them ... 𝕿𝖍𝖊 𝕷𝖔𝖗𝖉 𝖎𝖘 ... My shepherd? Rust had entirely dislodged the rest of the scroll. 'My defence', perhaps. Whatever it was it lay in dark flakes somewhere in the grass.

A little farther on he came to a pile of fresh, dark earth and it gave him a disagreeable shock when he realized that this was where Angela was to be interred. As he passed he was unable to resist a glance down into the neat oblong trench along the sides of which the white knuckles of roots showed like nuts in a slice of fruit-cake. Down there, in the course of a year or two, these slender white fingers would grow out again and wrap themselves round the wooden box imprisoning this unfortunate English lady (poor Angela, he was sure that her thoughts had always been returning like little lost dogs to such places as Epsom and Mayfair, Oxford and Cowes) for ever in Irish soil. He moved on now into the deep blue shadow cast by the tower of the church, a structure as modest as the headstones in the churchyard and made of the same grey, granitic stone quarried on the coast (Edward had once told him) ten or so miles away. The Roman Catholic chapel, as it happened, was also made of this stone.

The Major slipped into a pew at the back and, lulled by the organ's soft piping and rumbling and creaking of pedals, fell into a pleasant and confused day dream about a hiking holiday he had taken before the war, remembering how he had lain on a hillside on a sunny day like this, the long grass combed flat by the wind. It was very peaceful here.

When he looked up at last he saw Edward. Although his face was stony and expressionless he must have been weeping a few moments earlier, for his normally bristling moustache had become sodden and was drooping towards his chin; a drop of water clinging to it caught a ray of sunlight as he passed and glittered like a diamond. With Edward were two slim girls in identical black dresses and black veils that scarcely dimmed their shining blonde curls. They stood there, tall and straight, one on each side of their father, their lovely faces sad and composed as they began to move up the aisle in step with Edward who had an arm over each of their shoulders and was lurching slightly, in the manner of a prize-fighter being helped from the ring. At the end of the aisle they neatly supported him into the front pew, even tilted him forward a little to pray, before kneeling themselves and bowing their shining heads.

The service took its course. The rector had begun to talk about Angela and was evidently having difficulty, not merely in marshalling the dead girl's qualities, but even in thinking of anything to say about her at all. A shaft of blood-stained sunlight crept from the dusty hassock on to the gleaming toe of the Major's shoe. The devoted sister, the rector was saying, of these two lovely children (and of ... of this fine young man, he added as an afterthought). The Major's mind slipped away to the windblown hillside, with its scent of clover and wild thyme. The model of the Christian lady, gentle, firm and devoted, whom the Lord in His inscrutable wisdom ...

'Ah,' thought the Major, 'inscrutable wisdom ... ' The grey-faced man lay on the pavement spattered with scarlet, a gold watch clutched in his fingers. Goodbye, Angela. He sighed and tried to struggle back to the windblown hillside. He fell asleep, though, before he could get there. He was woken again almost instantly by the crash of his hymn-book which had closed itself and fallen between his knees. The rector was saying: 'When Duty called her she answered with firmness and devotion ... '

Before the day of the funeral was over the Major had once more left Kilnalough. An hour or two after he had returned to the Majestic with the other mourners word arrived that his elderly aunt in London (whose health had been poor for some time) had taken a definite turn for the worse. Her doctor had decided that it was necessary to summon the Major, who happened to be her only surviving relative. He sought out Edward, who was wandering around the hotel in a sort of agonized daze, trying to avoid the old ladies who kept bounding out of the shadows to present their condolences. Edward squeezed his arm and said that he quite understood — which possibly meant quite the opposite, namely, that he took the Major's dying aunt to be a polite fiction. But there was nothing the Major could do about *that*: to have gone into detail would have made things worse than ever. Since he had missed the afternoon train Murphy was ordered to take him across country in the trap to Valebridge from where he might catch a later train which, with luck, might get him to Kingstown in time to catch the boat.

Edward raised his leonine head and squared his shoulders with an effort.

'Angela gave me this for you. A few days before she ... you know ... '

The Major glanced at the envelope and, although he had felt very little throughout this day of black ties, pale faces and subdued voices (only perhaps a vague dread, a muffled sadness), the sight of his name written in the familiar, meticulously neat handwriting abruptly squeezed his heart. And at last Angela was really dead.

'I'd better get a move on. I must say goodbye to Ripon and the twins.'

The twins were in the writing-room being comforted by a pair of portly gentlemen in tweeds; they had clearly been reluctant to remove the gossamer-black veils which suited them so perfectly and now they sat on sofas, pale and brave, their eyes shining and their slender hands being patted by the rough, hairy paws of their escorts. The Major decided not to disturb them (after all, he had never set eyes on them before today) and instead, while Murphy waited outside the front door with the trap, searched from room to room for Ripon.

He was not in the Palm Court, nor in the dining-room (where one or two pale but hungry-looking mourners were gravely feeding on a cold collation), nor in the residents' lounge, nor in the ladies' lounge, the ballroom, the breakfast room, the coffee room or the gun room. He stood in the corridor, baffled, trying to think where Ripon might be. He ascended to the Imperial Bar, but Ripon was not there either. It was some time since the Major had been here; a new litter of kittens were romping on the floor, charming little ginger fellows. The previous litter had grown considerably in his absence and had abandoned the carpet to the new arrivals. Instead, they dozed on dusty chairs or picked their way among the bottles on the bar, their eyes blazing. The Major was still holding Angela's letter in his hand. He put it down on the bar and stooped to pick up one of the ginger kittens. It squirmed in his palm, mewing feebly, and dug its tiny claws into his fingers. With a sigh he dropped it and looked at his watch. He must hurry. Where on earth was Ripon? He decided, as a last resort, to try the billiard room.

There he found him, throwing a jack-knife from one end of the room to the other trying to make it stick in the oak panelling. His hand was raised to throw as the Major stepped across the threshold.

'Steady the Buffs!'

'Oh, it's you. I just thought I'd come down here for a while. All those morbid old ladies, you know.'

'Just called to say goodbye. I've got to go back to England to see a relation who's been taken ill.'

'Oh, I see,' nodded Ripon, putting on his jacket and for some reason patting his pockets anxiously. 'I don't blame you, really. It's awful here, isn't it? I'm thinking of trying to get out myself while the going's good before the bloody ship sinks, so to speak. Matter of fact I'm glad you came because I've been wanting a word with you.'

For the second time in less than ten minutes the Major considered defending the innocence of his motives for leaving, but thought better of it.

'Well, I haven't got much time. In fact, I haven't got any time at all. You see, I missed the train from here and I've got to get myself over to Valebridge before, let me see ... ' He looked at his watch.

'You've heard the news, of course,' stated Ripon, ignoring the Major's remarks. 'It's all over town, I expect.'

'Heard what news?' demanded the Major anxiously.

'About me and Máire Noonan. I'm sure that little bitch Sarah will have told you.'

'Yes, I did hear something. But look here, Ripon, you mustn't go around calling girls bitches like that ... I mean, really! Besides, she's a cripple, more or less, and if *you* had her disability ... '

'I suppose you know Máire's a fish-eater ... an R.C.?'

'Yes.'

'So there's going to be an unholy row sooner or later. Or maybe I should say a *holy* row. And just at the moment it's not such a good time, you know, what with poor old Angela and so on ... But old man Noonan has been putting on the pressure, d'you see, and something's got to be done.' Ripon paused and jabbed the knife violently into the oak panelling. 'Can you lend me a couple of fivers, by the way?'

'No.'

'Just one fiver would be a help.'

'No.'

'It doesn't really matter, of course, if you're short.'

'Why has Mr Noonan been putting on the pressure?'

'It's this R.C. business. He thinks that maybe I'm not going to ... Well, what it all boils down to is that he wants me to make it public and the main thing is ... '

'To tell your father?'

Ripon nodded gloomily.

'Well, I'm sure it will all turn out all right. After all, the Noonans are rather wealthy from what I hear. I don't see why Edward would have any real objection once he knows you're serious.'

'It's this stupid religious business, Major. The point is, you see, that I've been trotting along to see the old priest for what they call "instruction" (they're frightful sticklers for the rules). Not my idea, I can assure you. Old man Noonan insisted on it. It's a lot of rot, really. I mean, frankly it doesn't make an awful lot of difference to me where we're married, couldn't care less about that sort of thing. The snag is that Himself is going to get into a fearful wax when he hears about it ... and to tell the truth, I don't quite know what to do.' He paused, avoiding the Major's eye. 'Fact is, I was rather hoping you might do something to help me ... tip the wink to Himself and so forth.'

'Oh really! That's out of the question, Ripon. Look here, I'm in a dreadful hurry at the moment and I simply can't afford to miss this train (this business with my aunt is perfectly genuine, I can assure you). If you want me to give you advice I'd be glad to help you in any way I can; in fact, I'll give you my card and you can put it all down in black and white.'

Ripon took the Major's card and looked at it without optimism.

'If you spoke to Father he might not take it so hard, you know. If you pointed out that it's not the end of the world and so forth. I know he respects you. I'm afraid he won't listen if I tell him.'

'I'm sorry, but it's out of the question,' repeated the Major, becoming agitated. 'It won't do at all if I miss this train, as I'm sure to do if I stand here talking any longer. And so, well, I just wanted to say goodbye ... I'm sure everything will turn out all right in the end. Goodbye, Ripon.'

And without looking back the Major hastened along the corridor, up the stairs three at a time, through the residents' lounge, took a short cut through the orangerie and emerged beside the statue of Queen Victoria where Murphy was waiting for him with the trap.

As they reached the last point of the drive that afforded a view of the building the Major looked back at the grey, battlemented mass that stood there like a fortress among the trees.

'Stop, Murphy!' he cried suddenly. He had just remembered: he had left Angela's letter in the Imperial Bar!

The old manservant dragged on the reins and turned slowly to look back at the Major, his discoloured teeth exposed in a ghastly rictus. Was it the effort of reining in the pony that made him look like that or was he laughing hideously? The Major gazed fascinated at the old man's fleshless skull and sunken eyes.

'Never mind. Drive on or we'll miss the train.' And he thought: 'I'll get Edward to send it on to me. At this stage it can't contain anything very urgent, after all.'

IN PRAISE OF BOXING

A man's last line of defence is his fists. There is no sport, not even cricket, which is more essentially English than boxing. Wilde is a national hero because he has shown that in the great sport which is ours, and now is the property of the whole world, we can still produce a champion when it comes to a fight. There is no sport in the world which demands cleaner living. There is no more natural sport. Low cunning will not help him, but a quick, clear brain, a hard body, and perfect training will carry a man a long way.

The Major now found himself sitting beside his aunt's sickbed in London and not in the best of tempers. He had very quickly reached the conclusion that his aunt was less sick than he had been led to believe, which irritated him and caused him to suspect a conspiracy between this lonely old lady and her doctor (it was the doctor who had sent the telegram which summoned him). And although within a few months his aunt vindicated herself by dying, the Major was never quite able to discard the faint irritation he had felt at being greeted, as he raced up a beautifully polished staircase (everything looked so clean after the Majestic) beneath sombre, heavily varnished portraits of distant dead relations, and burst into her bedroom, by a wan smile rather than a death-rattle. Meanwhile he sat beside her bed with her loose-skinned, freckled hand in his and murmured rather testily: 'Of *course* you'll get better ... You're only imagining things.' But even while consoling his aunt his thoughts would very often revert to Edward, 'If I'd stayed a little longer,' he kept thinking, 'I might have been able to cushion the shock and make him see reason about Ripon and his lady-friend. After all, it can't be as serious as all that.' Nevertheless he knew instinctively that the possibilities of mutual incomprehension between Edward and Ripon would be prodigious, and he continued to ruminate on them as he held a glass of verbena tea to his aunt's faintly moaning lips and commanded her brusquely to take a sip. To tell the truth, he felt rather like a man who has walked away from a house drenched in petrol leaving a naked candle burning on the table.

Here he was in London and nobody seemed to be dying. What was he doing here anyway? The doctor appeared to be avoiding him these days and when they did meet he wore an apologetic air, as if to say that it really wasn't his fault. But at last the day came when the doctor, with a new confidence, informed him that his aunt had had a serious haemorrhage during the night. And even his aunt, though pale as paper, looked gratified. This news upset the Major, because he was fond of his aunt and really did not want her to die, however much he might want her to stop being a nuisance. However, in spite of the haemorrhage, his aunt still showed no sign of passing on to 'a better life' (as she unhopefully referred to it herself when, for want of another topic of interest to both of them, she embarked, as she frequently did, on conversations beginning: 'All this will be yours, Brendan ... ').

The news from Ireland was dull and dispiriting: an occasional attack on a lonely policeman or a raid for arms on some half-baked barracks. If one was not actually living in Ireland (as the lucky Major no longer was) how could one possibly take an interest when, for instance, at the same time Negroes and white men were fighting it out in the streets of Chicago? Now *that* gripped the Major's imagination much more forcibly. Unlike the Irish troubles one knew instantly which side everyone was on. In the Chicago race-riots people were using their skins like uniforms. And there were none of the devious tactics employed by the Shinners, the pettifogging ambushes and assassinations. In Chicago the violence was naked, a direct expression of feeling, not of some remote and dubious patriotic heritage. White men dragged Negroes off streetcars; Negroes fired rifles from housetops and alleyways; an automobile full of Negroes raced through the streets of a white district with its occupants promiscuously firing rifles. And Chicago was only a fragment of the competition that Ireland had to face. What about the dire behaviour of the Bolshevists? The gruesome murders, the rapes, the humiliations of respectable ladies and gentlemen? In late 1919 hardly a day went by without an eye-witness account of such horrors being confided to the press by some returned traveller who had managed to escape with his skin. And India: the North-West Frontier ... Amritsar? No wonder that by the time the Major's eye had reached the news from Ireland his palate had been sated with brighter, bloodier meat. Usually he turned to the cricket to see whether Hobbs had made another century. Presently the cricket season came to an end. A rainy, discouraging autumn took its place. Soon it would be Christmas.

One day the Major received a telegram. To his surprise it was signed SARAH. It said: DON'T READ LETTER RETURN UNOPENED. The Major had not yet received any letter and waited with impatience for it to arrive. Next morning he was holding it in one hand and tapping it against the fingertips of the other. After a brief debate with himself he opened it.

She had no reason for sending him a letter (she wrote) and he didn't have to read it if he didn't want to. But she was in bed again with 'an unmentionable illness' and bored to tears, literally ('I sometimes burst into tears for no reason at all') and, besides, her face was so covered in spots that she looked 'like a leopard' and she had become so ugly that little children fled wailing if they saw her at the window and nobody ever came to see her these days and she had no friends now that poor Angela had died and (that reminded her) why had he not come over to say hello to her on the day of Angela's funeral ... after all, she (Sarah) didn't bite, but then she supposed that he was too high and mighty to be seen talking to the likes of her and he probably, anyway, couldn't read her writing because she was scribbling away in bed, her fingers 'half frozen off' and surrounded by stone hot-water jars against which she kept cracking her 'poor toes' and which were practically freezing anyway ... and besides, besides, she was positively bored to distraction with everything and there was simply nothing to do in Kilnalough, nothing at all, and she would certainly run away if she could (which, of course, she couldn't, being a 'poor, miserable cripple' into the bargain ... and full of self-pity, he would surely be thinking) ...

But enough of that, about herself there was nothing of interest to say. The Major must be wanting to hear what was happening in Kilnalough and at the Majestic and the answer to that was ... ructions! ! ! Edward Spencer challenging Father O'Meara (practically) to a duel for improper association with Ripon. Old Mr Noonan threatening to horsewhip the young pup (Ripon, that was) if he didn't stop playing fast and loose with Máire (did the Major remember the fat pudding of a girl they had met one day in the street?) and show whether he was a gentleman or what he was, anyway, begod ... And as to what *that* might mean the Major's guess was as good as hers ... only it wouldn't surprise anyone to learn that the above-mentioned fat pudding was pregnant with triplets by the young pup. And to make matters worse Fr O'Meara was threatening to sue Edward for something the twins had done to him, she didn't quite know *what* but she'd try and find out and let him know. Anyway, there was surely worse to come.

However, she was pretty certain that such provincial matters would hardly interest him now that he was back in the big city ... Was it true that in London even the horses wore leather shoes? But she was only teasing him, of course. The English (that was to say, 'the enemy') were so serious one could never risk making a joke in case they believed you.

Had the Major heard the very latest, God forgive her (in fact, God forgive everybody), that had been happening right under her nose all this while ... which was that one of her father's clerks, a red-faced lad up from the country with a smathering of the 'mattermathics' had dared, had had the temerity, had made so bold-faced as to get up his nerve to, in spite of her spots (which must show what strong stomachs country people had), actually *fall in love with her*! ! ! Without so much as a by-your-leave! He, the Major, would undoubtedly be as amazed as she was that even a country lad who only knew about cows (and himself smelled like a farmyard) could have his wits so deranged as to consider marrying a 'total cripple' like herself.

Himself: 'Will ye walk out with me, Miss Devlin?'

Me: 'How can I, you peasant oaf, with no legs?' And now every time she went out of the house she would find her 'rural swain' touching his forelock and blushing like a ripe tomato and the whole thing was positively sickening and disgusting. There surely must be something wrong with someone (apart altogether from the things which immediately greeted the eye and the nose) who would marry someone like her sooner than one of the millions of girls who could churn his butter and wash his clothes and thump his dough and have a brat a year like a pullet laying eggs from dawn to dusk without so much as batting an eyelid. And what did the Major think of such a thing anyway? Wasn't she right to treat the whole thing as nonsense? But the worst was yet to come.

One could hardly believe it, but the 'rural swain' had had the temerity to approach her father with his 'bovine proposal' and had even inquired if there might not be a little bit of a dowry now to sweeten the bargain, a couple of heifers and a few quid, perhaps, or a brace of pigs and a few auld hens and then maybe later on a wee share in the bank (which he seemed to think was something like a farm for growing money) and so on and so forth, with lots of blushes and his breeches hanging off of him like potato sacks on a scarecrow! And the very worst was yet to come!

Incredible though it might seem, her father, instead of sneering at the young bog-trotter's pretensions to his fair daughter's hand, boxing his ears and sending him back to scratching in his ledgers or whatever he did (stoking the boiler for all she knew), had said that, by Jove, in such circumstances one did well to treat all proposals with serious consideration and though, of course, it would never occur to 'me or your mother' to influence her in any way, it nevertheless seemed unwise to send likely lads packing, up from the country or not (after all, they could be groomed and citified to cope with Kilnalough's undemanding standards), before one had given them a fair run for their money! The Major would hardly believe it, but there was even worse to come!

The 'bovine suitor', greatly encouraged by her father's attitude, had now taken to lurking beside the gate whenever she went outside, greeting her with familiar winks, and had even approached her near enough to suggest that she should play him 'a bit of a tune' on her piano and even, no doubt considering the conquest effected, had placed a hand like a gelatine lobster on her 'fair shrinking shoulder', murmuring that she should accord him 'a hug'. Naturally, he had received a tongue-lashing for his trouble. Yet he had stood there grinning and red-faced (the blush, she realized, was permanent) quite unabashed. What did the Major make of her predicament? Did he not agree that it would be better to accept the rigours of spinsterhood and penury ('your mother and I won't always be here to look after you, you know') rather than submit to such a grisly fate? Indeed, her only support in the matter had come from a totally unsuspected source, namely the incredibly ancient and insufferable Dr Ryan whom she had always thought of as her 'arch-enemy'. He had told her father flatly that he would as soon see her marry a gorilla in the Dublin Zoo as the above-mentioned peasant Lothario and that if he so much as heard mention of the matter again he would see to it that all his patients in Kilnalough transferred their business to some other bank. So for the moment there was an armistice. But for how long? The more he thought about it the more her father wanted to marry her off. So no wonder that she had been overtaken by her 'unmentionable illness'. Perhaps, like poor Angela, she would just wilt away and probably no one would care. The Major, she was certain, wouldn't care in the least.

And who knew? Perhaps her parents were right. Perhaps there was no real difference between one man and another. After all (she sometimes found herself thinking, sinful though such thoughts were), after all, are we so very different from animals? And animals made less fuss about such matters.

By the way, she had forgotten to mention one curious thing about the 'rural swain' (whose name was Mulcahy, incidentally): in his lapel he wore a plain gold ring. She had asked him what it meant. '*An Fáinne*', he had replied. Oh, she had eyes in her head, she had told him impatiently. But what was it *for*, that was what she wanted to know? Oh, so she 'had the Irish'? Just a little, she had admitted, not wanting to encourage his respect. Well, it was like a circle for Irish-speaking people, he had explained, so that they might recognize each other by the ring and talk to each other in Irish rather than in the tongue of the foreigner. They had a retreat, it appeared: a number of young men and women anxious to perfect themselves in the ancestral language of Ireland, all off in a cottage in the depths of the country somewhere chattering away in Irish from morn till night. Had the Major ever heard of such a wonderful idea? She had to admit that that was one point in Mulcahy's favour (admittedly, the only one). He had even asked *her* to join the circle (though no doubt his motives were impure). So the 'rural swain', though he did not do at all, though he was impossible, at least had gained a meagre point.

A few days later she had met a young Englishman, an officer from the Curragh camp staying with his uncle for a few days, and she had told him about this idea of people speaking Irish to each other. 'How bizarre!' he had exclaimed. 'How delightful! How original!' and he had told her about a club he had joined at Oxford which specialized in trying to make contact with poltergeists in haunted houses.

Ah, but the Major wouldn't be interested in all this dull tattle from the provinces since he was in London at the very centre of things, at the very centre of the Empire, of 'Life' even! She had abused his good nature by rambling on so long about herself and her own petty problems. He must think of her as she herself thought of the bovine aspirant for her affections, Mulcahy. And besides, besides, her fingers were now frozen to the point where they were practically 'dropping off', the hot-water bottles were lumps of ice on every side of her, her ink-well too was freezing over and her room was so cold that with every breath the paper she was writing on would disappear in a cloud of steam. The weather was quite appalling, cold and damp beyond belief, and the days so dark that even at midday one had to turn up the gas mantle in order to read a book or do some sewing. What misery, the Major must be thinking, to be an Irishwoman, to be living in Ireland, to live all of one's life in Ireland beneath the steady rain and the despair of winter and the boredom, the boredom! But no, she was *glad* she was Irish and he could think what he liked! She thought of him, however, with affection and remained truly his.

Having read this, the Major stood up and then sat down again. He turned over the thick, crinkly sheaf of writing-paper. The coffee pot had grown cold on the breakfast table. Well, he thought, what a remarkable letter ... I must answer it immediately.

And so he sat down, ignoring his aunt's faint cries from upstairs, and wrote a long and slightly delirious reply as if he too were in a fever, gripped in the claws of boredom, passionate and intense, surrounded by icy hot-water bottles. He said in substance that even with spots (and he couldn't believe that they were as bad as she claimed) nobody but herself could ever for a moment consider her ugly. That it was, alas, only too natural that the moth should be attracted by the flame, that the 'rural swain' (not to mention other young men) should become besotted with her charms; nevertheless, he agreed with Dr Ryan (the 'senile old codger', as Ripon called him) that, splendid fellow though Mulcahy no doubt was, it would be a shame to waste her on someone so little able to appreciate her culture, refinement and intelligence. Had she no relation in London whom she could stay with for a while with a view to stimulating 'une heureuse rencontre', as the Frenchies put |it, with a young man worthy of her? If not then she must certainly come and stay with him, duly chaperoned, of course. He would be only too glad to do everything in his power to rescue this 'cultured' pearl from the Irish swine.

In the meantime she must write and tell him everything that was going on at the Majestic. And she must write immediately. He was on tenterhooks. The thin, starving rats of curiosity were nibbling at his bones. As for London, though it was indeed the centre of the Empire it was no more the centre of 'Life' than, say, Chicago, Amritsar, or Timbuctoo—'Life' being everywhere equal and coeval, though during the winter in Kilnalough one might be excused for thinking that 'Life's' fires were banked up if not actually burning low—certainly, if one happened to be in bed with an unmentionable illness.

With that, he hastily sealed the letter with dry lips and posted it. Then he sat down with impatience to await the reply. But the days passed and no reply came.

Dispatches from Fiume this morning state that Gabriele D'Annunzio's expedition has succeeded beyond the most sanguine expectations of those who took part in it. All along his march the poet was joined by military contingents which broke away from their camps. He summoned the Allied Commanders and troops to withdraw ... The Italian commander, General Pittaluga, immediately tried to stop the advance, but in vain. He sent out troops to meet those of D'Annunzio and to order them to stop outside the town, but his own men immediately fraternized with those of D'Annunzio, and embraced one another. The general twice sent out nineteen armoured cars with machine-guns, but they also immediately went over to D'Annunzio. A dramatic scene then followed. General Pittaluga, with his last detachment, went to D'Annunzio at the point where he was entering the town. He halted a few paces from the advancing column, and his own soldiers remained a few paces behind. D'Annunzio ordered his car to stop and jumped out. The troops on both sides stood at the halt, impassive and silent.

An Animated Conversation

There were a few minutes of animated conversation between the general and the poet. General Pittaluga saluted D'Annunzio and then said to him: 'This is the way to ruin Italy.' The poet replied instantly: 'You will ruin Italy if you oppose destiny by an infamous policy.'

The general asked what were the poet's intentions. The reply was: 'Not one shot shall be fired by my men if their passage is free.'

The general retorted: 'I have strict orders and must prevent an act which may have incalculable consequences for my country."

The poet replied: 'I understand your words, General. You will order your men to fire on my soldiers, their brothers. But before you do so, order them to fire on me. Here I am. Let them first fire on me.'

Saying this he moved towards the soldiers, exposing his breast adorned with the medal of military honour. There was a movement among the troops, who approached the poet and cheered him. The general saw that his opposition was useless. He walked up to the poet and complimented him. The soldiers on both sides immediately cheered the poet and the general, and without further orders they crossed the road which divides Fiume from the suburbs and entered the town. General Pittaluga withdrew alone and the soldiers opened a way for him.

Mr Noonan, though a miller by profession, was an admirer of the military life and liked to wear clothes that gave him a soldierly air. He arrived at the Majestic wearing his most severe garb, a suit of khaki material garnished with black epaulettes. He unwisely parted company with his chauffeur at the gates of the Majestic (he had never visited the place before) and started to walk up the drive. He had been delayed on some business matter and Edward, who had long since ceased to expect him, had changed into his gardening clothes and was digging a flower-bed, thinking that some exercise might benefit his liver. Since he had never met Mr Noonan, he assumed that this was merely a somewhat elderly and irascible telegraph boy and told him to go on up to the house. Mr Noonan, believing he had just had an encounter with a particularly insolent gardener, did so but with bad grace. Pausing for a moment to acknowledge the statue of Queen Victoria, he then proceeded to climb the steps and be swallowed up by the front door of the Majestic, in whose various tracts and organs he wandered, increasingly furious, while Edward dug peacefully in the garden and wondered whether he would lose face (and establish Ripon's guilt) by going to pay a visit on Mr Noonan at his home.

Edward and Mr Noonan probably had more in common than they ever had a chance to realize. Neither, at this stage, was the least enthusiastic about a union of their respective children. Mr Noonan, looking round the mouldering caverns of the Majestic, no doubt saw immediately that only a massive transfusion of money could keep the place habitable for a few years longer; in a material sense it was a poor match for the daughter of Noonan's Flour. As for the quality which Mr Noonan had once found faintly appetizing when he considered the prospect of having Ripon Spencer for a son-in-law, the quality of 'breeding' (and with it automatic entry into the ruling class in Ireland from which Mr Noonan, in spite of his wealth and influence in business matters, was virtually excluded), he had now become extremely dubious as to whether Ripon possessed it in adequate quantities. Besides, by the autumn of 1919 it had become clear to everyone in Ireland with the possible exception of the Unionists themselves that the Unionist cause had fallen into a decline. Add to that Ripon's taint of Protestantism (which in Mr Noonan's view no amount of 'instruction' could scrub off) and the lad was a truly unsavoury prospect.

Edward's feelings were virtually a mirror-image of Mr Noonan's. He had a profound lack of interest in money, never having been sufficiently short of it, and was positively chilled by the idea that his daughter-in-law (buxom and rosy-cheeked) should be represented on packets of flour available to the grubby fingers of the populace for a penny or two. He was by no means anxious to dissolve the 'breeding' of the Spencers in a solution of Irish 'bog Catholicism' (a daughter of Cardinal Newman might have been another matter). In these troubled times one clearly had to close the ranks, not open them ... or so he thought as he set off to wander around the corridors of the Majestic in search of the 'dratted' elderly telegraph boy (he supposed it *was* a telegraph boy). The two men failed to meet immediately, however, since Mr Noonan, tired of waiting, had struck off towards the west wing, Edward towards the east.

Little by little, as they moved back towards each other, Edward's thoughts turned to the main and unbridgable chasm, the Roman Catholicism of the Noonans: the unhealthy smell of incense, the stupefying and bizarre dogmatic precepts, the enormous families generated by ignorance and a doctrine of 'the more souls the better' (no matter whether their corporeal envelopes went barefoot or not), the absurd squadron of saints buzzing overhead like chaps in the Flying Corps supposedly ever ready to lend a hand to the blokes on the ground (and each with his own speciality), the Pope with all his unhealthy finery, the services in a gibberish of Latin that no one understood, least of all the ignorant, narrow-minded and hypocritical priests. Well, such thoughts do not actually have to occur by a process of thinking; they run in the blood of the Protestant Irish.

At this point he found himself at the foot of the staircase leading to the servants' quarters and remembered that the maids had been complaining about a supposed colony of rats. There was no shortage of them in the cellars, of course, but who ever heard of rats in the upper storeys? The whole thing was plainly nonsense; all the same, since he was there on the spot he might as well have a look round.

The inspection did not take long and it came as no surprise to him that no rodent crossed his path. He peered with distaste into the cramped little rooms with their sloping ceilings. They had a curious and alien smell which he could not quite identify; perhaps it came from a lingering of cheap perfume on Sunday clothes (seeing the maids out of uniform in Kilnalough, he very often failed to recognize them and stared in surprise if they acknowledged him). Wherever it came from, he associated it with the distressingly vulgar holy pictures on the wall, with the chocolate-coloured rosary beads on the table, with the crucifix above the bed.

'Education is what these people need. And they think they're fit to govern a country!'

Satisfied that the rats were imaginary, Edward resumed his languid search for the telegraph boy.

Mr Noonan had just had a curious experience. He had met a maidservant hurrying down a corridor carrying a tray of teacups and toasted scones together with a large and (it must be admitted) desirable seed-cake. He had beckoned her, summoned her to his side. 'Come here to me now,' he had said to her. But, to his surprise, hardly had the girl seen him when she turned and fled back the way she had come. Not knowing what a business it was to get afternoon tea at the Majestic, the bribes and cajolery that had to be administered, the deadly feuds that could be sponsored by one guest spotting another settling down to a clandestine sup of tea and bite of toast in a remote corner, Mr Noonan was astonished at this behaviour.

'Where is the master?' he called after her. But she had scurried away and he was left listening to the fading clatter of her shoes on the tiles. A little later, however, he realized that there was a person following him, though very slowly, along the corridor. It turned out to be an old lady, a gentle-woman to judge by her clothing, moving forward with two sticks which she planted firmly in front of her one after the other in the manner of an Alpine guide. He halted and allowed her to catch up, her eyes on the ground, her breathing stertorous.

'Where is Mr Spencer?' he demanded.

The lady lifted her watery eyes and surveyed him; then she raised one of her sticks in a trembling, arthritic hand. The brass ferrule that tipped it performed a wavering figure-eight a little above his head. He took her to be indicating that his way led upwards.

He was not a young man himself. His chest had been giving him trouble. His blood-pressure was too high. He'd started with nothing, d'ye see, and done it all himself. Self-raising, like his own flour, was what they said in Kilnalough.

'Now what I'd better be doing is ... '

He was alone once more and, one way or another, had climbed to the floor above. The only reason he knew this for certain was that he happened to be standing at a surprisingly clean window looking down on the drive and, incidentally, on Edward's Daimler. It was raining very hard—so hard that a mist of spray was rising off the roof and bonnet of the car. Where was he? When had it started raining? He shouldn't let himself get in a rage because these days there was always a thick mist, bloody and opaque, waiting to roll in and blot out the landmarks. Now wait, the motor car had been left in front of the building, he remembered seeing it. Well, the great staircase with the chandelier was in the front of the building too ... so that meant that he was on or beside the staircase.

He was squeezed by a really breathtaking grip of anger when, on looking round, he found that this was not so. There was no staircase in sight. It was unfair and spiteful — a real British trick, the kind of murthering, hypocritical ... Mother of God! he would like to have smashed a window, he had even raised the heavy ash handle of his furled umbrella to shatter the glass. He was restrained, though, by the sudden thought that the Englishman might consider it bad form. Besides, the window was already broken ... that is, had obviously been broken on some other occasion, since it lacked its pane entirely. He could not have done it himself. There were no jagged edges. That was why it looked so clean. The rain, moreover, was pattering on the window sill and had darkened the faded crimson carpet (strewn with tiny three-pronged crowns) in the shape of a half-moon.

Having regrouped his forces, Mr Noonan set out along a carpeted corridor (while Edward continued to search disconsolately for him on the floor below), peering through the open doors of the many rooms he passed — nobody made any attempt to close doors here, it appeared — at double beds, enormous and sinful, without a trace of religion, at wash-basins and towels starched like paper and grey with dust. And this was what his only daughter was supposed to be marrying into!

In one room he came upon a vast pile of stone hot-water bottles, maybe two or three hundred of them. In another a makeshift washing-line had been stretched and forgotten, the clothing on it dry and riddled with moth-holes. In yet another he heard voices. He stopped and listened ... but no, he had been mistaken (Edward at this moment was peering into the room directly below). At the next door, however, he definitely heard voices, so he entered with some confidence. He found himself, not in a bedroom but on a gallery that ran round beneath the ceiling of a large book-lined room. The voices were coming from below. He peered over the railing (as Edward, moving away from him once more, started towards the west wing).

Below, two identical girls were sitting on a studded sofa with books in their hands. Opposite them, in an armchair but sitting very straight, was a small elderly lady wearing a lace cap. Her milky eyes were directed towards the girls, while her hands, constantly moving and apparently disconnected from the rest of her body, knitted away tirelessly in her lap.

'Are you sitting up straight, Charity?'

'Yes, Granny.'

'Faith?'

'Yes, Granny.'

The two golden heads turned towards each other with their tongues out.

'A lady never slouches in her chair as if she had no backbone.'

'No, Granny.'

Faith let herself sink back with her mouth open, miming inertia, while Charity shook with silent laughter.

'Sit still!'

'We *are* bally well sitting still.'

'Don't answer back! You'll be kept here all afternoon unless you behave. Charity, are your knees together?'

'Yes, Granny.'

Charity pulled her skirt up over her knees and threw one leg over the arm of the sofa, exposing pink thighs.

'I'm sitting up straight, Granny,' she said, and snatching a pencil from Faith's hand began to puff on it as if it were a cigarette-holder. While flicking the ash she happened to lift her eyes and saw Mr Noonan.

'Good girl,' said the old lady.

The twins stared up at Mr Noonan and he stared down at the twins. At length Charity said: 'There's an old man with an umbrella in the room, Granny.'

'An old man? What does he want?'

'What d'you want?' demanded Faith firmly.

'Where is Mr Spencer? I won't stand for it,' stuttered Mr

Noonan furiously. 'I'm looking for ... I shall speak to my solicitor!'

'What is he doing up near the ceiling?' the old lady wanted to know.

'We're in the library, Granny. There's a sort of balcony ... '

'Well, whoever you are, I'm sure you won't find your solicitor up there. Show him to the door, Faith. You stay here, Charity, it doesn't take both of you.'

Faith was already half-way up the spiral iron staircase to the gallery. Without a word she grasped Mr Noonan by the sleeve and towed him back the way he had come, down a dark flight of stairs, along a corridor, through a deserted cocktail bar, into the lobby and up to the front door which, with an immense effort, she dragged open.

'Peeping Tom!' she hissed and, placing a hand on his back, gave him a violent shove which propelled him out into the rain at a reluctant gallop.

A few moments later Edward, looking out of a window without a pane on the first floor and thinking that all this rain would give his Daimler a good wash, noticed the elderly telegraph boy hurrying away down the drive. The fellow halted for a moment and shook his umbrella angrily at the Majestic.

'Good heavens!' murmured Edward. 'I don't suppose that could have been old what's-his-name, by any chance ... '

THE HORRORS OF BOLSHEVISM

Irish Ladies' Terrible Experiences

Reuter's representative has just had an interview with two Irish girls, the Misses May and Eileen Healy, who have just reached London, having escaped from Kieff with nothing but the clothes—thin linen dresses—they were wearing.

They tell a terrible story of the Bolshevist outrage, of

which they were personal witnesses. They said that the mental strain was awful and one, Miss Eileen Healy, has lost 3 st. in weight.

'In a side building, a sort of garage, I saw a wall covered with blood and brains. In the middle was cut a channel or drain, full of congealed blood, and just outside in the garden, one hundred and twenty-seven nude, mutilated corpses, including those of some women, who had been flung into a hole ...

'Ten Bolshevists occupied rooms next mine. There was a beautiful drawing-room filled with valuable furniture. There, night after night, they carried on drunken orgies of an unspeakable character with women whom they brought from the town, and I lay on my bed with the door barricaded until from sheer exhaustion I went to sleep ...

'The terrorism of the Reds is really much worse than anything I have read of, and to those in this country who believe the story is exaggerated I would only say go out and see for yourselves.'

❧

THE PSYCHOLOGY OF TRIUMPH
Marshal Foch's Analysis

In conversation with a representative of the *Echo de Paris* Marshal Foch said that he had won the war by avoiding unnecessary emotions and conserving all his strength so as to devote himself whole-heartedly to his task. 'War requires an ingenious mind, always alert, and one day the reward of victory comes. Don't talk to me about glory, beauty, enthusiasm. They are verbal manifestations. Nothing exists except facts and facts alone are of any use. A useful fact, and one that satisfied me, was the signing of the armistice.'

In conclusion Marshal Foch said: 'Without trying to drag in miracles just because clear vision is vouchsafed to a man, because afterwards it turns out that this clear vision has determined movements fraught with enormous consequences in a formidable war, I still hold that this clear vision comes from a Providential force, in the hands of which one is an instrument, and that the victorious decision emanates from above, by the higher and Divine will.'

Nineteen-twenty. One, two, three weeks of January — grey, cold weather, fog in the streets, dirty snow underfoot — elapsed before the Major finally found another letter from Sarah propped against the toast-rack on the breakfast table.

'Dear Major,' she wrote, 'it was wrong of you to read that letter when I told you not to. I was ill when I wrote it and had a fever, as I'm sure I said. You needn't expect me to apologize, however, since I took the trouble of warning you not to read it. It's your own fault if you came across something that didn't please you. About Mr Mulcahy, I regret very much making fun of him as he's a decent enough sort of person and I exaggerated a great deal. As for being rescued from the Irish swine, as you remark, I can assure you that there's really no need for that as they and I agree very well (perhaps because I'm one of the same swine myself). Also, as regards London, I'm perfectly content where I am. Nevertheless, I must thank you for your offer, because, though unsuitable, I'm sure it was kindly meant.'

'Ah,' thought the Major, chastened, 'she's angry with me and no doubt thinks that I'm contemptuous of Kilnalough. Perhaps my letter was tactless.' And he hurriedly wrote to apologize, pleading with her to forgive his tactlessness. Would she not satisfy his curiosity anyway? He was devoured with curiosity to know how the affair between Máire and Ripon had come out? And what was this thing that the twins had done to Fr O'Meara? And how was Edward bearing up under the strain?

All *she* knew (Sarah wrote back) was that Ripon and Máire were living in Rathmines with 'a little one' on the way. Had he run away in the middle of the night with his fiancée? Had he been thrown out of his father's house without a penny? Nobody knew for sure, but several stories were circulating in Kilnalough. According to the one she believed (or liked to believe, anyway) Ripon had half run away and half been ejected. What had happened (so this story went) was that Edward had given him a sum of money, driven him to the railway station and put him on the train for Dublin with strict orders to stay there and get up to no mischief until he, Edward, had settled the affair in Kilnalough. This done, he had arranged to meet Mr Noonan at the Majestic to talk things over. Meanwhile Ripon had only allowed the train to carry him to the next station up the line. There, after a long argument, he had finally succeeded in extracting a refund from the station-master on the rest of his ticket to Dublin. Then he had returned with all speed to Kilnalough, climbed the Noonan's garden wall causing poor Máire to faint (she thought he was a tinker), revived her, informed her she was liberated (she had been 'confined to barracks' by her military-minded father), helped her to pack a suitcase, bribed a man he saw standing at the gate whom he supposed was one of Noonan's servants (but who was merely a bystander) and finally fled with her to the station while her father was still at the Majestic. By all accounts (or rather, by this particular account) the Kilnalough station-master came close to having a heart attack when young Ripon, whom he had only just seen go off on the last train to Dublin, appeared in time for the next one and went-off on that one too, accompanied by a heavily veiled lady whose ample proportions and pink ankles suggested that it might not be impossible that this was 'a certain person', he'd say no more; as he was handing this veiled lady up into the carriage he had caught 'a whiff of something not unlike chloroform ... but, mind you, I'm not saying it was nor it wasn't though, begod, it was as like as the divil!' Well, that was a story the Major could believe if he liked, the English (or 'the enemy', as she preferred to think of them) being so literal, the Major in particular being as literal as a lump of dough, she had no doubt that he'd believe it all.

As for the attack of the twins on Fr O'Meara, here was another story that the Major could try out on his digestion. The brave and worthy Fr O'Meara had taken it into his head one day to pay a visit on Ripon whom he had been grooming spiritually (the Major being a 'beastly Prod' would fail to see the need for this, she was sure) for the marriage he contemplated with the miller's daughter. He had cycled up the drive past two identical girls of such radiant countenance that he had at first mistaken them for 'angels from heaven' (he was later said to have explained, while still in a state of shock). However, when one of them made a disagreeable remark he quickly perceived his mistake and pedalled onwards out of earshot disturbed, in particular that a young girl should know such words, in general at God's habit, frequently observable here below, of mixing the fair with the foul, the good with the evil, and so on.

Before reaching the front door he had come upon Ripon in the orangerie, apparently in the act of upbraiding a flustered girl in maid's uniform who had no doubt neglected some household chore (though she, Sarah, had her own opinion of what the rogue was doing). Ripon had appeared startled and suggested a 'stroll'. Fr O'Meara, who envisaged a reflective promenade discussing extra-terrestrial matters, agreed immediately and they set off, Ripon heading at a great pace towards the bushes and looking round somewhat furtively the while. Fr O'Meara had trouble keeping up with him, but after the first hundred yards or so the pace slackened and Ripon asked him a few distrait questions about the catechism. Then somewhat abruptly he said he'd have to be going and marched off without even conducting his visitor back to his bicycle. The kindly priest, acknowledging to himself that he was more at home with ecclesiastical than with social etiquette, promptly forgave the lad. On second thoughts he also forgave the young girl who had addressed the obscenity to him. His mind at rest, he clambered back on to his machine and cycled down the drive.

It seemed, though versions of this particular version of the story differed, that disaster struck him at some point before he reached the gate. As he pedalled on his way, it seemed, he was lassoed from the overhanging branches of an oak tree. According to the most dramatic version of the version he was plucked out of the saddle and hung there swinging gently to and fro while his bicycle sailed on into some rhododendron bushes. More probably, however, the noose missed him (luckily, since it might have broken his neck) but caught on the pillion, shrunk rapidly, tightened, halted the bicycle suddenly and tipped Fr O'Meara over the handlebars. Stunned though he was by his fall he was willing to swear that as he unsteadily tried to pick himself up two smiling angelic faces were looking down on him from above. It was a matter for the police, no doubt about it. Charges of assault were prepared for the R.M., together with counter-charges of trespass (Ripon having assured his father that the priest was nothing to do with him) and theft (some apples had been stripped from trees in the orchard). Other charges were being considered and had there been a magistrate to hear them this sudden sprouting of litigation might have grown so dense and confusing as to become, inside a few days, entirely beyond resolution. But there wasn't. This representative of the foreign oppressor had received a number of menacing letters from the I.R.A. and had wisely retired. A new R.M. was expected but in the meantime criminals of all hues, including the twins, were running the streets at liberty. In fact Fr O'Meara had learned with satisfaction that while he was still removing the gravel from his grazed palms these two violent girls had been stripped and caned by their father as if they'd been boys; the thought of this retribution did something to mollify him. As for Sarah, although she had to admit that the 'odious brats' had some spirit, she sympathized entirely with the unfortunate priest. Almost everything with those two girls, she said, had a habit of beginning amusingly and ending painfully.

Now, had that satisfied the Major's curiosity? If he wanted to hear the other versions he would have to come to Kilnalough, because she was getting writer's cramp ... Yes, and as for his question about Edward, she never saw him these days ... Since Angela was dead she no longer had any reason to go to the Majestic. Indeed, she was bored, frightfully bored, and looking forward to being amused by the Major ...' Amuse me, dear Major, amuse me!' Life was intolerable in Kilnalough.

But wait! She had an idea. The Major must reply and tell her precisely, yes or no, whether he believed the stories about Ripon and the twins. He must do so immediately. It was essential, so that she'd know what sort of man the Major was ... though, of course, she really knew that already. Still, he must write and tell her anyway. And by the way, perhaps she would visit him in London after all. There was a chance she would go to a clinic in France for a while. Her walking had improved greatly and she wasn't nearly such a 'miserable cripple' as she had been when the Major knew her. She still, in spite of his dull letters, thought of him with affection and remained truly his.

The Major didn't know what to do about this letter. If he said he *did* believe the stories about Ripon and the twins she would accuse him of being 'as literal as a lump of dough'. If he said he didn't, she would almost certainly accuse him of having no sense of fun, no imagination. After two or three days' deliberation he wrote back to say that he believed parts of them (and enjoyed the other parts). A postcard was all he got in reply. It accused him of having made a cautious and typically British compromise. And it ended with the words: 'I despise compromises!'

All the time this correspondence was taking place the Major's aunt continued to linger in a twilight stage between living and dying which he found most unsatisfactory. At the time of her first haemorrhage a night-nurse had been taken on, a sombre lady of middle age who had a habit of enjoining his aunt to 'put a brave face on it, my dear', commenting that 'Madam's pain won't last for ever', or informing her that her 'only hope is in the Lord', while discreetly averting her face to eat steadily throughout the night. Though most of this woman's remarks had a religious cast and few of them were sequential she occasionally spoke of other deaths she had witnessed, invariably those of ladies in comfortable circumstances. One of them, a Mrs Baxter, had 'died in the arms of Jesus'. Another had provided her with food that was unsuitable. Yet another had beautiful daughters who 'went to dance at balls during their mother's agony.' One story she often repeated concerned the lovely and youthful Mrs Perry, far gone with tuberculosis, whose husband, a ravening brute, had claimed his marital rights until the very end, causing her to leave the sick-room for hours at a time, so that very often it would be nearly dawn before she was allowed back to comfort his victim — who had been uncomplaining, however. Describing this, she would aim black looks at the Major as if he were responsible.

Somehow this story made a very painful impression on the Major. He imagined the lovely Mrs Perry and her husband quite differently. He was sure that they had been passionately in love. What other reason could the husband have had for making love to a woman with tuberculosis? The physical act of love remained the one crumbling bridge between them. He pictured the slow nights of despair. He wondered whether the husband had also hoped to fall ill with tuberculosis. One night he had an agonizing dream about Mrs Perry and the next morning he felt so disturbed that he sought out the night-nurse and dismissed her with a month's pay. He thought: 'Really, I'm still a young man ... there's time enough to become morbid when I'm old.'

135

At about this time he read about the siege of the R.I.C. barracks at Ballytrain – half a dozen constables overrun by a massive horde of Shinners – over a hundred of them, like the dervishes at Khartoum. Edward had called them individual criminals out for what they could get. Never, thought the Major with a smile, never had so many individual criminals been seen together in one place!

The Major had invited Sarah to stay at his aunt's house as she passed through London on her way to France. Would this not be considered improper? she wanted to know. What would his aunt think? The Major replied that his aunt would certainly find nothing amiss in Sarah staying with them. Indeed, she would act as chaperone (his only worry was that the old lady, having survived so long, should die prematurely now that her services were needed). So presently Sarah arrived.

The Major, sunk in a slough of despond, his mind as barren as the frozen snow that lay on the streets, had been awaiting her arrival with indifference, even a vague dread. But Sarah appeared to have left the malicious side of her nature in Kilnalough. She was so affectionate and ingenuous, so excited to be in London, so obviously impressed by the Major's air of authority and distinction in these new surroundings as she clung to his arm (the confidence with which she was walking these days astonished him) that in no time at all he was disarmed. In restaurants she was apprehensive lest she be 'noticed'. The Major mustn't let her use the wrong knife and fork or she'd die of mortification. And how did all the diners (how did the Major himself?) look so much at ease in front of these august waiters? It was a mystery to her. And the ladies wore such lovely clothes! Was the Major not ashamed to be seen with such a scarecrow as herself? On the contrary, the Major was delighted to be seen with such a pretty girl.

The splendid shops, the elegant streets ... Amused and touched by her enthusiasm, the Major found himself seeing London with new and less world-weary eyes. It was perfectly true, London could be an exciting place if one allowed oneself to notice it. In the evening after dinner they sat and talked in front of a blazing fire. For a while they discussed Kilnalough. The Major had been hoping to hear more of the Majestic, but Sarah had nothing to add to her letters. Ripon and Máire were married now and living in Rathmines, but she knew no more than that. She thought that Edward and Ripon were having no more to do with each other. There'd been some terrible rows but she didn't know the details. She'd hardly seen Edward for ages, she added, gazing into the glowing embers. And then she grimaced and said that she didn't want to talk about Kilnalough, she wanted the Major to tell her about himself. And so the Major, feeling strangely at peace, found himself talking about the war. Little by little, random names and faces began to come back to him. He told Sarah first about one or two curious things that had happened: about a young Tommy who had been found dead in his bunk and the only thing they had been able to find wrong with him was a broken finger; about the shouted friendly conversations with the Germans across No-Man's-Land; about a man in the Major's regiment who had had his leg blown off and had sat in a shell-crater tying up the arteries by himself and had survived ... And soon the Major was telling Sarah about incidents that until now had been frozen into a block of ice in his mind. In the warmth of her sympathy he found he could talk about things which until now he had scarcely been able to repeat to himself. A little drunk and tired, sitting there in the flickering firelight, the bubble of bitterness in his mind slowly dissolved and tears at last began to run down his cheeks for all his dead friends.

The following morning Sarah left for France. She would send the Major her address, she said.

The Major had written to Sarah an enormous letter, crammed with confidences, packed with poetic observations on life and love and every other subject under the sun. He had at last found someone to talk to! He had found someone who understood him and shared his view of the workings of the world. Everything which for want of a listener he had been unable to say for the last four or five years came foaming out of his head in a torrent of blue-black ink, all at once. The leaves of writing-paper became so thick that they would no longer fit in an ordinary envelope and, besides, he had still more to say ... by the time he had finished he would be obliged to wrap up his letter in a brown-paper parcel. Not that the Major was waiting to finish his letter exactly (because the kind of letter the Major was writing is seldom voluntarily finished before the Grim Reaper bids us lay down our pens); his difficulty was more practical than aesthetic: he was unable to send Sarah his letter in instalments because she had forgotten to send him her address. As time went by, as winter turned into spring, the Major became less and less hopeful that she would remember to rectify this oversight. His flood of confidences declined to a trickle and finally dried up altogether. The Major became gloomy and sensible once more. And the grey world returned to being as grey as it had always been. In due course his aunt died.

Meanwhile, in Ireland, the troubles ebbed and flowed, now better, now worse. He could make no sense of it. It was like putting out to sea in a small boat: with the running of the waves it is impossible to tell how far one has moved over the water; all one can do is to look back to see how far one has moved from land. So in the case of Ireland all one could do was to look back to the peaceful days before the war. And they already seemed a long way away.

INDIAN UNREST

Lord Hunter's Inquiry

The Indian newspapers received by the Indian mail, says

Reuter, contain further reports of the proceedings of the Hunter Commission which is inquiring into the Indian disorders of last year. On December 3rd Captain Doveton, who administered martial law at Kasur, in his evidence, while admitting that he did invent some minor punishments during the martial-law administration, punishments less severe in form than the usual martial-law sentences, denied that he ordered any persons to be whitewashed, or made people write on the ground with their noses ...

Sir Chiman Lal Setalvad turned to the feeling of the people regarding martial law. 'You say the people liked martial law?' he suggested.

'Very much so,' was the witness's reply.

Sir C. Setalvad: 'You say the people would have liked it to become practically permanent?' 'That was the impression that was given.'

'Did the people actually tell you this—that the summary courts were things they liked?' 'They liked people being tried by martial law, without any right of appeal. They preferred that to spending money on appeals.'

Questioned in regard to the story of women of loose character having been compelled to witness flogging sentences, witness said that it was a misrepresentation, although not a deliberate one ...

Continuing, Captain Doveton said that as regards his order requiring convicted persons to touch the ground with their foreheads, he had heard of this being done before. He did not mean it to be debasing.

At this stage General Barrow, addressing Lord Hunter, suggested that witness was a young officer doing his duty to the best of his ability under rather trying conditions, but that he was not a criminal.

❧

The Major returned to Kilnalough in the middle of May,

expecting the worst. Since early in the year the number of violent incidents had steadily increased. An official return of 'outrages' attributed to Sinn Fein had just been published and the Major had read it with apprehension: it listed the total number of murders for the first quarter of the year as thirty-six; of 'firing at persons' eighty-one; three hundred and eighty-nine raids for arms had taken place, and there had been forty-seven incendiary fires. Tired from his journey and nervous in spite of the peaceful and familiar aspect of Kilnalough station, the Major started violently when a hand was put on his shoulder. He turned sharply to find the grinning and friendly face of the station-master, who wanted to inform him that Dr Ryan was waiting outside in his motor car and would give him a lift to the Majestic.

With Dr Ryan there was a youth of sixteen or seventeen with black hair and a pale, beautiful face. The doctor, his face almost totally obscured by a muffler and a wide-brimmed black hat, muttered an introduction. This was his grandson Padraig. They were going to tea at the Majestic, he added disagreeably, and Edward had asked them to ... In short: 'Get in, man, there's plenty of room. We've been waiting long enough already.'

Soon the long, unkempt hedges of the Majestic were un-reeling beside them; beyond lay the dense, damp woods. There was an air of desolation on this side of the road, a contrast with the loose stone walls and neatly ploughed fields on the other side. But a little farther on even the open fields degenerated; unploughed, the meadows empty of cattle, the potato fields abandoned to the weeds that devour the soil so voraciously in the damp climate of Ireland. By a gate leading into one of these fields a man wearing a ragged coat stood, motionless as a rock, his eyes on the ground. As they passed he did not even raise his eyes. What was the fellow doing standing motionless in an empty field, staring at the ground? the Major wondered.

Edward must have been watching for them, because hardly

had they turned in a sweep of gravel and come to a halt by the statue of Queen Victoria before he was hastening down the steps to greet them. The Major was the first to alight. Edward gripped his hand tightly and pumped it vigorously, his mouth working but unable to utter a word except 'My dear chap!' Then he turned away to the others.

Only as he greeted the doctor and his grandson did the Major have a chance to notice how much Edward had changed since their last meeting. His face had become much thinner and the contours of his skull more pronounced; in manner too he appeared strangely on edge, exaggeratedly cheerful and voluble now that the initial greetings were over, and yet at the same time weary and apprehensive as he set about extricating the old man from the front seat of the motor (Dr Ryan was tired also, it seemed, but his grandson proved as nimble as a gazelle). Edward, shoving and pulling with energy at the doctor's feebly struggling limbs, cried that he had something to show his visitors, something that they couldn't help but find delightful, something that was really outside the normal orbit of the Majestic, something that was, in fact, a new departure for himself as well as for the hotel and might, who knew?, turn out from a commercial point of view to be the foundation of something big ... in a word, they should all come while it was still fine (if they didn't mind waiting a few minutes before taking their tea) they should all come, before it started to rain, and see ... his pigs.

The boy Padraig, who had allowed himself to look faintly interested at this extravagant preamble, pursed his lips gloomily and appeared to be unexcited by the prospect of viewing some pigs. As for Dr Ryan, he seemed positively annoyed (or perhaps he had not yet had time to recover from the indignity of being dragged out of his seat by the lapels). 'Ah, pigs,' he muttered testily. 'To be sure.' His heavy, wrinkled eyelids drooped.

The old spaniel, Rover, came up and sniffed the Major's trouser-leg.

'See, he recognizes you,' exclaimed Edward cheerfully. 'You recognize your old friend Brendan, don't you, boy?'

The dog wagged its tail weakly and, as they set off, plodded after them, the long hairs of its stomach matted with dried mud.

As they turned the corner of the house a long bloodcurdling shriek ripped through the silence.

'What on earth ... ?'

'The peacocks,' explained Edward. 'Normally they only cry at dusk or after nightfall. I wonder what's got into them.'

Dr Ryan said querulously: 'It's going to pour again any minute.'

'And where are they, the peacocks?' Padraig wanted to know. 'Could I have some feathers off of them?'

'Of course. Remind me after tea.'

The Major looked out over the sea to where a black, massive cloud-formation was swelling towards them from over the invisible Welsh coast. It was going to pour. 'They have beautiful feathers, those birds,' he mused aloud. 'Why should they shriek like that?'

The land on this side of the hotel, Edward was explaining to Padraig with the old man limping along morosely a few paces behind them, was where the guests had diverted themselves in the old days. Was it not splendidly suited for the purpose? Look at the way it dropped in a series of wide terraces towards the sea. Each terrace had been reserved for a different recreation. This flat green meadow through which they were now passing had been reserved for clock-golf and bowls; the one below for lawn tennis, a dozen separate courts, each one of fine quality and, like the hard courts round by the garages, angled so that the westering sun would never shine into the eyes of the server ... and it worked, assuming, of course, that none of the guests were stricken by an irrational craving to get up and take some exercise before, say, half eleven in the morning (but few, if any of them, Edward added with a sour chuckle, had ever been greatly discomfited by the rising sun, or so he understood). The soil for these courts, the draining system and the grass lawn itself had been imported from England, installed specially and with enormous care in order to emulate the heavenly growth that cloaked the courts at Wimbledon. Edward might have gone on with his explanation but at this moment Padraig spotted a peacock sitting on the broken wall that snaked down from one terrace to another, protecting them from the north wind. As he skipped over to investigate, Edward muttered: 'A fine lad, Doctor, a fine lad.' But the surly old doctor merely grunted disagreeably, refusing to be mollified.

Padraig returned and together they descended a wide and imposing flight of stone steps lined at intervals with cracked urns bearing coats of arms but containing nothing more regal than a few tufts of grass, thistles, and in one of them what appeared to be a potato plant. Between the stone steps green whiskers sprouted unchecked in every crack and crevice. On the next terrace a young man stood smiling cheerfully out to sea. At the sound of footsteps he turned and, smiling down at the earth, went through the motions of digging with the spade he was holding.

'Ah there, Séan,' Edward called to him.

'Good day, sor.'

The Major noted with surprise that the foot which had come to rest, after one or two token digging motions, on the shoulder of the spade was shod in a gleaming shoe, the trouser-leg above it was neatly creased, and thrown over the young man's shoulders and knotted round his neck was what looked like a Trinity cricket sweater.

'I say, Edward, you have a very well-turned-out gardener.'

But Edward was busy telling Padraig (who showed no sign of being interested) that the land here was ill-suited to the growing of potatoes: the soil contained a good deal of clay and held the moisture so that if it rained too copiously the potatoes would rot in the ground, likely as not, before they could be dug up and eaten. Taking this fact into account it would appear to have been a mistake to dig up the tennis courts (for, in an effort to make the land pay, one or two had been dug up). True, the ones that had been left had forgotten their aristocratic origins and 'gone Irish', the delicate grass becoming thick and succulent in the damp climate, more suitable for feeding cows than hitting forehand drives off. Not that it mattered very much since the twins ('my two little girls ... about your age') didn't seem to care very much for the game.

'Do you play tennis?'

Padraig, after his moment of enthusiasm for the peacocks, had become sullen once more. 'Indeed I do not.' Padraig hated all games; he stated as much in a loud and satisfied tone. Particularly games which involved contact with other people's bodies.

'But tennis ... ' began Edward.

Having arrived at the lowest terrace, against which the sea lapped in chilly grey waves, they turned to the right, following a gravel path along the water's edge. This path was lined by monstrously unclipped privet hedges and ended at a boathouse complete with slipway and the half-exposed rotting ribs of what had once been a large yacht; built against the boat-house was a taller square building which Edward said was the squash court. (And what, Padraig wanted to know, was a 'squash' court when it was at home? It sounded mighty unpleasant whatever it was.) It was in the squash court that Edward apparently kept his pigs. He opened the door and went inside, making cooing noises. Padraig, wrinkling his nose, followed. Dr Ryan heaved a sigh and turned his ancient, lined features to the Major.

'Ach, it's a long way for a man of eighty to walk with no tea inside him.'

Before following him inside the Major turned to look back at the hotel, which at this point was much nearer; the ground fell away sharply and one crenellated wing of it hung almost directly above. Edward's voice from inside the squash court was calling him to have a look at his beauties, his three remarkable piglets. The building consisted of a small ante-chamber and an enormous oblong room with peeling white walls and a rotting wooden floor. The roof was of greenish glass that filled the place with a murky submarine light. In addition, Edward had lit two hurricane lanterns which hung from great metal arms riveted into the walls; the light from these poured down on mounds of straw, mud, excrement and pig-swill. The stench was intolerable.

Three piglets, glowing pink in the cascade of light from the lanterns, frisked around Edward, who was kneeling on a pile of steaming straw and doing his best to tickle their stomachs, though they were in such an ecstasy of excitement that they could hardly hold still for a moment, nipping and suckling at his fingers and tumbling over his shoes.

'Look at them, did you ever see such wonderful little fellows in all your life? Here now, calm down a bit and show your visitors how well you can behave. Here, Brendan, this is Mooney, that's Johnston, and the one sniffing at your sock is O'Brien. We feed them mostly with stale cakes from the bakery, you see ... ones that haven't been sold. We get a couple of sacks sent down from Dublin on the train once a week: iced cakes, barm bracks, Swiss rolls, oh everything! lemon sponges, almond rings, currant buns, Battenbergs, Madeira cake ... A lot of them are so fresh you wouldn't mind eating them yourself.' And Edward gazed down with tender-ness at the plump pink animals that were still whirling and somersaulting about his feet before turning to the Major for corroboration.

The Major cleared his throat for a favourable comment on the piglets. But he was silenced by a growl and an ear-split-ting squeal. It was Rover, of course, who had followed them into the squash court undetected. For a few moments there was chaos while the other two pigs joined in the squealing and Edward tried to soothe them. The piglet Mooney, unaware that any creature on earth might wish him ill and perhaps thinking that the old spaniel was merely a somewhat hairy brother-pig, had playfully performed a somersault which had landed him within range of the dog's sharp teeth. A painful nip had been administered. For a moment the piercing noise, the grovelling figure of Edward, the swaying lanterns and the asphyxiating ammoniac stench all combined with weariness from his journey to make the Major wonder whether his reason had not become unhinged.

He poked his head out of the door and took a deep breath of cool, unscented air. The relief was extraordinary. There was the sound of footsteps. A buxom girl wearing an apron was skipping towards them along the path.

'The master?' she called. 'Is he there? A gentleman does be at the door.' The Major nodded and re-entered the building to tell Edward that he was wanted. The piglets had calmed down and were lying in a row on their backs having their stomachs rubbed. Getting to his feet with a grimace of annoyance, Edward said: 'Look here, why don't you have a good look at the pigs and then follow me up to the house for a spot of tea when you've finished? See you up there in a few minutes.' With that he hurried out. A moment later he returned to say: 'By the way, would you mind dousing the lanterns before you leave?' Then he was gone again.

Dr Ryan and the Major exchanged a glance but said nothing. Padraig made a sour face and began to wipe one of his boots with a clean handful of straw. The three piglets, gradually becoming aware that the flow of pleasure over their fat pink stomachs had been interrupted, rolled over and sat up. Their three visitors stared at them grimly until, one by one, the animals crept away to a heap of oozing mud and straw in the farthest corner of the court and settled themselves with their backs to the strip of tin. From there they eyed with suspicion and alarm the hostile creatures who (in appearance, anyway) so much resembled their beloved Edward.

When he judged that they had gazed at the animals for a suitable interval the Major doused the lights (which turned the piglets as grey as rats) and ushered the doctor and his grand-son out into the fresh air. The old gentleman looked very weary indeed now and his movements had become more trembling and tentative than ever. They began to climb in silence towards the looming house, with the old man leaning heavily on his grandson's slim shoulder and thrusting at the ground with his stick. 'Really,' thought the Major, 'it was most inconsiderate of Edward to bring the "senile old codger" all the way down here for this pig nonsense.'

On a flight of stone steps between two terraces they stopped for a rest. They had gained sufficient altitude to afford the Major a view over the strip of park-land to the south-west, and beyond to the meadow. From the next terrace up, or from the one above that, he should be able to see clear to the tenants' farms and the rolling hills behind them. The farmhouses — he remembered them perfectly — would be clustered there on the green slopes looking, at this distance, like grey sugar cubes.

They were now taking a short cut across the penultimate terrace, which led them past an immense swimming-pool, a splendid-looking affair which for some reason the Major had never noticed before. Here and there bright blue tiles were visible through the green lichen that veiled its sides and they passed the peeling white skeleton of a high-diving-board; beside it a springboard hung over the black water on the surface of which, by accident or design, lay the green discs of water-lilies. 'It must be fresh water,' he thought. 'Rainwater, perhaps.'

As he watched, something heaved powerfully beneath the surface. 'Looks as if there might be good fishing. Pike, I wouldn't be surprised. Too bad Edward hasn't got a decent cook.'

Turning a corner of the pool brought a reflection of the sky down on to the water for a moment and left the water-lilies floating in azure. He glanced back once more to see if any fish were rising, but the surface was glassy smooth. He was tempted to go back and try the springboard to see whether it had rotted through — but undoubtedly it had. And it was fitting that it should have. From here the fashionable young men, his erstwhile comrades in arms, had taken one, two, three steps, a jump, and jack-knifed into the azure. There was something moving about this remnant of a happy youth; the Major, at any rate, felt moved.

But at last they were on the final flight of steps and soon they would be sitting in armchairs drinking tea.

'We've scaled the Matterhorn, Doctor!' But the old man, head and shoulders bowed forward on to his chest, was too spent to reply.

The Major looked towards the meadow and sure enough the farmhouses were scattered like grey sugar cubes on the rolling, quilted fields. Much nearer, though (indeed, near enough to have been visible from the lower terrace if he had looked more carefully), not far from the wall of loose, flat stones which divided the park from the meadow, a man in a tattered overcoat was standing motionless, facing towards the Majestic but with his eyes on the ground. The Major wondered whether it was the same man he had noticed earlier and, as they went inside and their footsteps echoed beneath the great glass dome of the ballroom, the incongruous but disturbing thought occurred to him that perhaps this man also would not object to sharing some almost-fresh cakes with Edward's piglets. Before going off to wash and change his shirt he told Edward that there was some fellow hanging around in the meadow and Murphy was dispatched to tell the chap to buzz off. It was probably that bane of all respectable folk in Ireland, a tinker.

On an impulse he went inside. It was very dark. The heavy curtains were still half-drawn as he had left them six months earlier, only allowing the faintest glimmer of light to penetrate. The bottles and glasses on the bar glowed in the shadows; there was a strong smell of cats and some silent movement in the darkness. Looking up, he was taken aback for a moment to see a pair of disembodied yellowish eyes glaring down at him from the ceiling. It was only when he had moved to the window to draw back the curtains that he realized that the room was boiling with cats.

They were everywhere he looked; nervously patrolling the carpet in every direction; piled together in easy chairs to form random masses of fur; curled up individually on the bar stools. They picked their way daintily between the bottles and glasses. Pointed timorous heads peered out at him from beneath chairs, tables and any other object capable of giving refuge. There was even a massive marmalade animal crouching high above him, piloting the spreading antlers of a stag's head fixed to the wall (this must be the owner of the glaring yellow eyes that had startled him a moment ago). He had a moment of revulsion at this furry multitude before the room abruptly dissolved in a shattering percussion of sneezes. A fine grey cascade of dust descended slowly around him. 'Well, I'll be damned, where the devil did this lot come from? All the cats in Kilnalough must be using the Majestic to breed in ... and not all of them are wild either.' Indeed, led by the giant marmalade cat which from the stag's brow had launched itself heavily into the air to land on the back of a chair and thence to slither to the floor, they were moving towards him making the most fearful noise. In a moment he was up to his shins in a seething carpet of fur.

He moved brusquely, however, and the animals scattered and watched him in fear. The smell had become nauseating. He tried to open the window but the wooden frame must have swollen with the dampness; it was wedged tight, immovable. He was about to leave when his eye fell on the envelope which lay on the bar. It was the letter from Angela which Edward had handed to him on the day of her funeral; his name was written on the envelope in the precise handwriting which had once been so familiar. He thought of it lying here, Angela's final message to him, through the long months he had been away, the cats multiplying around it, the seasons revolving.

Uneasily he opened it ... but he did not read it. It was much too long. He put it in his pocket and picked his way sadly through the cats to the door.

In the Palm Court the Major was greeted by Edward with a fresh burst of enthusiasm, as if the few minutes which had elapsed had been yet another long separation. No sooner had the Major forced his way through the new and astonishing growth of bamboo that threatened to occlude the entrance entirely (for here too the seasons had continued to revolve) when Edward was on his feet calling: 'Here he is, the man himself. Come here, Brendan, and explain why you haven't been keeping in touch with us all this time ... Eh? Let's hear his excuses, what! Damned if the fellow hasn't been too busy chasing the ladies to give his old friends a thought. Doctor, what d'you think? What d'you make of a friend who won't write letters, poor sort of a chap, isn't he? And I'm dashed if he hasn't put on weight into the bargain. A bit of riding is what he needs, I should think, and a few early mornings out with a gun and a dog ... How does that sound to you, Brendan? Not so bad, eh? I thought you'd get tired of being citified sooner or later. Now then, come and tell us all your news, old man. Sit here so we can have a look at you. Yes, that one looks solid enough ... pull it up a bit and I'll do the honours. Och, yes, I have to do it all m'self these days, I'm turning into an old woman so I am, a real old woman. We started. You don't mind, do you? Thought we wouldn't wait for the tea to get cold ... '

While the Major sipped his tea and peered curiously around at his scarcely familiar surroundings Edward fired questions at him, flitting from one subject to another, as often as not without waiting for replies. Such was his state of excitement that he could scarcely keep still. Indeed, he kept jumping to his feet to make unnecessary adjustments to the table.

'What was Ascot like last year?' he would cry gaily, handing everyone an extra teaspoon. 'You must have been there ... now don't tell me you weren't. Yes? Yes? No, wait a minute, try a fill of this and see how you like it. I got the man in Fox's to make it up specially ... a special blend, my own concoction, thought I'd try it out on you, see how you like it. No, wait, have a slice of cake first. Bewley's. They say it's very good, don't know much about cake m'self, but they say it's a good one ... Did I tell you I'd taken up science again? Have to keep the old brain from getting rusty, don't we? Body and mind. Body and mind. Body and soul, as Sammy would tell you. Never had any time for Ascot, Brendan. Ascot is for the ladies, m'father used to say, the men just stand there like stuffed parrots. Give me a good point-to-point any day where there's none of that nonsense. Used to let poor Angie and her mother bully me into it sometimes. (Poor Angela, echoed the Major in his thoughts, feeling a remote ache of compassion from the folded wad of paper in his breast pocket.) Didn't care for it, though ... Now, young man, what'll you have? Another slice of cake to put some muscle on you, eh? And you, Doctor? More tea? Now, Brendan, frankly I don't know what this country is coming to ... Have they gone mad over there in London? You tell us, you've just come from there ... have they gone mad or what? The bloody Shinners are getting away with murder. Land-grabbing is the latest. Pious articles in the papers about what they call 'land-hunger in the west' and d'you know what it is? They're forcing chaps to sign over their land at gunpoint for a pittance ... '

'Don't be a damn fool, Edward!' the doctor said distinctly.

'There, you see, Brendan,' Edward went on grimly. 'You see what I mean. The good doctor and I have been having words about this already. D'you know that they've even been trying it on with me?' And leaping to his feet once again Edward seized a bread-knife and began to slash away at the foliage with it as if it were a machete. And it was true that the growth of ferns, creepers, rubber-plants and God only knew what had become so luxuriant as to be altogether beyond a joke. Whereas previously the majority of the chairs and tables had been available, here and there, in clearings joined by a network of trails, now all but a few of them had been engulfed by the advancing green tide. While Edward slashed away with the bread-knife the Major, anxious to change the subject, observed politely that he had never in his life seen indoor plants 'succeed' so well. Edward, his exuberance subsiding abruptly, murmured something indistinct about the system of irrigation, then something further about sewage and the septic tank. 'A devil's own job' something would be 'and frankly the expense ... ' With a sigh he kicked the slashed leaves and twigs into a pile beside the table and slumped back into his chair.

'And anyway, what does it matter in the long run?' the Major understood him to murmur very softly, eyes raised, mouth open, to the great skylight above them, itself almost obliterated by vegetation. Rover, who had been dozing with his chin on the Major's instep, went over to inspect the pile of leaves, lifted a leg to sprinkle them with a few drops of urine before, inertia overcoming him, he rolled over on to his side to doze off once more.

There was a long silence as they sat there in the greenish gloom. The old man was motionless, deeply sunk in an arm-chair just as the Major remembered him from his first visit and, for all one knew, fast asleep behind the drooping lids. The Major noted with dismay that the doctor's flies were undone; a fold of flannel was protruding like the stuffing from a broken doll. Really! someone should have reminded the poor old fellow; at his age one couldn't be blamed for such a lapse. And why had nobody thought of removing his hat? He looked absurd sitting there at the tea-table wearing a hat (though it was true that the foliage made one feel as if one were out of doors).

'You said I could have some peacock feathers,' Padraig said plaintively, but Edward made no reply and silence fell once more.

A faint rustling sound became audible, as of someone making his way with caution along one of the trails through the thicket. There had previously been a way through, the Major remembered, from one end of the Palm Court to the other (leading to a spiral staircase down into the cellars). It seemed, to judge by the steadily approaching rustle of leaves, that against all probability this trail was still practicable. The noise of movement stopped for a moment near at hand, and there was a deep sigh, a long exhalation of breath, almost a sob. Then the noise started again. In a moment whoever it was would step into view from behind an extraordinarily powerful tropical shrub which seemed to have drilled its roots right through the tiles of the floor into the oozing darkness below. No sound but for the rustling footsteps. Even the doctor appeared to have stopped breathing. The Major tried to see past the hairy, curving, reticulated trunk of this tree, to distinguish (between succulent, oily leaves as big as dinner-plates) the tiny figure that slowly shuffled into sight. It was old Mrs Rappaport.

She stopped in the clearing opposite the tea-table and turned her sightless eyes in their direction.

'Edward!'

Edward said nothing but continued to sit there as if made of stone.

'Edward, I know you're there,' the old lady repeated shrilly. 'Edward!'

Edward looked agonized but said nothing. After a long pause the old lady turned and began to move forward again. For what seemed an age they listened to the decreasing rustle of her progress followed by a prolonged wrestling with the grove of bamboo shoots. Listening to the interminable thrashing as she tried to escape from the toils of bamboo, the Major wondered whether he should go to her assistance. But at last the thrashing stopped. Mrs Rappaport had won through into the residents' lounge.

Silence returned and it seemed to the Major that the greenish gloom had deepened into an intolerable darkness. If only the famous 'Do More' generator had been working they could have repulsed this aqueous darkness with a cleansing flood of electric light. He looked round for the tall-stemmed lamp which Angela had once switched on in this very glade, but although it was no doubt still somewhere near at hand (few things being ever deliberately changed at the Majestic) there was no longer any way of telling which of these leafy shrubs possessed a tubular metal trunk and glass corolla.

'Have you had enough to eat, old chap?'

'Eh?' said the Major.

Edward was talking to the dog, however. After a moment, though, as if the sound of his own voice had startled him into activity, he stirred uncomfortably and looked at his guests. He stood up for an instant, without pushing his chair back, then sat down again.

'Glad to hear you're something of a sportsman,' he said to Padraig with an effort. 'Good for a young fellow ... cricket, hockey and so forth. Mind you, I was never much of a cricketer myself ... Too impatient with it all, I suppose.'

'I hate cricket,' Padraig said sullenly.

Whether or not this exchange served to clear the air, Dr Ryan now also began to speak, though so softly that it was all the Major could do to make out what he was saying. Several moments passed before he realized that the old fellow had begun to speak hoarsely, comfortingly, consolingly to Edward of someone who had died ... and several more moments before he realized that that someone was Angela, as if she had only been dead for a matter of hours rather than months.

People are insubstantial, he understood the old man to be saying, a doctor should know that better than anyone. They are with us for a while and then they disappear and there is nothing to be done about it ... A man must not let himself become bitter and defeated because of this state of affairs, because really there is no point to it ... There is no rock of ages cleft for anyone and one must accept the fact that a person ('You too, Edward, and the Major, and this young boy as well') ... a person is only a very temporary and makeshift affair, as is the love one has for him ... And so Edward must understand that this young girl who had just died, his beloved daughter Angela whom he, Dr Ryan, had assisted into the world, even at the height of her youth and health was temporary and insubstantial because ... people are insubstantial. They really do not ever last ... They never last. A doctor should know. People never last.

Edward laughed heartily and, lighting a candle, said: 'I remember one time some fellows in Trinity asked me to bowl in the practice nets with them (used to like to keep myself in trim during the vacations) and I'm damned if I didn't have such a swelled head in those days that I made up some cock-and-bull story about being a demon bowler. Well, they had the nets up against the wall, of course. First ball I bowled (fella called Moore was batting, later played for the Gentlemen of Ireland), first ball, mind you, I'm dashed if it didn't sail clean over the batsman, over the back of the net, over the wall, bounced on the roof of a carriage in Nassau Street and went half-way up Dawson Street! Eh? What? How about that for a piece of bowling, eh? You can bet my face was like a beetroot and, by Jove, did they laugh at me ... Och, after that I stuck to the gloves, I can tell you.' Bubbling with mirth Edward gradually subsided once more.

On an impulse the Major had slipped Angela's letter out of his pocket and (overcome by curiosity and a vague dread as to what it might contain) was straining his eyes in the candle-lit gloom to read it, while the doctor began a rambling and incoherent monologue about there being a new spirit in Ireland (it was clear that the old chap was so exhausted and his mind so fogged that he no longer knew where he was or what he was talking about).

Ah, it was as he thought, *Dearest Brendan* — the regular handwriting, line after line like small waves relentlessly lapping a gentle shore. *On my dressing-table* — the mirror, the brushes, the jewellery-cases, even a photograph of himself. *From the window of my bedroom I can see* ... but what could she see? Only two elms and an oak, reputed to be a hundred and fifty years old, the second or third oldest tree on the estate, the edge of a path where the dogs sometimes wandered, but at this distance she could hardly recognize them ... Foch or Fritz? Collie or Flash? They were too far away, in a sense (thought the Major) they were too particular now ... only a generality like the circling of the planets could hold her attention now. But *at twelve minutes past eleven the doctor came* and he and Angela had a long chat which, for all that, didn't prevent her noticing and recording that *one of his waistcoat buttons was dangling by a thread* and that there was a copious spot of what was undoubtedly porridge on his jacket ... (Meanwhile the doctor muttered in the querulous tones of a tired old man: 'There's a new spirit in Ireland, I can feel it, you know, and see it everywhere. The British are finished here. The issue is no longer in doubt, hasn't been for the last twenty years. There's nothing now except a huge army that'll keep Ireland under the British yoke. If you take my advice, Edward, you'll give in gracefully now while you still can, you'll give them the land they're asking for, because, if you don't, they'll take it anyway ... Parnell was the last man who could have preserved some sort of life for the British in Ireland but the damn fools didn't realize it, thought he was their enemy! Serves 'em right. I've no sympathy for them, they've lived here for generations like cocks in pastry without a thought for the sufferings of the people. Now it's their turn and I'll shed no tears for them ... Ach, things have changed since I was a boy ... they have a different look to them, the people, it would take a fool not to see it.')

'But this is an enormous letter,' thought the Major, appalled, hefting the wad of crinkly paper in his hand. 'It would take a prodigious effort even to write such a letter if one were weakened by illness, if one were unable to take proper nourishment (he thought with a pang of the untouched trays of food ferried up and down the stairs) and ... and the detail in it is intolerable.'

('Of course, I was a child then, too young to remember those days, but my father had seen it and my uncles too, God rest them, they were old men before thirty with the worry and the trouble ... and I remember the way people talked of it, you know. It must be God's will, they'd say. He sent it to punish us, d'ye see? so what is there for a man to do? Sure we'll have to go to another country, says he, to America on a ship because in Ireland we'll never do any good; we'll die for sure and there'll be no help for it ... Man, I'd say, what need is there to leave? The hunger is over and there's food enough. But sure it'll come again, says he, you'd never know ... 'tis best to leave Ireland. B'the Lord Harry, in those days they were leaving so quick they were even starving there on the quays of New York. There's no luck in Ireland, they'd tell you ... ')

'There's no luck in Ireland,' agreed Edward, winking at the Major, who was thinking: 'Such detail is intolerable,'—the design of the carpet over which the shrinking white feet of the patient still continued to patter day after day, morning and evening, to perform her ablutions ... till the day inevitably came (he had been waiting for it with despair), till the page inevitably came when the pitcher and the bowl and the sponge came to *her* over the carpet and the carpet dropped out of her world and she too prepared to drop out of her world. 'Such detail is quite obviously intolerable,' thought the Major as Edward reached out in the gloom to feel whether the teapot's plump belly was still warm, at the same time absent-mindedly handing the sugar-bowl to the doctor, who did not need it and was muttering incoherent words to the effect that if Edward or anyone else laughed at what he was saying it was because he or they, was or were, British black-guards and fools (some part of the Major's brain had remained on duty to straighten out the grammar while he thought: 'Really, when I arrived and attempted to kiss her hand she flinched away from me as she might have flinched from some uncouth stranger.').

'Those were the days,' declared Edward absently, perhaps

157

still thinking of the day he had bowled a cricket-ball up Dawson Street.

'They certainly were *not*!' snapped the doctor.

So why should she write all this? Page after page to some-one she scarcely knew. The relentlessly regular handwriting lapped rhythmically on. Only on the last few pages did it begin to waver a little.

I shall not die now.

Brendan, if I die who will look after you when I am gone? And there were a number of other observations, feebly scratched out, which the Major had not the heart to decipher.

'People are insubstantial,' murmured the doctor, as his bowler-hatted head drooped sleepily on to his chest. 'They never last. Of course, it makes no difference in the long run.'

It was signed, without the usual qualification about the 'loving fiancée', quite simply: *Angela.*

'The old chap's fallen asleep,' Edward said. 'Such a lot of rot he talks ... I'm afraid he's becoming a bit you-know-what.'

Getting to his feet he shouted deafeningly to Murphy to bring more candles because it had become infernally dark. The Major returned the letter to his pocket. Glancing down, he noted with dismay that his own flies were undone. He fumbled with them hastily before Murphy arrived with more candles.

'Can I have some peacock feathers?' demanded Padraig stubbornly. 'You promised.'

'Of course, of course,' Edward told him genially. 'Look, why don't you go and ask the twins for some; I'm sure they have lots of that sort of thing. Murphy, show this young man where he can find the girls.'

When Padraig had departed with Murphy the Major asked: 'What are the twins doing at home? Shouldn't they be at school?'

'They were sent home,' replied Edward sombrely. 'A spot of bother at school.' He sighed but did not elaborate.

They waited in silence for Padraig to return. Presently they heard the thrashing and rustling of his advent. A few moments later he appeared out of the darkness. The Major stared at him. His face was flushed and indignant and he seemed close to tears. His hair had been ruffled and his shirt was hanging out at the back. In one hand he clutched a bunch of peacock feathers.

Edward looked at him with concern, seemed about to say something but changed his mind. At length he sighed again and said that he thought it was about time to wake the doctor and send him home.

Before leaving, the doctor, who had been restored by his brief nap and now remembered why he had come, said: 'For the last time, Edward, will you come to some arrangement with the farmers about the land, for your own good as much as for theirs?'

'So far I have received two threatening letters. Both of them I have given to the District Inspector. There happens to be a law in the land which protects a man's private property and I have no intention of giving in to threats.'

'Is that your last word?'

'Yes,' Edward replied curtly.

LENIN AND POLAND

'*To be delivered from her Oppressors*'

The Paris *Matin* says: 'A wireless message has been transmitted from Moscow announcing in glowing terms that the whole of Russia is rising to fight Poland. On May 6th the majority of the Moscow garrison of 120,000 men left the Soviet capital for the Dnieper front. Lenin and Trotsky addressed the troops. Lenin said: "We do not want to fight Poland but we are going to deliver her from her oppressors. Death to the Polish landlords! Long live the Polish Workers' and Peasants' Republic!"'

Ladies Terrorized by Armed Men

Late on Monday night considerable excitement was caused in Kilkenny by the news of the 'hold up' at Troyswood a mile outside the city, by masked men armed with revolvers, of a number of motor cars and horsed carriages which were taking ladies and gentlemen, in whose number were included Major J. B. Loftus, D.L., J.P., Mount Loftus, and Sir Hercules Langrishe, Bart, Knocktopher Abbey, to a ball at the house of Captain J. E. St. George, R.M., Kilrush House, Freshford, about ten miles from Kilkenny City. A barricade of large stones was placed across the road.

Some of the cars did not pull up immediately when called upon to stop and several shots were discharged, but no one was injured, although some of the passengers say that the bullets whizzed very near them.

All the parties, who were in evening dress, were huddled together under a ditch while the destruction of the engines was carried out, and some of the ladies were very much frightened. Other horsed carriages came on the scene shortly afterwards and the raiders decamped, leaving their victims to get home as best they could.

Yesterday morning six motor cars were lined up on the side of the road, and the engines appeared to have been smashed with some heavy, blunt instrument. In the corner of the field where the drivers and passengers were placed there were remnants of chocolate boxes and cigarette packets.

❧

Little had changed in Edward's study since the Major had first seen it on his first day in Kilnalough when they had come to arm themselves against 'the Shinner on the lawn'.

There was the same solidly tangled mass of sporting equipment on the sofa. The drawer containing ammunition still lay on the floor, though the Persian cat (wisely disdaining the community in the Imperial Bar) had forsaken it for the superior comfort of an enormous greyish-white sweater that lay in one corner like a dead sheep. From under the window there came a steady creaking sound: the Major leaned out to investigate. In the yard below was a circle of brick surmounted by a huge horizontal cartwheel with worn wooden handles; against these handles two men were toiling, heads bowed with the exertion, round and round, straining like pit ponies.

'What on earth are they doing?'

'Pumping water up to the tanks on the roof. The other well by the kitchens is for drinking water, fills up from an underground spring. Lovely water ... though for some reason it makes a weird cup of tea. You may have noticed, Brendan, that we sometimes get peculiar objects in the bath-water. Can't be helped. One of the old ladies was complaining she had a dead tadpole the other day. Better than a live one, I suppose.' Without changing his tone he added: 'Life has been hell these last few months.'

'I've been meaning to ask you about Ripon. I heard they were living in Rathmines.'

'Ripon is a wash-out,' Edward said bleakly. 'I don't want to hear his name mentioned again. It's not that he took up with a Catholic girl, it's not just that. I'm not so narrow-minded that I don't know there are decent fellows among the Catholics in Ireland and plenty of 'em. I'd have put a stop to it if I could, of course, because mixed marriages don't go down well in this country, with one lot or the other ... Besides, I don't want grandchildren of mine to be brought up believing all that unhealthy nonsense they teach them. All the same, if that's what the boy had set his heart on I wouldn't have stood in his way. He could have come to me and talked it over, man to man. He knew that. I may be an old fogey but I'm not a tyrant ... ' Edward paused and moodily looked at his watch.

For a moment there was silence, then he said: 'Come along to the lodge with me. There's something I want to show you.'

They put on their hats and set off down the drive. The day was mild, overcast; although it had not been raining there was a smell of damp grass which the Major now always thought of as the smell of the Irish countryside.

'Ripon's a wash-out,' Edward repeated. 'I suppose everyone knew that except me. I suppose you realized it, Brendan, as soon as you set eyes on him ... '

'Well, no,' murmured the Major diffidently, but Edward was not listening.

'Going behind my back and doing what he did ... playing the cad with an innocent young girl (and a Catholic at that!), getting her in trouble as if she were a common housemaid, that's something I'll not stand for. He's disgraced me and he's disgraced his sisters.'

They walked on in silence. The Major could hear the dull continuous roar of the sea from somewhere behind the trees which were thickening into dense woods, matted with undergrowth and strung with brambles like trip-wires. They reached the end of the drive and the ruined lodge came into sight. Edward led the Major through some low bushes to the side of the building that faced the road. Here, high up on a part of the wall that had not been engulfed by ivy, a notice had been stuck.

'How d'you like that for cheek?'

The Major stepped forward to read it.

1. Whereas the spies and traitors known as the Royal Irish Constabulary are holding this country for the enemy, and whereas said spies and bloodhounds are conspiring with the enemy to bomb and bayonet and otherwise outrage a peaceful, law-abiding and liberty-loving people;

2. Wherefore we do hereby proclaim and suppress said spies and traitors, and do hereby solemnly warn prospec-

tive recruits that they join the R.I.C. at their own peril. All nations are agreed as to the fate of traitors. It has the sanction of God and man.

By order of the G.O.C.
Irish Republican Army

The Major had read of these posters in the newspapers but this was the first he had seen with his own eyes.

'The ruffians slip in during the night when they think they're safe. Murphy should be here in a minute; I told him to bring along something to scrape it off with.'

'But what I don't see', said the Major with a smile, 'is why they should think that "said spies and bloodhounds" are anxious to conspire in your drive. After all, they could surely have found a more visible spot.'

'We have a few young chaps staying at the hotel at the moment,' Edward told him. 'Ex-army officers brought over from England to give a hand to the R.I.C. They're supposed to be the first of a new auxiliary force they've started recruiting. You won't have seen them about yet, I expect, because I've quartered them in the Prince Consort wing by themselves. They didn't get on with the old ladies. The Prince Consort wing is over the stables, can't see it from here, of course. They have their own mess there and so forth. We had them in the main building at first but they were rather boisterous, just schoolboys, really (though they've done their bit, mind you, they've been in the trenches) ... Trouble was they kept teasing the old girls; one of them kept on whipping out a bayonet and pretending to cut their throats ... But they're not a bad lot of chaps. Expect you'll run into them round about. They use the tennis courts a bit. Ah, there's Murphy.'

Murphy had appeared, carrying a hoe. Edward directed him to scrape off the notice and the old manservant advanced on the lodge feebly brandishing his implement. But the notice had been stuck well up on the wall and was out of his reach.

'We need something to stand on,' the Major said.

'Right you are,' said Edward. 'Come here, Murphy. Major, you hand me the hoe and I'll climb on Murphy's shoulders.' He gave the hoe to the Major. 'Come on, man, we haven't got all day,' he added to the decrepit manservant, who was shuffling forward with every sign of reluctance. The Major looked dubiously at Murphy's frail shoulders.

'Maybe we'd better get a ladder from somewhere.'

'Nonsense. Now hold still, Murphy. Hang on to the trunk of this tree while I'm getting up. For God's sake, man, we're never going to get anywhere if you're going to wilt like that every time I touch you.'

But time and time again, just as Edward seemed on the point of throwing his glistening shoe and beautifully trousered leg over the old servant's thin shoulders, he would begin to wilt in anticipation. Edward stormed at him for having no backbone and ordered him not to be so faint-hearted — all to no avail. In the end they had to leave the notice where it was. Edward stalked angrily up the drive. Murphy, relief written all over his cadaverous features, vanished into the trees. And the Major was left to his own devices.

He spent the afternoon in the company of the twins. There was a row going on between them and Edward; he did not know what it was all about but suspected it had something to do with their being sent home from school. In any event, Edward was taking a firm line with them (or so he told the Major). Any disobedience or lack of respect should be instantly reported to him and they would be dealt with. Part of their punishment, it seemed, was to spend the afternoon with the Major (who was offended by the idea); they were to go with him in the Daimler and show him the whereabouts of a remarkable trout stream. These days the Major was only faintly interested in fishing, but he had nothing better to do. Though Faith and Charity had a chastened air they looked remarkably pretty in their navy-blue dresses with white lace collars encircling their slender necks. The Major felt sorry for them.

'Which is which, and how can I tell?'

'I'm Charity and she's Faith,' one of them said. 'Faith is bigger there,' she added, pointing at Faith's chest. Both girls smiled wanly.

Throughout the afternoon, as they motored through the low rolling hills, the twins sat on the back seat in attitudes of meek dejection, slim fingers lifted to entwine the braided velvet straps, each the mirror-image of the other. 'What charming girls! Edward is being much too hard on them.'

He modified this opinion a day or two later, however. As an additional punishment a daily lesson with Evans, the tutor, had been ordained by Edward to take place in the writing-room. Passing the open door one afternoon, the Major paused to listen.

'How do you say in French, Mr Evans, "The buttons are falling off my jacket and I need a clean collar"?' one of the twins was asking innocently.

'How do you say, "I've got boils on my neck because I never wash it"?'

'How do you say, "I have ideas beyond my station"?'

'What does "*amavi puellam*" mean?'

'How do you say in Latin, Mr Evans, "My pasty white face is blushing all over"?'

'Sharpen my pencil, Evans, 'fraid I've just broken it again.'

'Any more of this and I'll report you to your father.'

'Any more of what? We're only asking questions.'

'Aren't we even allowed to ask questions?'

The Major moved on. He had heard enough.

Later that same afternoon, while taking a stroll with old Miss Johnston in the Chinese Garden ('If you ask me it's an Irish Chinese Garden,' Miss Johnston said with a sniff, looking round at the thick beds of tangled weeds and seeded flowers), their path crossed that of a young man in khaki tunic, breeches and puttees, wearing on his head a tam o'shanter with the crowned-harp badge of the R.I.C. The Major's eyes were drawn to the bandolier he wore across his chest and the black leather belt holding a bayonet scabbard; on his right thigh rested an open revolver holster. It was shocking, somehow, to meet this man in the peaceful wilderness of the garden, a sharp and unpleasant reminder of the incidents the Major had read about in the newspapers but could never quite visualize, any more than he could now visualize the shooting of the old man in Ballsbridge that he had witnessed. As they passed, the young man grinned sardonically and, winking at the Major, drew a finger across his throat from ear to ear.

'Gutter-snipe!' hissed Miss Johnston indignantly. 'To think the R.I.C. is taking on young men like that!'

And it took all the Major's considerate inquiries about her nephews, her nieces and the state of her health ('Chilblains even in midsummer in this hotel, Major. I've never known such draughts … ') to smooth her ruffled plumage.

And yet they were all ex-officers, these men, so Edward assured him later. One had to remember, though, that to be an officer in 1920 was not the same thing as being an officer in 1914. A lot of the older sort (their very qualities of bravery, steadfast obedience to the call of duty, chivalry and so forth acting as so many banana skins on the road to survival) had disappeared in the holocaust and had had to be replaced. It was also true that these new men, and the great number who would soon be following them to a meagre six weeks of police training at the Curragh, were among the least favourably placed of the countless demobilized officers who now found themselves having to earn a living once more. All the same, though one made allowances (and Edward was always ready to make allowances for men who had served in the trenches), there *were* limits. The old kind, the officer who was also a gentleman, would never have gone about frightening old ladies. So thought Edward. What did the Major think?

The Major agreed, but thought to himself that these 'men from the trenches' who were being paid a pound a day to keep a few wild Irishmen in order might well have trouble taking anything very seriously—whether the Irish, the old ladies, or their own selves.

At the same time he was disturbed by their presence. These men (individually they were charming, Edward told him) were unpredictable and still estranged from the accepted standards of life in peacetime—not that one could call Ireland very peaceful these days. As he was passing the Prince Consort wing a day or two later a window exploded in a sparkling burst of splinters, a laughing head appeared and a hand was held out to see if it was raining. Occasionally too one heard pistol shots and laughter in the long summer evenings; Edward had laid out a pistol-range in the clearing behind the lodge where the I.R.A. notice had been posted. In no time at all the notice had melted away under a hail of bullets and hung in unrecognizable shreds. One day the Major picked up a dead rabbit on the edge of the lawn. Its body was riddled with bullets.

This rabbit, as it happened, had been a favourite of the Major's. Old and fat, it had been partly tamed by the twins when they were small children. They had lost interest, of course, as they grew older, and no longer remembered to feed it. The rabbit, however, had not forgotten the halcyon days of carrots and dandelion leaves. Thinner and thinner as time went by, it had nevertheless continued to haunt the fringes of the wood like a forsaken lover. Poor rabbit! Moved and angry (but the 'men from the trenches' were not to know that this was not a wild rabbit), the Major went to break the news to the twins, who were down by the tennis courts trying to persuade Séan Murphy to teach them how to drive the Standard (though Edward had forbidden this until they were older). The twins were not as upset as the Major expected them to be.

'Can we eat him?' they wanted to know.

'He's already buried.'

'We could dig him up,' Faith suggested. 'Aren't rabbits' feet supposed to be lucky?'

But the Major said he had forgotten where the grave was.

'Were the bullet-holes bad?'

'How d'you mean? They were bad for the rabbit.'

'No, I was just thinking we could have made a fur hat', said Charity, 'if there weren't too many holes in him.'

'I say, Brendan, you aren't any good at arithmetic, are you? Daddy has set that dreadful tutor person on us and now he's threatening to look at our homework when it's been corrected.'

'Try Mr Norton. He's supposed to be good at that sort of thing.'

Mr Norton was a man in his seventies, a recent arrival at the Majestic; he had the reputation, fostered by himself, of having been a mathematical genius, drained in his youth, however, of energy and fortune by a weakness for beautiful women.

'We asked him ... '

'But he always wants us to sit on his knee as if we were children.'

'And his breath smells horrid.'

Now that the Imperial Bar had been rendered uninhabitable by the colony of cats the Major sometimes took one of Edward's motor cars into Kilnalough in the evening for a drink at the Golf Club. There one evening he met Boy O'Neill, the solicitor, who greeted him like an old friend, although it was almost a year since the Peace Day parade when they had last met. O'Neill's appearance had changed dramatically and the Major could now scarcely recognize the timid, bony invalid he had first met at Angela's tea-party. Dressed in a baggy tweed jacket with bulging pockets, O'Neill appeared more swollen and aggressive than ever. There was a subdued irritation about the man which made one ill at ease when talking to him; one had the feeling that O'Neill was capable at any moment of abandoning reason altogether and finishing the argument with an uppercut. The Major sat watching the wads of jaw-muscle thickening as he talked: he had just finished eighteen holes, he declared, and had never felt better in his life. A hot shower, a drink, and now he was off home for a good meal. He unslung the clinking golf-bag from his shoulder and heaved it into an armchair, showing no impatience to depart. Eyeing the golf-bag, the Major noticed nestling between a mashie niblick, a jigger and the bulging wooden head of a driver what he at first thought was a club without a head—but no, it was the barrel of a rifle.

'No half measures, eh?'

'I can see you haven't been reading the papers, Major. Couple of army chaps were shot down on a links in Tipperary the other day ... unarmed men. Didn't have a chance out there with no shelter, nobody passing by. The Shinners are brave enough when the other fella doesn't have a gun. They'll run like rabbits if they know you're armed.'

The Major only glanced at the newspaper these days, tired of trying to comprehend a situation which defied comprehension, a war without battles or trenches. Why should one bother with the details: the raids for arms, the shootings of policemen, the intimidations? What could one learn from the details of chaos? Every now and then, however, he would become aware with a feeling of shock that, for all its lack of pattern, the situation was different, and always a little worse.

Satisfied with the Major's look of dismay, O'Neill was now saying confidently that there was no need to worry. 'All this will be cleared up now within five or six weeks, you can take it from me.'

'How d'you know?' asked the Major hopefully, thinking that perhaps O'Neill had heard something. 'Two reasons,' declared O'Neill. 'One, reinforcements are coming from England with this new recruiting campaign. Two, because of the nature of the Irish people. The Irish are a quick-tempered lot but they don't hold a grudge for long. They're good at heart, you see. Besides, they're too inefficient to get anywhere by themselves ... I speak, mind you, of the Southerners; Ulstermen are a different kettle of fish. Besides, all Ireland's best leaders have been Englishmen; look at Parnell.'

'Yes, yes, to be sure,' agreed the Major dubiously. 'It must end soon. That's what we used to say in the trenches,' he added with a faint smile.

'Of course, of course,' O'Neill said, failing to perceive the Major's irony. 'You can take my word for it. I've just been having a drink with the army lads we have here now and I don't think they'll stand for much nonsense from Paddy Pig.'

'You mean the men staying at the Majestic? I didn't think they had much time for us locals.'

'They're splendid chaps, you can take it from me,' replied O'Neill, who was now taking off his bulging jacket and showed less sign of leaving than ever. 'It's just that they don't really know who they can trust over here and, frankly, I don't blame them for that. Come in with me now to the bar and I'll introduce you.'

'Really, thanks all the same ... ' protested the Major, but O'Neill was already on his feet and beckoning imperiously with a forearm as thick as a leg of lamb. The Major followed him reluctantly. O'Neill's studded shoes clicked on the tiles of the corridor and bit into the worn wood of the locker room where a fat naked gentleman was vigorously towelling his quivering bottom. They passed through into the Members' Bar.

'Just a minute,' the Major said. 'There's someone I must say hello to.'

Mr Devlin, dapper and smiling, was hastening towards him. He was delighted to see the Major back amongst them once more and must express his thanks for the kindness he had shown to his daughter Sarah on her way to France and how was the Major's dear auntie who had also been so kind ... ('Ah, deceased is she? Indeed now, I'm sorry to hear it.') And was the Major himself in better health than he had been? It must have been a great worry and a terrible grief for him to be losing his auntie like that ... And as for Sarah she would be back one of these days and he knew that she would look forward to seeing the Major as much as he himself did and besides they would probably be meeting here at the links from now on because he had 'a little job to do' ... He paused expectantly.

'Oh?'

Yes, he'd be spending some considerable time here in the evenings because he had been elected treasurer, there was a notice on the notice-board, the Major probably hadn't had a chance to see it yet. 'And it's all thanks to the influence of a certain person who has been very good to me and my family, very good ... I'll say no more ... it's a great honour.'

The 'men from the trenches', four of them, were sitting together at the curve of the bar by a window looking out over the eighteenth green and the gently ascending slope of fairway that led up to it. None of the members, apart from O'Neill, were sitting near them, and for a good reason. They had caused some dismay, the Major had heard, by installing themselves here without invitation; after all, there was a lounge available for ladies and non-members (providing that they were respectable); the secretary had affably pointed this out on the occasion of their first visit. They had listened politely enough; there had not been a scene. But though there had not been a scene the trouble was that they had not moved either. The secretary's smile had to some extent congealed on his lips but, as he explained to a special meeting of the committee, these fellows were, after all, over here risking their lives to maintain law and order in Ireland (not to mention the fact that they also happened to be armed to the teeth), so one did not want to deal too harshly with them, throw them out on their ears and so forth. The committee had pondered the problem and come up with a solution brilliant in its simplicity. The 'men from the trenches' should be invited to become members. The secretary had been dispatched there and then, on the spot, to deliver this generous invitation ... But he had returned almost immediately with the news that they had declined. Once more they had listened politely while he talked about members' fees, rules, rights and obligations and then said. 'No thanks.' It was preposterous, everyone agreed that it was. All the same, the objection to dealing harshly with them, the one about risking their lives to maintain law and order (as well as the other one), remained and one could not simply ignore it. In the end, after much discussion, a notice had been posted on the bulletin board announcing that all *senior* personnel of the R.I.C. had been declared honorary members for the duration of the emergency (one couldn't, of course, open the doors to a horde of other ranks, splendid fellows though some of them no doubt were). The Major, who thought the secretary a pompous ass, had enjoyed this affair. But now that he saw the men sitting there, cold and calm, he had to admit that he would not like to have been the person with the job of ordering them to leave.

'Back again like a bad penny,' O'Neill was saying with chilling heartiness. 'Want you to meet an old pal, Major Archer. Now I wonder if I can get this straight ... Captain Bolton, Lieutenants ... let me see, Pike, Berry, and Foster-Smith. How's that for a memory, eh?'

'Sergeants now, old boy,' said Foster-Smith, whose prominent teeth and thinning hair gave him a foolish appearance; he was very slight, his breeches hung in folds from thighs that were no thicker than wine-bottles.

It was Pike whose head the Major had seen appearing through the broken window at the Majestic; he looked a jolly fellow, but the eyes above his plump blue cheeks showed a disturbing intelligence and his frequent laughter seemed perfunctory. Berry was younger than the others; his sandy hair was cut so short that it stood up like the bristles of a hairbrush.

'Bit of a comedown,' he was saying. 'Not so much hob-nobbing with officers now that we've joined the unwashed O.R.' He glanced slyly at the Major. Everyone laughed except Captain Bolton, who merely smiled faintly. O'Neill, red with mirth, laughed louder than anyone.

Captain Bolton's eyes moved from one or other of the lieutenants to the Major in a detached, incurious way. There was something about his powerful jaw that was familiar to the

Major; it was a moment before he realized what it was. These were the strong regular features (a face without any particular identity) which he had observed that sculptors frequently chose for war memorials. He could easily imagine Bolton frozen in bronze into some heroic posture. Put a helmet on his head, a bronze flag in his hand, drape a few dying bronze comrades around his knees ... But Captain Bolton was very much alive and proved it by saying to the barman in a mild tone:

'Another round quick sharp, Paddy, you dirty Shinner, and put it on our account ... '

'And send it to the King,' added Pike. 'If he won't pay send it to the Lord of Wipers.'

O'Neill explained the reason for introducing the Major to them: namely, the fact that they were neighbours. The Major too lived under Edward Spencer's roof at the Majestic.

'Spencer has two lovely daughters,' Foster-Smith said, showing no interest in O'Neill's information.

'I've got a lovely daughter too,' offered O'Neill winking broadly. 'Want to see her picture?' And after a moment's fumbling he produced a tattered photograph of Viola. While 'the men from the trenches' were studying it O'Neill winked again, this time at the Major. The Major turned away. As he was leaving Bolton called after him: 'Tell the old grannies that the next one we catch we'll cut her up in pieces and put her in a sack.'

Laughter echoed after him as he made his way through the empty changing-room towards the lounge. Before he reached it O'Neill, who had hurried after him, took him by the arm and asked eagerly: 'What d'you think of them? They'll give the Shinners something to think about, won't they?'

'I'm sure they will,' the Major said coldly. 'But the cure may be as bad as the disease.'

When O'Neill had departed the Major wearily climbed the stairs to the tea-room on the first floor. It was empty at this hour, but there was a veranda with a splendid view over the links and beyond to the cornfields that lined the road to Valebridge. The sun was already low in the sky and black shadows crept far out into the flowing grass. Down below, by the club-house steps, four late arrivals were preparing to set out for the first tee, the breeze ballooning their plus-fours as they waited. There would still be time this evening for nine holes, or eighteen if one was not too particular about the fading light.

As they moved away from the club-house a great number of ragged men and boys materialized around them raising a piercing, pitiful clamour. Some of these tattered figures were so old and bent that they could scarcely hobble forward to press their claims, others mere boys who were scarcely bigger than the golf-bags they were hoping to carry. The golfers looked them over and made their selection. Those who had been rejected retired disconsolately to the shadows where they had been lurking. There was little hope now that another party would set out that evening.

The Major sighed, stretched, yawned and presently went home, disturbed that old men and children should have to hang around the club-house until late at night in the hope of earning a sixpence. He thought: 'Really, something should be done about it.' But what could one do?

STATE OF IRELAND

A Conspiracy Against England

On the motion for the adjournment of the House of Commons yesterday, Sir Edward Carson said that he could not help thinking that the English and Scottish people—he hoped he was wrong—had begun not to care a spark what happened in Ireland. He imagined that a few years ago they could not have seen policemen serving their King shot down like dogs from day to day and

174

soldiers who had fought their battles returning home to be treated like criminals because they had performed their heroic duties with very little being done for their protection. It was difficult to understand the paralysis that had come over the people of England in relation to these crimes. There was ample evidence that what was going on in Ireland was connected with what was going on in Egypt and India. It was all part of a scheme, openly stated, to reduce Great Britain to the single territory she occupied here, and to take from her all the keys of a great Empire. They would find, if they looked into it, that the same American-Irish who were working this matter in Ireland, and who visited Ireland last year, had an Irish Office, an Egyptian Office, and an Indian Office in New York. It was well known. It had been stated in the American papers that there was this great conspiracy going on—of which Sinn Fein formed only a part — not out of love for Ireland but out of hatred for Great Britain, fanned by Germans everywhere ... He believed that the whole of this murder campaign, or a great part of it, was directed from America, and he believed the funds largely came from there.

❧

GIRL'S HAIR CUT OFF

A New Way to Free Ireland

The outrage near Tuam when the hair was cut off Bridget Keegan by masked men who entered her father's house in the early hours of the morning was strongly condemned by magistrates.

Mr Golding, C.S., who appeared for the Crown said it was a blackguardly act. Seven men entered the girl's house about a quarter to one in the morning. One of them had a revolver and the others had what looked like revolvers. They took the girl, who had fainted, in her nightdress out to the yard, and cut her hair off with a shears, telling her sister, whom they threatened with the same fate, that that was what she got for going with Tommies. While the man with the shears was cutting off the hair he sang: 'We are all out for Ireland free.'

All I can say is, said Mr Golding, God help Ireland if these are the acts of Irishmen, and God help Ireland if these are the men to free her.

❧

LAND AGITATION MAINTAINED

Roman Catholic Bishop's Appeal

The Most Rev. Dr O'Dea, Roman Catholic Bishop of Galway, preaching at Killanin, where he administered Confirmation, entreated the people to be calm and united, and above all to do everything in accordance with the rules of justice laid down by the Church, and the precepts of honesty which the Commandments require. With regard to shootings and outrages he would say little. Shootings were always dangerous, and even if shots were fired without any attempts to kill or wound, were they not threats? Did not the shots fired in the air threaten, and was not a threat sinful?

With regard to the taking over of land, continued his lordship, all I shall say is this: Let not the love of land, or riches, or anything else in this world, make us break God's law, for land stained with God's blood is unlawfully got, and is branded with God's curse.

❧

A day or two after the Major's visit to the Golf Club Edward assembled his staff and what remained of his family to make an important announcement. The Major was also present, as were a number of the old ladies. Indeed, certain of the old ladies (particularly the Misses Bagley, Archer and Porteous) had lived at the Majestic for so long and in such penurious circumstances that somehow, since Edward no longer felt able to bring up the subject of payment of bills with them, they had metamorphosed themselves into members of the family. This situation was unsatisfactory for Edward who himself was no longer as wealthy as he had been. But one cannot turn a gentlewoman out into the streets to beg for her living. Besides, he found any discussion of money distasteful. As for baldly asking a lady to pay her bill, he would as soon have committed sodomy. His only resource, as the Major saw straight away, was to make their life so unpleasant that they might want to leave of their own accord. But naturally he was too much of a gentleman to do this deliberately, even though his expenses never seemed to stop mounting. In these circumstances it was probably a good thing that even at the best of times the discomfort of living at the Majestic was close to intolerable.

Edward's gaze wandered absently around the room while he waited for everyone to assemble. Presently he stifled a yawn; he did not in the least look like someone about to make an important announcement. When at last a hush fell on the room he cleared his throat. He just wanted to say, he said, that he was on the point of—he paused a moment to let his words sink in—on the point of beginning an economy drive.

An 'economy drive'? The old ladies flashed inquiring glances at each other, as if to say that they had been under the impression that this economy drive had already begun, indeed that it had already been going on for rather a long time. Some of the servants too betrayed signs of alarm: was this the end of their employment? So many people were out of work these days that it seemed more than likely that one day their turn would come. The cook, who had a houseful of drunken relations to support in one of the Dublin slums, gasped inaudibly; the massive façade of her bosom began to rise and fall rapidly. Evans turned pale and the boils on his neck glowed like cherries above the worn fringe of his stiff collar. Only one

177

or two of the youngest maids who had barely arrived 'from the country' blushed shyly and smiled their acceptance, as they would have even if Edward had decreed that they were to be whipped. As for Murphy, hitherto frozen into a cast-iron lethargy, his eyes were now racing to and fro across the carpet like terrified mice.

Edward cleared his throat. They expected him to continue, to amplify and explain ...but no, he said nothing. The heavy ticking of the grandfather clock became audible. At length he sighed and asked: were there any questions?

Well, no, there were not. The air of dissatisfaction in the room deepened, however, and Miss Bagley looked quite cross. One really did not know where to begin with one's questions when such an outlandish idea as an 'economy drive' was proposed. In the old days ... Silence had fallen again. It was interrupted by old Mrs Rappaport, who was sitting straight-backed as ever in a rocking-chair by the empty fireplace, a lace cap pinned on her thin grey hair. She began to rock herself peevishly back and forth, faster and faster, until at last she cried: 'It's scandalous!' and everyone brightened a little.

But with Granny Rappaport one could never be quite sure whether she had altogether pinned down the subject under discussion or was talking about something totally different. Edward chose to ignore her and said that, all right then, that was all he had wanted to say and, by the way, thanked them for their co-operation. So they were dismissed ... and still did not know at whose hard-won comforts the thin rats of economy were about to begin gnawing.

Edward, of course, was the sort of person for whom words and deeds are the same. Perhaps, the Major reflected, he would consider it sufficient to announce the economy drive without actually putting it into practice. That afternoon, however, while Edward and the Major were taking an after-lunch stroll on the terrace outside the ballroom, the twins were noticed fishing in the swimming-pool with an old tennis racket. They were brusquely summoned.

'Stand here and let's see how tall you are. Oh, stand up straight, girl! D'you need clothes?'

'Yes, Daddy. Ours are all in flitters, mine especially.'

'Mine are worse.'

'Mine are ten times, twenty times, a hundred times—' Charity held up the darned elbow of her cardigan—'a million million times worse.'

'How long have you had the clothes you've got?'

'Absolutely *ages*.'

'A billion years.'

'All right then, follow me. You come too, Major, and see fair play.'

Edward turned in through the grimy desert of the ballroom and they followed him across it and up an unfamiliar staircase, seldom used, to judge by the spiders' webs which garnished the banister. As they climbed the twins pestered Edward with questions: what were these clothes? Had he been to Dublin to the shops? Was it Switzer's, or Pim's, or Brown Thomas's, or what was it? How did he know their size and did he realize that Faith was a bit bigger in her bosom? Edward made no reply; he was short of breath and flushed. As they struck off down a corridor he murmured to the Major: 'Getting old. Must take it easy these days.'

The twins had run ahead; every step they took raised a puff of dust from the carpet, so that their footprints appeared like smoke, glittering in the stripes of afternoon sunlight that filtered through half-open doors. Underfoot loose floorboards creaked and shifted ominously.

'If I get dry rot I'm done for,' Edward continued as if still discussing his health.

'Oh?'

'Bally place'll fall about m'ears.'

One hundred and twenty-one, one hundred and twenty-two, one hundred and twenty-three ... The next room had no brass number screwed to the door but once there had been one; its darker shadow remained on the varnished wood. It was at this door that Edward halted. He took a key from his pocket and unlocked it.

'In *there*?' exclaimed Charity, mystified. It was dark inside. Edward crossed to the window and threw open the closed shutters. Abruptly everything took on shape, colour and meaning. Although he had never been here before, everything he saw was perfectly familiar to the Major. He knew whose room this had been. His heart sank.

The twins had not been in here before. The room seemed to be occupied. They peered around curiously but already their excitement was melting into suspicion. They looked at the unmade bed, sheets and eiderdown roughly pulled up as if the chambermaid had not had time to make it properly. They wrinkled their noses at the pitcher and bowl, the sponge dried as hard as the pumice-stone beside it. They eyed their lovely reflections in the mirror and looked at the dressing-table with its silver hairbrushes and the silver frame containing a photograph of, well ... the truth had dawned on them now but for a moment they were speechless with disbelief.

'Now let's see ... where ... ?' Edward said quietly. As he spoke the Major glimpsed a shadow of pain, as if he had been hurt behind the eyes (but why did he have to bring *me*? he wondered bitterly). Edward stepped over to the wardrobe and opened it experimentally. It was empty. A large white moth flew wearily out for a little way until it vanished from the air under a vicious downward smash of Faith's tennis racket. A puff of powder from its wings hung in the room.

'Daddy, how *could* you?' cried Charity. 'You surely don't mean us to wear *Angela*'s things!' Edward said nothing, but his face darkened as he turned away and looked round the room. His eye came to rest on a chest of dark polished oak which, to the Major's excited imagination, looked remarkably like a coffin. In fact it was an old dower chest which had probably belonged to the Spencers for generations. Edward had dug up the old metal clasp and lifted the lid; inside it was lined with another kind of wood, lighter and fragrant, cedarwood perhaps. Another lid was lifted. In a moment Edward was scooping piles of neatly folded clothing on to the carpet.

'We *can't*, Daddy, it's too creepy,' insisted Faith, wiping the strings of the tennis racket on the bedclothes to clean off the minced remains of the moth.

'Not a *corpse's* clothes,' pleaded Charity. 'It's awful. Just the thought of it makes me feel funny.'

'We must save money, my dear. Now be a good girl and take your dress off so we can try them on. If they don't fit we'll have to get the cook to work with her needle and thread — they tell me she's very handy at that sort of thing. Besides, you'd do well to take a few lessons from her while you have the chance since you don't seem to have learned much at school ... One of these days you'll have homes of your own and maybe, I don't know, the way things are going you'll not always have servants to look after you ... in any case,' he added weakly, 'a bit of sewing never did anyone any harm.'

'I think I'm going to faint,' Faith said grimly and sat down heavily on the bed, making its springs creak.

'Ugh! That's the corpse's death-bed you're sitting on, Faithy.'

'You'll speak of Angela with respect,' snapped Edward, 'or you'll both get a hiding and be sent to your rooms.'

'Why *me*? It was Catty that said it,' Faith said grumpily. 'And what's more I *am* feeling sick and will probably start spewing any moment.'

'Faith, don't be dis*gu*sting,' Charity said, grinning in spite of herself. 'You've started me feeling peculiar too.'

'Shut up, both of you, and pick one of these dresses before I lose my patience. They're as good as new and some of them were never worn.'

'Which ones?' asked Faith dubiously, poking at the heap of clothing with her tennis racket.

The Major had lit his pipe and was watching the twins as they rummaged in the pile of clothing, holding dresses up to see what they looked like. It was clear (one of the countless things the Major had never known about her) that Angela had dressed extravagantly. Almost all her dresses had tucks in descending horizontal tiers; there was a heavy afternoon dress of velvet embossed with chrysanthemums which reached to the ground and trailed in a swallow-tail behind; there were heavy woollen dresses with overdresses, all with a great deal of frogging and embroidery; there was a blue satin evening dress with a band of black velvet that trailed as a sash behind; there was a dress of black taffeta or chiné silk with a vast amount of braid; and there was a moleskin cape and muff.

'It's all so horribly old-lady!'

'Come on, we haven't got all day,' Edward told them. 'Make up your minds. If you don't pick one of these dresses each within thirty seconds I'll pick them for you.'

Under this threat the twins reluctantly made their selections: Charity a simple blue linen morning dress with a white organdie collar, Faith a silk jersey afternoon dress with a belt of gold cord and tassels to the ankles.

'I feel a bit sick, Daddy ... '

But Edward's patience was now clearly at an end and the twins retired sullenly to change.

Slumped in an armchair, the Major was wondering whether he might ask Edward for the photograph of himself which stood on the dressing-table (a picture taken in Brighton in 1916 showing a relatively carefree youth who bore little resemblance to the stoically grim head which these days accompanied him to the mirror). He wanted this picture merely to remove it from the room, from the neighbouring hairbrushes and other relics, to destroy it ... he did not know why he wanted to do this. In any case, he was afraid that Edward might look askance at such a request.

Edward was kneeling among the bundles of clothing and rummaging through them abstractedly.

'Poor Angie! There's lots more somewhere: petticoats and knickers and corsets and so forth ... she liked clothes, used to buy things nobody'd ever wear out here in the country.'

He held up a dress of black velvet that billowed emptily in his hands, empty of Angela.

'Wore this the day she was presented at the Viceregal Lodge. For a joke we went out to Phoenix Park on the tram instead of hiring a carriage, both of us dressed up like dog's dinners. How people stared at us! Bit of fun we had, you know, pretending to be Socialists. Angie said she was ashamed to be seen arriving on the tram, but she laughed about it afterwards like a good sport.' He stood up and went to stare at himself moodily in the mirror, picking up one of the silver brushes (tarnished blue-grey by months of neglect) and rubbing his thumb over the bristles.

'They're only kids and it doesn't really matter what they wear so long as it keeps them warm,' he added defensively. 'Got to get hold of a bit of spare cash one way or another if I'm to give that blighter Ripon a helping hand.'

'Is that the reason?'

'Well, you said yourself that with a wife to support he'd be needing some cash to set himself up.'

The Major could remember saying no such thing but could see no point in denying it.

'But don't you think his wife will have something?'

'I doubt it. Anyway, Ripon's not the sort to accept charity, whatever his faults. In some ways, you know, he's a chip off the old block. I suppose I should sell off these brushes and things as well. They're not much good to poor Angie now. These trinkets might fetch something. Hate to do it, though.'

They lapsed into a lugubrious silence. Presently, with a sigh, Edward began: 'You know, the one time in my life when I was really happy ... ' But at this moment the twins entered.

'My! Don't they look smart?' cried Edward in genuine admiration. 'Well, what d'you think of that, Brendan? Aren't they lovely?'

The Major had to agree with him. The twins looked more

lovely than ever standing there, identical, outraged, each holding up her skirts in small clenched fists. They uttered a simultaneous gasp.

'But we look like *freaks*, Daddy!'

'We can't wear things like this. People will laugh themselves sick at us.'

'Nonsense, you look absolutely charming, you can take it from me. Young ladies knew how to dress themselves before the war.'

'Daddy, you surely don't want us to look like freaks,' pleaded Faith, close to tears.

'That's going too far! I refuse, I simply refuse!'

'Faith, I warned you! Charity! You'll go to your rooms this instant,' shouted Edward, losing his temper. His anger impressed the twins sufficiently to quell them. They glared at him tearfully for a moment and then stamped out.

The soft-hearted Major hurried out after them and handed each a bar of chocolate (he had recently taken to carrying chocolate in his pockets to give to the ragged, famished children he encountered on his walks). They looked at the chocolate, sniffed, but finally accepted it.

The following day the Major came upon the twins in a deserted sitting-room sifting through a mountain of hats, muffs, boas and shoes. The hats were hopelessly lush and exotic, they told him peevishly. Who could possibly wear such things?

'Look at this!' Faith showed him a broad-brimmed felt hat swathed in yards of orange satin with a bird clinging to the back.

'Or this, it looks like a whole farmyard,' she said, throwing him another hat of black leghorn trimmed with a jungle of osprey feathers and real oats. They appeared to be mollified, however, by the boas; indeed, the Major found himself having to adjudicate a squabble that developed over a magnificent boa of magenta cock feathers. It went to Charity on the understanding that Faith should have first claim over a matching hat, tippet and muff of peacock feathers (the muff even had a beak and brown glass eyes on the alert), together with first choice of the silk parasols. Finally, the twins made another discovery: Angela's shoes fitted them to perfection! Unfortunately, however, old Mrs Rappaport happened to hear about the shoes and caused a dreadful scene. They must wear their button boots up to their calves for the sake of their ankles! Otherwise they would look like milkmaids when they grew up. The old lady achieved the support of Edward in this matter (although, to tell the truth, he was losing interest in the twins' clothing) and shoes were forbidden. The twins became spiteful and for days refused to go near their grandmother. But presently all was forgotten and nobody (except the Major) seemed to notice that they had gone back to wearing Angela's shoes. Certainly no one thought of mentioning the fact to old Mrs Rappaport.

This incident marked the beginning and also, really, the end of Edward's economy drive. The simple truth was that the old ladies were right: it was as if an economy drive had already been in operation. There was nothing much left to economize *on*. True, one could sack a few servants, but they were paid so little anyway it hardly seemed worth while. Besides, the place was already in a scarcely habitable state. If, into the bargain, the servants were sacked what would it be like? Well, probably, not much different, as a matter of fact, because the problem of keeping the place clean had long since gone beyond the point where Murphy and the blushing young girls 'up from the country' could make a significant impact on it, even if they had wanted to (which they did not, particularly).

Murphy had been behaving oddly of late. At Edward's meeting he had shown signs of abject terror lest his meagre income be stifled by the proposed economies. But now there came to the Major's ears one or two extraordinary rumours about the aged manservant's truculent behaviour; rumours, of course, which anyone who had set eyes on the chap could scarcely credit.

According to a story circulated by Miss Staveley, one of the oldest and deafest but not least talkative ladies in the hotel, Murphy had been asked to assist her up the stairs to her room on the first floor where she had the feeling she might find her pince-nez. The impudent old rascal was reported to have told her bluntly that she would do better to stay where she was ... before padding away down some lonely corridor with a wheezing chuckle. Unable to believe her ears (she was distinctly hard of hearing, it was true) she had waited for him to come back. But there had been no sign of him. He had disappeared into the dim recesses of the interior and it was hopeless to look for him (nobody, not even the twins, not even Edward himself, knew the geography of that immense rambling building better than Murphy who had spent his life in it). She had not set eyes on him again for two days, by which time she had found her pince-nez in her sewing basket and lost them again (this time the Major was conscripted to help in the search and found them on the nose of the statue of Venus in the foyer). This rumour reached Edward who rebuked Murphy. But Murphy denied all knowledge of the affair and clearly did not know what pince-nez were; he seemed to have a vague idea that they were a reprehensible form of underwear worn by foreign ladies. One just had to give the fellow the benefit of the doubt and, besides, Miss Staveley ... Edward tapped his forehead and rolled his eyes.

But whatever one might say about Miss Staveley one was obliged to add that she paid her bills regularly. This made her a person of consequence among the guests at the Majestic. However confused her apprehension of the world around her might seem at times, she was always listened to with respect. Another rumour, promoted this time by Mr Norton, the mathematical 'genius', had it that Murphy was well known for speaking seditiously in public houses. Miss Johnston remarked despondently: 'No doubt we shall all be murdered in our beds by the wretched man,' but scarcely anyone took

Murphy to be a serious menace, even full of whiskey and Bolshevism as he was reported to be. Nevertheless the old ladies and the Major agreed that it was a sign of the times. And what terrible times they were! At no point in recent history, reflected the Major (who was slumped in an armchair in an agreeable after-lunch torpor), at no point in the past two or three hundred years could the standards of decent people have been so threatened, could civilization have been so vulnerable and near to disintegration, as they were today. One just had to open the newspaper ...

Another sign of the times was the derelict state of the fields that lay around the Majestic. Not planted in the spring because of Edward's quarrel with the farm-workers, they now wore a thick green fur of weeds. The Major sometimes saw tattered children dragging aimlessly through these fields in a doleful search for something edible: a little corn that had seeded itself from last year's harvest or a stray potato plant. Edward too seemed oppressed by this sight and although he said: 'It's their own damned fault. I told the silly beggars what would happen if they didn't plant those fields,' he made no move to have the children chased away and even one day sent Seán Murphy out with a washing-tub full of windfalls from the orchard. The children fled, of course, at the sight of him and he was obliged to leave the tub there in the middle of the field. When he went back for it half an hour later it was empty.

'I sometimes wonder', mused the Major, 'what would happen if one caught one of those little brats young enough, taught him how to behave, sent him to a decent public school and so on. D'you suppose one could tell the difference between him and the son of a gentleman?'

'You might just as well dress up a monkey in a suit of clothes,' replied Edward shortly.

The findings of the Hunter Commission in regard to the disturbances in the Punjab in the spring of last year were issued last night as a Blue Book ... General Dyer's career as a soldier is over. All the members admit that firing was necessary. Even the Indians recognize that the riots could not have been quelled by any other means. They condemn General Dyer, however, in the first place, for firing without warning, and, in the next place, for continuing to fire when the necessity for drastic action had disappeared ... Six months after an event it is very easy to weigh its circumstances in a delicate balance and to apportion approval and blame. No doubt, General Dyer acted rashly; but he probably had about two minutes in which to make up his mind. He was confronted with a fanatical Oriental mob, fired with anti-European frenzy. He knew that hundreds of white women and girls were dependent on him for their safety. Rightly or wrongly, he believed that the fate of India was at stake. Therefore, he gave the order to fire. We quite agree that he went beyond his brief. The 'crawling' order was merely stupid. General Dyer was neither a politician not a moralist. He was a soldier and, moreover, an Anglo-Indian. He thought of the *memsahib* who had been assaulted, and in India the *memsahib* is sacrosanct. The Hunter Report will have far-reaching consequences in India. We are not at all certain that they will lighten the task of the Indian Government. General Dyer's condemnation, although inevitable and strictly correct, will be remembered in India when his unfortunate decision has been long forgotten.

NIGHT OF TERROR IN DERRY

Fierce Fighting in the Streets

Armed parties of Unionists and Sinn Feiners took possession of some of the streets and rifle and revolver fire was almost continuous during the greater part of the night. Our Londonderry Correspondent, telegraphing last night, says: 'The fiercest and most fatal rioting of modern times in Londonderry occurred on Saturday night when several people were killed and many wounded. A state of the greatest terrorism prevailed throughout the night. On Sunday morning looting took place on an extensive scale and there were instances of actual and attempted incendiarism.'

❧

CONNAUGHT RANGERS IN INDIA

A Reuter's Simla message states that three-quarters of the men of the Connaught Rangers at Jullundar refused duty and laid down their arms upon receipt of a mail giving news of Irish events ...

The detachment at Jutogh, six miles from Simla, is perfectly quiet. The whole affair is regarded as being entirely due to political causes and the Sinn Fein agitation.

❧

In Kilnalough, as elsewhere in Ireland, it rained all that July. The farmhouses were now empty except for two or three old men, the rest of the workers having decamped after their abortive attempt to induce Edward with threats to hand over ownership. It was no doubt thanks to the fact that a contingent of Auxiliary Police were billeted at the Majestic that Edward escaped without harassment or injury. Other landowners in various parts of the country were prudently giving in to the demands made upon them at that time, but Edward remained inflexible and contemptuous. Given the state of the country and the frequency of terrorist attacks, any vindictive farm-labourer with a gun might have shot Edward down with impunity. In the meantime, however (provided he could find men willing to harvest them for him), Edward still had two meagre fields of slowly ripening corn.

The Major could see both of these fields from the window of his room; they lay one on each side of a gently sloping valley, separated only by a rutted cart-track that swept round by the farm and on to join the road to Kilnalough. Pale green at the beginning of August, the corn seemed to grow a little more blonde morning by morning. He had brought with him a pair of excellent field-glasses, made in Germany, which he had removed from the massive punctured chest of an apoplectic Prussian officer with waxed moustaches whom he had come upon lying upside down in a shell crater. Every morning he used these glasses to scan the countryside and derived a particular pleasure from examining the shining, iridescent surface of the corn as it flowed this way or that along the valley in waves of syrup.

'Strange,' he thought one morning. 'How did that get there?' A large boulder which he had never noticed before had appeared at the edge of one of the fields. Why should anyone go to the trouble of carting an extremely heavy boulder to the edge of a cornfield? He decided to take a walk over there later in the day.

But immediately after lunch the twins pounced on him. They wanted him to 'be the man' while they practised some new dance steps; in particular, it seemed, they were anxious to learn 'The Joy Trot' and 'The Vampire'. They had succeeded in borrowing a gramophone and some new records from old Mr Norton, whose relentless pursuit of youth was truly amazing when one considered his physical decrepitude. At first Mr Norton had demanded that he should 'be the man' in return for the use of his gramophone. But the twins were unenthusiastic. Besides, it was found that the rhythm was too lively for his arthritic joints and the twins absolutely refused to dance at half-speed as he proposed. Somewhat disgruntled, he settled for a 'squeeze'. Each twin in turn was given a hug that squeezed a groan of air out of her, while the Major frowned and puffed at his pipe, wondering whether he shouldn't intervene. But at last Mr Norton let them go and sat down gloomily to watch the Major's clumsy efforts to do as the twins told him. For unfortunately the Major was a very poor dancer and found new steps difficult to acquire. Not that there was anything particularly difficult about the one-step or the fox-trot—they were remarkably like walking; the difficulty lay in matching his movements to those of his partner. He also sometimes had trouble turning corners.

'Not with your pipe,' said Faith, seizing it from his lips and taking it away while Charity busied herself with winding up the gramophone. 'Now, hold me tighter for heaven's sake.'

'Hm, I told you I wasn't frightfully good at this sort of thing,' murmured the Major, discountenanced by the removal of his pipe. 'Now let me get this straight ... '

'Forward with your *right* foot!'

'Ah ... '

'Dear God!'

'Sorry, I got mixed up.'

'You'd better let *me* lead. Now just listen to the rhythm and don't bother to look at your feet ... Oh, you're perfectly hopeless!'

But the Major, although he was aware that music was being played, was at first deafened by the scraping of his own feet on the grimy floor of the ballroom and listened in vain for some sign which would tell him when to make his movements. He had started off with one softly yielding hand in his own horny palm and another resting like thistledown on his shoulder; but in no time at all he was being towed, pushed and dragged without ceremony this way and that, first by one twin, then by the other. For such slender, delicate creatures they were really amazingly strong: when Charity spilled a box of gramophone needles and dived under the piano to pick them up the Major involuntarily glimpsed the back of her smooth, firmly muscled thighs and (while fox-trotting swiftly forward to block this disturbing sight from Mr Norton's avid gaze) found himself thinking that, physically at least, one could hardly still call her a child.

By now the Major was beginning to warm up and get the hang of things and did not need so much pulling and pushing. They changed the record to 'By the Silver Sea' and while he had a rest the girls danced together most prettily, taking it in turns to be the man.

'The little darlings,' whispered Mr Norton hoarsely to the Major who had sat down beside him. 'Butter wouldn't melt in their mouths.'

The Major too was watching them with admiration as they spun round whirling their skirts and shaking their ankles in the air and doing all sorts of amusing and fanciful things without ever losing the rhythm or getting in each other's way. With the exertion (the Major changed the needle and wound up the gramophone as quickly as he could, so that they would not stop this enjoyable display) they gradually became flushed and flirtatious. Their eyes sparkled. They flashed lingering smiles at the Major as they danced round. They licked their lips with delightful pink tongues and demurely lowered their lashes over moist, shining eyes. Dimples appeared in their cheeks and their teeth had never glistened more pearly white. 'How perfectly charming they are,' thought the Major, 'as they try out their attractions on me—though not in the least seriously—like young birds learning how to fly: the same attractions that one day they'll use on the young men whose hearts they choose to break ... How charming!' But a glance at Mr Norton's puckered walnut face told him that the old rascal obviously considered that *he* was the target for the lingering smiles and licked lips and lowered lashes. He was returning the smiles with a roguish one of his own, a peeling back of the lips to exhibit unusually large yellow false teeth. The man was truly amazing. Really, one almost had to admire him for the tenacity with which he held on to the remnants of his youth.

Once more it was the Major's turn. Dancing could really be quite enjoyable, he decided, and one girl melted into another so smoothly from one record to the next that he had trouble remembering which twin he was dancing with. It came as something of a shock when he realized that Mr Norton had fallen asleep on his chair (worn out by the sexual electricity in the air) and that the time was five o'clock and that he himself was exhausted.

'Just one more!' cried the twins, but the Major said no, he hadn't realized the time, and picking up his pipe made for the door, ignoring their entreaties. It was only later, while he was thirstily drinking a cup of tea in the company of Miss Bagley and Miss Porteous, that he remembered the curious boulder which had appeared from nowhere at the edge of the cornfield. By that time it was too late to walk over and have a look at it. If it turned out to be still there—he fancied it might disappear as magically as it had arrived—he would go tomorrow. Having made this decision, he put the matter out of his mind in order to give his full attention to Miss Bagley and Miss Porteous, who already seemed to have discovered how he had spent the afternoon. Yes, he agreed, the younger generation's love of dancing might well be one of the reasons for their disrespect for their elders; on the other hand, it was all in good fun, they really meant no harm by it. It was all very harmless. Yes, he would like another cup of tea, he had a 'terrible thirst on him', as the Irish would say.

He was still in pyjamas the following morning when he removed the German field-glasses from the cardboard box in which he carried them (the Prussian officer had inconsiderately bled all over the original velvet-lined leather case) and raised them to his eyes. The boulder was still there, of course, lying beside the waving ears of corn. He had not really expected to find it gone. But it had now been joined by another and much more startling object. The Major adjusted the focus of the glasses to make sure that it really was, yes—but how could it possibly be?—a tree stump, the stump of a tree, which quite positively had not been there yesterday, neither tree nor stump. But there it was, as large as life, beside the densely packed corn.

When he had finished dressing he went downstairs, but he was too early. Edward and the rest of the household had not yet even begun their breakfast; morning prayers were still being said. Outside the breakfast room the Major listened with a faint smile as Edward began to recite the list of things for which on this morning of 1920 one should give thanks to God. He lingered for a moment, leaning against the cold stone wall of the corridor and thinking that Edward's voice sounded tired and disabused. And over the last few months the list seemed to have grown shorter. Edward's voice ceased. Now he would be moving to the War Memorial to open the hinged leaves. Still smiling, the Major tiptoed away; the ranks of tiny accusing eyes would once more look for him in vain. Moreover, he would be first with the *Irish Times* and would not have to wait his turn through the long morning while the old ladies pored over the 'Births and Deaths' column to see which of their contemporaries they had managed to survive.

When he saw Edward later in the morning he said: 'I suppose you know there's a clandestine harvest going on.'

To his surprise Edward nodded gloomily. 'I thought as much, but I wasn't sure. Now I shall have to do something.'

'What will you do?'

'God knows. I shall have to stop them one way or another.'

'Why not just let them take it! They must need it badly if they come out to cut it at night.'

'That's quite out of the question. It'd never do to let them know that they can get away with stealing my property. The whole bally place would be stripped in two shakes.'

'Oh, surely not.'

'Look, it's not my fault they cleared off. If they want to follow the wretched Shinners then let the Shinners feed them. Another thing, the corn isn't even properly ripe yet. Any fool can see that.'

'I suppose they can't wait,' said the Major with a sigh. 'Mind you, I agree that it's their own fault.'

'Really, Brendan, there's such a thing as law and order, you know. If the country's in such a mess at the moment it's because people like you and I have been slack about letting the blighters get away with it.'

'Oh, hang law and order! Two miserable fields of corn which the poor beggars planted themselves anyway. You don't mind letting them go hungry so long as your own pious principles are satisfied.'

There was a sudden silence. The Major was as surprised at his outburst as Edward. Edward flushed but said nothing.

He must have brooded about the matter, however, because after lunch he took the Major aside and told him that he would try to make arrangements to have it harvested and milled by people in Kilnalough and then distributed to the people round about who most needed it. He would also make sure that Dr Ryan and the parish priest heard of his intentions, so that they could warn the people to leave the corn alone until it was ripe. That way they wouldn't be obliged to break the law, nor would his own 'pious principles' (he smiled wryly) be offended. He had already sent Murphy into Kilnalough with the news.

For some time the Major had been impermeable to the rumours that circulated in the Majestic, having had his fill of them in the damp of the trenches where they grew like mushrooms. But now he found himself listening again, since the old ladies gobbled them up greedily and loved to share them with him (it was a mystery where they originated unless they were somehow generated by the revolutionary sentiments said to be bubbling in Murphy's brain). The I.R.A. had planned to assassinate His Majesty, Miss Archer (no relation) assured him one day, with a dart tipped with curare fired from a blow-pipe by some form of savage imported specially from the jungles of Brazil.

'Oh, what nonsense!' the Major chaffed her (she was one of his favourites). 'I'm surprised at you, Sybil, for believing such a cock-and-bull story.'

'But it's perfectly true. I have it on the best authority.'

'Oh *really*!'

Miss Archer lowered her voice. 'D.C.'

'D.C.?'

She clicked her tongue, despairing of the Major's power to comprehend. 'Dublin Castle.'

'Absolute rot,' laughed the Major.

But no, Miss Archer insisted that it was nothing less than the truth. And that wasn't the half of it ... Not only had the I.R.A. planned this dastardly act, they had come within a whisker of carrying it out. The Brazilian savage, wearing his own feathers and disguised as a tipster, had been placed beside the course at Ascot. As the Royal Carriage swept towards him he had raised his blow-pipe. The King had come nearer and nearer, had drawn level, the savage's cheeks were actually bulging when ... he had been taken by a fit of coughing (unused to the climate, he had died of pneumonia two days later), the dart had slithered out of the pipe and stuck harmlessly in the turf! Miss Archer had abandoned the pretence of seriousness and finished her story in a gale of maidenly giggles, her dim, rheumy, once beautiful eyes streaming with tears of laughter, so that the Major no longer knew whether she had ever intended him to take it seriously. Perhaps she no longer knew herself.

'I shall never believe another word you say,' the Major told her sternly.

There was another rumour believed by old Mrs Rice and the Misses Johnston, Laverty and Bagley (and at least half believed by the other ladies) to the effect that all the I.R.A.

leaders spoke fluent German and that those mad women (Maud Gonne and the Gore-Booth girl who had married the man with the unpronounceable name) had both been mistresses of the Kaiser. As a supplement, Mr Norton indicated *sotto voce* to the Major that poor old Kaiser Bill had found them insatiable and had permanently impaired his health in an effort to uphold his honour.

Miss Staveley, as befitted her status at the Majestic, had a rumour vended and believed exclusively by herself but which nevertheless chilled for a moment any old lady who heard it: a scheme was afoot whereby every butcher in the country, whether pork or beef, would rise as one man and take their cleavers to the local gentry.

Yet the rumour which the Major liked most of all came from no less a person than Edward himself. He had heard, though it was probably 'utter bilge', that Dublin Castle's water supply had been deliberately poisoned and the entire Executive laid low with the exception of a handful of the heaviest whiskey drinkers. These latter were desperately trying to conceal the situation while they coped with it. But what could they do? They were in a situation reminiscent of classical tragedy. The very elixir which had saved their lives now had them groping through an impenetrable alcoholic fog. As one cheerful intoxicated manoeuvre followed another, Sinn Fein prepared to strike a mortal blow at Ireland's heart.

'Fatuous,' smiled the Major.

'It does seem a shade far-fetched, but one never knows, particularly these days.'

Yet if the Major was tempted to smile at some of these rumours he was always sobered quickly enough when he opened the newspaper. Since his return to Kilnalough not a single day had gone by without news of a raid or shooting or terrorist attack somewhere in Ireland. Indeed, these raids had become so numerous that since the end of May only the major disasters found their way into the main columns of the *Irish Times*, the remainder being relegated to a brief numbered list which appeared daily under the heading CATALOGUE OF CRIME or CAMPAIGN OF OUTRAGE.

1. Londonderry City. At 10.50 p.m. on Thursday, while Constables McDonough and Collis were on duty, they were fired at from a revolver, the bullet striking a wall beside where they were standing.

2. On the morning of Wednesday John Niland, Co. Galway, found that during the night the tails had been cut off nine cattle, some two or three inches of the fleshy part having been cut off in each case.

3. At 11.35 p.m. on Thursday three masked men, two of them armed, entered the house of Thomas Flattery, a candidate for the district councillorship, and asked him to sign a paper not to contest the election. He refused. The leader then said: 'Go on your knees and make an Act of Contrition.' Mr Flattery said: 'I am prepared to die.' Two raiders kept revolvers pointed at him, a third kept his wife from moving, and a fourth from outside the door said: 'Shoot the dog.'

4. On Monday, at Ballyhaise, Co. Cavan, a large glass panel was broken in the Protestant church, and a bottle of wine stolen from the vestry.

5. Co. Cavan. Samuel Fife, postman, Cavan district, received the following letter through the post: 'Fife, you have escaped the Huns, but should you come to Arvagh your days are numbered. Take this as final and prepare for death. The White Boys.'

6. On Wednesday the house of T. Box, Mountbellew, Co. Galway, was fired into. Last week his potato ridges were torn up and destroyed.

7. Co. Mayo. Patrick McAndrew, water bailiff, received a letter: 'Death notice. I think it has come to the time of the day when no man will be allowed to save the fish for an English dog. If you do, you are doomed. Rory of the Rivers.'

8. Co. Kerry. Sergeant Coghlan received a letter: 'You

have been a good and diligent servant of the Crown so it is high time to end your gallop. I now advise you not to chance a sin on your soul as the reward we give good and faithful servants is ½ oz. of lead dead weight. For the future you are branded as a traitor. Our governor, Sinn Fein, has decided it.'

Before getting into bed that night the Major doused the candles and stood for a moment at the window looking out towards the invisible cornfields. In an hour or so, perhaps, men would appear out of the shadows like rodents out of the woodwork, and set to work reaping Edward's corn by the dim, intermittent moonlight. Perhaps they were already out there. He yawned and got into bed. In a way it was pleasant to fall asleep thinking of the men working out there—silently, a faint swish of reaping sickles, a soft whisper, the muffled creak of a cartwheel. But of course by now they would know that Edward was on to their game and they would not come. It was pleasant, the summer night. A silent gale of sleep blew over the dark countryside, inclining the corn in waves, now this way, now that. He was happy, in spite of everything. Edward had been about to tell him, waiting for the twins to appear wearing Angela's clothes, about the one time in his life that he had been really happy. 'I must ask him,' the Major told himself as he fell asleep.

The Major was asleep on his back in a stiff military posture, feet together, hands by his sides, dreaming of Sarah. Later he lay on his stomach and for a while was almost conscious. The room was dark but there was a pink glow on the wall opposite the window. He sat up. There was a scraping sound by the dressing-table.

'Who's there?' he whispered.

A match flared and dipped towards the branched candlestick, lighting first one candle, then the other. It was Edward, haggard, in a dressing-gown.

'Ah!' exclaimed the Major joyfully. 'I was just going to ask you something ... ' He stopped, unable to think what it was.

Edward threw open the window. With his hands on the sill he leaned out. Gradually coming to his senses, the Major sleepily pulled on his bedroom slippers and reached for his dressing-gown. Even before he reached the window he had begun to realize that something was wrong. He had not been asleep long enough; it was too dark for it to be dawn. He stared past Edward's head at the distant lake of flame. The cornfields were blazing furiously on each side of the valley beyond the sloping ridge. All around them the blackness was perfect and impenetrable.

'Did you do this?'

'Don't be a damn fool!'

'But why should *they*?'

'How the devil should I know?'

By now there was nothing to do but watch it burn. It took hardly any time at all.

Now in the Prussian officer's field-glasses there was no waving corn to be seen, only an expanse of blackened earth. Here and there, where the corn had been still a trifle green, the stalks had not burned to the ground but stood up in scabrous rings and patches, making the Major think of the worm-eaten scalps of young boys whom he had seen trailing round the golf-links. 'The wanton burning of food,' he thought. 'As senseless as the plague.' Word had spread in the neighbourhood that Edward had burned the crop himself so that the country people should not have it. The Major guiltily remembered that this had been his own first thought and would have liked to make amends, particularly as Edward had taken on his disabused air.

'Naturally everyone thinks me capable of burning my own crops,' he said wryly to the Major. 'Why, I'll burn the blessed house down out of spite one of these days, I shouldn't be surprised.' And he went off chortling grimly.

But if Edward had not set fire to the field, who had? Surely not the peasants themselves, they needed the corn too badly.

'Brendan, you're not listening!'

'Yes, I am. I've heard every word you said. It's about a bathing-costume.'

And still, it could have been an accident, a dropped match, perhaps, or a smouldering cigarette. Or perhaps it was one of those spontaneous fires that sometimes occur in hot weather, a fragment of broken glass catching the rays of the sun, or some such thing.

'Brendan, do you understand, we want eightpence. You're not listening again!'

'Yes, I am. What d'you want eightpence for?'

'Oh, how many times have we got to tell you? For the pattern. Read it to him again, and for heaven's sake listen this time!'

' "Bathing-Suit 1149 (a Practical Bathing-Suit). This is a remarkably simple pattern. The knickers are cut in one piece and joined on to a plain bodice, while the overdress is on the lines of a coat-frock, with a back ... " '

(In summer such fires are always possible. There had been a spell of warm, dry weather; the earth was brittle and broke into powder underfoot. But the Major did not really believe that it had been caused accidentally. It had started in the middle of the night and no fire was ever generated by the rays of the moon. Edward was convinced that it was the work of the Sinn Feiners, who were anxious to turn the peasants against him. If they became hungry enough they could be persuaded to do anything. It seemed the only realistic explanation.)

' " ... with a back, front, short sleeve, and straight stole collar. A plain belt buttoned over in front holds in the fullness round the waist, and gives the suit a neat finishing touch. (To the knee, with shoes and a cap.) Pattern eightpence." '

'But why tell me all this?'

'Faithy, I swear that I'll kill him if he says that just once more ... Because we want eightpence to buy the blessed pattern with!'

'Certainly,' chuckled the Major, fumbling in his pocket. 'Why didn't you say so in the first place?'

The Major had not yet managed to divest himself of his peculiar habit of patrolling restlessly from one room to another. Wandering aimlessly one day, he entered the writing-room, which was hardly ever used these days, and had a look round. The walls were panelled in dark oak but partly obscured by vast greyish tapestries depicting hunting scenes. Above the mantelpiece, for example, stretching up to the dim ceiling was an immense doe lying on its side on a table laden with fruit and round loaves of bread. One of the animal's hind legs was twisted up at an angle to the table while in the foreground the graceful head lolled on its long neck. Once scarlet, the blood which dripped picturesquely from the slit white gullet was now as grey as the fruit on the table, as grey as dust. Tables, chairs and desks were distributed here and there in clusters.

A faint sound alerted him. Edward was fast asleep in a cavernous winged armchair of worn leather, his head lolling on one side, mouth open, face collapsed by weariness, by the beginnings of old age and despair. The Major stood there for a long moment in the silent room, appalled to see Edward looking so vulnerable, so disarmed. Then, as he was preparing to tiptoe away, a black shadow slipped from beneath a dusty escritoire and settled itself comfortably in Edward's abandoned lap (for the great army of cats from the Imperial Bar had recently begun to commandeer certain other little-frequented rooms in the Majestic). Edward woke up, saw the Major watching him, muttered: 'Fell asleep,' and cleared his throat with a long weary hooting sound which might have been the cry of a dying animal. Neither of them could think of anything to say.

Since the burning of the fields the weather had taken a turn for the worse: perhaps this was adversely affecting Edward's spirits. In any case, it was clearly no comfort to him that the burned crop would very likely have been flattened by the rainstorms that howled around the Majestic and left shining puddles on the floor of the ballroom, even if it had escaped the fire. The storms retired to lash and grumble their way over the Irish Sea towards Wales, leaving a steady, interminable downpour that seemed to hang from the sky like a curtain of glass beads.

'Where's my revolver?' demanded Edward one morning of one of the maids, having spent an hour rummaging through various drawers in his study.

'The cook has it, sir. She does have it safe in the press in the kitchen.'

'What the devil does she have it for?'

'She does be afraid of the Volunteers.'

Edward wasted no time in recovering the weapon—it was covered in floury fingerprints and wrapped in buttered paper—but told nobody what he intended to do with it. As the days passed, the old ladies continued to huddle in shivering groups like nomads round a camp-fire while the Major's breath steamed up one window after another in various parts of the house. From one or other of these windows he would spot Edward stalking down the drive, oblivious of the water that beat heavily on his tweed cap and raised a faint spray from the shoulders of his trench coat. Very often this trench coat sagged heavily on one side and the Major glimpsed the butt of a revolver protruding from the pocket. Once he hurried after Edward with an umbrella, afraid that he might be about to do something foolish. But Edward was simply making his way towards the pistol-range. There the Major saw him standing at the edge of the clearing under the dripping trees, his cheeks scalded purple by the cold deluge, right arm raised stiff and straight to fire at ... it was by no means clear what he was firing at, perhaps at a dandelion that grew uncomfortably from a crevice in the lodge wall. The hand on the end of this stiff arm wobbled violently between the explosions, but

Edward's face was impassive, dead. A thin needle of water streamed without interruption from the metal eye on the end of the butt. The Major withdrew into the sodden shrubbery and made his way thoughtfully up the drive with the rain drumming on his umbrella.

On the following day, however, the rain came to a stop and gave way to weak intermittent sunshine. The change in weather seemed to improve Edward's spirits, for, as the Major was being dragged off by the twins for a swim, he called out cheerfully from the library window: 'Don't let those two little beasts drown you, Brendan.'

The two little beasts looked adorable. Their attempts to make practical bathing-suits from the pattern had ended in failure and tantrums of impatience, but by a lucky chance new bathing-suits had been sent to them by a remote aunt in London, a half-sister of Edward's, reputed to be rather 'fast' although married to a clergyman. The bathing-costumes she had chosen, certainly, were the most daring the Major had ever seen, sleeveless and with only the most perfunctory of skirts. Hardly had the rain stopped when the twins donned these scanty garments and set out for the strand. The Major himself was a poor swimmer and although he had pulled on a woollen costume borrowed from Edward (Edward being considerably stouter, it hung loosely over the Major's flat stomach) he lacked enthusiasm; besides, he had heard that the water on the coast of Wexford was freezing even on the hottest day of summer. Consequently, he hoped to avoid entering it.

As it turned out, the twins had no serious intention of swimming either. They shrieked as the surf boiled over their ankles. When the Major, who was sitting on a rock and smoking his pipe, commanded them to go deeper they clung to each other and wailed piteously as a wave washed up to their knees. And that was as deep as they would go.

Presently the Major noticed the cadaverous features of Murphy peering down at him from behind an outcrop of rock.

'What is it you want?'

A lady was asking for him up at the house.

'A lady? Who the devil is it?'

But Murphy had already turned away and no doubt considered himself to be out of earshot.

The Major set off across the beach to the gravel path that led to the boat-house and squash court, then turned to climb the steps towards the first terrace. Looking up, he saw that Edward was waiting for him at the very top of the final flight of steps, on a level with the house. And with Edward was Sarah.

The Major brushed the sand from the blue-and-white stripes of his costume and began to run, springing up one flight of steps after another. Edward and Sarah waited motionless as he toiled steadily upwards, the empty bag of cloth (which Edward's swelling chest and paunch normally filled) flapping in front of him. On one of the lower terraces he overtook Murphy, who was scurrying along with his head down as if he too were in a great hurry. He uttered a gasp of fear when the panting, blue-striped Major suddenly sprang from behind him, taking three stone steps at a time, his bare feet making no noise on the smooth surface. The aged manservant was swiftly left behind to labour up the steps alone—and, indeed, soon vanished altogether along some alternative route.

As the Major reached the last flight of steps, from the top of which Edward and Sarah looked down at him smiling, he slowed to a more dignified pace and thought: 'Why am I in such a hurry? Really, she's only a friend. She'll think me a silly ass for running all the way.'

He reached the top at last. Edward was saying: 'A very dear friend of ours, Brendan, has come to see us ... ' and he smiled at Sarah with an expression of great warmth and kindness.

'Ouf!' gasped the Major. 'I'm out of breath ... ' And he was silenced again by the need for air.

'It's nice to be back. How are you, Brendan?'

'Oh, fine, fine.'

'Sarah and Angela used to be great friends, you know,' Edward explained unnecessarily, eyes sadly lowered for a moment to the still heaving, sagging stripes of the Major's chest. 'Angela used to think the world of you, my dear.'

'And I of her,' Sarah said calmly, almost indifferently.

And the Major, while nodding piously to indicate that of course everyone thought the world of everyone, as was only natural, and there need be no doubt in anyone's mind on that score (he was still flustered from his rapid climb and anxious to agree with everyone), made a rapid and oblique appraisal of her and decided that she looked older and less beautiful. It was a number of months, mind you, since he had last seen her and sometimes a girl in her twenties will change enormously, yes, just from one year to the next, he had often heard it said ... something to do with the glands, most likely. Her eyes were still a delightful grey, of course, and her face and hands still attractively sunburned (the Major not being the sort of indoor fellow who likes his ladies lily-white) but her features had a fretful cast; she was probably still weary from travel. What changed her appearance most of all was her hair, which no longer fell freely over her shoulders but was now very neatly secured in a chignon. It was that, more than anything, which made her look older. It made her look like a governess — which was exactly what she had become.

Edward had asked her a polite question about her stay in France (although he already seemed to know all about it) in order to give the Major time to recover his breath, and Sarah was saying that the family had been charming and as for the children, her charges, leaving them had been (the Major listened in vain for a change in her measured, indifferent tone) ... had been heartbreaking. Now it was the Major's turn to say something and both Edward and Sarah turned to him. But he could hardly express the critical thoughts which had been passing through his mind with regard to Sarah, so he panted artificially a little longer. At last he exclaimed: 'I must have left my pipe on the beach,' but then he noticed that his fingers were still curled round a dark wooden object. He stuck it in his mouth and then removed it. Both Sarah and Edward burst out laughing.

Sarah said: 'Brendan, you look positively absurd in that bathing-suit.'

Sarah was expected home, she said, and had just looked in for a moment. But she seemed in no great hurry, so the Major went upstairs to wash the sand from his skin and change into more suitable clothes, rubbing macassar oil into his hair and brushing it meticulously smooth. This effort was wasted, however. By the time he went downstairs there was no sign of Sarah. The twins had come up from the beach but they were sulking for some reason and when he asked them if they knew where Sarah was they shrugged their shoulders and said that they hadn't the faintest. Nor was there any sign of Edward.

He noticed that some of the old ladies were throwing meaning glances in his direction. 'What's the matter with them now?' he wondered irritably. Whatever it was, he had no time for them at the moment. Moreover, he was tired of being considered their protector. Presently, however, he came upon the reason for their meaning glances. Peering into the ladies' lounge he saw that it was empty except for the broad uniformed back of Captain Bolton. He had his feet up on a sofa and was reading a magazine.

'You may not be aware of the fact, but this room is reserved for ladies.'

Bolton turned slowly. In his hand he held a lady's lorgnette. He lifted it to his eyes and surveyed the Major for a moment in silence. Then he tossed it aside and turned back to his magazine, saying: 'Tell someone to bring me some tea, old boy.'

The Major turned away angrily. There was nothing he could do except find Edward, which was what he was trying to do already. At last he came upon him in the foyer.

'Where on earth have you been? I've been looking for you everywhere.'

'Taking Sarah home. I say, you do look smart, Brendan. Remind me to ask you for the name of your tailor.'

'Yes, yes, by all means ... The thing is that one of those Auxiliary fellows, the one called Bolton, is upsetting the ladies by sitting in their lounge. I tried to get him to leave but it was no go. Maybe you could have a word with him.'

The Major would have accompanied Edward but at this moment one of the maids came to tell him that Miss Porteous was summoning him to the Palm Court. She had been driven out of the ladies' lounge, she told him when he had at last located her amid the foliage, by that awful man. What was it that she wanted? inquired the Major patiently. Oh yes, she wanted two things: one was for him to kill a spider which had been making repeated attempts to climb on to her shoe and was causing her great distress. And the other? She would tell him the other in a minute ... wait ... she put a small, swollen-jointed wrist to her brow and tried to think what it was.

'I can't see this ravening beast, Miss Porteous, that's been trying to attack you,' the Major said, peering on the dusty, shadowy floor. And then, imagining that he had perhaps seen something scurrying away, he murmured, 'I see it,' and stepped heavily forward, crushing something beneath the sole of his shoe. He made no attempt to examine the remains of his victim. 'I suppose that means bad luck for me, doesn't it?'

'Oh dear, I hope not,' said Miss Porteous. 'I've just thought of what I wanted: someone to help me wind my wool.'

A few moments later, as he sat there, hands raised in an attitude of surrender or benediction with the skein of wool diminishing between them, a roar of angry shouting broke out from the direction of the ladies' lounge. It was Edward losing his temper.

Later in the evening a story circulated among the jubilant old ladies to the effect that during his confrontation with Bolton, Edward had threatened to call the police. When Bolton had pointed out that he *was* the police. Edward, outraged, had telephoned to Dublin Castle where he had an influential friend. The matter was being dealt with and it was likely that Bolton would lose his job or, at the very least, be reduced in rank.

There was a curious supplement to this story. After Bolton had been evicted from the ladies' lounge he had retired, vanquished (at least, in the eyes of the old ladies), to the Prince Consort wing. On his way he had passed through a small antechamber where a number of ladies had gathered while waiting to reoccupy their rightful territory. He had appeared unperturbed by his encounter with Edward, at most a trifle preoccupied. He might have passed through without noticing the ladies had not Miss Johnston abruptly hissed: 'And I should think so too!' Captain Bolton had paused then and, smiling politely, had plucked a pale pink rose from a vase on one of the tables. Then, holding it delicately between finger and thumb, he had walked over to where the ladies were sitting. The more timorous ladies had looked away. Miss Johnston, however, was far from supine by nature (the Major had heard that her father had died on the Frontier, taking with him some astonishing number of the dark-skinned persons who had sought to oppose his will). She had straightened herself resolutely. Captain Bolton had stood there for a moment, bowed politely, and offered her the flower. Naturally she had refused it. He had continued to stand there, still smiling. It was an agonizing moment. At any instant, one felt, he might fly into an uncontrollable rage and, drawing his revolver, wreak his vengeance on the defenceless ladies. Instead of that, however, he had done an even more extraordinary thing. Slowly, methodically, petal by petal, he had begun to eat the rose. The ladies had watched him munching it in amazement and alarm. He was in no hurry. He did not wolf it as one might have expected (the man's reason was clearly unhinged). With his lips he had dragged off one petal after another, masticating each one slowly and with evident enjoyment until at last there were no petals left. But he had not stopped there. With his front teeth he had bitten off a part of the stem, calmly chewed it, swallowed it, and then bitten off another piece. In no time he had eaten the entire stem (on which there had been two or three wicked-looking thorns). The ladies had stared at him aghast, but he had merely smiled, bowed again, and strolled away.

The Major sighed when he heard this and agreed that it was an incredible way to behave. Later he asked Edward if it was true that he had telephoned to Dublin Castle. Edward nodded.

'There's something rather odd I've been meaning to tell you. D'you remember we had a good laugh the other day when I told you a rumour I'd heard about the water supply at the Castle?'

'I remember. Only the whiskey drinkers survived.'

'That's right. Well, it's probably just a coincidence but the fellow I spoke to on the telephone was quite definitely tipsy ... in fact, he was as drunk as a lord!'

Part 2

TROUBLES

THE TUAM MURDERS

Preaching in the Roman Catholic Cathedral, Tuam, on Sunday, the Most Rev. Dr Gilmartin said that he came to sympathize with the people of Tuam in the sickening horror and terror of last week. A foul murder of two policemen was committed within three miles of the town on the previous Monday evening. Had no reprisals been taken, he said, there would be a great wave of sympathy with the police. Commenting on the wrecking of the town, His Grace said that he need not add that one crime did not justify another ... in this case the police had taken a terrible revenge on an innocent town. No matter from what quarter the encouragement came, the policemen committed a fearful crime in gutting a sleeping town with shot and fire. The town was vengefully and ruthlessly sacked by the official guardians of the peace, and if the Government did not make immediate compensation and reparation for the damage done, the sense of crying injustice would remain as a further menace to peace and good will.

All this time the hotel building continued its imperceptible slide towards ruin. The Major, though, like Edward, had almost come to terms with living beneath this spreading umbrella of decay. After all, the difference between expecting something to last for ever and expecting something, on the contrary, not to last for ever, the Major told himself, was not so very great. It was simply a question of getting used to the idea. Thus, when he put his foot through a floorboard in the carpeted corridor of the fourth floor, which these days hardly anyone ever visited, he sprang nimbly aside (the carpet had prevented him from making a sudden appearance on the floor below) with a muttered oath and the thought: 'Dry rot!' But a glance at the ceiling was enough to tell him that for all he knew it might just as easily be wet rot. He informed Edward, of course. Edward sighed and said he would 'consider the matter'. In the meantime the Major set about adapting himself to the fact that he was living in a building with rot, of one sort or another, in the upper storeys.

On another occasion, while leaning with his hands on a wash-basin and gazing in contemplation of his freshly shaved cheeks, he felt the basin slowly yield under his weight. It slid away from the wall, twisting the lead pipes so that it hung upside down and emptied a deluge of water over his slippered feet. For a few moments the plug swung gently to and fro on its chain like a clock pendulum. The Major dried his feet carefully and moved his belongings next door. This was by no means his first move. Since the episode of the decaying sheep's head on his first visit he had moved a number of times for one reason or another.

It was true that the Major had the advantage of already having become accustomed during the war to an atmosphere of change, insecurity and decay. For the old ladies, on the other hand, who had lived all their lives with solid ground underfoot and a reliable roof overhead, it must have been a different matter. The Major sometimes lurked in the residents' lounge, spying on them as they read of the day's disasters in the newspaper. What must they be thinking as they read that a patrol of a dozen soldiers had been attacked in broad daylight between College Green and Westmoreland Street? The very heart of Imperial Dublin! In July alone there had been twenty-two people murdered and fifty-seven wounded, the majority of them policemen. While the Manchester Regiment suffered heavy losses in Mesopotamia (but there had always been some corner of the Empire where His Majesty's subjects were causing trouble) were they relieved and gratified to read, that August, of the Restoration of Order in Ireland Act? Trial by court-martial (since locally conscripted juries had long ceased to be reliable) and the withholding of grants to local authorities which refused to discharge their obligations — the Major did not think for a moment that this would restore order in Ireland. Nor perhaps did the old ladies, for none of them looked in the least cheered as, with quivering cheeks, they read about it. On the first of September the partridge season opened. Birds were reported to be numerous.

One morning the Major and Edward found themselves standing in the potato field which lay within the boundary wall of the Majestic on the far side of the orchard. They stood there in silence, looking round at the rows of green plants in which stark, mysterious craters had begun to appear overnight, like the empty sockets of missing teeth.

'They're even climbing the wall now. Next thing we know they'll be sitting down at the table with us.'

'They have nothing to eat. What d'you expect?'

'It's not my fault they have nothing to eat.'

'Oh, I know that. All I'm saying is that you can't expect someone willingly to starve to death. What would you do in their shoes?'

'Don't be absurd, Brendan. I wouldn't allow myself to get into such a mess in the first place.'

The Major turned away to watch the crows flapping in lazy circles, looking for some nourishment from the newly turned soil. Between himself and Edward there was a long, dissatisfied silence.

Early in the afternoon the weak sunshine was masked with cloud, the sky crept nearer to the treetops and a drizzle began to fall. The warm, clammy breath of autumn hung by the still open windows, but Edward, with absent-minded munificence, called for turf and log fires to be lit. It was not so much against the chill in the air as against the melancholy; everyone was touched by it. By half past four it was already quite dark outside, thanks to the drizzle. The Major, transfixed by sadness, was slumped in an armchair in the gun room with his elbows on a level with his ears, gazing into the fire or watching its reflection flicker in the shining, varnished scales of an immense stuffed pike. In the hotel's heyday this pike had succumbed to a gentleman with a title, name and date illegibly inscribed with spidery flourishes on a brass plate, and now it rested on the mantelpiece, its small, vicious mouth frozen open in impotent rage and despair.

The ladies never came into this room; it was a masculine preserve. In Ireland, of course, the distinction between the sexes had become blurred in recent years. Many young women were crack shots, the Major had heard, and would fire off both barrels without batting an eyelid. Someone he knew had a niece who was a fast bowler. Another girl, the young sister of one of his army friends, had been given a rhinoceros-hide whip for her sixteenth birthday; by the time she was eighteen she could flick a cigar out of a man's lips at twenty paces.

And of course there was the Countess Markievicz who day and night wore a pistol on her hip, it was said, and thought nothing of shooting a man between the eyes. He had heard, too, that these days girls smoked cigars and drank port. But all that was the younger generation. Older ladies had been brought up with different ideas on how it was seemly to behave. It was rather a relief to know that here in the gun room he was protected from them — because after all, he couldn't spend *all* his life with old ladies. Of course, young ladies (if there had been any) would not think twice about barging in here for a smoke and a chat. But against *them* the Major did not particularly feel he wanted to be protected.

He sighed. He had been avoiding the Majestic's ladies all day. This evening they would feel they had been neglected. At dinner he would very likely be snubbed by Miss Staveley. He would receive vinegary glances from some of the others. It had happened before.

Edward came in and sat down in an armchair beside him. Having taken a spill from a pewter mug on the mantelpiece, he proceeded to light his pipe, saying between puffs that he would be going up to town tomorrow to see Ripon, was there anything the Major wanted?

'No thanks.'

'Sarah has to see her doctor, so I may as well give her a lift. Save her the train journey.'

The Major sighed enviously, thinking how much he would like to motor up to Dublin in Sarah's company. There would be room for him in the Daimler, moreover. But Edward showed no sign of inviting him to join them and for some reason he felt unable to broach the subject. He sighed again, disgruntled. She was only a friend, of course. The pike's small bad-tempered mouth and wicked teeth expressed his mood to perfection.

'Will it be safe travelling by yourselves?'

'Oh, I should think so,' Edward replied blandly. After a moment he added reflectively: 'What a state the country's in!

You know, Brendan, I sometimes think "to hell with them all" ... The way they've ruined life in this country I sometimes feel that I'd welcome a holocaust. Since they want destruction, give it to them. I'd like to see everything smashed and in ruins so that they really taste what destruction means. Things have gone so far in Ireland now that that's the only way they can be settled with justice, by reducing everything to rubble. D'you understand what I mean?'

'No,' said the Major sourly.

After Edward had left for Dublin on the following morning the Major took a walk with Rover (who was getting old, poor dog) as far as the summer house and then looked back across the lawns towards the Majestic. How dilapidated it looked from this angle! The great chimneys towering over the hulk of wood and stone gave it the appearance of a beached Dreadnought. The ivy had begun to grow, to spread greedily over the vast, many-windowed wall adjacent to the Palm Court ... indeed, it appeared to spread out from the Palm Court itself, through a broken pane in the roof: one could just make out a trunk which emerged thick and hairy as a man's thigh before advancing multifingered over the stone. Rusting drainpipes bulged on the southern walls like varicose veins. 'Maybe', thought the Major, 'the ivy will help hold the place together for a bit longer.'

Ripon stood beside the statue of Queen Victoria with one elegantly shod foot on the running-board of a shining Rolls-Royce. His eyes shielded by a tweed cap, he was staring up uncertainly at the windows of the first floor. His manner, the Major thought, was oddly furtive as he started towards the front steps. He stopped abruptly when he saw the Major and seemed disconcerted.

'Oh hello.'

'Hello.'

'Didn't know you were back here. Thought I'd just drop in ...'

'Your father's not at home. In fact, I understand that he's planning to visit *you* today.'

Ripon's eyebrows shot up, miming surprise and despair. 'What a nuisance!'

'He'll be back this evening so why don't you stay? I know he's anxious to see you.'

'That's a bit difficult, actually. You see ... ' The Major waited, but Ripon's explanation lapsed into silence. Over his shoulder he glimpsed the motionless silhouette of a chauffeur behind the steering-wheel. Meanwhile Ripon, in turn, was looking over the Major's shoulder with curious longing at the half-open front door. But the Major, half turning, assured himself that there was nobody standing there, only the dog Rover and one of the maids cleaning the brasswork on the massive front door. Could it be that the boy was homesick? wondered the Major, touched.

'You really should stay.'

'Wish I could, old man. Only wish I could ... Fact is ... ' But again the explanation was still-born.

'Well, at least come in for a moment. You can write him a note or something.'

But Ripon paid no attention to this suggestion. Instead, he turned towards the motor car and with gloomy animation began pointing out its virtues to the Major. The size, the speed, the comfort ...

'It looks a splendid vehicle.'

'Not mine, of course. Old man Noonan lent it to me for the day to motor over and see the old parent. Very civilized of him. Thoughtful.' He advanced on the motor car, summoning the Major.

'This is Driscoll. Come and meet him, Driscoll's a brick.'

The chauffeur was a thin sandy-haired youth with bulging eyes and the abnormally solemn face of the impudent; the Major had seen his type in the army, where trouble-makers reveal themselves as surely as acid on litmus paper. He nodded curtly. Driscoll lifted his peaked cap with more deference than the situation required. Ripon was once more gazing greedily at the front door. Reluctantly dragging his eyes away, he said: 'Splendid driver, aren't you, Driscoll?'

'If you say so, sir.'

'See you at Brooklands one of these days, eh? Almost hit a heifer on the way over ... I tell you, Major, he's a real bright spark. Hey, on parade!' And Ripon, lunging forward, knocked the peaked cap off Driscoll's head on to the gravel. Driscoll instantly dropped into a boxing stance, right fist guarding his chin, left fist pumping exaggeratedly back and forth, chuckling as Ripon feinted in one direction and tried to land a blow from the other. The Major watched, in dismay.

'You'll find me in the house,' he said sharply and turned away, thankful that Edward was not on hand to see his son skylarking with the chauffeur.

'Hey, wait a minute. Wouldn't you like to go for a ride in her? Wait, Major ... look, I thought Driscoll might take you for a drive around while I'm writing a note for the old man.'

'No thanks.' The Major had already reached the door. He turned and glanced back. Driscoll was picking up his cap. Ripon's round cherubic face was looking towards him in consternation. 'Whatever is the matter with the fellow?' wondered the Major.

Feeling tired and somewhat feverish (he believed he must have a cold coming on), the Major went upstairs to his room and lay on his bed. But presently he got up again, searched through the drawers of his dressing-table for a cigarette, found one and lit it. The tobacco tasted dry and stale. He put it out almost immediately.

A few minutes later he made his way along the dusty corridor towards a room which looked out over the drive. The Rolls-Royce was still standing there. Driscoll was sitting on the running-board flicking gravel. Ripon was talking earnestly to one of the maids under the orangerie door; the Major could just see the white starched cuff of her sleeve moving against the black material of her uniform.

A few more minutes elapsed before he made up his mind to go downstairs again. But Ripon was no longer to be seen. Wearily the Major set off to look for him, trailing through one room after another. Rover, uncomfortable in Edward's absence, trotted at the Major's heels, as anxious as he was himself to find whoever it was they were looking for. The Major stopped. He felt delirious and thought: 'I must have caught a chill. It's like being in a maze. I've walked for miles. Are those footsteps I can hear or am I imagining things? I must avoid the rooms where the old women will be at this time ... Really, I feel quite ill.' He turned and retraced his steps swiftly. It was Murphy.

The Major was astonished, never having known Murphy to follow anyone. On the contrary, the old rascal usually made himself scarce. Murphy stood his ground, though irresolutely, avoiding the Major's eye. But the Major was in no mood to be trifled with and, grasping the old man by the lapels of his faded, stained livery, he said harshly: 'Well?' Murphy made an incoherent reply. What was he trying to say? The Major shook him. But no, the old fellow was merely caught in the spasm of a long and wheezing cough that dampened the back of the Major's hand.

'Where's Ripon?'

Murphy pointed upwards and whispered: 'Fourt' floor.' His wizened skull of a face with its bushy yellow eyebrows peered up at the Major, lips contracting back over empty gums in which stood two or three discoloured teeth. Shocked, the Major stepped back a pace. The old blackguard was smiling! Clenching his fist, he all but drove it into Murphy's face. With an effort he restrained himself. He turned on his heel and strode rapidly towards the foyer, Rover at his heels. He was conscious that Murphy was following at a distance.

He climbed the stairs painfully. He was suffocated. Murphy had vanished up some dark ancillary staircase of which perhaps only he knew the secret. But on the second floor he glimpsed him again, motionless, watching, half concealed by a linen-room door. The Major ignored him. What did the rascal want spying on him all the time?

At last he reached the fourth floor. He paused after a few paces along the corridor and steadied himself, thinking: 'I must be feverish.' He had a sore throat. His throat was painfully dry. He had to keep swallowing.

Rover had been waiting for him to move forward but now pricked up his ears, alerted by some faint sound. Nose to the carpet he surged forward without waiting for the Major. He stopped outside one of the rooms and scratched at the door. A few feet away the Major halted and watched. Rover scratched the door again.

The door was opened a few inches. Rover vanished inside. The door closed again.

For a few moments the Major tried to visualize the scene that Rover would now be confronted with. Then he turned and tiptoed back the way he had come, stood for a while on the landing, thinking: 'After all, it's none of my business,' and finally made up his mind to retire to his own room. An hour or so later he got up and went to look down into the drive. The Rolls-Royce was no longer there. At six o'clock one of the maids pushed a note under his door. It was from Ripon and said: 'Please don't mention my being here to Father. Ripon.'

His incipient cold had taken away his appetite, so he did not go down for dinner. Instead, he got between the sheets fully dressed (the room was chilly) and dozed fitfully until late in the evening when there was a knock at the door. He sat up.

It was Edward. He stared in surprise as the Major, fully clad in waistcoat, collar and tie, threw aside his bedclothes and swung his trousered legs over the side of the bed.

'Look, about Ripon ... ' the Major began, dazed and forgetting Ripon's instructions.

'Oh, he was in splendid form,' Edward told him cheerfully. 'Spent the afternoon with him while Sarah was with her surgeon fellow in Harcourt Street. Mind you, he'll need a bit of a helping hand .... '

He was interrupted by a deafening volley of sneezes from the Major, whose head drooped wearily between his knees while he groped for a handkerchief.

'I say, you seem to have caught a bit of a cold,' Edward said sympathetically.

The Major nodded, his eyes streaming. On second thoughts he decided to swing his legs back into bed and pull the blankets up to his chin.

'You got your hair cut,' the Major mused.

'Eh? Yes, so I did. Stopped in at Prost's this afternoon before going out to Ripon's place in Rathmines. I mean, I couldn't very well turn up there looking like an organ-grinder's monkey, now, could I?'

'Of course not,' agreed the Major grimly.

All next morning Edward was in a terrible rage. His anger crashed and boomed around the Majestic, rattling the windows and scaring the wits out of servants and animals alike. A small dent had appeared in one of the wings of the Standard while he had been away in Dublin. Small though it was, it appeared to be this dent which was stimulating his explosions of passion. Naturally suspicion centred on Faith and Charity, although they wasted no time in swearing on their mother's grave (and, when that failed to work, on their sister's) that they were innocent. The Major was summoned to inspect the damage, but was unable to mollify Edward by saying that he thought it trivial. The twins, meanwhile, were darting covert glances in his direction, trying to warn him by telepathy not to mention it if he had seen them by the garages.

'Besides', the Major lied weakly, unable to resist feminine distress, 'they spent most of the day with me.'

The twins looked comforted, but Edward merely glanced at the Major in scornful disbelief. The twins were banished to separate rooms, locked in, and given only bread and water for lunch. Edward retired to the squash court to brood in the company of his piglets. It was the not owning up afterwards or, in other words, the telling of lies which was the real crime. He had made that quite plain. This was something he would not tolerate in his children.

The Major listened to this pronouncement with an expression of cold surprise, with one eyebrow sardonically raised, and with a running nose. Besides, given the hotel's state of disrepair he considered it eccentric to notice a small dent in a motor car.

As for the Major, his cold was much worse and he had just decided to spend the rest of the day in bed when a message arrived from Sarah to say that she was bored and would like to come to the Majestic 'to see everyone' and would he come and collect her? He was ill. He had a considerable fever (such that at times he found himself wondering whether he hadn't simply dreamed the events of the day before). His nose was red, sore and still streaming. Every now and then he was convulsed by shuddering sneezes. At intervals he felt giddy. But now that the opportunity presented itself nothing would prevent him from seeing Sarah. Inflamed equally by his fever and by some whiskey that Edward had made him drink, he stopped on the way to buy some flowers and a box of chocolates.

'The blighter must have been waiting for me,' he thought peevishly as Mr Devlin hurried out of the bank to intercept him at the gate. The flowers and chocolates he was holding made his intentions all too plain. Mr Devlin's eyes rested on them for a moment, expressionlessly. Then he was greeting the Major with his customary effusion.

He and Mrs Devlin (and a certain young lady too) saw far too little of the Major these days, he informed the Major, and for this reason he must insist, indeed he wouldn't take no for an answer, that the Major should accord him a few moments of his precious time now that he had finally had the good luck to set eyes on him ... a piece of good luck which occurred all too seldom since the Major undoubtedly had a great number of good friends here in Kilnalough ... so he shouldn't mind, rather he should expect to be 'kidnapped' by those who suffered from the deprivation of his company.

The Major nodded moodily at this extravagant preamble, looking at his watch. But Mr Devlin did not mean to be deterred. He steered the Major firmly into the bank, along a corridor in which there hung a smell of boiled cabbage, and into a comfortless office. On entering the Major sneezed explosively and had to mop a trail of mucus from his sleeve. He sat down in misery while once again Mr Devlin's eye rested on the flowers and chocolates.

Did the Major have a cold? It was plain that he paid too little heed to his health. He must partake of a sup of something to warm him. The Major protested feebly, but Mr Devlin had already seized a bottle of whiskey and a glass. Sweating, the Major felt once more that he must be having a dream.

'I'm afraid that Sarah may be waiting for me.'

'Not at all at all,' Mr Devlin reassured him, smoothing his already smooth hair with a delicate white hand. 'We have time for a nice little chat now.'

The Major drank some whiskey and blew his nose unsatisfactorily.

And how was Mr Spencer getting along these days? There was another of his good and generous friends ... very generous, he had done more for 'a certain young lady' (he winked roguishly, distressing the Major) than could ever be repaid, more anyway than *he* would ever be able to repay, and all out of the kindness of his heart ...

A sudden pause ensued, as if Mr Devlin had just asked a question, which of course he had not. The Major, in any event, could think of nothing to add to his remarks.

Not only with money (Mr Devlin gave the Major some more whiskey), not only with money, though to give that 'certain young lady' the proper care would have been beyond his own means with medical expenses being what they were, no, not only with money, though the Major was probably unaware of the extra expense involved in having a semi-invalid in the house whose prospects for marriage ... ah, well, that was a different story and one couldn't blame her for that, now, could one? it was the luck of the draw ... but she was a self-willed girl and though he and Mrs Devlin saved what they could they would have to provide for their old age and even with a fortune behind her an invalid would be hard put to it to make a decent match but that was life ... not only with money, though he prided himself on knowing its value, but with acts of kindness, sure, he would go out of his way to help someone, would he not?

'He would,' assented the Major, the whiskey providing him with an Irish turn of speech.

He'd do anything for you and that was the truth, one had only to look at the way he had taken her up to Dublin in his motor car yesterday ... but of course the Major would know all about that, since he had most probably gone up to Dublin with them?

There was a long pause until the Major said: 'Really, no more, thank you. I've already had more than is good for me.'

Oh, he could manage just a little drop to boil the germs out of him, sure he could, it was rare to find a man who'd do a Christian act like that out of the goodness of his heart, so to speak, and he understood that the specialist had taken a fair old time about it, keeping the young lady waiting around annoyingly for a good part of the day, the morning anyway (?), but that he'd given her a splendid report in the end so that it was worth waiting all that time (?) ... irritating though it must have been to Mr Spencer who probably had a hundred and one things to do, and to the Major?

'No trouble to me, Mr Devlin,' the Major burst out with sudden irritation, 'because I wasn't there. But I think I can say quite honestly—I won't drink any more, thank you—that I wouldn't have minded waiting all week if it had helped Sarah to walk again as she's walking now.'

'To be sure, that's very kind of you. So you weren't in Dublin with them?'

'No, I wasn't. As for it being kind of me, why, anyone would do the same.'

'Ah, I suppose ... '

Mr Devlin fell silent, his troubled eyes on the Major's face as if he were anxious to confide something in him but not quite able to bring himself to speak. The Major, in any case, had got to his feet, having disposed of his glass, and was walking directly to the door with a plain determination not to be stopped.

'Still, she's a worry to her mother not being married yet at her age, a great worry, it's only natural ... '

'Natural or not, Mr Devlin,' said the Major sharply, having lost all patience, 'it's ... ' But he could think of no way of ending the sentence. He left it hanging ominously in the air and strode out of the office with Mr Devlin fussing somewhere behind him and muttering deferential instructions: to the right here, there's a door, yes, then up the stairs and ...

'What a frightful fellow!' thought the Major giddily. 'And to have such a nice daughter.' He looked round, but Mr Devlin had retired and he was outside a door he recognized as that of Sarah's room.

He had barely rapped on it when Sarah opened it, caught him by the sleeve and pulled him inside, saying: 'Why have you taken so long, Brendan? I heard your car arrive ages ago.'

'Well ... '

'Oh, you're so slow,' Sarah said impatiently, 'and you have a cold. Really, you're such a child! What can you expect if you wander around in that absurd bathing-costume in the middle of winter? You'll catch your death, I expect, and serve you right.'

'Your father gave me a drink.'

'My father? He said something to you? He asked you something about me?'

'Well, not really ...

'Ah, I knew as much. He wouldn't dare say anything to my face!'

'But no, I assure you, he merely wanted a chat.'

Sarah had sat down awkwardly and without ceremony, ignoring him. She stood up again and made for the door.

'Are we ready then?'

'No. Wait here. Ah, these dratted stairs ... D'you know why they give me a room up here? They think they'll keep me a prisoner,' she muttered furiously, and went out, dragging the door closed behind her. The Major was left standing there with the chocolates and flowers (which were blood-red roses); he had just cleared his throat, on the point of presenting them.

A moment later he heard the sound of angry voices from below. He held his breath but was unable to hear what was being said. 'Heavens!' he thought wretchedly, 'I've started another family row.'

Sarah called from below that he should go down, they were ready to leave, she didn't want to climb the 'dratted stairs' again. Still clutching his roses and chocolates, the Major made his way down. He was following Sarah into the street when Mr Devlin materialized at his elbow and whispered: 'You mustn't mind her. She gets excited. She's very high-strung, you know, Major, but she means no harm ... Indeed, it clears the air ... Her music makes her temperamental, you see, it's always the way ... '

The Major nodded curtly but showed no inclination to pause and discuss the matter. Mr Devlin dropped back into the shadows of the corridor from which he had appeared, murmuring that the Major should call more often, that he was always welcome under their ... Under their what? The Major did not wait to hear. 'Roof,' he supposed.

'What on earth are you carrying, Brendan? Are you going to visit someone sick in bed?'

'They're for you.'

'For *me*?' Sarah exclaimed, laughing. 'How ridiculous you are! What on earth shall I do with such things? But, very

228

well … I'll accept them. It's really very kind of you. In fact, you are a terribly kind person, I can see that plainly. With your flowers and chocolates you remind me of Mulcahy.'

'Oh? The rural swain?' asked the Major, offended.

'Now I've hurt your feelings, Brendan. It's just like the old days.'

As they motored through the tranquil streets of Kilnalough the Major, eyes blurred, nose red and mouth gaping like a fish, peered gloomily at the peaceful shops and houses, some of which already had turf-smoke rising from their chimneys, and wondered whether one day there would be trouble in these streets too.

On the outskirts of Kilnalough a shabby old man hurled a stone at them as they went sailing by—but feebly. It missed by a considerable distance. The Major pretended not to notice.

The twins had not been liberated. There was no sign of them in the writing-room, where a fire was blazing in the hearth and where card-tables covered in green baize had been set up, each with a neat stack of playing-cards, a scoring pad and a sharpened pencil.

'I say, you don't really feel like playing whist, do you?' asked the Major, his eyes closed to the merest slits in an attempt to avoid surrendering to another volley of sneezes. He hoped that she felt as reluctant as he did.

'But of course! That's what I came for. What a frightful smell of cats there is in this room.'

The Major could smell nothing because of his cold, but he had already noticed that one or two cats, presumably ejected by the servants who had put up the card-tables, were pressing discontented faces against the closed windows.

'Something will have to be done about the cats. Miss Staveley found a litter of kittens in her knitting-basket the other day. And at night they have the most fearful battles up and down the corridors. One can hardly get any sleep.'

Hitherto whist had been informal, merely a way of crossing

some of the great expanses of time that stretched like deserts over the afternoon and evening at the Majestic, deserts through which the lonely caravan of old ladies (together with Mr Norton and, on occasions, the Major or Edward) was obliged to make its way. But this time everything was different. Not only had real card-tables been set up and the cats expelled but the ladies, forewarned that this was to be a social occasion, had dressed up in their most splendid clothes and most luxuriantly feathered hats. A glorious riot of coloured plumage waved beside extravagant creations inspired by the garden and executed in silk, satin, leghorn and organdie. And of all the magnificent hats that greeted the Major's weeping eyes none was finer, as was only to be expected, than the golden pheasant, perfect in every detail, which was riding Miss Staveley's thin white curls.

'We must cheer ourselves up some way or another,' Edward told him. 'Keep up morale and so forth.'

The Major went up to his room to get some dry handkerchiefs and lingered there morosely for a while. When he came downstairs again he found that Mrs Rice, Miss Porteous and Mr Norton were all impatiently waiting for him to join their table. The cards had been dealt. The other tables were already playing.

Sarah was at a table with Miss Staveley, Edward and the Reverend Mr Daly. As for the Major, he was expected to partner Mrs Rice throughout the afternoon. He already knew from past experience that her grasp of the principles of the game was anything but firm. He mastered with difficulty a great explosion of rage as she led with her trumps on the first hand, but he knew that the real reason for his irritation was the deprivation of Sarah's company, for which, feverish and vulnerable, he felt an acute longing.

For most of the afternoon he sat at the same table (for Edward had organized the contest so that winners moved to the next table, losers stayed in their seats), periodically convulsed by sneezes which had opponents and partner wincing away from him, eyes barely open, light-headed, moustache bedraggled, miserable beyond words. And yet this rare social occasion was undeniably a brilliant success. The ladies of the Majestic had been in poor spirits recently. With the approach of winter, aches, pains, insomnia and bowel discomforts proliferated; under the compulsion of shortening days the ladies were once more funnelled towards the dreadful gauntlet of December, January and February which most of them had already run over seventy times before, reluctantly forced through it like sheep through a sheep dip—it was appalling, this ruthless movement of the seasons, how many would survive? Looking round bleakly, the Major was sorry for them and for a moment, as his mind strayed from his own misery, was glad that they were enjoying themselves. Troubles forgotten, shawled and feathered, they sat round the card-tables chattering and squabbling like great plump birds around a feeding-trough, laughing, teasing young Padraig (who had appeared with his grandfather) and forgetting what they were saying and whose turn it was to play and all talking at once and no one really listening. The men too were enjoying themselves. Mr Norton had allowed his preference for youth to lapse for the occasion and flirted with any lady who appeared at his table. The Reverend Daly beamed cheerfully and encouraged his partner to greater efforts. Even old Dr Ryan who, chin on chest and grumbling constantly, seemed positively unable to keep his eyes open, nevertheless won consistently in company with Miss Archer, hand after hand after hand—which caused immense difficulties since his body, if not his mind, was to all intents inert and had to be carried, chair and all, from one table to the next (the rule that winners moved, losers stayed where they were, being quite inflexible). Murphy, naturally, was selected to do all the carrying, but he mumbled and groaned and heaved to such pitifully little effect that Seán had to be called from the garden, springing immaculately groomed from the neighbourhood of the compost heap, to help.

Of the gentlemen only the tutor, summoned from his room above the kitchens to make up the numbers, seemed ill at ease, perhaps because Miss Bagley was cross at being given him as a partner: after all, he was 'practically one of the servants', she whispered to the unsympathetic Major when they found themselves at the same table. She watched him like a hawk and rebuked him sharply if his attention appeared to wander, calling him 'partner' with bitter irony. A faint flush crept up Evans's pale pocked cheeks. The Major sighed, feeling sorry for the man (Miss Bagley, besides, was by no means his favourite among the old ladies), but at the same time he was irritated. After all, the fellow could surely afford to buy himself a new collar or two to replace the thing like a dish-rag that he was wearing.

Old Mrs Rappaport was blind, of course, and so could not play. She sat on a straight-backed chair by the fire, glum and disapproving, refusing to admit that she was comfortable and warm enough, refusing to answer the pleasant remarks that were spoken into one ear or another as the winning players shuffled past her in the periodic changing of tables. Shortly before tea was served, a thickset marmalade cat (which the Major thought he recognized as a former inhabitant of the Imperial Bar) emerged from the forest of chair- and table-legs and jumped on to her lap. It was greeted with cries of surprise. Where had it come from? Windows and doors were shut. The room had been diligently searched beforehand. There was a fire in the fireplace, so it could hardly have come down the chimney (a favourite trick of the cats at the Majestic), it was absolutely impossible that the beast could have got in ... yet here it was! The Major, as it happened, knew the answer to this problem. He had earlier noticed that evil, orange, horridly whiskered head poking itself out of a rent in the side of a massive velvet sofa on the far side of the room. The creature presumably lived in there. The Major took a perverse pleasure in keeping this knowledge to himself, merely smiling in a superior way at the general bafflement. Nor did he relent when

Mr Norton genuinely alarmed some of the ladies by saying that there must be a witch in the room, that the cat was quite plainly a witch's familiar and that he for one had already had a spell put on him by one of the ladies present (he glanced roguishly at Sarah and attempted to place a trembling hand on her knee). A witch in the room! The ladies laughed nervously and tried to avoid looking too plainly into each other's haggard, wrinkled faces.

'What piffle,' said Edward. 'We'll soon get rid of the animal.' And getting to his feet he made to remove the cat from Mrs Rappaport's lap. But she would have none of it, demanding petulantly that 'her' cat should be left in peace. She even went so far as to call it 'Pussy'; the cat narrowed its acid green eyes and flexed its claws, which were as sharp as hatpins.

'You're all enjoying yourselves,' she cried. 'I just sit here ... I don't know, why haven't I got any tea?'

'No one has yet,' Edward soothed her. 'Tea will be served in a few minutes.'

Mrs Rappaport sniffed ill-temperedly. The attempt to remove the cat was abandoned and it remained where it was, relaxed but alert, flicking its tail from time to time as it watched the swaying feathers and nodding plumes of the ladies' hats.

After tea the Major sank into a nightmarish daze in which it no longer seemed to matter when Mrs Rice played an ace or a trump to make doubly sure of tricks he had already won. He even gave up trying to win enough tricks to progress to the next table where Sarah and Edward had been losing steadily for some time; all his attention was taken by sucking in air through his parched lips and dealing with the steady trickle of fluid from his nose with sodden handkerchiefs. Slumped in his chair, he thought wearily: 'What a disgusting animal I am!' But at that moment Mrs Rice eagerly tugged his sleeve and alerted him to the fact that they had won at last. While he had been day-dreaming she had played her cards with the cunning of a fox. At last they could move. Moreover, Sarah and Edward had lost yet again, so they would be at the same table.

'You poor thing,' Sarah said to him cheerfully, putting cool fingers on his damp brow. 'You do look a mess! Edward must fill you with whiskey after supper and you must go to bed.'

'Oh, I'm all right.'

'Don't be so grumpy.'

'I'm not.'

'You certainly sound it.'

'I can't help that.'

Sarah grimaced with annoyance and turned away to talk to Mrs Rice, who was still flushed and jubilant over her victory.

They began to play. The Major played his cards at random, no longer able to remember what his partner and opponents had played. Sarah glanced at him one or twice but said nothing. He fell into a gloomy reverie until suddenly, without warning, Mrs Rice asked: 'And how was dear Ripon, Mr Spencer? I hear you went to see him when you were in Dublin yesterday.'

The Major glanced from Edward to Sarah, who was studying her cards serenely as if she had not heard the question. A faint flush, however, had tinged her neck and cheeks. What could Edward say? The Major coldly watched the troubled expression on his face as he framed a reply. He was on the point of answering Mrs Rice's question when he was prevented by a sudden and most terrible commotion.

The recent rearrangement of opponents had brought Miss Staveley to within a few feet of where Mrs Rappaport was sitting with the cat on her lap. For the past few minutes the cat's bitter green eyes had been glued to the plump pheasant which clung defencelessly to the crown of Miss Staveley's magnificent hat. With each movement that she made the bird's sweeping tail-feathers trembled deliciously. At last, tantalized beyond endurance, the cat sprang from Mrs Rappaport's lap, hurtled through the air in a horrid orange flash and pounced on Miss Staveley's black velvet shoulders, sinking its hideous claws into the bird's delicate plumage. Miss Staveley uttered a shriek and sank forward on to the card-table while the cat, precariously balanced on her shoulders, ripped and clawed savagely at her headgear in an explosion of feathers. There was pandemonium. The ladies cried out in alarm. The men voiced gruff barks of astonishment and leaped to their feet. But still the beast savaged its prey. At last Edward and the Major, knocking chairs aside, stumbled to the rescue. But before they could reach Miss Staveley the tutor sprang forward and dealt the beast a terrible blow on the back of the neck. It gave a piercing wail, thin as the shriek of a child, and dropped senseless to the carpet.

Silence fell. Everyone in the room froze. In the sudden stillness the crackling of a log in the fireplace seemed unnaturally loud. The tutor stooped and picked up the cat. For an instant, as he held it high over his head, there was a savage rictus on his white pocked face. Then he hurled it across the room with terrible force. It smacked against the wall with a sickening thud and dropped lifeless to the floor. There was a sharp intake of breath, and everyone peered at the shapeless marmalade bundle.

The Major was not quite sure what happened next. He saw the fierce exultation slowly fade from the tutor's face. His eyes dropped to the carpet and he shuffled back to his table, flushed and self-conscious. Nobody said a word to him. He began to study his cards with unseeing eyes.

Meanwhile Edward and the ladies were bustling around Miss Staveley with smelling-salts and sympathy while she sobbed fitfully and tried to unpin the shattered remains of her hat from her white curls. The doctor was applied to for advice and although he murmured disagreeably: 'Och ... give her some air. She'll be all right,' nobody was prepared to accept that this was all he had to say. The Murphys were summoned to pick up his chair and he was carried bodily across the room (muttering unheeded protests) to be deposited at Miss Staveley's side. There the lids came down over his eyes and he appeared to fall asleep. Miss Staveley, in any case, was coming along splendidly and really had no need of medical help. She was even beginning rather to enjoy being the centre of attention and presently she was describing what it feels like to be pounced on and to have 'cruel claws' digging into one's shoulders. What a business! Everyone was trying to make himself heard over the babble, to describe how it had looked to *him*, from where he was sitting, that ruthless feline thunderbolt which had sped across the room to attack Miss Staveley's hat. In the hubbub of voices only Mrs Rappaport, grim and catless on her chair by the fireside, remained silent.

'Would you like some more tea, Mrs Rappaport?' asked the Major, who felt sorry for her. But she merely shook her head. The corners of her mouth drew down as if she were about to cry.

As interest in Miss Staveley subsided people remembered the cat which had been the cause of the commotion. It was still lying there against the foot of the wall. Its mouth was partly open; through its wickedly sharp teeth a little blood was leaking on to the parquet floor. The elder Murphy was told to dispose of it but he refused, saying he didn't dare touch it. Edward grimaced with annoyance but did not waste time arguing the point. There was a moment of tension as he turned it over with his shoe, as if everyone expected it suddenly to revive and start tearing him to pieces. But the animal was quite plainly dead.

'Mr Evans, I wonder, would you mind?' The tutor looked up from the cards he was studying. He hesitated for a moment, his face expressionless, then he got to his feet without a word, picked the cat up by its dark-ringed orange tail and left the room.

'The strength of some of those fellas is positively fr-frightful ... ' Mr Norton said to the Major, who was not sure whether he was referring to the tutor or to the cat.

When Evans returned Edward said that, rather than end on such an unfortunate note, everyone should sit down and play another hand or two, if they felt like it, and try to forget this unpleasant little episode. And presently, though in a rather subdued fashion, the players began to chatter about other things. The odour of fear and violence gradually dissipated.

When he had thrown a few more pieces of turf and wood on to the fire Edward sat down and said cheerfully: 'Now whose turn was it to play and what were we talking about?'

'Your turn. Mrs Rice had just asked you about your visit to Ripon when you were in Dublin yesterday.'

'Ah yes,' said Edward and once more a strained expression appeared on his face. But before he could say a word Sarah exclaimed: 'Oh, we had a lovely time, Mrs Rice, and Ripon is getting along wonderfully. Did you know that he married a friend of mine, Máire Noonan, from Kilnalough? Such a nice girl ... ' and she went on to talk about Máire, though Mrs Rice, who believed she was missing one of her cards (how many did everyone else have?) was not really listening. As for the Major, he lowered his jealous eyes to the fan of cards in his hand and said no more. He thought: 'That evening with me in London must have meant nothing to her after all.'

Certain of the guests, including Dr Ryan, his grandson and Sarah, had been invited to stay for supper. Padraig had begun the afternoon affecting a cautious and supercilious manner. He had relaxed, however, on hearing that the twins had been locked up and soon became expansive, even voluble. Like the Major he appeared to be partial to older ladies. The Major, who was looking for the doctor (his cold was at its zenith and he was afraid he had pneumonia), overheard the lad describing to Miss Bagley in minute detail the martyrdom of Saint Sebastian. Miss Bagley murmured 'Dear me!' at intervals, genuinely horrified.

The doctor had vanished, as he had a habit of doing when the old ladies might want to discuss their ailments with him. But he was so old and infirm that the Major was confident that he would be able to track him down without much difficulty—and so it proved. He came upon him sitting in the Palm Court, little frequented these days for a number of reasons: one, of course, was the usual difficulty of the foliage having swallowed up most of the chairs and tables; another was the lack of light, since there were no gas mantles and the 'Do More' generator had been idle for many a month — there were oil lamps, of course, but they gave the place such an eerie and frightening atmosphere (all those weird shapes and shadows lurking beyond the circle of light) that it was almost better to do without. Yet another, and even more conclusive, reason was the fact that Miss Porteous had some-how convinced herself that she had been bitten in there by a poisonous spider. The Major had declared this to be non-sense, but curiously enough Miss Porteous did have an enormous blue swelling on the wrist over which the offending spider was supposed to have walked. At any rate, after dark none of the ladies would have considered going in there for a moment—which was why the Major was not in the least surprised to see the doctor there, sitting in a cane chair beside the glass door into the lounge. This door afforded enough light for the Major to see that the doctor was awake. He explained that he had a cold, a very bad cold which he was afraid—he added ominously, seeing the doctor stir with impatience—might turn into something worse.

'A cold, is it?' grunted the old man querulously. 'Sure, we all get 'em ... a cold is nothing at all.'

And he went on to say something confused about things not being the way they used to be ... or perhaps people weren't the way they used to be, one or the other, or perhaps both, it was hard to make out precisely.

'But I just want to know what medicine to take,' the Major interrupted him plaintively. He had been going hot and cold by turns and felt that at any moment he would be suffocated by fever or roasted alive, if he was not actually poignarded to death by the painful 'absence-of-Sarah' that had suddenly started to afflict him—indeed, the pangs of self-pity and

Sarahlessness became appallingly acute as he listened to the old man grumbling on. A wave of fever clutched him. His shirt and underwear clung damply to his skin.

'Thought you'd come sooner or later,' the doctor was saying contemptuously. 'This is no place for the likes of you ... You must leave Ireland, leave Kilnalough, it's no place at all now for a British gentleman like you. Clear yourself out of here, bag and baggage, before it's too late!'

'But I only asked about my cold,' protested the Major petulantly. 'I suppose I shall have to go to bed before it gets any worse.'

'Yes, go to bed, go to bed, that's it,' sneered the doctor. 'You're as right as rain, just sorry for yourself.'

The doctor, splendid old chap though he no doubt *was*, thought the Major indignantly, was really becoming a tiny bit tiresome.

The great gong boomed for dinner. The Major dolefully wandered along a corridor. Padraig was still talking volubly to the alarmed Miss Bagley as they passed on their way to the dining-room. Did she know ... did she know ... did she know then what had happened to Héloise and Abélard? he was asking slyly, well, to Abélard anyway, since nothing much in *that* line could happen to Héloise? Well, he'd better not be telling her because it might spoil her appetite ...

The Major decided not to go in to dinner. Instead he sat down dizzily in an armchair in the residents' lounge, not his favourite room at the Majestic but he felt too weak to go any farther. His mouth open like a dying fish, he fell asleep. His last conscious image was of Dr Ryan pottering past, grumbling to himself, his stick held in a knobbly, freckled hand.

'Go on out of it, the whole bally lot o' ye,' he might have been muttering as his boots scraped by on the other side of the Major's drooping eyelids—but before it had time to consider this, his waking mind had slipped away into a quieter and darker area beyond.

MESOPOTAMIA

Serious Agitation on the Lower Euphrates

The situation in Mesopotamia shows some improvement in the disturbed areas, but is becoming more tense in the districts not yet in open rebellion. The Lower Euphrates and Hammar Lake neighbourhood are being seriously affected by the agitation now breaking out among the Muntafik Arabs. The besieging forces are said to be increasing in numbers.

❧

TERRIBLE OUTBREAK IN BALBRIGGAN

Town Partially Destroyed by Fire

During Monday night and Tuesday morning there was a violent outbreak in Balbriggan, following the murder of Head Constable Burke in that town. Head Constable Burke, with other police in plain clothes, had motored from Dublin on their way to Gormanstown. At Balbriggan they stopped for refreshments, which were refused by the publican. In the disturbance which appears to have ensued, revolver shots were discharged, and the Head Constable was shot dead, and his brother, Sergeant Burke, was wounded. Subsequently, it is stated, a number of auxiliary police stationed at Gormanstown came into Balbriggan. Many houses were burned and shots fired in the streets. Two civilians were killed during the night. In the morning large numbers of the panic-stricken population left the town by road and railway and apparently only those who were unable to get away remained.

EYE-WITNESS STORY

An old gentleman resident, describing what followed the shooting, said: 'Myself and my wife went to bed, and some time later we were awakened by a tremendous knocking at the door which greatly alarmed my wife. We thought it was some persons intruding. On going down to the door, I found there two "black and tan" policemen, with two children of the barber, James Lawless. One of the children was suffering from pneumonia and the other was an infant of not more than two years old. I took the two children upstairs and put them into my own bed as they were. I was told that the house of Lawless, the barber, had been wrecked, and this morning I learnt that Lawless was dead — that he had been taken from his house and shot, and also that a young man named Joe Gibbons, a dairy farmer, had been killed.'

❧

GOVERNMENT TO PREVENT REPRISALS

The *Pall Mall Gazette* last evening published the following telegram from Sir Hamar Greenwood, Chief Secretary for Ireland.

Monday   *Dublin*
There is no truth in the allegations that the Government connive in or support reprisals. The Government condemn reprisals, have issued orders condemning them, and have taken steps to prevent them. Nearly one hundred policemen have been brutally murdered, five recently in Clare on one day, by expanding bullets, resulting in horrible mutilation. In spite of intolerable provocation the police forces maintain their discipline, are increasing in number and efficiency, and command the support of every law-abiding citizen. The number of alleged reprisals is few and the damage done exaggerated.

(Signed) HAMAR GREENWOOD

❧

If the ladies at the Majestic had needed something to improve their morale before, now, with the country 'put to the fire and the sword', as Miss Johnston expressed it not without satisfaction, with 'the troubles' yesterday at Balbriggan, tomorrow perhaps in Kilnalough itself, how much more they needed this something! Once again whist proved to be the answer. A couple of tables were started in the residents' lounge, although without the circumstance and the finery of the occasion in the writing-room. These tables rapidly became the centre of social life in the hotel; each player found a retinue of advisers and confidantes at her elbow providing a constant stream of conflicting advice and encouragement and when she became weary her place would promptly be filled by someone else. Within a day or two this epidemic of whist had taken such a grip that play began immediately after breakfast on the green baize tables (opportunely salvaged from the writing-room but dispensing, nevertheless, a faint odour of cats) and continued almost without interruption throughout the day and on into the night. There was an excellent spirit at these games: an air of gaiety and abandon, almost of recklessness, reigned over the chattering groups. By the end of the chilly autumn evening, with dampness and dark beyond the window panes, the hooting of an owl in the park or the lonely cry of a peacock, when one of the ladies irrevocably dozed off with the cards in her ancient arthritic fingers and there was no one at hand to replace her (which meant the end of the game, of course), one pair of players might add up the score and find that they were winning or losing by some prodigious number of tricks accumulated during the day, several hundred perhaps ... And everyone would climb the stairs chuckling to their rooms and dream of aces and knaves and a supply of trumps that would last for ever and ever, one trump after another, an invincible superiority subject to neither change nor decay nor old age, for a trump will always be a trump, come what may.

Around these tables rumours continued to circulate and prosper. One day it was thought that a brigade of Cossacks, émigrés from Russia whose fiendish Bolshevists they no longer found it worth their while to quell, had been hired en bloc by Dublin Castle to subdue the Irish. Someone else announced confidently that a hungry mob in County Mayo had seized and eaten a plump Resident Magistrate; because this story, absurd though it was, happened to coincide with the actual disappearance of an R.M. (though not from County Mayo) it gave all the ladies a dreadful frisson and a kaleidoscope of bad dreams. But then the R.M. was discovered, in a coffin left on a railway line, and all was well. It said in the *Irish Times* that he had been buried and dug up again (reprisals had been threatened if his whereabouts were not made known), but there was no mention of cannibalism.

But while the ladies gossiped cheerfully and playing-cards continued to snow down on the green baize tables the Major was at his most despondent. Above all, he took a gloomy view of the reprisals at Balbriggan and elsewhere. The result of this degeneration of British justice could only be chaotic. Once an impartial and objective justice was abandoned every faction in Ireland, every person in Ireland, was free to invent his own version of it. A man one met in the street in Kilnalough might with equal justification (provided it fitted into his own private view of things) offer you a piece of apple pie or slit your throat. But given the way things were going (the Major could not help feeling) he would be more likely to slit your throat.

If no throats were actually slit in Kilnalough in the first days after the disturbances, there were, nevertheless, some ugly incidents. Miss Archer was rudely barged into the gutter by two mountainous Irishwomen clad in black and wearing men's boots. She then dropped her muff, which was trampled on and kicked around like a football by a group of urchins. Wisely she left it to them and fled before anything worse happened. Not long afterwards a young hooligan in Kilnalough put his stick through the spokes of Charity's bicycle, causing her to fall and graze her knees and palms. Stones were thrown at the people from the Majestic but without causing any great harm. Viola O'Neill, while buying buttons in the haberdashery (Boy O'Neill informed the Major), had had some obscene words spoken into her innocent ears which, naturally, she had failed to comprehend.

But presently the Major's sense of shock and dismay over the degeneration of British justice evaporated, leaving only a sediment of contempt and indifference. After all, if one lot was as bad as the other why should anyone care? 'Let them sort it out for themselves.'

He was bored, he was lonely, and one day he realized that Edward was getting on his nerves. The more the Major thought about this, the stronger his aversion grew. Strange that he had never noticed before how he disliked the fellow. These days the mere sight of Edward was enough to set him grinding his teeth. Everything about him was capable of awakening the Major's irritation: his overbearing manner; the way he always insisted on being right, flatly stating his opinions in a loud and abusive tone without paying any attention to what the other fellow was saying; and the unjust way in which he dealt with the twins, locking them up for telling lies when he himself was in the process of telling them, tyrannizing them unmercifully whenever the whim crossed his mind. But no less offensive were Edward's demonstrations of tenderness towards these same twins, the mildness and self-mockery that cohabited uneasily with his ferocity and conviction of always being in the right. 'He's weak and sentimental,' the Major would think on these occasions. 'How can I have ever liked the chap?' Even Edward's clothes, the impeccable cut of his suits and the creases in his trousers, became an affront. 'Don't you think that Edward looks like a tailor's dummy?' he remarked one day to Miss Archer as Edward sauntered past. Indeed, the only satisfactory thing about Edward was his evident liking for the Major. 'He can't help but admire me because I did what his wash-out of a son should have done. What a joke!'

Perhaps it was inevitable that sooner or later the Major and Edward should have a row.

'The Black and Tans who sacked Balbriggan should be punished,' the Major said one day after he had glimpsed Edward and Sarah walking together on the terrace outside the dining-room. Edward looked at him, irritated and surprised —it had obviously never occurred to him that the Major might not approve of reprisals.

'Or perhaps you think that there should be one law for them and one law for other people?' went on the Major aggressively.

'But, Brendan, a man was killed in cold blood.'

'That's still no reason for going on the rampage.'

'A man was murdered. These people have to be taught a lesson.'

'By all means let the culprits be taught a lesson. And leave law-abiding people alone.'

'Ach, they're all the same. They laugh behind their hands when one of our chaps is killed.'

'That's not against the law. Burning people's houses is.'

'But how can the police possibly be expected to find who's guilty and who isn't when they're all in it together?' shouted Edward, losing his temper. 'Dammit, man! Be reasonable.'

'If they don't know who's guilty they should find out before going berserk and punishing people at random the way they did at Balbriggan.'

'I don't want to hear any more of this. If you don't care about the poor fellow who was killed doing his duty, I *do*!' And with that Edward strode away, clenching and unclenching his fists furiously. After a few strides he paused and shouted back: 'Are you disloyal, Major, or what?' Then he departed without waiting for a reply.

Edward muttered an apology later in the day for this last abusive question and the Major, who was ashamed of himself, murmured sadly that that was quite all right, he hadn't taken it to heart. Later the Major wondered why he should feel ashamed of himself. After all, he genuinely believed in what he had said to Edward.

'If the R.I.C. take to behaving as badly as the Shinners,' he remarked to Miss Archer, 'pretty soon the whole country will be in chaos and it'll be every man for himself.'

Later again the painful image of Edward and Sarah walking together on the terrace came to his mind.

'She's a Catholic and he's old enough to be her father,' he told himself sourly.

'This is no place for a young man to spend his time, surrounded by a lot of old women,' Miss Archer said to the Major with a smile.

'Yes, perhaps I shall still go to Italy ... Florence maybe, or Naples. But I hear that travelling abroad is becoming impossible. All the papers one needs ... not like before the war when all you needed was a ticket. But you're quite right, Sybil. I must make up my mind.'

And yes, the Major was seriously thinking of leaving Kilnalough. Now that relations were strained between himself and Edward there was even less reason to stay. He could go anywhere in the world. He no longer had any ties, either in London or elsewhere. Yet this was precisely the trouble. In all the aching void of the world where should he go? Why should he choose one place rather than another? For wherever he went, Sarah would not be. Sarah would remain behind in Kilnalough.

The Major still had hopes, although now somewhat insubstantial, of establishing once more the intimacy which had existed between them during Sarah's brief visit to London the previous winter. He still sometimes, at his writing-desk or in bed with a book open on his chest, fell into a reverie for minutes on end, day-dreaming delightfully about Sarah in the Strand with her arm through his, asking him questions, Sarah in a restaurant not knowing which knife and fork to use, sad and sweet, page after page of an old photograph-album ... with himself at her side, amused, paternal, indulgent, and a tiny bit world-weary. He still had hopes.

She often came to the Majestic in the afternoon. He did not know what to make of her relationship with Edward: it was not as if she took any trouble to be alone with him. She seemed to enjoy the Major's company just as much. Of course, the wide-eyed Sarah whose excitement at finding herself in a strange city he had found so touching was a very different person from Sarah in Kilnalough where she was so sure of herself. She was sometimes impatient with him. Sometimes, it was true, she laughed at him as if she found him ridiculous (he was still nettled by the thought of the bunch of roses and the chocolates). She enjoyed teasing him but she enjoyed flirting with him too, sometimes.

'You may kiss my hand, Brendan, if you want to very badly, as I can see you do,' she would say, laughing.

'Nothing could interest me less,' the Major would reply gruffly, laughing also but in a rather strained manner (he dimly divined that if he was to get anywhere he must refuse these tempting little offers, although the effort of doing so wore him out).

In front of the fire in the gun room stood an old leather sofa, a first cousin of the one in Edward's study, buttoned and bulging like a sergeant major. Sitting on this one evening while Edward was away at the Golf Club, idly playing with a large family of new-born kittens that lived in the turf-basket, the Major suddenly found himself being kissed by Sarah. When they paused for breath elated thoughts sped through the Major's mind like scared antelope. He was unable to speak. Sarah, however, merely remarked: 'Your moustache has a taste of garlic,' and went on with what she had been saying a moment before about the races at Leopardstown. This comment staggered the Major but he said nothing. It was clear that he was a traveller through unmapped country.

On the other hand she was also quite capable of falling into a cold rage for no reason that he could perceive. At such times she could be very cruel. One day when he had been speaking, though impersonally, about marriage and its place in the modern world, she interrupted him brutally by saying: 'It's not a wife you're looking for, Brendan. It's a mother!' The Major was upset because he had not, in fact, been saying he was looking for either.

'Why are you so polite the whole time?' she would ask derisively, while the Major, appalled, wondered what was wrong with being polite. 'Why are you always fussing around those infernal old women? Can't you *smell* how awful they are?' she would demand, making a disgusted face, and when the Major said nothing she would burst out: 'Because you're an old woman yourself, that's why.' And since the Major maintained his hurt and dignified silence: 'And for Jesus' sake stop looking at me like a stuffed squirrel!'

After one of these outbursts the Major might climb tragically to his room and in front of the mirror decide that it was all over, his hopes had been illusory. And then perhaps he would draft a curt note explaining that circumstances obliged him to leave Kilnalough never to return — debating with himself for half an hour whether one *could* actually say: 'Circumstances oblige me to leave Kilnalough never to return,' or whether it did not sound a bit foolish. Anyway, by the time he descended the stairs again, armed to the teeth with polite, coldly glinting words which would skewer Sarah's heart like a shish kebab, well, her mood would have changed completely. Without the slightest hesitation she would grasp his wrist and say that she was sorry, that she was a pig, that she hadn't meant whatever awful thing it was she had said. And no matter what stern resolutions the Major had taken five minutes earlier, he would allow himself to be mollified with indecent haste. Later he would be sorry that he had allowed himself to capitulate so quickly because, here again, he had dimly begun to perceive that it was poor strategy.

Until now, incredible though it may seem, the Major had never considered that love, like war, is best conducted with experience of tactics. His instinct helped him a little. It warned him, for instance, against unconditional surrender. ('Do with me as you see fit, Sarah.') With Sarah he somehow knew that that would not work. He was learning slowly, by experience. Next time he had a love affair he would do much better. But to the love-drugged Major that was not much consolation.

All the same, he had hopes, mainly of a practical nature. He was wealthy and independent. He had no relations to placate. Sarah was entirely without money; and about her 'family' the less said the better, for even his present state of narcosis was powerless to furnish the unspeakable Devlin with attractive qualities. Could the girl refuse such a dazzling opportunity? Well, the Major gloomily fancied that she *could* — but all the same, and however undernourished, he did have hopes, in spite of everything.

While the Major, with neither chart nor compass, was thus wandering at large through the minefields of love, a letter arrived for him. He recognized neither the postmark nor the handwriting. 'Curious!' he mused, and tore it open. It was from a girl he had known before the war. She said that she was going to get married and that she hoped he didn't mind. (Not only did the Major not mind, for a few minutes he could remember nothing about the girl at all; even the circumstances of their meeting escaped him.) But she had waited for him — that is, if at a certain stage he had made the right move, or rather (the letter was somewhat confused, as if written while intoxicated), any move ... that is to say, it had become clear to her, after all one can only wait so long, but she would always think of him, would always remember him with love and affection ... one can't, after all (why should one want to?), pretend that the Past hasn't happened ... tear it out of one's life by the roots ... the fun they had had together. She could close her eyes even now and still see him, Lieutenant Brendan

Archer, as she knew he would always be. She hoped he would also. Life goes by so quickly.

The Major did remember her now, of course. She had been someone's sister, not particularly attractive but with a reputation among the young men of that circle. He was glad that she had managed to find a husband in spite of the reputation (which had turned out to be justified, he recalled). He had liked her, really. She had been a good scout, in spite of the other thing. She had oppressed him, though, by the intensity of her feeling for him, and that was the principal thing he now remembered about her. She had had a tendency to hug him violently, squeezing the air out of his lungs — it's distressing to be squeezed very hard if you are not trying to squeeze the other person back. One feels trapped. The Major had felt trapped. As to what had inspired this passion he had no idea; in those days, not long after leaving school, he had been an intolerably stuck-up young prig. Well, perhaps that was what women liked. Insufferable young prigs striking attitudes. 'But no, I mustn't be bitter. And the insufferable young prig was *me*! That should make a difference.' Well! But women liked other kinds of men too. The thought of Edward crossed his mind again. 'Women have appalling taste in men,' he decided gloomily.

The Major sat down then and there and unscrewed the cap of his fountain pen, thinking how strange it was that all this time a girl, whom he could still only think of as someone's sister, should have been harbouring fond thoughts of him and now, after so many years, should send him a letter saying she hoped he didn't mind that she was going to get married.

He wrote to her immediately. He said that *of course* he minded (after all, one could hardly say that one didn't mind in the least), but he hoped that nevertheless she would be very happy. In fact—he wrote, warming to the task—in fact, he was positively gnashing his teeth with despair, but richly deserved to be passed over in favour of someone who was, without a doubt, a better man than he. It served him right—

he wrote, feeling a flood of compassion for this other person wandering, like himself, at large in the minefields—that she should choose someone else and leave him for ever outside in the cold and clammy darkness. And, it went without saying, he would always cherish his memories of the good times they had had together. He remained, with devotion, her Lieutenant Brendan Archer.

He sealed this letter and posted it. As he retired to the residents' lounge to wait and watch for Sarah he wondered lugubriously how it was that the tyrant one moment could become the slave the next. Moreover, certain misgivings began to awaken. Had he not written with too much haste and warmth?

'My God, supposing she regards it as a counter-proposal, calls off the wedding and comes over here to get me!' He wondered whether he should not dash off another letter disclaiming the first. But no, he could hardly do that. Fortunately, however, the days passed without any word and it gradually became clear that he would not be held to account for his rash outburst of sympathy.

'At the first favourable moment I shall propose and the business will be settled one way or the other.' But his efforts to lead up to the subject were constantly disappointed. It seemed as if Sarah could hardly hear the word 'marriage' even in the most theoretical and general way without being seized by one of her cruel moods. Naturally the Major was dismayed, but persevered nevertheless, telling himself that it was just a question of finding the right mood.

One afternoon, sitting on a sofa in the residents' lounge and screened by an ornamental pillar, he almost brought himself to broach the subject. They were at the farthest extreme from the ladies playing whist by the fire. Sarah had been unusually warm and affectionate following a dire clash the day before (stimulated by some observations the Major had attempted to make about the Islamic wedding ceremony). For some moments they had been sunk in a contented silence, Sarah had idly slipped her hand into his, nothing was happening, she seemed rather sleepy. There was unlikely to be a better opportunity, so the Major cleared his throat.

'Look here ... ' he began (he had chosen his words days ago and knew them by heart). But at that moment a blue-veined, bony hand, fingers bright with diamonds, appeared from behind a bay tree in a tub (a refugee from the Palm Court next door, brought into the lounge on Edward's instructions so that it could 'breathe'). The hand knocked rather sharply against the ornamental pillar, then caressed it. A moment later old Mrs Rappaport was standing there, her head on one side, listening.

'Is that you, Edward?'

'No, Mrs Rappaport, it's me, Brendan Archer.'

'I could hear you breathing.'

The old lady stepped forward; her other hand, dry and freckled, held a walking-stick. She advanced cautiously until she was standing beside the Major, looking down at him with her empty, unfocusing orbs.

'Angela's Major,' she breathed, reaching forward with her free hand. 'Where are you, my dear?' The Major frowned with annoyance but grasped her hand and guided it rather roughly (he was still keyed up from his attempt to propose) on to the top of his head, where it remained for some moments. He glanced at Sarah out of the corner of his eye. She was grinning at his discomfiture.

'Angela will be so glad you've come,' the old lady murmured, and her hand, delicate as a moth, began to model the Major's features. 'How handsome you are, Major!' she whispered, fingers spreading like cream over his forehead, rimming his eyes and returning to slither down his nose, smoothing outwards over the firmly clipped bristles of his moustache and on to the jawbone. She paused again, still holding the Major's chin lightly between finger and thumb, listening.

'There's someone with you. It's not Angela, is it?' Her

252

hand left the Major's face and began to make slow sweeps beside him, reaping the air, nearer and nearer to Sarah. The Major got to his feet. Sarah was looking up at Mrs Rappaport with an expression of revulsion, mesmerized by the bony diamond-clad fingers that were groping towards her.

'There's no one there, Mrs Rappaport,' the Major said abruptly, taking her by the elbow. But she shook off his hand and edged nearer to Sarah, her fingers still desperately trawling back and forth through the empty air. Sarah was shrinking right back now, holding her breath, unable to retreat further.

'Come along now. Let me show you to the fire.' Grasping the old lady's arm firmly, he pulled her away, still clawing at the air. As they made their way across the lounge the corners of Mrs Rappaport's mouth came down and a single tear stole over her powdered cheek. When she had been deposited in her seat by the fire the Major hastened back to the sofa hoping to resume his proposal. But Sarah was no longer there.

The glass in the towering windows of the residents' lounge was already stained blue-black, but the ladies, engrossed in their interminable game of whist, had not yet thought to summon Murphy or one of the maids to draw the curtains and stem the tide of night seeping into the room. Far overhead, beneath the white ceiling encrusted with plaster roses, laurels, fleurs-de-lys and three-pronged crowns, a trapped sparrow fluttered helplessly from one darkening pane to another. Deep in an armchair, the Major, no less helpless, pondered Sarah's bizarre behaviour. That afternoon she had been even more taunting and capricious than usual. In particular she had let fall two remarks which he was finding difficult to interpret: 'I should be mad about you, Brendan, if we had more in common,' and a few minutes later: 'Who should I like to marry? I should like to marry someone just like you, Brendan, only with brains.' Should these remarks be regarded as increasing or decreasing the chances of his proposal being accepted?

He sighed. Soon it would be time for dinner. He attempted to decide whether he was hungry or not, but even the answer to this question eluded him. Compared with his feelings for Sarah all his desires were tepid. Cries and laughter at some incident at the whist-table awoke the echoes of the cavernous room. The sparrow fluttered out once more to beat against the dark glass. There was silence then, except for the beating of its wings and presently a rapid, heavy tread that the Major had come to recognize at great distances. He pictured the gleaming leather shoes with dove-grey spats which were making the tiles of the corridor ring louder and louder. In a moment Edward's massive and elegant frame ('the tailor's dummy', as the Major was in the habit of describing him these days) — silk tie and snowy shirt, silk handkerchief in top pocket — would make its appearance. Edward would smile mechanically in the direction of the ladies, who would probably be too busy to take any notice of him; maybe he would add a puzzled frown in the direction of the Major, as if to ask: 'What ails the fellow?'

But Edward's collar was hanging by a thread and completely divorced from his tie, the knot of which had shrivelled to the size of a raisin. His shirt was ripped and muddy; one lapel of his jacket had been torn out at the seam and hung to his waist; his trousers too were mudstained and the spat of one shoe flapped like a broken bird over the instep. The other shoe had lost its spat altogether. A bruise had swollen and darkened one of Edward's prominent cheekbones; a trail of blood leaked from the corner of his mouth and there was a black congealed mass beneath his nostrils. He waved one closed fist at the Major, stared wildly about the room for a moment, then turned and departed the way he had come. The ringing footsteps started again in the corridor outside, now diminishing. The ladies had noticed nothing.

The Major got to his feet and hurried after Edward. He found him in his study, examining himself in the mirror with his back to the door. From behind, his jacket's elegance was unimpaired; a rapid swelling and shrinking was visible below the armpits but there was no noise from his breathing. He heard the Major enter and turned, waving that same closed fist.

'Out for a walk,' he said harshly. 'Two men tried to attack me.'

'My God! Where?'

'On the way up from the beach a mile or so away.'

'Here, let me get you a drink!'

The Major poured whiskey into a glass and handed it to Edward. He took it with trembling fingers and drank it rapidly, as if he were thirsty. He sat down then but stood up again immediately, pacing back and forth and still waving his clenched right fist threateningly in the Major's direction.

'Did they want to rob you?'

'I've no idea. For all I know they were trying to kill me. It was odd ... Not a word! They didn't say a word. Neither threats, nor abuse, nor argument ... Only heavy breathing and an occasional grunt during the scuffle. I couldn't even see what the blighters looked like. There was a big man whose clothing was ragged and I heard something tear while we were struggling ... and there was a smell of dirt and turf-smoke about him ... but they all smell that way. There's only one thing I know about him for certain. Come here to the light and have a look.'

Edward had paused, holding his tightly clenched fist under the oil lamp. Curious, the Major went over. Edward slowly opened his fingers—a tuft of red hair lay in his palm.

'That's not much help,' he laughed. 'I must know two dozen men with hair that colour around here.' Now that he was standing near to the light the Major could see that he was very pale. But he continued in a strong and cheerful tone: 'Must have wrenched this from the beggar's scalp. Didn't realize I had it in my hand till I was back here.'

Far from getting better as time went on, the situation was plainly getting worse. Hardly a day passed now without some fresh instance of disagreeable behaviour on the part of the

255

local population: a tradesman deliberately ignoring you in his shop, a child putting out its tongue at you without being scolded by its parents, a door that nobody thought of holding open for you, a seat that nobody offered you while you were waiting to be served ... Trivial things, perhaps, but when one thought of how obliging the people of Kilnalough *used* to be! In short, it became wearing for the nerves. Who could blame Miss Staveley for delivering a long, rambling rebuke to the sniggering shop-girls of Finnegan's?

The ladies from the Majestic no longer ventured into Kilnalough alone these days; one was too vulnerable to insult. If anything was needed, a few ounces of wool or a jar of peppermints, perhaps, or something from the chemist's — smelling-salts or senna pods or lavender water — the problem was discussed over the whist-tables and an expedition was mounted. Six eyes, of course, all sharply on the look-out, proved far better than two for spotting insults while in the drapery or the tea-rooms, three tongues far better than one for putting someone back in his place.

In no time at all the ladies developed a remarkable skill for discerning traces of insulting behaviour in the townspeople. A lack of respect would be detected (in a turned back, in a 'saucy' smile, in a cheeky 'Good day!') and quick as a flash it would be dealt with. Miss Johnston rapidly established herself as the champion in both detection and retribution and accordingly became the most sought-after person to accompany shopping expeditions. Miss Bagley and Miss Staveley were also reliable performers. Miss Archer and Miss Porteous however, were frankly not much good; the latter was particularly erratic in detection and tended to become incoherent with rage once she was aroused. As for poor Mrs Rice, she was completely hopeless.

'She wouldn't notice if someone called her an old aitch ... ee ... en to her face,' sighed Miss Johnston. 'We shall simply have to make sure she isn't left alone.'

One afternoon the Major happened to accompany an

expedition which included Miss Devere, Miss Johnston and Mrs Rice, all of whom had some business to conduct at the post office. He was astonished by the speed with which battle was joined. Half-way across the bustling market square, without a moment's hesitation, Miss Johnston locked antlers with a craggy-faced old farmer whom she had observed spitting on the ground some twenty yards away with obvious reference, she said, to herself and her companions.

'Oh really!' protested the Major. But Miss Johnston was already berating the surprised farmer and even waving her umbrella in his face in a threatening manner. Later there was more trouble when a clerk at the post office spoke to her with his hands in his pockets.

It didn't take long for the Major to perceive that the ladies found these expeditions a source of rare excitement. Almost every afternoon a party was formed to go and buy something in Kilnalough. Those left at the whist-tables would await the return of the shoppers with eager anticipation, and rare were the afternoons when the returning ladies had no encounters to report. The Major was dubious about most of these alleged insults. Miss Johnston, in particular, stimulated by the admiration of her companions, already appeared to have refined her skill to the point where she could sense an insult before it was delivered. He suspected that, as with the unfortunate farmer in the market square, she very often administered correction to entirely innocent passers-by.

One day, genuinely alarmed by their immoderation, he permitted himself to suggest to the ladies that this 'lack of respect' was more imagined than real ... but that if the shopping expeditions continued to behave like war-parties there really *would* be trouble. The ladies received this suggestion coldly, but perhaps it had some effect. In his company, at any rate, the subject was brought up less often. It had never been mentioned, except obliquely, when Sarah was present. Dimly he was beginning to realize that the old ladies of the Majestic had little affection for her.

The Major had grown weary of whist, although the fever for the game showed no sign of relaxing its grip on the old ladies. Besides, the ladies themselves with their snobbish gentility and complacency had begun to grate on his nerves. Anyone would think, to see them whispering, that Sarah was nothing but a servant-girl! Not, of course, that individually they still could not be as charming as ever. All the same, one could have too much of a good thing.

These days he wanted to be alone in order to think clearly, more clearly, about Sarah. But where? His room was without comfort, the Imperial Bar overrun by cats, all the other rooms in the hotel (of which there was, of course, no shortage) seemed somehow wrong. He hardly knew why. There would be one thing or another which failed to please him. He would simply look at them and see that they were unsuitable, hardly bothering to detail the reasons to himself. But at last, on the second floor, he opened a door he had not tried before—and found exactly what he wanted.

It was a linen room, long and narrow and rather dark. Sheets and pillows lay in piles everywhere. Blankets, hundreds of them, were stacked to the ceiling against each wall; no doubt they had been there since the old days when every room in the place was in use. It was dry here, too, and rather warm, which was a great advantage now that the weather had turned chilly. At certain times of day it became positively tropical because the master chimney from the kitchens passed along one wall. But the Major did not mind; he would simply take off all his clothes and lie naked on a pile of blankets, reading a magazine and perspiring gently while he sipped a whiskey and soda requisitioned from the seething Imperial Bar. It was perfect. Nobody ever came here (except once when Edward, who must have heard a noise, poked his head in, gave a grunt of surprise at seeing the naked Major and withdrew hastily). In no time at all he had fashioned himself a huge, warm and slightly dusty nest of blankets and pillows.

As he lay day-dreaming in this nest he sometimes pictured

Sarah (though without permitting himself any indecent reflections) lying there also, naked and gently perspiring like himself. How splendid that would be! He knew without having to ask that she would enjoy it as much as he. He understood her so well when she was no longer present; it was only when they were actually together that he experienced some difficulty. As time went by they would undoubtedly become more attuned to each other's presence. In the meantime, particularly at equatorial noon and in the late afternoon (except on those days when the cook decided to send back to the dining-room, cut up cold, the unconsumed meat from yesterday's dinner), Sarah lay there, delightfully insubstantial, naked and content by his side in the hollow of dusty pillows.

Once or twice, indeed, she even managed to be both in the linen room at his side and down below (flesh and bone, blood, cartilage, muscle, mucous membrane and whatnot) playing whist with the old ladies and perhaps with Edward too—for Edward, although some time ago he had forsaken the whist-table for the pistol-range come rain or shine, had recently suffered a relapse and was frequently to be seen shuffling and dealing with no less fervour than the old ladies. But in general the fantasy tended to weaken and vanish in the vicinity of flesh and blood. Besides, the thought of Edward disturbed him. So when he knew that Sarah was there he would pull on his clothes and go downstairs to watch them play.

When Sarah was present Edward liked to play as her partner; 'the old firm' he called it. They would both become very boisterous, greeting their cards with cries of mock grief or joy, encouraging each other to all sorts of extravagant behaviour. In this mood Edward often made the ladies roar with laughter and even towards Sarah they adopted a less frosty attitude. The Major would laugh at Edward's jokes too, of course, but with bad grace. He seldom enjoyed himself. Only Mrs Rappaport, sitting grimly on her straight-backed chair by the fire, never smiled.

Mrs Rappaport would have cast a cloud over the proceed-

ings, no doubt, if the whist fever had been any less intense —
but one got used to her presence. Besides, she sat a little apart
from the main group. One day, however, she did cause a slight
stir and a few cries of dismay because it was noticed that
another cat had magically appeared in her lap. Once again it
was a mystery as to how it had got there. Normally everyone
made a point of hunting cats out of the residents' lounge with
walking-sticks or parasols or whatever lay to hand, because
one had to draw the line somewhere. Even more disturbing
was the fact that the cat in question had the same marmalade
fur as the frightful beast which had attacked Miss Staveley's
hat in the writing-room. Old Mrs Rappaport was blind, of
course, so she could not possibly have selected it deliberately.
The ladies' concern might have been greater but for the fact
that this cat was clearly not dangerous. Indeed, it was only
a kitten — a tiny, mewing bundle of orange fur with its eyes
barely open. If anything, it was a rather attractive little
creature. One felt immediately that one wanted to stroke it.
Some of the old ladies did so, bending stiffly to fondle its
tiny ginger ears, and if the kitten promptly reacted by gripping
these loose-skinned, jewelled fingers with the miniature needles
of its claws, why, any healthy kitten would do the same.
'It's only natural', said Miss Bagley, 'and hardly hurts at all.'

All the same, it did have one faintly disturbing quality:
namely, the speed at which it was growing. It was almost as
if during the night someone picked it up by its wisp of a
black-and-orange-ringed tail and blew a deep breath into it,
inflating it like a gaudy balloon. With each day that passed it
appeared a little more swollen and when it stretched and
yawned the span of its claws reached a little farther. Moreover,
when its eyes were more fully opened it was remarked that
they were of a bitter, sea-green hue. Grim and impassive Mrs
Rappaport sat there day after day with the kitten under her
palm swelling into a ... well, into a cat. Nobody took much
notice of either of them; Edward had become so amusing
these days, almost like a comedian.

The Major envied him. No matter how grey the afternoon, no matter how despondent the whist players had become about the state the country was in, Edward had only to sit down at the table for five minutes and everyone would be shouting and laughing, their ailments and prophecies of disaster forgotten. A current of energy accompanied him. When he left the table it was as if all the lights had been turned out. He dominated everyone, even the indomitable Miss Johnston. One could hear his voice three rooms away. His cheerfulness rattled the window-panes. He was like the ring-master of a circus: not one of the old ladies would be allowed to sulk or sink into herself. Miss Devere or Miss Bradley might try to resist him, remembering a loved one who had died on that particular day, perhaps, or thinking of the onset of winter, but ... Crack! The whip of Edward's massive personality would sail out across the ring and tickle her into action once again. Crack! Even the Major was forced to go through his paces or appear impossibly surly. He might be thinking: 'I'm stronger than Edward because he can't help admiring me whether he likes me or not ... ' but then, crack! He would find himself having to jump through a blazing hoop.

But still the Major was convinced that he was stronger than Edward. It was simply that Edward was so hearty and extro-verted these days (but the Major had not forgotten the days when he was moody) that he made the Major seem dull and cautious by comparison. 'It's all show,' the Major would think lugubriously as he noticed that Sarah's glistening eyes seldom left Edward's face. But then, crack! It would happen again. He scarcely had time to build up his animosity before he would be forced to laugh grudgingly at whatever Edward was saying. 'Very funny!' he would mutter to himself. 'But we shall see ... ' Once or twice since the day that Edward had been set upon in the dark the Major had seen a hint of un-certainty in his eyes, he was sure of it. 'We shall see what we shall see.' And to his surprise he found that he was grinding his teeth. 'Good heavens, the fellow is my friend after all,' he reproved himself.

'If I haven't an ace in this hand I'll eat my pipe,' cried Edward. And sure enough he pulled out a pipe and wolfed it in a flash. The ladies shrieked and gasped in pain, holding their ribs, so funny did they find this (the pipe, of course, had been made of liquorice). The Major watched them with dismay, afraid that Edward might give them all heart attacks. But in between these humorous sallies the Major more and more often believed he could discern a lost and frantic look on Edward's face. Sarah too sometimes stared at him with concern when she was not laughing at his antics. But then Edward would leave the room to attend to some business and everyone would feel dull and dispirited once again.

'It's a scandal!'

Silence fell immediately, an absolute silence in which everyone held his breath and the throbbing purr of the kitten could be distinctly heard. Mrs Rappaport had gone unnoticed for such a long time that they had almost forgotten that she could speak.

'You think that I don't know what's going on in this house,' shouted the old lady, her jowls quivering with fury. 'I shall not stand for it under this roof!'

The Major expected Edward to soothe her as he usually did, to ask her what was the scandal, what it was that she wouldn't stand for. But he said nothing. His eyes remained on the table. Nobody said a word for two full minutes. There was no movement except for the flicking of the kitten's ringed tail on Mrs Rappaport's lap. But at last her shoulders drooped, she sniffed and felt for the handkerchief tucked into her sleeve, her face went vacant once more. She had forgotten about her scandal, whatever it was.

But her outburst had a strange effect on Edward. He became morose and taciturn. Not only did he stop making jokes and infecting the ladies with hilarity, in a day or two he stopped playing cards altogether. Without any warning he abandoned the field to the Major. The Major was pleased, of course, since this meant that he could exercise his more subtle charm on Sarah without impediment, but somehow disturbed as well. Edward had begun to drink more than was good for him. More than once the Major had caught a whiff of liquor on his breath. One day he heard that Edward had been drunk at the Golf Club. He had got into an argument with one of the members and told him he was 'worthless'. Of course such things happen from time to time and a man in his cups is not to be taken seriously. But then, perhaps a week later, it happened again, this time at the Majestic. Edward, impeccably dressed as ever but with his mane of grey hair in disorder and a glass in his hand, confronted Mr Norton in the corridor and told him he was 'worthless'. Mr Norton fled indignantly to the residents' lounge but Edward, glass still in hand, followed him there and, although he did not say anything, stared at Mr Norton with a sarcastic smile, looking himself (as Miss Porteous later put it) like 'The Wreck of the Hesperus'. Presently, however, he tired of Mr Norton and, slumped in an armchair, stared balefully at the Major.

'Always playing cards with the ladies, Major?'

'That's right, Edward.'

'Fine occupation for a young man.' The Major said nothing.

'I said it was a fine occupation for a young man.'

'I heard you.'

'Well, I take it you agree with me.'

'Edward, please!' Sarah said. She had become very pale. She stared at Edward anxiously. The other ladies had become as quiet as mice.

'I'm sure *you* think it's a good idea to have young men playing cards with you,' Edward said harshly. 'I want to hear what the Major thinks.'

'Very well,' the Major said curtly. 'I think it's better than being in the trenches. Does that answer your question?' With that he put down his cards, got to his feet and strode out of the room.

The Union of South Africa is passing through a period of stress and danger. On Saturday last serious rioting broke out in Port Elizabeth ... The police showed admirable restraint but were powerless to cope with the frenzied crowd of maddened natives. Military came on the scene and opened fire, killing several of the rioters ... Every effort is being made to localize the trouble, but, in view of the fact that in the whole Union there are only one and a quarter millions of white people as compared with four and a half millions of natives, the possibilities of widespread disturbances cannot be ignored.

The dangers of a native rising are much greater than they would be if the white population were united ... To the Kaffir, Boer and Briton, Nationalist and Unionist, German and South African, are alike. There is not a white man in South Africa who does not recognize to the full the perils that lie dormant in the niggers' kraals. There is not a white woman from the Congo to the Cape who does not shudder at the thought of a native rising, and there is hardly a native in the country who would not rise tomorrow if he dared.

THE CAMPAIGN OF CRIME

The guerrilla warfare against the forces of the Crown has become general outside North-East Ulster. Already the R.I.C. has suffered as heavily as if it had held a front-line trench in France. Its efficiency is maintained only by its own indomitable spirit and by constant reinforcements ... The last three days have produced a truly appalling orgy of blood-stained lawlessness. In different parts of the country policemen have been assassinated and soldiers killed in ambush; every Irish newspaper has been turned into a catalogue of horror.

It was now that the first of the great autumn storms began to blow. The wind whistled in the chimneys and immense breakers rolled in to smash against the sea-wall, kicking clouds of white spray high into the air. Spray drenched the gravel paths and dashed against the squash court, so that Edward was in a state of constant anxiety lest his piglets (now as big as spaniels) be drowned. A great quantity of rain-water collected on the sagging flat roof of the Prince Consort wing and presently it relaxed under the pressure, allowing a cascade to empty itself with a musical roar into a grand piano which had been left open and on its side, with one leg amputated. By this time, in any case, the Auxiliaries billeted at the Majestic had removed to a barracks at Vale-bridge, either because the accommodation there was superior or because they judged the hotel indefensible.

'There are a devil of a lot of people about,' Edward remarked to the Major as they motored out to the golf links. 'Something must be up.'

There was a high wind, almost a gale, howling over the countryside, but the rain had abated. The roads were thick with people and vehicles, ponies and traps, carts with giant lumbering horses in the shafts, even some battered motor cars—passengers crammed inside and out, on the bonnet, on the running-board, even on the roof—bicycles pedalling in and out or way up on the grass verge with bells ringing—and hundreds of people on foot. It might have been an annual fair or point-to-point; but there was no talking or laughter, no singing, these crowds moved in silence, like refugees the Major had seen moving back from the Front.

'What a rabble!' he thought unsympathetically. He hated the Irish. He stared at the faces that floated by as the Daimler inched its way through against the tide of humanity sounding its horn. Dull, granitic faces, cheekbones sculpted like axe-handles, purple cheeks and matted hair, bovine, the women huge and heavy-breasted, arms dimpled and swollen like loaves of bread. But no, they did not look like refugees;

in their faces he read a strained, expectant look. Something was up. The Major shouted at a toothless old man dangling his legs on the back of a cart to ask him what it was all about. But the fellow did not seem to understand, merely touched his forelock and looked away furtively.

'Yes,' he was saying to Edward, 'I've written to Cook's to ask about hotels in Florence, but I may move farther south.'

Edward's face darkened, as if he were thinking: 'Disloyalty!', but he said nothing. The Major listened to the echo and re-echo of his own words and thought how false they sounded, how hollow! He no longer had the will-power to leave Kilnalough without Sarah; all he could do now was allow himself to drift with the tide of events. Some strange insect had taken up residence in the will-power of which he had always been so proud, eating away at it unobserved like a slug in an apple.

At the golf links they heard about the miracle. Nobody was out playing golf and for once there were no caddies to be found. But the Members' Bar was overflowing and there was an unusual air of excitement, with much laughter and joking. Only that corner of the bar where the Auxiliaries were normally to be seen remained empty. They'd gone off to perform a miracle of their own, someone said.

Boy O'Neill told them what had happened. Late on Saturday night a young seminarian, kneeling in front of a crucifix in prayer, had seen drops of blood flowing from the wounds of the Christ-figure. For a number of hours he had remained there in a state of ecstasy, unable to speak or move.

This miracle was clearly anti-British. Some member of the seminarian's family had been accused of complicity in the ambush of an R.I.C. constable. It was said in Kilnalough that the lad's family had been abused and threatened, dragged out of their cottage by the Tans and lined up against a wall as if to be shot; his sister had been made to dance in her night-shift in front of her father while the Tans made lewd remarks and jeered at her. Under such provocation of devout people a miracle was only to be expected.

'What d'you make of it, Boy?'

'Mumbo-jumbo.'

'Of course it's mumbo-jumbo, that's obvious ... What I mean is: are the beggars going to cause trouble? God knows, things are bad enough already without having a holy war on our hands.'

'Och, it's just a bit of nonsense. In a day or two they'll have forgotten about it. But look who's just come in, Ted. You'd have thought he'd be spending the day on his knees in front of the miracle.'

The Major turned. Mr Devlin had just come in and was standing uncomfortably at the door, smiling ingratiatingly in the direction of a group at the bar who, by accident or design, had turned their backs on him. Sarah was standing beside her father. For a moment her eyes met the Major's but her face remained expressionless. Mr Devlin, in turn, caught the Major's eye and began to make frantic signals of respectful greeting: would he be permitted to join the Major and his companions and perhaps have the honour of purchasing them a refreshment? The Major nodded curtly.

O'Neill said: 'I do believe the awful fellow is coming over here.'

'I invited him,' the Major said coldly.

'Well, well, you don't say ... '

Sarah, sullen and with downcast eyes, hesitated for a moment before accompanying her father. She barely moved her lips in response to the Major's greeting. Captain Bolton had come in silently behind the Devlins and followed them over to where Edward, O'Neill and the Major were standing. Boy O'Neill, meanwhile, was maliciously asking Mr Devlin what he thought of the miracle. Did he agree that it was mumbo-jumbo? Mr Devlin said cautiously that he really didn't know what to think, it was such a strange business.

'But you'd better believe what they tell you to believe,

Devlin, isn't that right? Or else the priest will send you to hellfire, eh?' O'Neill, barking with aggressive laughter, was somewhat drunk, the Major realized. 'So you don't think it's mumbo-jumbo then?'

Well, of course, in such matters one would want to be careful, because there was perhaps more to it than met the eye, at least, to his way of thinking ...

'To your way of thinking but not to mine. If you ask me it's a plain case of hysteria.'

'Well now,' began Devlin helplessly, 'I'm not sure about that...'

'If there's hysteria it's because innocent people are having their houses burned down,' burst out the Major suddenly.

Bolton said: 'There are no innocent people in Ireland these days, Major. If you put on a uniform like this you'll find that everyone's your enemy.'

There was silence for a moment. Then Bolton added: 'If any of you are brave enough to be seen with a man in the uniform of the Crown perhaps you'd care to come out to the seminary with me. I'm afraid that the Shinners are using your miracle to do some rabble-rousing with. It's a strange feeling to be in the middle of a crowd of innocent people, Major, any of whom may instantly become a hero by pulling a gun from his pocket and shooting you in the back without fear of being caught ... How about you, Mr O'Neill? Would you like to come with me?'

'I'd be delighted any other time, but I've arranged to meet my wife.'

'Too bad.' Bolton smiled faintly.

There was silence for a moment. Sarah had at last lifted her eyes and was looking with amusement from one face to another. Bolton's eyelids drooped sleepily.

'Of course I'm probably exaggerating the danger,' he added indifferently. 'There may not be a single person with a gun in the whole crowd.' He paused again and his eyes flicked towards Edward. 'How about it, Mr Spencer?'

'I really can't see the point in taking foolhardy risks,' Edward said harshly. 'That's the first thing they teach you in the army.'

'Of course. You're perfectly right. All the same, the Major here is an army man and I'm sure he'll want to come with me.' Bolton was smiling contemptuously once more. Without turning towards her the Major was aware of Sarah's eyes on his face.

'Certainly,' he said. 'I'm ready to go whenever you like.'

The wind that had been blowing since early morning continued without slackening throughout the afternoon, a solid rushing of air that kept the branches of the trees pinned back and combed the grass flat on the hill-slope where the Major was standing. The wind sifted through Captain Bolton's short fair hair and ballooned the jacket of his tunic as he sat on a shooting-stick, peering through binoculars. His wind-swollen shoulders gave him the appearance of a hunchback. After a moment he dropped the binoculars, removed the leather thong from round his neck and, without a word, handed them to the Major. The Major raised them to his eyes and looked down the slope towards the sea.

'Funny thing,' Bolton mused. 'I never cared much for the Irish even before all this. An uncouth lot. More like animals than human beings ... used to make me sick sometimes, just watching them eat.'

The Major had by now focused the binoculars on the seminary, which stood beside a rocky promontory. The crowd had assembled in a meadow in front of the grey stone campanile, whose bell, moved by the wind, struck an irregular, querulous chime, scarcely audible at this distance.

'I hope they all get rheumatism from kneeling in the wet grass.'

'They're standing up again now. A young man is making a speech by the look of it.'

'Let's have a look.' Bolton took the glasses, looked through them briefly and handed them back.

Even though earlier in the afternoon he had seen the roads packed with people and carriages, the Major was astonished by the size of the crowd. With the foreshortening of perspective the heads seemed to be piled one on top of another. A number of women stood on the fringes of the crowd and three or four carts in which invalids lay propped on mattresses had been dragged over the rough ground to the front of the seminary so that they could hear the speaker. At the upper windows of the seminary building white-faced boys craned to hear, grasping the heavy iron bars for support, while on the steps a group of black-skirted priests stood and stared and cupped their ears into the rushing gale of air. The young man now stood way out by himself on a jetty of rock that ran some distance into the sea.

He had a strong jaw above a thick, muscled neck in which the Major imagined he could see veins starting out, bulging furiously as the mouth opened and closed to articulate his soundless words of rage. He stood on a level a little below that of the listening crowd and the wind from the sea blew his matted hair forward over his face.

'Are we going down there?'

'You can go if you like, but I prefer not to get a bullet in the spine if I can help it.' Bolton stared mockingly at the Major and then went on: 'I get fed up, you understand, with all the heroes in the Golf Club. You must excuse me for not being able to resist calling their bluff from time to time.'

'I see.'

'Sarah Devlin was telling me the other day what a fine man Edward Spencer is. A man of courage and principles who would never be capable of a cowardly or unworthy act—a real gentleman, in fact. She compared him favourably with me, a ruthless and unprincipled fellow whose men harass innocent people, burn their houses and destroy their property as the whim takes them.'

'What she says is true, isn't it?'

Bolton smiled and picked up a dry twig, snapping it thoughtfully into small pieces between his fingers. 'I do whatever the situation requires, Major. What I tried to explain to Sarah was that people like you and Edward can only afford to have fine feelings because you have someone like me to do your dirty work for you. I become a little upset when people who rely on me to stop them being murdered in their beds start giving themselves superior moral airs.'

'As a matter of fact I think you're wrong about Edward. If anything he supports reprisals.'

'Perhaps, but without dirtying his own hands with them. That makes all the difference.'

The Major raised the binoculars and gazed once more at the young man on the rock jetty, wondering what he was saying to the crowd. Behind him as he spoke great towering breakers would build up; a solid wall of water as big as a house would mount over his gesticulating arms, would hang there above him for an instant as if about to engulf him, then crash around him in a torrent of foam.

'He looks a wild young fellow,' the Major said as he handed the binoculars back. Before turning away he watched another huge wave tower over the young Irishman, hang for a moment, and at last topple to boil impotently around his feet. It was, after all, only the lack of perspective that made it seem as if he would be swept away.

By the following morning the wind had dropped and mild autumnal sunshine bathed the old brick and woodwork of the Majestic.

With the milder weather the Major's nest of pillows in the linen room became hotter than ever, almost equatorial in fact. It was impossible to open the window, which had swollen with the rain and been painted shut many years ago. The heat mounted. After a couple of hours of tortured reflection on his relationship with Sarah, his naked body glistening like a savage's, he would be obliged to gulp down several pints of cold water. It was true that later, when the meal had been cooked and the stoves banked down for the night, the heat would drop to a more pleasant temperature – but by that time he had worn out his emotions, written two or three feverish letters with sweaty hiatuses on the paper where the ink refused to stay. In some of these letters, forgetting that he could not permit himself to be weak, he capitulated completely ('Sarah, I love you, you must come back to me, ah, the heat is intolerable'). But fortunately he mastered himself sufficiently never to post them, thinking: 'She'd only think me a bit of an ass.'

'I shall never see you again,' he groaned aloud one afternoon, sitting high up on one of the blanket racks with a glass of whiskey and swinging his damp hairy legs in the air. But at that moment there was a knock at the door.

'Who is it?'

'Me. Can I come in?' came Charity's voice.

'Certainly not.' The Major hastily jumped down and began to pull on his clothes. 'What d'you want?'

'That girl wants to see you.'

'Which girl?'

'The one you all make such a fuss of. The one with the spots and the limp.'

'You mean Sarah? Tell her I'll be down immediately.'

But Charity was still mooning outside the door when he opened it, and gave him a surly, reproachful look.

'How did you know where I was?'

'I saw you go in one day. What d'you do in there anyway?'

Although some days had passed since they had seen each other, Sarah seemed to be treating her visit as entirely normal. She greeted him as if unaware of the heartache that this separation had caused him. She was cheerful. She was delighted to see him. By herself she had been miserable. Why had he not come to see her?

'Eh?'

'I've been most horribly sick (ugh! It's disgusting to mention such things). You might at least have come and cheered me up.'

'Was it an unmentionable disease?' asked the Major gaily, infected by her good spirits.

'All diseases are unmentionable, Brendan, but I shall tell you anyway. I spent a whole night vomiting. Isn't that revolting?'

The Major laughed, although secretly somewhat taken aback by this frankness. Of course Sarah was a law unto herself.

But she was irresistible. She chattered away gaily to him as they strolled arm-in-arm back and forth over the dusty floor of the ballroom. Yes, she had talked to Captain Bolton ... What a strange, cold man he was! Those blue eyes of his! They said in Kilnalough that once he had glanced for a moment at a glass of water on Father O'Byrne's table and ice had formed on it an inch thick ... Oh, the Major was impossible! Of course it wasn't true *literally*, it was true in some other way, how should she know in what way it was true? And, and ... the miracle, had he seen the miracle after that absurd little scene at the Golf Club? Well, she'd taken a peek at the statue and there didn't seem to be much blood flowing anywhere but there were a couple of brown spots ... but *they* might have been anything, they might have been, say, oxtail soup. Oh well, if it was blasphemy to say so then so much the better, she'd have a sin to confess for once, which would make a nice change, her life was so dull ... she could never think of any sins to *commit*, let alone confess, particularly when she felt sick and vomited all the time, it left her feeling much too weak to do any sinning ... and anyway, since he, the Major, was a 'beastly Prod', she didn't see why he should mind her saying something blasphemous, in fact he should positively encourage her, but never mind about that, what was it she wanted to say, yes, she wanted to know everything, absolutely everything that had been going on while she had been sick ...

'You mean, going on here?'

'Of course I mean here. Where d'you think I mean?'

But the Major could think of nothing but the fact that he had spent three whole days hollow-eyed with love for her.

By now they were strolling in the residents' lounge, shielded from the curiosity of the whist players by a bank of potted shrubs which had been evacuated from the Palm Court by Edward.

'Take a look at this.' Grasping a heavy plush sofa that stood in the middle of the room beside a table of warped walnut, he dragged it aside. Beneath, the wooden blocks of parquet flooring bulged ominously upward like a giant abscess. Something was trying to force its way up through the floor.

'Good heavens! What is it?'

The Major knelt and removed three or four of the blocks to reveal a white, hairy wrist.

'It's a root. God only knows where it comes from: probably from the Palm Court – one of those wretched tropical things. There's a two-foot gap between this floor and the brick ceiling in the cellars, packed with earth and gravel and wringing wet from some burst drain or waste-pipe.'

'Why d'you think it wants to come up into the lounge?'

'Looking for nourishment, I suppose. There may be lots more of them for all I know. One shudders to think what it may be doing to the foundations.'

'Poor Edward! Come on. Let's see if we can find any more suspicious bulges.'

They set off immediately, walking from one room to the next, along corridors, upstairs and downstairs. In no time this looking for bulges became a marvellous game. They spotted bulges on the walls and floor and even on the ceiling. 'Bulge!' Sarah would cry gaily and point at some offending surface. And then the Major would have to get down on his hands and knees or place his cheek against a cold wall and squint along it in order to adjudicate. Although a number of these bulges proved imaginary, once one started looking for them at the Majestic there was no shortage of genuine ones. Did some of these bulges conceal thrusting roots sent out by one or other of the ambitious plants in the Palm Court? Probably not. However, without digging up tiles and making holes in plaster it was impossible to be sure. Even so it was great fun. Sarah was in the most delightful, effervescent mood and in between bulges she chattered away with all sorts of charming nonsense. What would she do without her gallant Major? How brave he must be to have won all those medals in the war (*what* medals? he wondered, perplexed)! And had he ever in his life seen a more delicately shaped ankle than hers (leaning a hand on his shoulder and lifting the hem of her skirt to show him not only her ankle but her knee as well)? It came from having been a miserable cripple in a wheelchair all her life, which had stopped her getting ugly muscles like a dairy-maid. And she was lost, she said, in admiration of the Major's moustache, which made her think of a privet hedge she had seen in Phoenix Park. What a fine couple they made! she exclaimed as their twin reflections floated over a grimy mirror. What a fine couple! The Major laughed and laughed, as happy as a schoolboy. The afternoon passed delightfully.

Tired out at last, they sank down on one of the red plush sofas in the foyer and chuckled about the grey veil of dust that rose as usual, and about the clock over the reception desk which only told the right time, by accident, once every twelve hours. It was tranquil here, and oddly private, as public rooms often seem when deserted. By the foot of the stairs the statue of Venus glimmered in the subdued light.

Still chuckling, Sarah leaned over and kissed the Major, partly on his moustache then, more seriously and from a better position, on the lips. The Major melted, but cautiously, remembering the remark she had once made about his moustache tasting of garlic. They continued to kiss for a minute or two. Then Sarah sat up abruptly, disengaging herself. The Major straightened up also, to see what was the matter. She was looking over his shoulder with an expression of shock. He turned to see what it was.

Edward was standing a few feet away watching them. He had evidently come down one of the corridors, his footfall muffled by the carpet—but no, the floor was surely tiled, there was no carpet, they should have heard him coming; perhaps, even, Sarah had chosen this very place because one could hear people coming. Edward continued to stand there for the briefest of moments, his face expressionless. Then he turned and vanished, his shoes ringing clearly on the tiles.

Sarah hurriedly got to her feet. As the Major made to do the same she pushed him back and said sharply: 'No, wait here for me. I'll be back in a moment.' With that she hurried after Edward. The Major was left alone.

The foyer had become very silent. The Major got up and went over to peer down the corridor. It was deserted. He listened, holding his breath. Very faintly he heard, or imagined he could hear, the sound of Sarah's voice. Then a door closed. He stood there for a moment or two, then went to sit down again. The minutes passed. Sarah did not come back. 'Really, that's a bit thick.'

He had been there for half an hour by now. The foyer was silent and peaceful. Nothing stirred. Nobody came or went. For a while he played hopefully with the thought that Sarah might have forgotten that she had said she would come back, that she was waiting anxiously for him in some other part of the building. But no, he had to abandon it. It did not hold water. So that was that.

He chose the corridor that led away from Edward's study and as he mechanically followed it he experienced a sharp craving for something sweet. There was a bar of chocolate in his pocket. He gobbled it rapidly. But the acid continued to eat into his soul.

In this unbearably sensitive state he took an unfamiliar route—through a grimy bar that no one ever visited, through a door like a cupboard that contained a flight of wooden uncarpeted steps. It was as if he had been skinned alive; the thought of contact with anyone was more than he could endure. The slightest banal word would produce a scream of agony.

The staircase took him up into a round, many-windowed turret, the floor of bare wooden boards, empty of everything except a carved lion and unicorn, worm-eaten and hanging from a nail. A strong smell of boiled cabbage hung in the air and somehow seemed to belong to the silence.

Another door led into a covered catwalk spanning thirty feet of empty air to another, identical turret. Below lay the dank, sunless remains of a rock-garden. The Major ventured circumspectly on to the catwalk, testing the wooden planks with his foot before putting any weight on them. There were no windows. Slatted trays of apples banked up from floor to ceiling allowed him barely enough room to squeeze through. The smell of apples was overpowering. He picked one up and, sniffing its wrinkled, greasy skin, somehow found this autumnal smell soothing. The turret at the end of the passage was as empty as its sibling. Steps led down from it on to an open veranda on which a man was standing, elbows on the iron rail, smoking a cigarette. It was the tutor.

'Hello.'

The tutor turned towards him and nodded without surprise. He was wearing roughly darned plus-fours and a tweed jacket with pleated, bulging pockets which reached almost to his knees. Since the education of the twins had lapsed once more the Major could not remember having set eyes on him. He was seldom to be seen about the hotel. He ate his meals in some other part of the building, perhaps with the servants. Presumably he was still responsible for cooking the stew of sheeps' heads for the dogs. If he had other duties the Major did not know of them. In all probability he had been forgotten in this remote part of the house and lived his own life, waiting for better days.

'They come here every evening at this time,' the tutor said. The Major had joined him on the veranda and having

277

had a look round now knew where he was. Below was a paved courtyard full of rubbish and dead leaves, although there was no tree in sight. Just round the corner would be the back door to the kitchens. Beyond that, on the other side of a wall, the dogs would be lounging, bored as the ladies of a harem, waiting for someone to come and give them some exercise. Immediately below the veranda yawned four giant, malodorous dustbins. A number of old women dressed in black were rummaging in these bins with fingers as gnarled as hens' feet, head and shoulders swathed in black shawls that concealed their faces.

'They're looking for food. They come up from the beach every evening when it begins to get dark—they can get in easily that way provided there isn't a high tide. I told Mr Spencer about it but he hasn't done anything.'

The Major stared down at the moving black figures, smelling the aromatic scent of the tutor's cigarette. A shrill, incoherent argument had broken out between two of the women over a greasy newspaper containing scraps and bones. Watching them, the Major thought with despair: 'She doesn't love me at all. She doesn't love me at all.'

Below, the argument was at last settled. One of the women withdrew and, squatting on the ground, opened the newspaper to pore over its contents, counting them over and carefully examining the fragments of meat. When she had finished she stowed them in an empty flour bag before returning to the huge bins.

'If you ask me, the cook sometimes throws away perfectly good food on purpose. They can get away with murder if no one keeps an eye on them.'

The Major nodded. His whole life would be spent without Sarah. Although it was now almost dark the black crones, oblivious of the Major's anguish hanging like a bitter fruit a few feet above them, continued to pick deftly through the rubbish.

Mr Lloyd George, speaking at the Guildhall banquet in London last night, referred to the situation in Ireland. He said: 'Before I sit down, if you permit me, I must touch on one of the few disturbed corners of the Empire. I am sure you will not guess what I am referring to (laughter)—Ireland (laughter). I hope soon it will be less disturbed. There we witness the spectacle of organized assassination of the most cowardly character (Hear, hear), firing on men who are unsuspecting, firing from men who are dressed in the garb of peaceable citizens and are treated as such by the officers of the law, firing from behind—cowardly murder (Hear, hear).

'Unless I am mistaken by the steps we have taken, we have murder by the throat (Hear, hear). I ask you not to pay too much heed to the distorted accounts by partisans, who give detailed descriptions of the horror of what they call reprisals but slur over the horrors of murder (Applause). I ask the British public—I am sure it is not necessary to ask them—I apologize for asking them—not to be ready to credit the slanders on the brave men (Hear, hear) who at the peril of their lives are tracking murder in the dark (Hear, hear).

'I am told that the result of the steps we are taking is that you have had more murders than ever in the last few weeks. Why? Before this action was taken in vast tracts of Ireland police were practically interned in their own barracks. They dare not go out. Terror was triumphant. We had to reorganize the police. But as long as men are in dug-outs the casualties are not as great as when they go out to face danger. And the police are going out seeking danger in order to stamp it out (Hear, hear). And believe me they are doing it. They are getting the right men. They are dispersing the terrorists.

'If it is necessary to have further powers we shall seek

them (Hear, hear), for civilization cannot permit a defiance of this kind of the elementary rules of its existence (Hear, hear). These men who indulge in these murders say it is war. If it is war, they, at any rate, cannot complain if we apply some of the rules of war (Loud cheers). In war if men come in civilian clothes behind your lines armed with murderous weapons, intending to use them whenever they can do so with impunity, they are summarily dealt with (Hear, hear). Men who carry explosive bullets are summarily dealt with in war. If it is war, the rules of war must apply. But until this conspiracy is suppressed there is no hope of real peace or conciliation in Ireland and everyone desires peace and conciliation — on fair terms — fair to Ireland, yes, but fair to Britain (Hear, hear). We are offering Ireland not subjection but equality. We are offering Ireland not servitude, but a partnership. An honourable partnership, a partnership in that Empire at the height of its power, a partnership in that Empire in the greatest day of its glory.' (Loud and prolonged cheering.)

❧

The Major should have left for Italy now, but he did not, of course. A letter arrived for him from Cook's answering a variety of questions about trains, hotels and steamers which he could no longer remember having asked. He dutifully read it through twice, but five minutes later he was unable to recall a single word. By this time it was almost the end of November. Icy draughts played around the rooms and corridors of the Majestic and sent their freezing breath up the legs of his trousers as he sat in the lounge.

After some deliberation he wrote Sarah a letter asking if they could meet some time to talk things over — but she did not reply. Presently, he wrote her another letter saying that whatever her virtues, constancy was not one of them (not that she had ever claimed that it was). The only conclusion he could come to, he concluded, was that she was simply a plain, old-fashioned flirt, which was fine, of course, if that was what she wanted to be. A little later he wrote yet another letter disclaiming the one before, which, he regretted to say, had been written in a spirit of bitterness. Neither of these subsequent letters achieved a reply, however, and he thought: 'All I've managed to do is to have an argument with myself in these letters. She'll think me quite mad.' And he forbade himself to write any more. At the very end of November, while getting dressed one morning, he became extremely depressed and one by one the buttons dropped off his shirt, like leaves off a dying plant.

This was also a bad time for Rover, who was gradually being supplanted as the favourite among the harem of dogs. By degrees he was going blind; his eyes had turned to milky blue and he sometimes collided with the furniture. The smells he emitted while sitting at the feet of the whist-players became steadily more redolent of putrefaction. Like the Major, Rover had always enjoyed trotting from one room to another, prowling the corridors on this floor or that. But now, whenever he ventured up the stairs to nose around the upper storeys, as likely as not he would be set upon by an implacable horde of cats and chased up and down the corridors to the brink of exhaustion. More than once the Major found him, wheezing and spent, tumbling in terror down a flight of stairs from some shadowy menace on the landing above. Soon he got into the habit of growling whenever he saw a shadow ... then, as the shadows gathered with his progressively failing sight, he would rouse himself and bark fearfully even in the broadest of daylight, gripped by remorseless nightmares. Day by day, no matter how wide he opened his eyes, the cat-filled darkness continued to creep a little closer.

To share his place another dog had been summoned from the yard, a spindle-legged Afghan hound with pretty golden curls. Little by little this animal usurped the affection dedicated to Rover. True, he had some bad habits. If one managed, in spite of the draughts, to doze off in an armchair after lunch, there was a good chance of being promptly awoken by a warm wet tongue licking one's cheek—but some of the ladies did not seem to mind this. Besides, compared with Rover he smelled like a rose.

As December arrived, a curious thing happened at the Majestic: in a steady trickle more guests began to appear. There had always been the odd one or two coming or going; someone would be stranded in Kilnalough and obliged to stay the night before going on to Dublin in the morning. But now the number of old ladies (and there were even one or two old gentlemen), was increasing noticeably. It was a little while before it dawned on the Major that what they were coming for was ... Christmas! He could not help thinking that far from enjoying a merry Christmas they would be lucky if the place did not fall on their heads. Of course they probably had some idea what to expect. They had heard, perhaps, that the place was not what it used to be; but the habits of a lifetime are hard to break. So many people, now elderly, had banked their few warm and glorious memories of childhood at the Majestic that, even though they knew it was not quite the same, they somehow found it hard to stay away.

At first the Major would sometimes be on hand when they arrived (neither Edward nor Murphy nor any of the servants would be) to cushion the shock. But soon he realized that it was easier to stay away like everyone else. The new arrivals would sort themselves out somehow or other. In the mean-time it was less embarrassing to keep out of their way. Still, the Major would give them a friendly thought as they stood in the shabby magnificence of the foyer beside their mountain of suitcases, probably in silence waiting for someone to come, listening, perhaps, to the heavy tick-tock of the clock over the reception desk (which the Major had wound as a token of welcome) and wondering, could that really be the time? (which of course it couldn't) or glancing with misgiving at the numbered rack of heavy room-keys which, ominously, seemed to be nearly all there—the only thing about the hotel that *was* all there, they might decide later, including Edward and the staff.

They would stand there looking round at the dusty gilt cherubs and red plush sofas and grimy chandelier and statue of Venus. While they waited uneasily for someone to come (for Murphy would have melted into the deepest jungle of the Palm Court at the sight of the carriage laden with heavy suitcases coming up the drive) they would taste the bitter-sweet knowledge that nothing is invulnerable to growth, change and decay, not even one's most fiercely guarded memories.

The Major's relationship with Edward had further dis-improved, no doubt as a result of the kiss in the foyer he had witnessed. Not only was the Major jealous of Edward, but Edward seemed to be jealous of *him*, a fact which for a little while helped the Major to extract a little comfort from Edward's coldness. One day he received an unpleasant surprise, however, when Edward abruptly said: 'Oh, by the way, Sarah's gone away for a couple of weeks or so.'

'Oh, has she?'

'She told me to tell you. And to thank you for your letters.'

The Major nodded calmly and turned away, but he was bleeding internally. He had been betrayed again.

Whatever satisfaction Edward might have got from tor-menting the Major, he appeared anything but cheerful himself. He reacted, moreover, to the increasing number of guests by making himself scarcer than ever. Although his appearance for breakfast, and dinner in the evening, remained inflexible, he was now seldom seen for the rest of the day. On one occasion he murmured to the Major (perhaps he was momentarily ashamed of himself for sadistically revealing the fact that Sarah had confided in him about the Major's letters), as a sort of oblique explanation of everything, that he was devoting himself to his biological studies. The Major had already noticed the parcels of books and equipment that had started to arrive from Dublin. Once or twice he came upon Edward in a remote bedroom surrounded by books and papers. On another occasion he stumbled upon Edward's makeshift laboratory, set up in the bathroom adjoining the bridal suite on the first floor. Afraid lest Edward should think he was snooping, the Major backed out again quickly—but he had had time to glimpse a microscope on the table beside the bath of peeling gilt and black marble in which, no doubt, many a bride of the last century had washed away her illusions of love. Beside the microscope there was a litter of glass slides, a Bunsen burner, some jars containing a greenish fluid, a few sticks of rotting celery and a dead mouse. It was not clear whether the mouse had merely happened, by accident, to expire there or whether it formed a part of Edward's experiments.

The Major was concerned, not only because Edward had become moody and hostile and peculiar again, but also for more practical reasons. After all, it was not *his* job to run the hotel. But it badly needed to be run by somebody. If there was an increase in the number of guests arriving (which was bad enough, since nobody seemed to want them) there were also one or two defections among the regulars, which meant that life at the Majestic was really getting beyond a joke. The Major ventured to suggest to Edward that if any more of the regulars left they might well start a stampede which would leave the place denuded after Christmas.

'I say, do you really think so?' Edward asked, brightening for a moment. But then: 'Some of them have nowhere to go, of course.' He became despondent once more and turned back to the tome he was reading.

'Oh well, if you actually *want* them to go ... ' the Major replied crossly.

The thing that most worried the Major was that the Majestic was literally beginning to fall to pieces. Edward was making no effort to keep it in repair. The Major supposed that the way he looked at the situation (if he looked at it at all) was logical enough. After all, the hotel had over three hundred rooms.

Even if half the building fell down he would still be left with a hundred and fifty – which was more than enough to house himself and the twins and the servants and anyone else who survived the strangulation of the hotel's trade. Meanwhile, no matter how much they might grumble, the residents adapted themselves remarkably well to the nomadic existence of moving from room to room whenever plumbing or furniture happened to fail them.

True, the amenities had gone from bad to worse (not that the Major really noticed any more). The foliage evacuated from the Palm Court now looked like taking command of the residents' lounge; the mirrors everywhere had become more fogged and grimy than ever; the gas mantles which had until recently burned on the stairs and in the corridors had now stopped functioning, so that the ladies had to grope their way to bed with their hearts going pit-a-pat; the soup in the dining-room became clearer and colder as the days went by, and as the cook was left more and more to her own devices bacon and cabbage followed by baked apples appeared more frequently on the menu; outside in the grounds a tall pine keeled over and flattened a conservatory with such a terrible crash that two ladies (Miss Devere and a Mrs Archibald Bradley) packed their bags then and there; on the few remaining tennis courts a peculiarly tough and prolific type of clover continued its advance, so that if anyone had been thinking of playing tennis (which nobody was) they would have found that even the most firmly hit service would never rise more than six inches. But Edward these days had that far-away look in his eyes and if one of the recent arrivals went to complain to him he scarcely seemed to be listening, though he would nod his head rapidly and say from time to time, almost with eagerness: 'I say, do you want your money back?' Or puffing at his pipe and looking at his shoes he would murmur: 'Really, that is most unfortunate ... Let me assure you that no charge will be made ... I mean, none could possibly ... ' and his voice would trail off.

One unseasonably warm day the giant M of MAJESTIC detached itself from the façade of the building and fell four storeys to demolish a small table at which a very old and very deaf lady, an early arrival for Christmas, had decided to take tea in the mild sunshine that was almost like summer. She had looked away for a moment, she explained to Edward in a very loud voice (almost shouting, in fact), trying to remember where the floral clock had been in the old days. She had maybe closed her eyes for a moment or two. When she had turned back to her tea, it had gone! Smashed to pieces by this strange, seagull-shaped piece of cast iron (she luckily had not recognized it or divined where it had come from). Edward made a feeble effort to penetrate the submarine silence in which the old lady lived, muttering an apology and tugging nervously at his thickly matted grey hair. She wanted an explanation, she said, ignoring his words (which she could not hear anyway) but mollified nevertheless to see that his lips were moving and that his expression showed alarm. For a while she continued grumbling and it gradually emerged that her main grievance was that her tea had been demolished along with the table. It appeared that she had spent a good part of the afternoon shuffling along distant corridors trying to find someone willing to take her order for afternoon tea. In the end she had come upon Murphy taking a nap on a royal-blue ottoman behind a screen of ferns in a remote sitting-room (it was probable that he was the only person to know of its existence until that moment). He had been aroused by a poke in the chest from the heavy blackthorn that the old lady had brought with her to punt her frail body over the vast, dustily shining expanse of the ballroom. Unmanned by this experience, he had gone to make tea for her himself. After getting lost a couple of times on the way back, and stopping for a rest at frequent intervals, she had at last regained the veranda. And now this hard-earned tea had been pulverized by a twisted piece of metal which had apparently fallen from the sky! It wasn't good enough.

Edward ordered fresh tea and, anxiously looking up at the other letters clinging insecurely to the building, suggested that she might like to move her chair along the veranda a little to where there was a better view.

As a result of this incident Edward seemed to abandon whatever ambition he might still have nourished of running the place as a hotel. It marked, at any rate, the end of that period during which guests might consider themselves encouraged to come to the Majestic. He did not lock the gates, however, and a trickle of Christmas guests continued to arrive, unencouraged, to claim hospitality.

The Major, unfortunately, was unable to match Edward's indifference. He worried about everything, about the cats proliferating in the upper storeys, about the lamentable state of the roof (on rainy days the carpets of the top floor squelched underfoot), about the state of the foundations, about the septic tank, about the ivy advancing like a green epidemic over the outside walls (someone told him that far from holding the place together, as he had hoped, it would pull it to pieces with all the more speed). It is true that the Major's nerves were in a poor condition; he sometimes wondered himself if he wasn't being unduly alarmist—the Majestic had held up splendidly in all weathers for many years. Presently, however, a piece of stucco ornamentation the size of a man fell from the coping of the roof into the dogs' yard. A foot or two to the left and it would have squashed Foch, a long-haired dachshund.

Anxious to report this, he went in search of Edward. The laboratory had been evacuated from the bridal suite; Edward had set up his table in the very middle of the ballroom. One needed space to allow one's thoughts to expand, he explained. In the bathroom he had felt compressed, his ideas had been restricted, had refused to flow freely.

While the Major told him about the near-disaster to the dog Foch, Edward picked up the dead mouse and absent-mindedly began to squeeze its thorax between finger and thumb like a piece of india-rubber.

'Missed him, did it?' he remarked brightly. 'Well, that was a stroke of luck.'

'Hadn't we better get a mason in to look the place over?'

'That's a capital idea. I expect there's some johnny in Kilnalough who does that sort of thing. I'll get in touch with him.'

That night the Major dreamed that he was in a dirigible. The captain and crew had fallen overboard, leaving only Mrs Rice and himself. Later Mrs Rappaport appeared in the uniform of one of the Bavarian line regiments, together with her marmalade cat, now as big as a sheep. Fortunately she took command and, after bombing Dublin, brought them down safely.

There was no sign of the mason. Instead, a plump and pretty girl wearing a straw boater over her stiff pigtails came wobbling up the drive on a bicycle. It was Viola O'Neill, come to play with the twins. The twins gave her a desultory kiss on the cheek and led her away upstairs. As she went her eyes lingered disconcertingly on the Major, who was standing in the foyer listening sympathetically to an old gentleman in stockinged feet. The Major watched her slender white hand trail up spiral after spiral of the staircase and heaved a melancholy sigh. 'Why couldn't Sarah want me like that?'

'Do you have any idea where they would be?' the old gentleman asked crossly, not for the first time.

'Where what would be?' The Major's mind had wandered again. 'Oh yes, of course, you've lost your shoes. I'll make inquiries.'

The old gentleman, a new arrival at the Majestic, had left his shoes outside his bedroom door. Not only had they *not* been cleaned, they had disappeared altogether! And all his other shoes were in a cabin trunk that had yet to be delivered from the railway station. The Major left him in the foyer and went to ask Murphy to ask the maids.

Later in the day, while hunting languidly for the shoes along one of the upper landings, he opened a door and was

288

greeted by cries of surprise and dismay: through a blue mist of cigarette-smoke he perceived three figures in petticoats. He closed the door again discreetly. He was shocked, however, and thought: 'I must tell Edward. If those girls go on the way they're going ... ' But he was annoyed with Edward and did not see why *he* should have to bring up his daughters for him; let him see to it himself! Besides, young women these days ...

The matter of the shoes was cleared up in the course of the afternoon. It seemed that the cook, on her way down to prepare breakfast, had noticed them outside the gentleman's door and had naturally supposed that he was throwing them away—a perfectly good pair of shoes! She had picked them up and given them to Seán Murphy, who had been digging energetically in them all morning.

At the end of the first week of December Padraig was also sent up to the Majestic to visit the twins, not by old Dr Ryan but by his father who, it turned out, was not only a staunch Unionist but something of a snob into the bargain. The Major intercepted Padraig (who was looking pale and anxious— it was clear he had little appetite for visiting the twins) to ask him about his grandfather.

'Oh, he's well enough. I don't see him so much now. He has a cook and a maid but he'll hardly let anyone into the house.'

'Is he still not speaking to your parents?'

Padraig nodded. 'He's very stubborn and bad-tempered. 'He's told my father he's a traitor to Ireland for approving the British the way he does.'

'I didn't know he was a Sinn Feiner.'

'Ah, you wouldn't mind him,' Padraig said, his eyes flickering uneasily to the landing above, where three pretty faces had appeared over the banister. 'He's very old.'

'Well, here's your guest,' the Major called up sternly. 'I hope you'll look after him properly and behave yourselves.'

Padraig mounted the stairs as if under sentence of death, was seized by the girls and whisked away. The Major went about his business.

Curiously enough, Padraig seemed to enjoy himself. He reappeared on the following day looking cheerful and confident, then again on the day after. Soon he became a frequent visitor. 'It was probably just a question of breaking the ice,' reflected the Major.

The Major's nerves were once more in a deplorable state. He could hardly bear to open the newspaper, for it seemed that the war, which he thought he had escaped, had pursued and caught him after all. Martial law was proclaimed in Cork, Tipperary, Kerry and Limerick. On the night of December 11th Cork was sacked by Auxiliaries and Black and Tans after a patrol had been ambushed. Reading about it, the Major was reminded of how Edward had once said to him that he would welcome a holocaust, that he would like to see everything smashed and in ruins so that the Irish would really taste the meaning of destruction. He read about the scarlet flames that lit up the night sky as the shopping district of Cork was set on fire: firemen's hoses cut by axes; uniformed police and military staggering through the flaming streets with looted goods; Auxiliaries drunk on looted whiskey singing and dancing with local girls in the smoke. It was said that the clock on the tower of the City Hall, rising out of an ocean of flame and smoke, went on striking the hour until dawn, when it finally toppled into the inferno below.

The Major's sleep was as short and disturbed as it had been during his convalescence in hospital, punctuated by nightmares which continually returned him to the trenches. Any sharp noise, a book clapped down flat on a table or a dropped plate, would have him ducking involuntarily like a new recruit. During the hours of daylight, unless he was in the open air or in the safety and warmth of the linen room, he felt himself compelled to keep moving from room to room, corridor to corridor, upstairs and down. Only now did he consider that this compulsion might stem from the irrational fear that a trench-mortar shell was about to land in the spot where he had been standing a moment before, invisible explosions that tracked him from the lounge to the dining-room to the library to the billiard room, on and on, perpetually allowing him to escape by a fraction of a second. 'I must pull myself together or Edward will notice that I'm showing the white feather.'

He needed some distraction—a visit to the theatre. He consulted the *Irish Times*. *Charley's Aunt* was being performed at the Gaiety and the advertisement said that it was 'Enough to make a cat laugh'. But the Major dolefully suspected that it would fail to work on him. Besides, there was a special notice which said that the performance ended nightly at 9.15 p.m. sharp, and the idea of snatching a few quick chuckles before hastening home through the lawless streets did not appeal to him. All the same, he must take himself in hand. For an entire morning he forced himself to remain sitting in one place. The ladies, rebuffed in peevish tones, watched him from a distance and supposed in offended whispers that he had 'got out of bed the wrong side'. After lunch, when he had satisfied his most urgent craving for movement, he did his best to restore himself to their good graces.

Shortly before tea-time he was strolling, hands in pockets, along a corridor on the third floor (since putting his foot through the floor-boards he seldom ventured higher) when a door opened round the corner, releasing a gale of laughter followed by footsteps and a rustling of skirts. A moment later and he had collided with a slim, dark girl who came running round the corner, laughing over her shoulder. In the dim light the Major failed to see her until the last moment. He just had time to catch her in his arms to prevent her falling.

'I beg your pardon!'

The girl's laughter changed to surprise and dismay. She disengaged herself and stood back awkwardly. The Major peered at her in the twilight. She was wearing a charming dress of black velvet with a white ruff and white lace cuffs; from the ruff her neck rose, slender and flushed, to a delicate pouting face. A fragrant perfume hung in the air. Abruptly, she turned and fled back into the room that the laughter was coming from. There was some urgent whispering (it was the twins and Viola, of course) and then the hilarity became greater than ever. The Major, also laughing, put his head round the door. By this time he had realized that the 'girl' was Padraig.

'Brendan, what d'you think? Doesn't he make a gorgeous girl?'

'We're all frightfully jealous of him.'

Smiling (though still a tiny bit dismayed by the pleasure he had derived from touching 'her' soft body a moment earlier), the Major agreed that black velvet suited Padraig to perfection. It was some time before the mortified Padraig could be enticed out of the adjoining dressing-room. Indeed, it took a great deal of cajolery from the girls and a hearty appeal from the Major before he would agree to show himself again. And then what laughter there was when Charity lifted the hem of his skirt to show the Major what slender, well-turned ankles he had! And his hair was so fine and curled so naturally that if he grew it a bit longer he wouldn't have to wear a wig at all! Besides, according to some magazine they'd been reading there were girls in London who had cut off all their hair and wore it short like men.

'So with his lovely soft hair ... '

'And his skin and colouring ... '

'And his dark eyes with their long lashes ... '

'And my ankles, don't forget them,' added Padraig.

'And his ankles, of course, we mustn't forget them, and his *hands*, just look how slender and white they are!'

'With all those things there's hardly any difference between him and a girl *at all*!' cried Viola enthusiastically.

There was a moment of silence after this remark, perhaps for reflection that there were, after all, one or two small but essential differences (although a well-brought-up girl like Viola might not be expected to know much about them). However, the general good humour was such that in no time at all everyone was bubbling over with laughter and compliments once more and Faith was showing the blushing but gratified Padraig how a girl should walk: this walking was more like gliding, the twins explained (and they ought to know, they'd been to enough different schools with enough deportment classes). They made him walk to and fro with a book balanced on the top of his head until he could move without it falling off. Padraig took to this with a splendid natural aptitude and soon they could safely balance a glass of water on top of the book without him spilling a drop.

Presently someone decided that Padraig should be taken on a tour of the hotel to see if any of the ladies recognized him. He should go on the Major's arm! What a brain-wave! But the Major turned out to be a spoil-sport and refused point-blank.

'Oh, oh, *why*?' pleaded the girls.

'Because.'

'Because *what*?'

'Just because.'

And there was no shifting him. Usually the twins could get round him without difficulty, just by telling him that they thought him handsome and interesting, that he looked like Alcock, say, or Brown. But this time, for some reason, he remained adamant. Well, never mind. They would take him on a tour themselves!

The Major, like the spoil-sport he was, tried to dissuade them, but he did not make his case very eloquently. He kept pointing out that although a joke was a joke, enough was enough, and that sort of thing. Padraig, he suggested hopefully, should put his clothes back on and then everyone should think of another, different, game.

'But he's got his clothes *on*!' screamed the girls indignantly. The Major was *too* boring!

'Yes, I've got them *on*,' agreed Padraig.

Were there any actual *reasons*, the girls wanted to know, enunciating carefully, as if to an idiot, why Padraig shouldn't be taken on a tour of the hotel? Well, yes, there were reasons, but they were so nebulous that the Major found it difficult to specify them. They were certainly not tangible enough to satisfy the girls.

So the tour got under way, Viola leading the way with long button-booted strides, displaying her pearly teeth like the principal boy in a pantomime. Padraig followed with a twin on each arm, chuckling or whispering into one ear or the other while he himself looked as radiant as Joan of Arc and prepared to respond to anything the situation might present.

And as it turned out, Padraig had an enormous success with the old ladies, which caused the Major to reflect that the twins were probably right: he was a stick-in-the-mud, a spoil-sport and a kill-joy. What a fuss they made of him! They patted his shoulder and kissed his brow and made minute adjustments to his wig, which was the only part of him that 'rather spoiled the effect', they thought (it was a cheap theatrical wig stolen by Faith from some school dramatic society). They delved into their handbags and gave him chocolates to nibble that had that rather peculiar musty taste of perfume and moth-balls that old ladies' chocolates always have. It was wonderful, they thought, how he seemed to know what to do just by instinct, keeping his knees together and sitting up straight and so forth. They were so delighted with him, in fact, that they were loath to let him continue his tour and made him promise to come back. He agreed, of course, and came back quite soon.

The rest of his tour had turned out to be something of an anticlimax. With his retinue he had marched into the ballroom and wheeled several times round Edward's makeshift laboratory. But Edward was engrossed in assembling some extra-ordinary piece of machinery with pipes and tubes and an old clockwork barometer with graph-drum and inking-needle and pieces of rubber, evidently for some experiment he wanted to make. Consequently he paid no attention whatsoever. The maidservants, of course, smiled at him and showed their dimples, but they were too shy to speak to him, so that was no good. Curiously enough, Mr Norton showed no interest at all; he merely glanced up from his newspaper and raised his wicked old eyebrows. One had to assume that after his life of debauchery he must know the difference between Padraig and the real thing, so this poor reaction dampened their enthusiasm a trifle. Back to the old ladies, then, to have their confidence restored. All in all, and taking, as one must, the rough with the smooth, they had reason to be satisfied.

By now, unfortunately, it was time for Padraig to go home for his supper and so he had to get changed back into his other clothes. But he would come again on the following day; there were still lots of different dresses for him to try on—all Angela's clothes, in fact, which the twins still stoutly declined to wear. Viola had to go home too and said she'd escort Padraig back to his house. With all the excitement and amusement they had been having, with all the good cheer, one tended to forget that these days the roads could be dangerous.

Soon it was time for dinner at the Majestic and the hotel guests began to assemble in the dining-room. It was cold there. A stiff east wind was blowing off the sea and, filtering in through the cracks between the French windows, caused the heavy curtains to move back and forth like impatient spectators in the shadows. In the branched silver candlesticks the flames constantly sputtered from yellow to blue under the compulsion of draughts; the light they provided was supplemented by an oil lamp on each table. One could see one's breath against the surrounding darkness; the tureen of soup on the table belched steam like a locomotive.

The ladies waited, pinched and shivering in layers of shawls and stoles, fingers buried in muffs, crowding all together around the moaning fireplace in which huge, unevenly cut sods of turf blazed without warmth. Now and again a backdraught of pungent whitish smoke would drive the ladies back with averted faces, but somehow this puff of smoke ascending into the darkness, and the smell of turf-ash, made the room seem fractionally warmer. The fireplace groaned mournfully and everyone waited for Edward to come.

It was his habit to appear punctually at seven o'clock. Except when he happened to be away for the day the Major had never known him to miss attending the evening meal. This punctuality of Edward's was the very spine of the hotel: in a sense, it held the whole place together. Slates might sail off the roof in a high wind, the gas mantles might stop functioning on the landings, but Edward's appearance at dinner was immutable. Was there something wrong? An accident? At ten past seven one of the maids appeared with a note asking the Major if he wouldn't mind taking charge. Edward was busy. The ladies exchanged significant glances. It was one thing (said these glances) to be in the trenches with one's commanding officer, quite another thing to be there when one knew that he was toasting himself in front of a warm fire behind the lines somewhere.

While Angela was still alive the Spencers had eaten at a table separated by the width of the dining-room from the guests, but now, drawn together by death, growing chaos, and the advancing winter, everyone ate together at two long tables, Edward normally at the head of one, the Major at the head of the other. According to the ritual the Major now picked up the heavy handbell and rang it vigorously, before crossing to the small door concealed in the oak panelling. He held it open and waited for Mrs Rappaport to step out. She did so, followed by the marmalade 'kitten' (now a powerfully built cat). Having taken hold of his arm, she allowed herself to be led to the table. In silence the Major helped her into her chair at the end of the table nearest to the fire, tied a napkin round her neck and put a silver spoon in her hand. A stool had been placed beside her chair for the cat, which had recently become too big and cumbersome to remain on her lap while she was eating. Disasters had occurred; hot soup had dribbled on to its striped back; once while it was sleeping peacefully a portion of scalding shepherd's pie had slid off a fork and dropped like a poultice into one of its ears.)

The Major said grace and took his seat at the other end of the table.

'Where's Daddy?' whispered Faith.

Beneath his thick growth of moustache the Major's mouth shaped the words: 'Busy. Eat up.'

'Busy doing what?'

The Major frowned but offered no reply. It hardly mattered what Edward was doing. The important thing was that he had broken one of his own rules.

'Cheer up, Brendan,' said Charity and reached under the table to pat his knee. The Major frowned more sternly than ever and, lifting a spoonful of tepid grey soup to his lips, drank it down with a slight shudder, like medicine. 'He's broken one of his own rules,' he thought again, not without a certain bleak satisfaction. 'He's beginning to go to pieces.'

Next day Edward was by turns impatient, irascible and resigned. His experiments were being baulked at every turn. The trouble seemed to be that Murphy, whom he wanted to perform his experiments upon, was being difficult.

'The man has no apprehension of the needs of scientific inquiry,' he said. The Major noticed that look of mild self-mockery, which had so surprised him at their first meeting, pass fleetingly over Edward's leonine features. But then his face hardened and he added petulantly: 'Pretty soon the bloody servants will be giving *us* orders.'

'What exactly is this contraption?'

On Edward's table lay the partly dismantled graph-drum from the barometer. The inking-nibs had been rearranged to connect with a tangle of wires and rubber pipes; one of these pipes was attached to a glass funnel containing water and a wooden float, terminating in a deflated rubber balloon.

'I've been trying to reproduce some experiments Cannon made before the war on hunger and thirst. He was the chap who discovered that hunger-pangs come from a periodic contraction of the stomach. He got one of his students to swallow a balloon like this, inflated later, of course ... then with each contraction the balloon in the stomach would be compressed, driving the air up along this tube, passing through the esophagus and in turn making the float rise by forcing up the water-level. Pretty ingenious, really. The trouble is that the wretched Murphy simply refuses to swallow the damn balloon.'

'Ah.'

'The point is that Cannon used a young man for his experiments. I wanted to see whether the average sixty-second period between contractions would be different in an old man like Murphy.'

Hands thrust in pockets, the Major gloomily surveyed Edward's machine. On his table there was no sign of the dead mouse. Presumably it had been devoured by the cats during the night.

'I took a lot of trouble building this,' Edward added with resentment. 'One feels badly at being let down at the last moment.'

'Look, Edward, I've been meaning to ask you about the mason. Did you ever get hold of him?'

'Who? Oh, yes, you're quite right. It went clean out of my head. Thanks for reminding me. I'll see to it today.'

Edward frowned and got to his feet, picking up a glass measuring-jar which he tossed absently from hand to hand. Presently he said: 'There's another experiment I'd like to try ... one on thirst. There are lots of conditions that result in thirst apart from the simple lack of water—wounds, for instance. Severely wounded men very often complain of a raging thirst. The one that interests me, though, is the sensation of being thirsty through fear, the mouth going dry and so forth. There are lots of instances recorded but nobody has ever actually measured it to my knowledge.'

'How can it be measured?'

'Just a question of measuring the amount of saliva available in the mouth in the normal everyday state and comparing it with the amount of saliva produced in a state of fear.' Edward's face became faintly animated. 'This might be a small but significant contribution to scientific knowledge. Of course Murphy's already deuced peculiar and one doesn't want to give him a heart attack ... '

'Look, you won't forget about the mason, will you? We don't want the place to fall down.'

'I'll see to it right away.'

Unhopefully the Major wandered out of the ballroom, leaving Edward to ruminate.

Meanwhile the days were slipping away towards Christmas and still nothing had been done about decorations. The ladies became sulky and despondent at the comfortless prospect of spending the festival at the Majestic. Miss Staveley talked openly of going to stay at the Hibernian in Dublin where they knew how to do things properly. She might have gone, too, had it not been common knowledge at the Majestic that respectable ladies were being raped by Sinn Feiners every day of the week in Dublin; indeed, the aunt of someone's friend had only the other day been violated by a Sinn Feiner posing as a licensed masseur. Miss Staveley had no desire to suffer a similar fate, so she stayed on at the Majestic, but with bad grace.

At length the Major decided that something must be done, so he took the twins, Viola, Padraig, and Seán Murphy into the park to collect holly and mistletoe, while he himself chopped down a puny and naked Christmas tree he had noticed near the lodge. At the sight of this activity the ladies cheered up and soon they were helping to make paper decorations. The residents' lounge became a hive of industry. Miss Johnston mounted the largest and most drastic shopping expedition hitherto, and returned from Kilnalough with a great supply of glass ornaments and coloured ribbons. In due course this enthusiasm spread to everyone, servants and guests alike; even the newcomers became eager to lend a hand. The old ladies underwent a gay metamorphosis and showed themselves full of energy, humming and singing as they worked, reaching up with trembling hands to pin mistletoe strategically over doors or intrepidly making their way up shivering step-ladders to hang coloured paper streamers. The Major watched them and admired their daring. Whenever a step-ladder began to get a fit of the shakes he would spring forward and anchor it firmly, but then perhaps another step-ladder would begin to rattle on the other side of the room and he would have to watch helplessly, with that mixture of resentment and admiration one feels as one watches trapeze artistes sailing dangerously here and there under the circus roof.

There was only one casualty. One of the less prominent ladies, Mrs Bates, fell off a high stool while trying to deposit a glass fairy on top of the grandfather clock in the writing-room and broke her hip. By an unusual stroke of luck there happened to be a young doctor staying in the hotel overnight on his way back to Dublin. He took charge of everything and Mrs Bates was whisked out of sight before her fate had time to affect the morale of her fellow-guests. A few days later the Major motored over to visit her in the Valebridge nursing-home ... but he was too late. She had caught pneumonia and died in the meantime. 'Poor Mrs Bates.' Ankle-deep in a drift of dead leaves, he stood outside the nursing-home and sucked his moustache distractedly.

In the midst of all this cheerful activity and confusion Edward moved like a sleepwalker, silent and remote. If you called to him: 'Where's the hammer?' or 'Have you seen my scissors?' he would shake his head wordlessly, not bothering to understand. He seemed unaware that the grim walls around him were blossoming into festive colour. He remained where he was, at his table in the middle of the cavernous ballroom, slumped in a chair with a book open on his knee. The ladies, awed by his silence, tiptoed around the perimeter of the room as they executed their decorations. One day Miss Archer came to the Major and said: 'He has a shotgun.'

'Who has a shotgun?'

'Edward. It's on his table in the ballroom.'

'Good God, what does he want that for?'

They stared at each other in consternation. Later, while Edward was out visiting his piglets, he went to have a look. It was perfectly true. On Edward's table there lay a shotgun, broken and unloaded. Beside it a dead frog lay on its back with its legs in the air, exposing a flabby white stomach.

All this time Padraig and Viola O'Neill visited the Majestic every day and roamed around with the twins, who had swiftly tired of helping with the decorations. For a few days they continued playing their game of dressing up Padraig as a girl. All of Angela's clothes were spilled out of their trunks, cupboards and packing-cases; the dresses that suited him were put in one pile, those that didn't in another. For a while they found this engrossing enough, but presently the job was finished. Just as interest was once again beginning to subside Viola remembered that they still had to consider the rest of Padraig's clothing, his underwear, petticoats, corsets and so forth. Soon they were all bubbling with hilarity as they struggled with eye-hooks and tugged on the strings of Angela's corsets – not that Padraig's shapely body needed any artificial correction of course, but they thought they might as well do the thing properly. After a day or two of trying to persuade the Major to go upstairs and have a look at Padraig clad variously in a camisole, a nightdress, and Angela's 1908-style swimming-costume (all of which invitations the Major declined firmly) the question of underwear similarly began to pall. It was clearly time to look for a new game.

The girls mooned about aimlessly for the next three or four days, telling people that they were bored and asking them for money – so that they could run away to Dublin and get raped like everyone else (they weren't too sure what this meant but it sounded interesting). Padraig, however, continued to dress up and sit with the ladies or glide along corridors with whispering skirts. Indeed, he had become such a familiar sight that scarcely anyone paid any attention to him now beyond, say, an absent-minded smile or a 'Yes, dear ... that *is* a lovely dress.' The truth was that most of the ladies had probably forgotten by this time that he wasn't, in fact, a girl. Only once did he provoke a strong reaction: Mr Norton unaccountably exploded with anger one day and shouted: 'Get out of my sight, you filthy little swine!' Everyone considered this to be amazing behaviour, but then old Mr Norton had always been considered uncouth, in spite of his mathematical genius. Padraig was made a special fuss of that day to compensate for his hurt feelings.

One bright, chilly December afternoon the Major came upon Padraig on one of the upper landings, standing mournfully by a window. He was dressed in a glistening evening dress of powder-blue satin with gloves to match and he wore a string of pearls round his neck. The Major felt sorry for him. He looked very lonely standing there by himself. With a sigh the Major moved to the window to see what he was looking at. The view from here was almost identical with that from Angela's room: there stood her 'two elms and an oak', the oak supposed to be a hundred and fifty years old, the edge of a path where the dogs sometimes wandered ... and beyond, beyond what Angela's clouding eyes had been able to descry, the ground sloped down to a wood. Walking up from this wood were the twins and Viola, escorted by a couple of young Auxiliaries who were laughing and prancing about them, throwing their berets in the air like schoolboys. The girls clung tightly together but looked charmed nevertheless. They had found a new game.

In the course of the next few days the Major glimpsed them all together once or twice again, walking and laughing in some distant part of the grounds. Sometimes Padraig would be in the vicinity too, not with them but sulking hopefully at a distance (ignoring them when they shouted at him, however).

The Major clicked his tongue. He should really tell Edward that the twins were meeting the young Auxiliaries. But these days it was no use telling Edward anything! Moreover, Edward was taking advantage of his good nature, there was no doubt about it, leaving him to do everything while he amused himself chopping up rats in the ballroom. Depression came down on the Major like a blanket of fog, suffocating him. What dreadful days these were! The future of the British Isles could never have seemed so dismal since the Romans had invaded; there was trouble everywhere. The ultimate stunning blow arrived just two days before Christmas with the news that, in spite of courageous resistance by Hobbs and Hendren, England had been defeated in the first test match in Australia by the appalling total of three hundred and seventy-seven runs.

And then it was Christmas, which, at least to begin with, turned out to be a more cheerful day than anyone had the right to expect. Edward, who had been expected to spend the day in the ballroom with his rats ignoring the festivities, surprised everyone by the way he bustled around full of cheerful greetings for whoever crossed his path. His good spirits persisted throughout the morning service in church: he lustily sang the Christmas hymns and repeatedly nodded with agreement during the sermon (the pleasure and virtue to be found in turning the other cheek). He cast twinkling glances at the surrounding pews and smiled indulgently at the young children fretting impatiently beside their parents. Certainly he talked too loudly at the church-door afterwards, and again during the gathering for sherry in the lounge before lunch, but compared with what one might have expected ... ! The Major heaved a genuine, though tentative, sigh of relief.

After lunch it occurred to the Major to ask Padraig how Dr Ryan was getting along. It was a considerable time since he had heard any news of the old man.

'Oh, much the same really.'

'Hasn't he made it up with your parents then?'

'No.' Padraig shook his head. He was ill at ease. His parents had given him boxing-gloves for Christmas and they were hung round his neck by their laces like swollen severed hands. A small fat boy in short trousers called Dermot had arrived two days earlier to spend the holiday with his parents and by a singular misfortune he had also been given boxing-gloves. The twins, aided by two attentive, curly-headed young men in mufti (whom the Major recognized, nevertheless, as the Auxiliaries from the garden), were ruthlessly trying to promote an afternoon fight between him and Padraig, an encounter for which neither of them had any stomach.

In the middle of the afternoon the Major took the Standard and motored over to the doctor's house to see how he was faring. Padraig had at first agreed to come with him in the hopes of avoiding his boxing-match with Dermot. But then Dermot's mother had intervened to say that she wanted her son to 'save' some of his toys for the morrow, otherwise he would quickly get bored and complain that he had nothing to do. After a period of reflection Dermot elected to save his boxing-gloves. Besides, as Miss Archer pointed out tactfully, it was wrong to fight on Christmas Day ... that sort of thing should be postponed until St Stephen's Day.

'Very well, then,' said Matthews (one of the curly-headed young men), 'the boxing will be for tomorrow.' The other curly-headed young man was called Mortimer and his curls were almost as blond as those of the twins. He had frank blue eyes, moreover, good manners and a pleasant smile, not to mention the fact that he had been to a public school. It was clear to the Major that Mortimer did not owe his rank simply to the war-shortage of officers: this young chap was quite plainly officer material and could certainly be trusted to keep his somewhat more dubious companion, Matthews, under control. The Major was relieved about this—there was no telling what the twins might get up to with a little encouragement.

Winking at Padraig, the two young men took the twins off to play touch rugger in the ballroom with Viola and another young man, using an old Teddy bear belonging to the twins as a ball. Dermot and Padraig shyly exchanged a glance of mutual dislike and despair.

The Major found Dr Ryan at home and by himself as he had expected. What he had not expected was to find the old man in the kitchen laboriously trying to prepare his Christmas dinner. Where on earth were the bloody servants? the Major wanted to know. They had no business leaving a man of his age to fend for himself.

'Sent 'em home,' grunted the doctor.

'But for heaven's sake! You can't cook for yourself! And how about your family?'

The feud with his family was maintained, it seemed. 'Unionists!'

'Look here, why don't you come back to the Majestic with me ... If you like we could take that chicken of yours with us and get the kitchen staff to see to it.'

But the old man was obstinate. He'd sworn he'd not go near the place again! He'd not sit down with the British! He'd not have fellow-Irishmen working to feed his stomach while they had nothing to put in their own! The Major listened to this nonsense with consternation. The old man was becoming a Bolshevist in his dotage!

While they talked Dr Ryan scraped feebly at a potato he was trying to peel. A man of his class peeling his own potatoes! This was too much for the Major. Elbowing the old doctor aside, he seized the potato from him and began to peel it in his place, and then another and another (by this time he had taken off his jacket). Dr Ryan, unable to leave well alone, tottered back and forth from the pantry collecting things.

'Will ye not stop and eat with me, Major?' But the Major had eaten already; his only interest was to see that the doctor ate. Still, he might stay to sample a little, see what it tasted like. And he became absorbed in the preparation of the meal—

305

which luckily presented no great difficulties since the servants had left the chicken stuffed and it had only to be put in the oven. Ah, but there was no bread, except for the remains of a pan loaf, hard as steel, that was serving as a paperweight in the doctor's study. They would have to make do with the potatoes and Brussels sprouts. And so he set to work again. But all that peeling and chopping took him an age, and Dr Ryan kept wanting to help, getting in the way and giving advice, as if the Major didn't know what he was doing, which was more than the perspiring and exasperated Major could stand.

'Look, why don't you go and sit down and leave it to me?' he exploded at last.

But the old man had become bad-tempered too. He was probably hungry, although he said he wasn't. His mind had begun to wander as well ... Fanny would soon be here, he said, with her mother and father, they were expected for Christmas. The Major did not know who Fanny was. He supposed she must be the doctor's wife, dead, though, forty years or more. And no one did come, which in the circumstances was perhaps just as well.

But then the doctor seemed to realize that he was being disagreeable and wandered away, returning almost immediately with two wine glasses and a bottle of sherry. So they had a drink and wished each other Merry Christmas ... However, while the chicken was in the oven and they were waiting in vague desperation (the Major, too, had become horribly hungry, as if he hadn't eaten for days) for the wretched thing to cook, the old doctor, although he was plainly trying to be nice to the Major, kept bursting out 'British blackguard!', which distressed the Major considerably.

Soon a tantalizing smell pervaded the kitchen, the smell of roasting chicken—but if anything this made them more hungry and bad-tempered than ever and, besides, there was still a great deal of work to be done. It was time, the Major judged, to put the vegetables on to boil. Should one put salt in the water with them?

'British blackguard!' muttered the doctor irritably. But then his mood changed and he murmured almost tenderly that the Major shouldn't worry, that life was a fugitive affair at best, he should know, he'd been a doctor for sixty years ... Then he shuffled away to the lavatory, for the cold weather and the port he had been drinking made him incontinent, and when he came back he was saying that, really, people are insubstantial, they never last. He himself wouldn't last much longer, but that was a law of Nature, the body wears out ... the Major wouldn't last very long either, but one had to accept it and make way for one's children and grandchildren ... he himself had accepted it long ago because he had had to, long ago, when he was still a young fellow of the Major's age. But here he was interrupted by the need to go to the lavatory once more, though he had only just been there, and the Major poked desperately with a fork at the bubbling potatoes and Brussels sprouts which were still as hard as stones. Strange, said the doctor coming back, to think that a beautiful woman who seemed like a solid thing, solid as granite, was really no more solid than a flaring match, a burst of flame, darkness before and darkness after ... People are insubstantial, they never last ... And so he rambled on while the Major ground his teeth and prodded the vegetables with a fork.

At long last everything was ready and they sat down to eat at the kitchen table. Once more they toasted each other and really, thought the Major as they began to eat, it wasn't half bad considering everything, though the potatoes were still not completely cooked. The doctor was tired, however, and could eat very little—the wine had no doubt made him sleepy. The Major helped him back to his armchair in the other room and made up the fire, banking it down with wet slack so that it would last through the evening. Then he carved some breast of chicken and left it on a plate by the old man's side with a glass of port, in case he should feel hungry later on. Dr Ryan was dozing already, his head lolling against one of the wings

307

of his armchair. The Major said goodbye, that he would call in tomorrow and perhaps bring Padraig. Without opening his eyes the old man made a faint, murmured reply that might have been: 'British blackguard!'

Edward had fired his shotgun at Murphy! He had gone berserk and tried to slay the elderly manservant. The strain had been too much for him.

All afternoon the downpour had continued, so that by now the roads were flanked with bubbling pools; the wheels of the Standard sent out great bow-waves that saturated the hedges and stone walls. But the Major's eyes were on the winding road ahead, alert for signs of an ambush. No civilized person, of course, would wait behind a hedge in a downpour on the offchance that an ex-British-Army-officer might come driving by. But were the Irish civilized? The Major was not prepared to risk his life on the assumption that they were.

Nevertheless he reached the Majestic without incident. It was as he strode cheerfully into the lounge and found himself surrounded by pale excited faces that he realized that something was amiss. Everyone was talking at once, so that it was a few moments before he was able to understand what it was all about. Edward had summoned Murphy about an hour ago. After a brief, heated discussion a terrible boom had reverberated throughout the building. A few minutes later Murphy had staggered out of the ballroom more dead than alive (though physically unscathed) and was now lying down somewhere.

'Where's Edward?'

'Still in the ballroom. But you'd better not go in.'

'Don't worry. It was probably just an accident. I'll go and have a talk with him.'

In the ballroom it was still light enough, thanks to the glass dome of the roof, for the Major to see Edward sitting at his table in the middle of the floor. He was scribbling rapidly on the top sheet of a thick stack of paper; a number of curling pages lay beside him, already written on. As the Major watched, he came to the end of a page, threw it aside without waiting for the ink to dry and immediately started on another, the nib of his pen making a faint rasping sound, barely audible against the dull, steady roar of the rain drumming on the glass roof.

The Major took a few steps forward. Scattered on the parquet floor around Edward's table were a number of pinging jam-jars, two or three of which were already brimming. But more jam-jars were needed. Here and there shining puddles had already formed.

'Edward.' The Major advanced with caution. 'What's all this I hear about you firing a shotgun at Murphy?'

'Eh? Oh, it's you, Brendan. Watch out where you're walking. There's a drop of rain coming in. Wait, I'll get some light.' He crossed to the grand piano and came back with some candlesticks which he arranged in a battery around his writing-table. He struck a match, touching off one candle after another until his desk shone like a lighthouse in the gathering gloom.

'It was just an experiment. Are they making a fuss?'

'They are a bit. You can't really blame them, you know.'

'They'll get over it. As far as Murphy's concerned it had to be a shock, mind you. There was no other way of doing it. But I gave him a couple of quid, so I don't suppose he has any complaints. He'll be as right as rain in an hour or two.'

Edward seemed calm and pleased with himself. The candlelight, however, throwing the lines and wrinkles of his face into sharp relief, gave him a haggard, insane look.

'It's never been done before. Never actually *measured*, that is ... so, of course, as far as science is concerned it hasn't strictly speaking existed until now. Plenty of subjective reports, but they won't wash for your scientist. If you want my opinion, Brendan, nobody has ever *dared* to do it before. In Cannon's book *The Wisdom of the Body* he mentions a person who was captured by Chinese bandits and thought he was going to be shot. *His* mouth went dry, of course, but he didn't bother to find out *how* dry ... He was a scientist too, I gather. Still, I suppose it's understandable.'

'You mean you threatened to shoot Murphy.'

'He believed me too. Went as white as a sheet. For a moment I was afraid he was going to pass out, which would have ruined the whole thing. I had to keep him talking for a while so that he could get a grip on himself ... but not too much of a grip. Told him the first thing that came into m' head ... that his service had been unsatisfactory and so forth, and that he had to be dealt with. Then I pulled both triggers. It made one hell of a noise ... even scared me. I'd taken the shot out, of course, so it was only the caps going off. Even so, it brought down a cloud of plaster from the ceiling ...' He gestured to a corner of the room where the Major perceived what looked like a snowdrift glimmering in the shadows. 'The place needs doing up a bit.' He cleared his throat and got to his feet as a drop of rain from a new leak in the roof hurtled into the area of light and drummed on the white stomach of the frog lying beside the ink-well. Picking up one of the jam-jars from the floor, he edged the frog aside with it, then sat down again.

'Anyway, I dropped the gun and got him to spit out what saliva he could manage into the measuring-glass. D'you realize that he could only produce four c.c.? It's incredible! Here, have a look. It may seem a bit more than that because I'm afraid a few drips of rain got into it before I realized what was happening.'

The Major looked dubiously at the white froth in the measuring-jar.

'I'm drafting a paper to send to the Royal Society. Maybe you'd like to see it before I send it off.'

'Yes, I would,' the Major said.

Above them, against the streaming, echoing bubble of blackness, the rain increased in intensity. Presently Edward said: 'I always wanted to make a contribution, however small.'

The Major said nothing. Together they listened to the steady, musical drips in the jam-jars around them.

Nineteen-twenty-one. The rain continued to fall virtually without interruption into the New Year. By now most of the seasonal guests had disappeared, manifestly dissatisfied with their stay. But oh, if they had only known (reflected the Major) how much worse it might easily have been! He himself was so hardened that he no longer found it easy to sympathize about such matters as cold rooms and cold food, dirty towels and damp sheets. Besides, the near-escape of the dog Foch was still at the back of his mind. Compared with death itself these things pale into insignificance.

In spite of the continuing bad weather Edward refused to remove himself from the ballroom. The Major looked in on him once or twice and saw him sitting there, calmly dissecting a toad under an umbrella. The jam-jars had proliferated around him, so that now, if one listened carefully, one could hear a symphony of drips against the percussion of rain from above. As for the toad, it reminded the Major only too horribly of things he still saw in his nightmares—indeed, for all its resemblance to a toad it might have been strawberry jam scooped out of one of the jars and thinly spread on Edward's marble slab. As for the old ladies, they now had no other resource than to grit their teeth and survive as best they could the awful weeks between Christmas and Easter, keep their noses above the surface somehow or other until the green leaves were back on the trees. As for Padraig, he had not been seen for a few days. Although Dermot had by now gone back to school with his boxing-gloves, the two young Auxiliaries, Matthews and Mortimer, claimed to have found another prospective sparring-partner for him, the son of a farmer of the region—a lad who, although only twelve years old, was reputed to have to shave twice a day. As for the Major himself, the start of the new year could not help but fill him with a young man's irrational optimism. Perhaps nineteen-twenty-one was the year he would get married (to Sarah, naturally, since matrimony involving any other girl was quite unthinkable) – but even if he did not (and he could not escape the unpleasant fact that for the moment he did not even know where she was), even if he did not, it was still a new year. Something new was sure to happen.

Moreover, any new year was a gift that the Major somehow felt that he did not deserve. Although the *Weekly Irish Times* no longer published those inky photographs of dead men on the front page, the last stragglers having by now made up their minds whether to live or die (and those that were going having gone), he still had the same grateful but uneasy sensation. 'You must do the living for all the others as well as yourself,' a kindly Scottish doctor had once said to him in hospital, trying to coax him back out of the cold areas of chagrin and indifference where his mind had chosen to stray. But of course that was easier said than done, particularly at the Majestic.

The weather continued bitterly cold for the next few days. Getting out of bed in the morning, taking a bath with an icy draught sighing underneath the bathroom door, became an agony. The Major's teeth chattered and he thought with physical distress of sunshine and Italy. People spoke little during this cold weather; the ladies curled themselves up in tight little bundles and compressed their lips to preserve every particle of warmth in their bodies. Twelfth Night came and went, but nobody thought of taking down the decorations. One had to keep one's arms tightly hugging one's sides these days; lift them for a moment and the chilly sword of pneumonia would run you through.

Not only for the ladies was this a bad time. Padraig too was in despair. His father was now talking of having him apprenticed as a clerk in a solicitor's office in Dublin, a prospect which no person of sensitivity could tolerate. Faith told the Major that Padraig was going about telling the ladies that he would prefer to dress himself in a scarlet cloak and leap from the battlements of the Majestic. The Major told her to tell him on no account to go near the battlements, they weren't safe. The ornamental façade might give way at any moment.

Wearing mittens and a Balaclava helmet, the Major sat in the residents' lounge on a bright February morning reading of the day's disasters in the *Irish Times*. Looking up, he noticed that Edward had come into the room. He gave a violent start. With Edward was Sarah! Her face was pale and tense; she looked unhappy. Edward stared sightlessly past her, but his lips were moving rapidly as he spoke to her in an undertone. Only for an instant, as he came to the end of what he was saying, did he allow his eyes to focus on her face before retiring to scan the empty reaches of the room once more. Sarah was protesting bitterly about something. The Major dropped his eyes and pretended to be engrossed in the newspaper. Sarah stood talking with Edward near the fire for a few moments. The Major was aware that her glance rested on him once or twice, as if waiting for the moment when he would look up and their glances would meet. However, he continued to scrutinize the *Irish Times*, frowning with concentration. Presently he was aware that she and Edward were moving away again through the chairs and tables towards the door. When he at last permitted himself to look up they were no longer there. 'What a fool I am! It would have been much better if I'd gone up to her and made some cheerful remark and then wandered away again, so that she'd have realized how little she means to me since she told Edward about the letters I wrote her.'

Edward's experiments were languishing once again. His toad, spread out invitingly on the marble slab, had been devoured during the night by the omnipresent cats—they had evidently been undeterred by the fact that the toad had been marinated in formalin, which had turned it a blue-black colour, more like damson jam than strawberry. Edward

313

still sat among his books and implements, lost in thought, his face extinct. But now sometimes his seriousness gave way abruptly to disconcerting bouts of hilarity; he became once more a player of mild practical jokes. To the Major, who had no sense of humour, practical jokes were disagreeable in the normal course of affairs; in cold weather they became intolerable—one simply had no energy left to cope with them. But nevertheless he was obliged to keep a constant watch on Edward, jokes or no jokes; he was obliged to haunt him, in fact, flitting along chilly corridors, taking walks in the grounds whenever Edward went to commune with his piglets, or repeatedly passing the ballroom windows to ascertain that he was still at his desk. The reason, of course, was that sooner or later Sarah would come again to visit Edward. Honour required the Major to seize the opportunity of making some casual remark to her which would indicate his indifference.

The three of them met head-on in one of the high-hedged privet alleys of the Chinese Garden.

'Hello, Brendan,' she said with a smile.

'Oh, hello ... you're back, are you?' replied the Major casually, turning pale. Even though he had been prepared for this inevitable meeting, it had still come as a dreadful shock. She looked very pretty in her winter coat of heavy grey wool trimmed with dark musquash, fingers buried in a fur muff, ears hidden by a fur cape. Her eyes remained steadily on the Major's, disconcerting him. In order to avoid this gaze he turned about and strolled in the direction they were going.

Edward himself seemed disconcerted for a moment; he had been talking with animation but had stopped suddenly on seeing the Major. Edward continued to look distressed until his eye fell on a bird-bath in the shape of a giant sea-shell proffered by a cement nymph. Her body was naked, clothed only in patches of yellow green lichen on her stomach and beneath her arms; one foot had been broken off, a rusty wire projected from the stump of her ankle. The Major studied her with feigned interest.

A great deal of snow had collected in the sea-shell and Edward was busy patting it together to make a snowball which he drolly pretended to throw at Sarah.

'Oh, for God's sake!' she muttered testily.

A little farther on they reached the terrace balustrade from where they could look down on the frozen swimming-pool. The twins had made a slide on the ice by shunting back and forth along a track to make it slippery. They were busy there now, skirts hitched up to their knees, running down the frosted grass and leaping over the lip of the pool to skid with gracefully flexed bodies to the other end. They stopped to watch this game for a moment, then Edward hurled his snowball as Charity was bounding forward on to the ice. Although it missed, it startled her, causing her to lose her balance and sit down heavily. There was laughter from Edward and soon a snowball fight was raging. Sarah forgot her bad humour and soon her slender fingers had left the warmth of her muff to dig into the freezing snow.

The Major loathed this sort of thing but joined in nevertheless. Sarah and Edward were enjoying themselves so much— besides, he did not want Sarah to think he lacked a sense of fun. Soon he got his reward. A snowball hurled by one of the twins struck him on the ear and made his head ring. He retired at that, laughing like a good sport—but displeased nevertheless, cupping his tender ear in the palm of his hand. Faith afterwards apologized: the twins had learned in a hard school and put stones in the middle of their snowballs. But the one that had hit the Major had been intended to flatten Sarah, not him. She was dreadfully sorry.

'Good heavens, why Sarah?' asked the Major, astonished that anyone could fail to like such a lovely girl.

'Oh, because she's so bloody awful,' Faith said vaguely. 'She's always hanging around Daddy.' The Major frowned then, to show his disapproval of swearing. He frowned later, too, on thinking it over. How he wished it were him instead of Edward that Sarah was always hanging around … !

What was going on between Edward and Sarah anyway? She still came to the Majestic quite frequently, but both she and Edward were always looking so grim these days. They did not behave in the least like lovers. Although his indifference to her had been amply demonstrated, the Major still could not prevent himself from haunting the couple, in the hope of getting further opportunities to demonstrate it. Thus it was that while flitting after them along a dim corridor one day he heard Edward exclaim: 'You're not the only woman in Kilnalough!'

'Who else would look at you twice?' jeered Sarah in a tone that the Major recognized only too well. After that she stopped coming to the Majestic.

TROUBLE IN INDIA

The centre of growing Indian unrest seems to have shifted from the Punjab to the United Provinces. Here, in the Oudh district, a serious land agitation has been in progress for the past month. It has given rise to violent outbursts and the United Provinces today are passing through a crisis not unlike that which reached its most acute phase in Ireland forty years ago. Hatred of the landlords is the cause of all the trouble and, undoubtedly, the peasantry has many grievances.

The trouble in the United Provinces has furnished a rare opportunity to Mr Gandhi. His object is the expulsion of the British from India, and he will welcome the aid of the Fyazabad farm labourers just as heartily as if they were Sikhs from the Punjab or Brahmins from Madras. Unless the dispute be settled quickly the agitators will succeed in convincing the rioters that their real enemy is the *Raj* ...

Throughout the Punjab, in Delhi, and now even in

Calcutta, this fanatical 'patriot' has proclaimed his boycott of British rule. He has transformed peaceful villages into hotbeds of intrigue and sedition, and his lieutenants, by their plausible sophistries, have fired the imaginations of young Indians with crazy ideas. Mr Gandhi is the author of his country's unrest. While he is allowed to preach his gospel India will continue to seethe with discontent.

*

THE GREATEST NEED

Ireland is being ground to powder between the two millstones of crime and punishment. For those whose sense of horror recent events have not blunted the daily newspaper has become a nightmare. The deliberate death-blow and the wandering bullet fired in attack or defence spare neither sex nor age. On Monday night a police officer's wife was murdered at Mallow and the officer himself sorely wounded. Immediately afterwards, in a fight with forces of the Crown, one man was killed and seven were wounded. Human life is cheaper today in Munster than in Mexico. The explosion of bombs has become a common sound in Dublin, where yesterday another attack was made on a police motor car in Merrion Square ... We believe that a national demand for a stoppage of murder and lawlessness, made with a single voice by our Churches, our newspapers, our public bodies, our farmer's unions, our Chambers of Commerce, would be the herald of a new day of hope and peace for Ireland. No man has a right to say that this great act of faith would be fruitless until it has been attempted. Who will give the lead?

*

By this time the Major was perfectly numb to the daily horrors printed by the newspaper. He had become used to them as he had once become used to the dawn barrage. He supposed that one day it would all come to an end, somehow or other, because the situation was by no means static. On the contrary, it continued to get worse. 'It has to get worse before it can get better,' remarked one of the ladies who was used to looking on the bright side. Early in January the sinister De Valera was reported to have returned to Ireland from America, having travelled, according to rumour, in, variously, a German submarine, a seaplane and a luxury yacht. Shortly afterwards there had been talk of peace negotiations between him and Lloyd George—but the days had gone by, multiplying into weeks. Nothing more had been heard. Instead, the Major congratulated himself on having resisted the impulse to visit the theatre in Dublin; a man sitting in the stalls of the Empire was shot in the chest while watching the pantomime *The House that Jack Built*. The advertisement for the show in the *Irish Times* carried the slogan: 'Not a dull moment from rise to fall of curtain.' Meanwhile the English cricket team continued to lose test matches in Australia by huge margins.

In mid-February a young widow appeared at the Majestic. Her name was Frances Roche. Though not exactly beautiful, she was a pleasant young lady, without airs or graces, the sort of person one felt inclined to trust instinctively. Her husband had died early in the war leaving her comfortably off, a fact which lent her considerable prestige at the Majestic. But she took no advantage of it. She was just as kind to impoverished Miss Bagley as she was to wealthy Miss Staveley. True, she aroused some criticism because in certain respects she was inclined to be 'modern' and lacking in finesse. But for the most part she was well received.

Mrs Roche had arrived accompanied by her mother, Mrs Bates, who in every respect was an older, more portly version of herself, though much less modern. Her mother was not in the least talkative, however. She listened and smiled but was hardly ever heard to utter a syllable. There was always a greater shortage of listeners than of talkers at the Majestic, and the new Mrs Bates (as opposed to the old Mrs Bates who had fallen off the stool before Christmas and long since gone to her reward) was as popular as her daughter. But it was, of course, in the daughter that Edward one day began to show an interest.

It was some time before the Major perceived what Edward had in mind, partly because he found it impossible to believe that any man in his right mind could prefer Mrs Roche, charming though she was, to Sarah – but then he remembered the jeering remark he had overheard and concluded that Edward was treating it as a challenge – and partly because Edward's method of courtship was a curious one, consisting of advances so discreet as to be virtually invisible to anyone but himself. For example, he treated Mrs Roche herself with decorous formality and instead engaged her mother in long conversations which soon became – since Mrs Bates only allowed herself an occasional smile or nod of agreement – a rather frantic series of questions and answers, both supplied by Edward himself. 'Ah, I see you're interested in that painting over there,' he would say if Mrs Bates's gaze wandered away from his face. 'It shows King William crossing the Boyne after the famous battle ... All the smoke in the background and so forth ... ' And then, shaking his head: 'You're wondering just what it was all about, I expect, apart from the religious aspect. Well, I'm afraid you have me there. We must ask Boy O'Neill. He's sure to know all about it.' 'Do we always have such a hard winter in Kilnalough? Now let me see: if I recollect rightly, last year and the year before that ... ' And so on.

For some time past Edward's appearance at dinner had become extremely erratic. As likely as not he would be content to eat off his knees wherever in the hotel Murphy, carrying a tray, happened to find him. But now he once more took to appearing punctually and presently he got into the habit of showing Mrs Roche to a seat at the end of the table where he sat himself, thereby dislodging old Mrs Rappaport to sit at the end of the Major's table. They were too far away to talk to each other, of course, but think of their position—one at each end of the table! It gave them such an air of being *en famille* that Edward was clearly embarrassed to be making his intentions so obvious; yet to his evident surprise Frances Roche showed no sign of being aware of them, chatting pleasantly as she had always done to the old ladies sitting on either side. There was no sign at all of blushes or swoons or melting glances (some of the looks the old ladies gave him, on the other hand, would have turned the milk sour). Was Mrs Roche perhaps rather stupid? Edward might have wondered. As a scientist, of course, he should have known that young ladies no longer functioned, physiologically speaking, quite as they had done when he was a young man: they no longer swooned in a difficult situation ('indeed', thought the Major gloomily, 'the modern young lady would be more likely to punch you on the jaw'). But Mrs Roche seemed even to be unaware that she was in a difficult situation.

He was getting nowhere. Like it or not, if this difficulty was ever to be resolved he would have to make his overtures even more brutally frank. Thus, at any rate, did the Major interpret the fact that Murphy was ordered to place the soup tureen and plates at Mrs Roche's end of the table so that she should serve the food. And she did serve the food—with Edward's dilated pupils fixed to her homely features, trying to find some trace of awareness in them. But Mrs Roche ladled the transparent, faintly steaming bouillon into one dish after another as if she were doing the most natural thing in the world, which indeed she was.

Edward was beginning to lose heart by now. He had taken to brooding darkly at his end of the table. He was bewildered, the Major could see. One had to feel sorry for him. But then the Major thought of Sarah and hardened his heart as with a sigh he turned back to sift through the watery hot-pot on his plate in search of a piece of meat suitable for Mrs Rappaport's marmalade cat, sitting on its stool and staring him down with expressionless, acid eyes.

The next thing was to take Mrs Roche for afternoon drives in the Daimler. These tended to be tedious and repetitive because, with the country in such an uproar, it was not safe to go far afield. The twins were usually present, conscripted at the price of violent scenes and sulks to chaperon their father. Sarcastic remarks were passed about the beauties of the countryside. Worse, the twins had recently become experts on the subject of sexual intercourse, thanks to a volume wrapped in brown paper lent to them by one of the young Auxiliaries. As a result they were inclined to take a disabused view of all relations between men and women, and this view even extended to their father's afternoon drives in the motor car. 'Oh, for heaven's sake grab her, Daddy,' the appalled Major overheard Faith groaning to her sister. 'Throw her on her back, that's what she wants!'

But Edward, of course, did nothing of the sort and gradually, although Mrs Roche continued to sit at the end of his table, the afternoon drives declined in frequency and were forgotten.

'One needs every now and then to escape from the company of women into a place from which women are excluded. After all, unless he has sisters or comes from the lower classes a young Englishman is likely to grow up entirely among males. Later in life he simply isn't accustomed to a heavy dosage of female company. And surely, if the English gentleman is respected throughout the world for his courtesy towards the gentler sex, it is because he takes care to provide himself with a room in which he can be alone in the company of other men.' So the Major was thinking as he sat in the gun room with Edward on a frosty moonlit night.

It was very quiet. There was no movement in the house or in the trees outside the window. Edward was gazing abstractedly into the fire, enjoying a rare moment of tranquillity. Presently, however, a small oak leaf of white plaster dropped from a

321

wreath on the dim ornamented ceiling and shattered into pieces on the tiles by Edward's feet. He gave a start and peered up at the ceiling.

'We really must do something, Brendan, about the old place. It needs doing up badly. One simply can't let things slide.'

The Major raised his eyebrows dubiously but said nothing. He remembered Edward's indifference about the piece of the façade which had almost crushed the dog Foch. By comparison the distintegration of the ceiling plaster was trivial. But Edward had begun to interest himself in what he was saying.

'There's so much wrong with the place no wonder we get complaints from some of the guests (because we *do* get complaints, Brendan, from time to time). Heaven only knows when we last had a lick of paint and some new wall-paper, not to mention the things like mending broken windows and replacing some of those old curtains that the moths have been getting at ... And then we need to have a look at the roof, I hear there was a positive waterfall cascading down one of the servants' staircases during that spell of rainy weather we had over Christmas. And of course we must get that M put back up there ... it looks too absurd the way it is ... 'AJESTIC' ... whoever heard of such a word? ... and make sure none of the other letters are going to fall off ... After all, if one's going to run a hotel it may as well be a good one, what d'you think?'

'I quite agree,' the Major said with a sigh, doubtful that Edward's enthusiasm would last long enough to become action. 'I should think the first job is to make sure none of the masonry falls on anybody's head.'

'Absolutely! That's the ticket. Really put the old place back on its feet again. We could clean out the swimming-pool and maybe try to get that wretched "Do More" generator working again ... '

'And maybe the Turkish Baths,' added the Major, who at that moment felt like taking a Turkish bath and was prepared to join Edward's romancing. Edward was being serious, however.

'The Turkish Baths might present us with a tiny bit of a problem, actually. We did try to get them going again some years back but it was a disaster. The boilers suddenly went haywire and before anyone knew what was happening half a dozen guests had suffered heat prostration ... Had to be carried out, poached like lobsters ... '

'Well, we must do something about the Palm Court before it undermines the foundations. And the squash court ... '

'Ah yes, and the squash court. Of course I'd have to find another place for the piggies, but that shouldn't be impossible. Really, the place has all the amenities ... all we need to do is to fix things up. Mind you, with the state of the country this may not be the best time to get people over here from England. But with luck the situation should be under control by the beginning of the season ... I hear that Dublin Castle has a plan to start shooting Sinn Feiners by roster until they stop attacking the police ... We could put an advertisement in *The Times* and do something about the tennis courts. Pity not to make use of them.'

Edward was on his feet now, his eyes gleaming with enthusiasm. As he talked he jingled some loose change in his pocket, which caused the Major to wonder where the money for all this splendid refurbishing would come from. But Edward's enthusiasm was infectious. How was it that he had never thought of this before? he was wanting to know. His eyes had been opened! The Majestic was no fantasy. It was solid. It was there! It had everything that was needed ... indeed, it had more than most places: it had electric light. It even had a firmly established reputation as a place of fashionable luxury – tarnished, doubtless, but a reputation nevertheless.

Dubious again, the Major listened as Edward talked on excitedly. At his feet Rover stirred and barked fearfully, peering with his sightless eyes into the threatening darkness all around. Poor dog! The Major dropped a soothing hand to scratch that fretfully acute silken ear. Rover allowed himself to sink back to the floor again and yawned, emitting a frightful smell.

Edward was too excited to sleep. It was all the Major could do to prevent him setting off there and then on a tour of the premises, notebook in hand, summoning from their beds masons and carpenters, plumbers, painters and glaziers. When in a little while the Major climbed the stairs to bed he left Edward wandering from one silent, sleeping room to another, raising branched candlesticks to gaze with inspired eyes at cobwebbed walls and dusty brocade curtains which, after all the years they had hung there, still glinted dimly with their heavy gold thread, woven into the dusty, tattered cloth like the thread of hope that runs from youth to age.

Edward continued to move through the house, treading softly as a ghost, staring and staring, his heart beating strongly, his eyes full of tears. He sat down once on the arm of a chair, as if he were drunk, overcome by exhilaration, gazing around at this house which he had somehow never really *seen* before. And he continued for a while to sit there with tears of joy coursing down his cheeks, thinking now of his wife, now of Angela, now of his friend the Major. He sat there until his candles had burned down to thin liquid wafers of wax. Suddenly the thought came to him that he should give a ball—a magnificent ball, the kind of ball they used to give here in the old days. His excitement surged to new heights. This would mark the rebirth of the Majestic! He must go and tell the Major immediately, wake him up if necessary. A Spring Ball will be held at the Majestic in Kilnalough. The pleasure of your company is requested ... the formal delicacy of this phrase enchanted him. The pleasure of your company.

Faintly from outside in the park there came the shattering, lonely cry of a peacock. For a moment the sound of that cry disturbed him—aching, beyond hope. As he got to his feet there was a threatening movement in the darkly swaying shadows. But it was only one of the multitude of cats, out for the purposes of hunting or mating in the Majestic's endless forest of furniture.

One evening towards the end of March Edward and the Major were to be seen standing together in the foyer, the latter smoking a thin Havana cigar, the former keeping an apprehensive eye on the drive. The Major was impeccably dressed in white tie and tails – it was easy to see that both he and his tailor were men of distinction. Edward was also dressed in tails, but of a more antique cut—which was strange when one considered the care he normally took about his appearance. Moreover, the contours of his body had changed somewhat over the years that had elapsed since the tailor had done his work: the years revealed themselves in the horizontal strain marks where the top of his trousers surrounded his stomach, in the severe grip that the coat exerted across his shoulders from one armpit to another, encouraging his arms to hang outwards, penguin fashion. Nevertheless he was an imposing figure. Evening dress suited his craggy, leonine features by putting them in a civilized perspective. They made him look both fierce and harmless, a lion in a cage. Even the red carnation he wore in his buttonhole—on Edward's person it gave one a mild shock, as if one had just come face to face with a prizefighter with a flower behind his ear.

'This looks like somebody.'

A Bentley had come nosing up the drive and now, at a walking pace, was making a wide turn in front of the statue of Queen Victoria. A pale glimmer of faces showed at its windows, staring out at the hotel.

'That's deuced odd. They're making off again. You don't think they might have changed their minds at the last moment, do you?'

But the Major did not answer. He was not worried about some guests who could not make up their minds out there in the darkness. He was listening intently. Had he just heard a deep, ominous miaowing issue from some distant reaches of the building?

Those wretched cats, the trouble they had caused! First they had tried hunting them out of the upper storeys with broomsticks, sweeping them out of the rooms, along the corridors and down the stairs into the yard. But it is impossible to control a herd of cats; each one makes up its own mind where it wants to go. You start off with a vast furry flock, terrified and resentful. But then, quick as lightning, they double back or flash between your legs or over your head, zoom up the curtains or on to the top of wardrobes, and sit there spitting at you while you try to reach them with your broom and the rest of the flock disperses. You are lucky if you succeed in ushering out one scarred old ginger warrior whom, likely as not, you find waiting for you once again at the top of the stairs, having slipped back in through a broken window or down a chimney.

'Hello, they seem to be coming back.'

The Bentley had reappeared on the lamplit crescent of gravel travelling slowly backwards, having locked antlers with an immense De Dion-Bouton on the narrow drive. Both motor cars stopped this time and disgorged their occupants, so Edward opened the door and with a welcoming smile on his lips moved out on to the steps. As the Major followed him he again heard that ominous caterwauling in the distance and remembered Edward's brainwave: 'Bring the dogs in from the yard and quarter them in the upper storeys ... that'll get rid of the bloody cats!' Well, they had tried this, of course. But it had been a complete failure. The dogs had stood about uncomfortably in little groups, making little effort to chase the cats but defecating enormously on the carpets. At night they had howled like lost souls, keeping everyone awake. In the end the dogs had been returned to the yard, tails wagging with relief. It was not their sort of thing at all.

The Major was now shaking hands repeatedly and smiling

as he was introduced. More carriages were arriving. Horns were sounding cheerfully. The Hammonds, the FitzPatricks, the Craigs with son and daughter-in-law, the Russells from Maryborough, the Porters, the FitzHerberts and FitzSimons, the Maudsley girls, Annie and Fanny, from Kingstown, Miss Carol Feldman, the Odlums and the O'Briens, the Allens and the Douglases and the Prendergasts and the Kirwans and the Carrutherses and Miss Bridget O'Toole ... The Major's head began to swim and his smile became fixed.

'One doesn't shoot cats' (he was thinking as his weary paw gripped that of Sir Joshua Smiley and he bowed pleasantly to his ugly brood of daughters), 'one doesn't shoot cats, other quadrupeds one may shoot without a qualm, but not cats.' Still, what else was there to be done? The blessed creatures had to be got rid of somehow (the distant caterwauling, meanwhile, was becoming intense; a whole chorus of tom-cats it sounded like, he could hear it even above the hubbub of the arriving guests) ...

So one day he and Edward had steeled themselves to climb the stairs with revolvers. The eucalyptus reek of cats was overpowering, so long had they had dominion over the upper storeys. Ah, the shrieks had been terrible, unnerving, as if it were a massacre of infants that they were about – but it had to be done, in the interests of the Majestic.

Edward these days had a shaky hand; several times he missed altogether, in spite of the long hours of practice he had put in at the pistol-range down by the lodge. Twice he wounded the cats he aimed at. It was the Major who had to seek out the moaning animals and finish them off. All this made a dreadful mess: blood on the carpets, there for ever, ineradicable, brains on the coverlets, vile splashes on the walls and even on the ceiling. Edward, in his excitement, shot out a couple of window-panes and caused a great plaster scroll bearing the words 'Semper fidelis' to plummet earthwards, taking with it a rotting window-box gay with crocuses from one of the ladies' rooms two storeys below. Apologetic for his poor marksmanship,

Edward had insisted on gathering up all the carcases and throwing them into a sack he had brought for that purpose. When they had been collected he threw the sack over his shoulder and descended the stairs. The Major followed, jingling the empty brass shells in the palm of his hand. By the time they had reached the second landing the sack was oozing dark red drops. Fortunately the carpet too was red. The drops scarcely showed.

By this time the Major's smile had become a painful grimace. One person after another; he greeted whoever stepped in front of him in the same mechanical way. Even if Kaiser Bill had suddenly shook him by the hand he would probably just have smiled and murmured: 'Jolly glad you were able to come.' But now, abruptly, face to face with the stout and venerable Lady Devereux (a second cousin of the Viceroy), he startled her with a brilliant smile and exuberant greeting. He had just realized what that dreadful miaowing was that had been so disturbing him: it was merely the orchestra tuning up in the distant ballroom. Tuned to perfection, or as near as one could ask, they had at last gathered themselves together and were playing a lively waltz, the strains of which wafted pleasantly into the foyer. Hearing this sound, a number of the guests, who had been met by hired flunkeys carrying trays of champagne but had lingered chatting more sombrely than one would have expected, brightened up a shade, as if with the thought that something they had been dreading might not, after all, turn out quite as badly as they had expected. There was a perceptible movement then, a venturing inwards away from this friendly antechamber to the mild spring night.

But the Major was still repeatedly having his hand shaken. 'There are some really splendid people here already. Perhaps it won't turn out so badly after all.' And then he mused: 'Why are people from abroad always so much more distinguished than people from Ireland?' His eyes fell on the distinguished figure of Mr Robert Cumming, a visitor from North Carolina, chatting with Mr Russell McCormmach and the beautiful Miss

Bond from Scotland. 'How courteous and enlightened they are! (They make the Irish look like oxen.) How naturally they wear their evening dress! What will become of all these splendid people?' he wondered, gazing rapt at Miss Bond's lovely face, her clear eyes and delightful smile, at the gay and charming Mrs Margaret Dobbs who had just come in at that moment, at the young faces that swirled by. 'What happens to such people? They never get old, that much is certain. They vanish suddenly one day. They change by magic into something different, utterly different. So that one moment there is a lovely girl and the next some other creature, as different from her as a frog is from the tadpole it used to be. What will become of us all?' he mused (including himself because, after all, he knew himself to be quite handsome too). And this unanswered question left him in a mood of melancholy which he rather enjoyed — because, of course, it was a problem he did not have to face immediately. (One day we shall vanish. But for the moment how lovely we are!)

Ripon and his wife arrived and while Edward greeted them, as stiffly as if they were people he scarcely knew, the Major concluded that his optimism regarding the success of Edward's ball had perhaps been premature. The young people were marvellous, of course, but there were *so few of them*! And young people, the Major knew by experience, were absolutely vital to the success of a ball.

At this moment, however, a large number of handsome young men arrived. The older guests who were still standing in the foyer turned to look at these newcomers and once again they brightened a little. The presence of youth, the Major reflected, very often raises the spirits (however grudgingly) of older people. His own spirits were not raised, however, even though his right hand was grateful for the opportunity of taking a rest. A curt nod was enough greeting for these young men. Two dozen of so of the ex-officers among the Auxiliaries had been invited by Edward, for the chronic shortage of young men in Europe was also felt here in Ireland (whose ruling classes, at any rate, had not waited for the conscription that never came). The result was this: one had to make do with the young men who had survived, whatever their quality.

'You look lovely, my dear.'

Charity was plucking at his sleeve. She and Faith were both dressed in splendid hooped white crinolines; too old-fashioned even to have been culled from Angela's wardrobe, they had been discovered, with cries of bliss, packed away in a forgotten trunk, abandoned by some guest from another era. All their dressing-up of Padraig had given the twins an idea of the dramatic possibilities of clothes; instead of sulking at the prospect of being unfashionable they had set to work with needle and thread — with the result that if their faces had been sufficiently grave and doleful they might well have passed for the elegant inbred daughters of a mad Spanish king.

'It's Granny. She's being frightfully obstinate. She simply refuses to give in.

'I don't know what I can do.'

'Please come and try. You *must*, Brendan! It'll be too shaming. Everyone will laugh themselves silly ... '

The Major agreed reluctantly; he wanted to be on hand to greet Sarah when she arrived. After a quick look outside to make sure that she was not on the threshold he followed Charity upstairs to the suite of rooms occupied by Mrs Rappaport on the first floor. The old lady was sitting bolt upright in front of her dressing-table, a flustered maid at her side.

'Well, Mrs Rappaport, what's all this I hear about you being in danger? I never heard such a story in all my life! I can assure you that nobody means to hurt a hair on your head.'

The old lady was wearing a long gown of black velvet, a dress (the Major had heard) which had formed part of her trousseau but which she deemed herself never sufficiently to have worn; the cloth had been quite unsuitable to the climate in India, yet by the time she and her husband had

330

returned to the more temperate climate of the British Isles her youth had fled, taking with it most of the social occasions at which it might have been suitable. Curiously, though unaltered, it still fitted her to perfection (unlike poor Edward's suit). This could only be a tribute to her relentless habit of sitting up straight and eschewing all forms of self-indulgence. It was strange to think that the proportions of her body were unchanged inside all that black velvet, the proportions, presumably (it could hardly have been her dowry), which old General Rappaport had once found irresistible.

The maid, Faith and Charity were all looking at him expectantly, waiting for him to work a miracle. He dropped his eyes from the glinting diamond pendant the old lady wore around her withered neck and with a sigh fixed them on the worn leather holster she had strapped around her velvet waist. Pulling up a chair, he sat down opposite her, repeating in a reassuring tone that there was really no danger, none at all. Moreover, even if there had been any danger, a whole platoon of young policemen were among the guests. Let a Shinner so much as sneeze out of place and hey presto! he would find himself handcuffed to the nearest grand piano in a brace of shakes.

'Oh do talk *sense*, Brendan,' pleaded Faith, close to tears. 'She hasn't the vaguest idea what you're talking about. Can't you be firm with her? The ball is going to be over before we've even found anyone to dance with ... '

'Look here, I'm doing my best,' replied the Major, offended. 'Besides, if you will interrupt me ... Why don't you both go downstairs and send Miss Archer up here. She'll know what to do, I expect. Or Mrs Roche if you can't find Miss Archer.'

The twins required no second bidding. They squeezed their crinolines through the doorway and raced ballooning down the stairs three at a time. The Major turned back to Mrs Rappaport. Few new notions succeeded in getting through to her these days, but when one did it tended to preoccupy her. All the more unlucky, therefore, that when someone

331

had happened to mention the 'troubles' to her a day or two earlier, her mind had been sent back to heaven only knew what lonely Indian station out in the middle of nowhere with a vociferous, gesticulating, hopelessly untrustworthy rabble of natives at the gates; the women had had to be armed, taught how to use a revolver and reminded to save the last shot for themselves. Now, sixty years later, on the one night in years that it mattered, the old lady had remembered her elementary weapon training, found her departed husband's revolver and, thin lips quivering, buckled it on.

As the Major reasoned with her gently, and drew his chair closer with the intention of disarming her when the time was ripe, the hideous marmalade cat leaped nimbly out of the hat-box in which it had been sleeping, stretched luxuriously, and bunched itself to jump into the old lady's lap. There it settled, obscuring the buckle which the Major had been hoping to undo. It fixed the Major with a bitter, hostile gaze. The situation seemed hopeless. But at that moment there was a knock on the door and Miss Archer came in, followed by Mrs Roche, both looking serene and capable.

'She mustn't be allowed to go downstairs wearing it or the twins will die of mortification,' the Major explained, and then hurried away, leaving the matter in their hands.

Since Edward's moment of inspiration as he roamed the building by candlelight a month or so earlier a great deal of work had been done at the Majestic. It was on a new carpet with new rods that the Major's patent-leather dancing shoes were now treading as he made his way downstairs, thick and blood-red (which was a good thing since the farther down the stairs they had gone the more copiously had the sack of cats oozed its morbid liquid). True, this carpet came to an abrupt end on reaching the first landing and gave way to the old threadbare and faded one—but in theory it might have come to an end just round the first bend of the banister, the last point that could be glimpsed from any part of the foyer unless one stood on a chair. It was a tribute to Edward's generous nature that no such parsimonious thought had occurred to him. Besides, although guests do sometimes climb stairs uninvited, out of curiosity, they really had no business going up there at all.

The Major paused for a moment at the foot of the stairs and surveyed the foyer, which, though now empty, was brilliantly lit, first by the crude blaze of the torch which had been lifted out of its iron bracket by the stairs, soaked and set ablaze as a fiery welcome to the guests; then by the great ninety-six-branched chandelier which had earlier been converted to electricity and now, with the failure of the 'Do More' generator, had been converted back again—candles had been softened and stuck where necessary on to the lifeless prongs of the empty bulb-sockets. Oil lamps with windows of coloured glass had been hung elsewhere and in the vast open hearth a log fire was burning.

All this blaze of light was picked up and reflected by the waxed and polished tiles on the floor (firmly cemented so that they no longer clinked underfoot); it glinted on the golden cheeks of cherubs, freshly dusted and holding mirrors (which were, however, still peeling behind their polished glass). The great sofas that slumbered round the walls had been dragged out on to the steps one morning and pummelled with carpet-beaters, which raised such a thick grey fog as to mask the sun to a pale amber disc, until at last no more dust would rise. But now they glowed a dark cherry red beneath the gilt oak leaves and tassels, and one could sit down without sneezing. The surface of the reception desk lay like a pool of dark water; had anyone leaned over to sign the register he would have seen his own distinguished features looking up at him as if from an ancient, much-varnished portrait.

The Major's eye moved back with a hint of anxiety to the dancing flame of the torch at the foot of the stairs. He was not accustomed to seeing a flame allowed to blaze unprotected in the middle of a room—but it was, after all, safe enough, firmly bracketed over tiles with nothing but the spiralling emptiness of the stairwell above. At his elbow, close to the torch, the gracefully inclined face of Venus had taken on a sly vitality with the dancing of light and shadow. What trouble she had caused, the Major mused, before they had been able to restore her to the softly glowing purity of white marble; that descent of dust which, year by year, had grown like black hair on her head and neck, on her shoulders and sloping breasts, had also found its way into the crevices of scanty marble cloth that failed to clothe her. Quite impossible to get at it with a feather duster! But he and Edward, fanatical and perfectionist, had decided she must be as white as snow; nothing less would suit them. So Seán Murphy had been summoned and the three of them, with starting eyes and bulging veins, had lifted her off her pedestal and staggered out of the door, around the house, down through the kitchens and into the laundry where the maids were waiting for her with scrubbing-brushes and a steaming soapy bath. They had set to work, blushing and tittering and teasing Seán Murphy as if what they were doing was somehow indecent. Then, rinsed and dried and wrapped in clean towels, they had taken her back and set her up once more.

All their spring-cleaning had been fun! The Major was smiling at the recollection. But as his eye wandered over the gleaming black and white chessboard of tiles his smile faded — for sitting on a white tile in the very middle of the floor was a plump grey rat. Almost immediately, startled by the Major's movement, it crept away under one of the sofas and vanished from sight. Frowning, the Major made his way towards the ballroom. This was something they had not envisaged when they had gone upstairs to make their grim harvest of cats. Those cats hadn't been eating the air! A steady grey stream of nourishment had been coming up into the house: rats from the cellars and the pond, mice from the fields and the barn. A cat, however wild and savage, can always be passed off as a pet. Not so with rats. Fortunately there was still a sizeable residue of appetites in the upper storeys. Perhaps the rats would remain out of sight until the guests had gone home.

The orchestra was playing a foxtrot. As the Major made his way towards the ballroom, the lively melody of 'Dreamland Lover' grew louder, blending with laughter and the chatter of voices, the rhythmic movement of the dancers on the parquet floor which was shining like a pool of ice. What a fine time everyone must be having! Once again he allowed himself a touch of optimism about the success of the evening.

In the doorway he hesitated. He had seen Sarah and, although his mind continued to register calmly a variety of impressions which had nothing whatever to do with her, he was aware of a solid pulse throbbing in his neck and chest. Tonight he would propose!

The ballroom was decorated with banks of violets which added a sweet fragrance to the faint odours of cologne and perfume drifting from behind the delicate ears of the ladies and the heavier aroma of tobacco-smoke from the thickly moustached lips of their companions. Sarah was sitting beside one of these banks of violets, her face slightly blurred by a mist of green ferns. Behind her chair, with his right hand over his heart as if posing for a photograph, stood Captain Bolton, watching the dancers (of whom there did not seem to be a great many). It was Bolton's other hand which caught the Major's eye; the palm rested on the back of Sarah's chair but the fingertips trailed carelessly forward on to her shoulder. As the Major watched, he bent his head to say something to her, delicately encircling her naked upper arm with finger and thumb as he did so. The finger whitened for an instant, but Sarah continued to look straight ahead. Her face was dark and closed. She might have been unaware that Bolton was standing behind her.

Having started in her direction, the Major now changed his mind. He had a great deal of dancing to do; he had cheerfully promised a number of the old ladies that he would dance with them. He began with a trembling but light-footed Miss Porteous, next came a waltz with the cumbersome Miss Johnston who made things difficult by wanting to lead, then it was time for a bewildered Mrs Rice to take the floor.

Edward was moving from one group of guests to another, making genial, incoherent remarks, red in the face and wearing an air of mingled triumph and discomfort in the tight grip of his tail-coat. The Major was afraid that this triumph might be premature. The guests had been carelessly chosen because, although there were a great many young men, thanks to the Auxiliaries, young ladies were in short supply. The twins, flushed and exultant, were besieged and claimed for every dance. Viola O'Neill was also discreetly holding court under the sharp eye of her parents, flirting with three or four young men at once. Even Sir Joshua's daughters were being paid considerable attention: their long, horse-like faces were turned continually to where their mother was sitting, for encouragement or advice. A doting smile would appear on her face, which was an older, more wrinkled version of theirs, and she would nod affirmatively. And this horse face—the Major's disabused eye noted as with flexed knees he foxtrotted a gasping and near-hysterical Miss Staveley round the floor— these equine features were repeated again and again all the way down the glittering ballroom, as if the Smileys had been reflected in a great hall of mirrors, from the oldest men and women to the youngest children. This was the face of Anglo-Ireland, the inbred Protestant aristocracy, the face, progressively refining itself into a separate, luxurious species, which had ruled Ireland for almost five hundred years: the wispy fair hair, the eyes too close together, the long nose and protruding teeth. 'Ripon was right, in a biological sense as well as in several others, to marry Máire Noonan.'

If only there had been more young people! No doubt it was this absence of youth which lent the guests the appearance of wax figures, museum curiosities, unconnected with the present era, the seething modern world of 1921. The Major peered round Miss Staveley's heaving shoulders. The handsome and distinguished young people from abroad were no longer to be seen. Even the lovely Miss Bond, who had briefly captivated him in the foyer, had vanished.

Thinking of the Auxiliaries, he cast a worried glance in their direction; they had stationed themselves near the buffet and were drinking copiously, becoming steadily noisier and more boisterous. But now they had discovered an amusing game: if there were no young ladies to be danced with, well, they would make do with the older ones. As the next waltz began half a dozen of them crossed the floor to bow and click heels in an exaggerated manner in front of as many old ladies. The ladies looked apprehensive. They perhaps remembered how these or similar young men used to threaten them with bayonets at the tea-table. Under the obligation to be good sports they accepted, nevertheless, and allowed themselves to be escorted on to the dance floor.

'The first time I came to the Majestic,' the Major was saying to Sarah, 'I went for a walk round the terraces with Edward and he told me about the hunt balls and regattas they used to hold here ... the violins and the chandeliers and the silver breakfast dishes ... I never expected to see it for myself.'

'It's lovely, Brendan. This is how it should be all the time—with candles and flowers. It's almost too good to be true. D'you think there'll be silver dishes for breakfast? What a long time there is still to go before then!'

She was smiling at him warmly, with a trace of that innocent enthusiasm which he had found so disarming during her visit to London. Dancing had made the Major thirsty. He drank a glass of cold champagne and then another. He was in a strange mood, both sad and somehow optimistic at the same time. He told Sarah, pointing at the blue-black glass on the roof, how, up on the balconies above, the nannies and the children used to watch the grown-ups dancing. That was in the old days, at the height of the season, when the ornate gilt mirrors in every room in the hotel were busy reflecting the corporeal envelopes of titled persons and the attics under the roof were positively bulging with their servants. Those were the days! (In those days too Sarah would have thought him too splendid a match to refuse.) He drank some more champagne and gazed into Sarah's grey eyes, thinking ... well, he didn't know *what* he was thinking ... perhaps of old women, black as ravens, rummaging through the rubbish bins.

Sarah dropped her eyes to her glass, which was empty; she flicked it idly with her finger-nail and drew from it one thin, clear note of a painful beauty, over which the honeyed sighings of the violins on the platform had no dominion.

'Come on, let's go upstairs and see what the nannies and the children used to look at.'

He gave her his arm. On the way out they passed Bolton, who was conversing politely with a feathered lady. He raised one eyebrow sardonically at Sarah as she passed.

Through the empty foyer and up the stairs Sarah clung tightly to his arm, humming under her breath.

'Well, you must tell me all the gossip, Brendan,' she said at last. 'I hear that Edward has been courting that sensible lady with the moustache.'

'Oh come now!' protested the Major feebly. 'She hasn't got a moustache. And besides, he wasn't really courting her in my opinion and anyway he's stopped now ... But why do you want to know? Are you jealous?'

'Look at me, Brendan. Isn't it plain to see that I'm head over heels in love with him?'

In consternation the Major stopped. For a few moments she gazed at him with a sombre, tragic air; then, seeing his expression, she abruptly burst out laughing – a fresh, mocking laugh that echoed cheerfully all around them.

They had now reached the second landing. Reassured, the Major steered her along the corridor and into one of the dark starlit rooms. They moved out on to the balcony; below them lay the ballroom, an immense, glistening bubble of glass. Another waltz was about to begin; the orchestra sat poised in its luxuriant garden of ferns, bald heads shining with perspiration, fingers crooked, bows at the ready. Hardly had the first few notes been played before the twins were out on the floor spinning round and round, disappearing every now and then into the fierce solar glare of one or other of the chandeliers. Presently three of the young Auxiliaries went spinning out on to the floor with their partners, Miss Bagley, Mrs Bates and a terror-stricken Mrs Rice. The Major watched, perturbed lest the young men might be taking their joke too far. A crash of breaking glass echoed up to them – but it was only some young chap who had clumsily swept a tray of empty glasses to the floor.

'I'm cold,' Sarah said with a shiver. 'Let's go inside.'

In the darkened room the Major took hold of Sarah's arm and, in concert with his strange mood, kissed her sadly yet optimistically. It was one of those nights, he had the feeling, when everything isn't (as it usually seems to be) already settled; when one doesn't have to say to oneself: given your character and my character what harmony shall we ever be able to achieve?

'The moon will be coming up soon. Let me show you my favourite room.'

As he opened the door of the linen room a great exhalation of hot air enveloped them. The night was mild, the kitchen ovens had been burning for several hours at full blast while the supper was being prepared, so behind this closed door the temperature had been mounting steadily all afternoon. Still, Sarah had said she was cold. The Major stepped inside and lit the candle beside his nest of pillows on the floor. He gestured for Sarah to sit down in the depths of the cocoon. She looked faintly surprised but did so, murmuring: 'It's frightfully warm in here.'

The Major was full of determination but uncertain quite how to proceed. He would have liked to take his coat off for a start (indeed he would have liked to take all his clothes off) but was afraid lest Sarah might put an unfortunate construction on any removal of clothes. He took his place in the nest beside her and for a few moments they kissed, thereby making real a scene which the Major had frequently evoked in his imagination. The reality however, turned out to be less satisfactory than the scene he had pictured. In hardly any time he was sweating profusely; his shirt clung to his back and his collar itched unbearably. Sarah was clearly also suffering from the heat; her brow was damp and shiny; as she raised a hand to brush away a stray lock of hair that was threatening to creep between their kissing lips he noticed that a dark stain had appeared under the arm of her grey silk dress. At any moment, he was afraid, she might decide that the heat was too much. While with a trace of desperation he continued to kiss her, he nerved himself to say what he had to say, to speak the words on which his happiness depended. He cleared his throat and ... but no, he retired again for one final revision of the words in his mind.

Presently Sarah disengaged herself and said: 'I'm afraid my dress will get crumpled.' She hesitated for a moment, half expectantly, then with a sigh she got to her feet. The Major leaped up also and, mopping the perspiration from his brow, said jerkily: 'Look here, I want you to be my wife.' He could say no more. He could not move. He stood waiting there like a pillar of salt. He could see, however, that it was going to be no go.

Sarah's face had taken on a bitter, sly expression he had seen many times before. She said crossly: 'Oh, I know you do, Brendan.' For a while neither of them said a word, then she added: 'This heat is frightful. I shall have to go and wash my face.'

She turned away. The candle on the floor threw hulking shadows over the ceiling and the walls.

'Really, you're such a child. You haven't any idea what I'm really like ... Oh, I'm sure you mean well, but it's quite out of the question ... D'you know that I'm a Catholic? Of course you do. But do you even know what a Catholic *is*? You probably think it's some sort of superstition or black magic or ... But no, forget all that, that's not what I want to say. It doesn't matter whether or not I'm a Catholic. It's simply impossible, d'you understand? And for heaven's sake stop staring at me with sheep's eyes like that! You're not the man I want and that's all there is to it ... That's that. So please don't mention it again. I thought you were cured of all that nonsense. Now I'm going to wash my face!'

'But why not?'

'I told you. Because you aren't the man I want! Isn't that enough for you?'

'I suppose you want Edward, then.'

'I want a man who isn't always trying to agree with people, if you must know. There! Now perhaps you'll let me go and wash my face ... And for heaven's sake don't look so wretched. I'm sorry ... but it would serve you right if I did marry you. You wouldn't like it in the least. No, don't come with me ... I'll find my own way.'

Left alone, the Major took off his coat and fanned his flushed, unhappy face with a pillow-case starched as stiff as cardboard. Craving sweetness, he delved into his pocket for the bar of chocolate he had put there. But the chocolate had melted into a mass of oozing silver paper.

When the Major had composed himself a little he went downstairs. The ballroom was empty except for an effete young man with a monocle who was strumming on the abandoned piano while a thick-set lady sat on a stool beside him eating trifle. This young man was G. F. Edge, the racing motorist, so the Major had been told (but somehow he found it hard to believe). In any case, they paid no attention to the Major and so, although he was not in the least hungry, he wandered towards the dining-room where supper was being served.

Not for many years had such a magnificent display been seen in the dining-room of the Majestic: the snowy linen that cloaked the tables, the silver winking in the candlelight, the golden-crusted battlemented pies filled with succulent game, pheasants and ducks in quivering aspic, brittle and juicy hams cured with sugar and cloves and crowned with white frills, spiced beef the colour of mud, and steaming pyramidal vol-au-vents overflowing with creamed chicken, mushrooms and sea-food. On long silver platters salmon stretched themselves, heads and tails shining and perfect as if caught a moment before (if one forgot the clouded, resentful eye) while, in between, all that glorious pinkness was gradually scooped away by the deft and deferential waiters imported from Dublin for the purpose. And besides all that, the salads and the soups, the pâtés and the hors d'oeuvres, the sucking pig (which at that very moment, as his eye fell on it, caused Edward to knit his brows pensively and think of his own plump darlings), the smoking pasties and pies, the delicate canapés, the cheeses that came not only from Ireland but from certain other countries as well (these cheeses, however, had been set at a table apart lest their smell offend the ladies). Nor must the desserts be forgotten: the mountainous creamy trifles that gave off the fumes of sherry and cognac, the trembling fruit and wine jellies, both clear and cloudy, aquamarine and garnet, pearly blancmanges and black fruit puddings smeared with melting slabs of brandy butter ... and, of course, many, many other things besides.

On all this the Major, for whom life had become empty, cast a listless eye. Instead, he stationed himself by the sugar bowl on the coffee table and into his mouth morosely popped one lump after another, crunching them noisily. Sarah was not in the room. He was glad. He would never be able to speak to her again.

The other guests, their appetites unimpaired by love, were doing full justice to the magnificent food prepared for them. The elderly guests ate with dignity but more than was good for them, remorselessly, a little of this and a little of that (the Majestic's old ladies making the most of this opportunity to acquire a little nourishment), the others out of a mixture of gluttony and surprise that Edward should do things so well. Only the very finest of the guests (Lady Devereux, Sir Joshua and his wife and a sprinkling of other titled gentlemen) were heard to murmur 'Wonderful!', 'Absolutely capital!' but were not seen eating anything. Such groaning tables, of course, were an everyday sight for them – besides, people without wealth are obliged to eat not only for today but a little for tomorrow as well, 'just in case' ... Aristocrats and millionaires (and men of letters), on the other hand, scarcely have to eat at all: they can survive for days on a finger of toast and a plover's egg. The Auxiliaries ate with the zest of youth, their appetites sharpened by the wine they had drunk. They had gathered into a rowdy group of their own, full of laughter and horseplay; a movement of this group afforded the Major a glimpse of white crinoline: the twins were standing there like queen bees at the centre of a swarm; tasting everything but too excited to eat, they laughed louder than anyone as the young men ribbed each other and played the fool. On the far side of the table a veil of steam from the tureen of turtle soup failed to conceal the pale elfin face that watched them, brooding. The Major caught Charity's eye and beckoned her over.

'Why haven't you asked me to dance?' she cried as she came skidding to a stop in front of him.

'You seem to be too busy,' smiled the Major. 'I just wanted to tell you not to forget about poor Padraig. He looks lonely and he's probably too shy to talk to anyone.'

'Oh all right, where is he? But I'm sure he could talk to the old women if he really wanted to. What happened to Granny?'

'She's sitting in the lounge. Mrs Roche disarmed her, I gather.'

Edward passed at this moment, tweaked Charity's ear painfully and whispered to the Major: 'Would you mind holding the fort later on, Brendan? A few things I must do ... have a word with Ripon and so forth ... ' He bent closer to the Major's ear and, tapping his breast pocket, added: 'I have a cheque for him. The rascal must be getting short by now.' He winked at the Major and moved on. Meanwhile Charity had departed and was dragging Padraig by the sleeve into the throng of young men. The Major, whose heart was still aching, did not feel in the least like holding the fort for Edward and was wondering peevishly whether he should not go and tell him so. Edward had halted not far from the table of foreign cheeses. He was standing by himself, hands behind his back in the 'at ease' position, which was probably the most comfortable, given the tightness of his coat. He was gazing at his guests with a look of wistful satisfaction. 'This', he seemed to be thinking, 'was the way it used to be in the old days.' But then his attention was taken by the large and jovial figure of Bob Russell, the timber merchant from Maryborough, who had come up to congratulate him. Arm in arm and puffing cigars, they sauntered back to the ballroom where coffee and liqueurs were being served.

'Why have you left those beautiful daughters of yours at home?' Edward was inquiring amiably as they passed the Major. 'But of course! They're still at school in England!'

He turned briefly before leaving the dining-room and his face clouded for a moment. Perhaps he too was thinking that the shortage of young ladies was acute.

A few moments later it became more acute than ever, because the twins hared off somewhere with shrieks of laughter, dragging Padraig with them. Left to drink by themselves, the Auxiliaries' merriment declined and although there was now a general movement back to the ballroom they remained morosely where they were. Since the servants were no longer filling glasses they seized bottles of champagne and served themselves, moving out on to the terrace through the open French windows. The Major followed them and stood on the threshold looking out. The moon had now risen, washing the stone parapets with a pale light; farther along, outside the open French windows of the ballroom, a galaxy of coloured lanterns swayed in the mild night air. The orchestra had begun to play once more, the sound of violins mingling sadly with the distant thud of waves from the darkness below. With a shiver the Major went back inside. He stood, hands in pockets, in the middle of the dining-room, which was now empty except for the servants clearing away the tables. He wished the ball were over so that he could be alone.

The Major stood irresolutely at the door of the ballroom. He still had some old ladies who had to be danced with. But, knowing that he must come face to face with Sarah, he was unable to bring himself to enter. Instead, he climbed the stairs to the second floor with the intention of returning to the balcony over the ballroom where he had been earlier.

The room was still in darkness but the door was open. A faint murmur came from the moonlit balcony that lay beyond the window. He paused — afraid that Sarah might have returned here with someone else — but now the speaking voice rose querulously, becoming audible; a confused string of obscenities reached his ears. The voice was unrecognizable, but an image flashed into the Major's mind — of a man he had seen mortally wounded sitting hunched in a shell-hole with his intestines in his lap like a mess of snakes, his blue lips still quivering with an unending rigmarole of curses while his eyes turned milky.

The Major blundered forward and stepped out on to the balcony. There was only one person there: a man leaning over the balustrade, his face illuminated by the bright pool of glass that lay beneath. It was Evans. A bottle stood on the stone parapet beside him. He paid no attention to the Major, perhaps had not even heard his footfall, but continued his muttered, gulping commentary on the dazzling scene below. On the whores and whoremasters, the bitches in heat and the lecherous old goats, the cowards and the swine who thought they were so high and mighty, their day would come, the wheel would turn ...

The Major grasped him by the frayed collar of his shirt and

wrenched him back from the balustrade with a hiss of splitting cloth. He was swaying on his feet and the Major had to hold him up, fingers dug into the stained lapels of his jacket. Sudden anger gripped him. He shook Evans with all his strength; all the growing bitterness of the last hour, of the weeks and months of receding hope, all the tragedy and despair of the years in France exploded in one violent discharge of hatred concentrated on the loosely swaying head in front of him. Slowly the pale lids crept down over the tutor's bleary eyes and a tear trickled down to the corner of his mouth.

'I hate them! I hate them all!' And he shuddered convulsively, his chin sinking on to his chest. The Major's anger abated suddenly. Evans's knees sagged and the Major had to stagger forward to keep his own balance. It was all he could do to keep him from falling. For a long moment he stood there, holding the tutor upright by the lapels. But then, with a sudden access of strength, Evans straightened up and tore himself free, throwing his head and shoulders forward over the parapet. The Major lunged after him, afraid that he was about to throw himself over. But Evans had begun to vomit copiously, a thick yellow fluid that splattered on the illuminated glass below. Unaware, the black and white gentlemen on the other side of the glass continued to revolve mechanically with the softly flowing silk and taffeta of the ladies.

'You're disgusting.' The hand that the Major reached out to grasp Evans by the shoulder and help him back was shaking. Evans's eyes were closed and his features had relaxed into a strangely peaceful expression. It was difficult to get him back through the window and across the dark room. 'You'll hear more of this tomorrow.'

In the corridor a shadowy figure detached itself from a doorway. 'Murphy, come here!' the Major shouted. 'What d'you think you're doing there anyway?' But then he remembered that the uncouth old manservant had been instructed to keep himself out of the way until the guests had departed, for fear that his cadaverous appearance would upset the ladies.

'Never mind. Take Evans back where he came from and put him to bed. And clean him up while you're at it. You'd better lock him in his room until tomorrow morning.'

The tutor's sour breath still seemed to hang in the room as the Major moved back to the balcony to retrieve the bottle left on the parapet. It was empty. He left it where it was. There was a pause in the dancing. The music had come to a stop; the musicians were mopping their shining heads and consulting each other. Suddenly across the empty floor the twins came into sight, towing the beaming but reluctant Padraig ... and Padraig was dressed in a black velvet gown that reached to his ankles, with a string of pearls round his slender neck. The twins had decided to remedy the shortage of young ladies. With a grunt of dismay the Major watched them sweep out on to the moonlit terrace to join the young men, then he turned and hurried back downstairs.

But on his way back to the ballroom he was diverted for a moment by Bolton, who was lighting a cigar from the flaming torch at the foot of the stairs. He was just leaving, he informed the Major, since he had to be on duty early in the morning. Perhaps the Major would be so kind as to thank Edward on his behalf for a most pleasant evening—for the moment their host was not apparently to be found.

By now there were only a few couples dancing; among them were the twins with the young men they had selected and Viola O'Neill dancing with her father. Old Mr Norton was also there with a lady of middle age who wore a long-suffering expression as he ferried her hither and thither, his gleaming bald head stooped to the level of her bosom. With so few of the guests dancing one might have expected that the surrounding tables and chairs would be overflowing, but this was not the case. The Major looked at his watch anxiously: not yet two o' clock. Could it be that the guests had begun to leave already? The Major's worried eyes moved from one group to another, trying to account for the guests who were missing. But he soon gave it up. There was Padraig to be seen to, and the twins must be given a sharp word, they were dancing in an outrageously abandoned fashion, brushing against their partners and throwing their heads back with wild laughter while the other guests watched them with pursed lips ... they both must have had something to drink on the sly. But first, Padraig!

He was standing with several other people by the open French windows and there was something on the floor at which they were all looking with interest. Avoiding Mr Norton, who went trotting swiftly by, head and shoulders industriously lowered like a man pushing a wheelbarrow, the Major crossed the floor to see what it was. At first sight it might have been a blue-green muff or feather boa let fall by one of the ladies; but then, looking over Padraig's shoulder he saw that it had a pair of feet, a long neck and a tiny head crowned with a sparse diadem of feathers; the neck had been twisted round several times like a piece of rope.

'Where on earth did that come from?'

But before anyone had time to reply a gale of drunken laughter echoed from the darkness beyond the terrace and the Major understood. Padraig turned a pale, disconcerted face towards him.

'I asked one of them if he'd give me a peacock feather. Then they threw that in!'

The Major stooped and picked up the dead bird; its body was still warm. As he carried it outside the neck swung to and fro, unwinding a few turns, and the long tail-feathers trailed on the floor. He dumped it on the terrace and returned. Again, from outside where the Auxiliaries were roaming with bottles in the darkness, there came that gale of laughter.

He cursed Edward silently for not being present, but, determined to remain calm, he lit a cigarette and made some bland remarks to the Prendergasts and Colonel Fitzgibbon, who had noticed the dead peacock. Then, excusing himself, he moved away, beckoning to Padraig. The boy must be made to go upstairs and change his clothes instantly!

But before he had time to speak there was a further unfortunate diversion. Charity, in full view of everyone, swinging herself round more and more recklessly in the arms of her grinning young man, had finally lost her balance and fallen heavily, bringing her partner sprawling on top of her. The orchestra faltered and stopped playing.

'The poor thing is *stōshus*!' cried one of the maids in the sudden silence. And the appalling silence continued while Charity, flushed and bemused, tried to extricate herself from her partner's limbs and get to her feet. The Major, mortified, signalled to the orchestra to go on playing and hurried over. By this time Charity, giggling helplessly, was being assisted to her feet by Faith and her partner.

'You and your sister had both better go and lie down,' the Major told Faith sternly. 'And see that they have no more to drink,' he added to the blue-eyed Mortimer, who had been dancing with her and was now dusting off his companion Matthews. 'I thought I could rely on you.'

Faith and Charity were escorted from the room, crestfallen; the Major could not help feeling sorry for them.

The music had resumed. Mr Norton tirelessly continued to criss-cross the floor with his lady of middle age. The Major turned to the maid who was anxiously trying to attract his attention.

'What is it?'

'There's a gentleman and lady would like to say goodbye to Mr Spencer before they leave, sir.' Lady Devereux had apparently already left. The Smileys were all on their feet and waiting expectantly. No doubt their departure would start a general exodus. Already two or three couples were consulting each other interrogatively.

'I'll see if I can find Edward. But do you really have to go so soon? The party's only just beginning.'

By half past two the number of guests anxious to leave had swollen considerably, but still there was no sign of Edward. The ladies had long ago exchanged their flimsy dancing-shoes for more solid footwear and waited wrapped in furs. The men had found and used Edward's telephone to summon their chauffeurs and now stood, conspicuously overcoated, silk hats in hand, at the door of the ballroom, peering in distractedly in the hope of seeing, if not Edward, at least the Major. But by this time even the Major had disappeared.

The presence of these guests at the door (so obviously leaving but taking such a long time about it) had a debilitating effect on the resolution of those in the ballroom who had decided to stick it out until breakfast was served ... for, after all, not everyone has the chance of attending as many balls as the Devereuxs and the Smileys. Every now and then someone would turn his head casually to see if the overcoated defectors were still there (and yes, they *were*!), then, looking thoughtful, would return his gaze to the almost empty expanse of dance-floor where old Mr Norton, stooped and perspiring but feet twinkling as industriously as ever, continued to plough his lonely furrow. He would have been altogether alone had it not been for the fact that there were a handful of the least distinguished guests (the young Finnegans for example whose grandfather owned the drapery) for whom a dance was a dance, no matter what.

By now it had occurred to several of the guests that, although it might be embarrassing to leave so early, it might be even more embarrassing to stay and find oneself eating breakfast *en famille* with the Spencers at a breakfast table set for two hundred.

'Where *is* the dratted fellow?' demanded the overcoated and outspoken Captain Ferguson in a loud voice from the door. He was no longer even referring to Edward, given up for lost and completely mad, but to the equally elusive Major.

'Well, we can't wait all night!'

And at last the defectors moved in a convoy of fur, perfume, silk hats and cigar-smoke towards the foyer. Dragging open the massive front door (the servants had evidently vanished to their own more amusing below-stairs revelry) they found themselves face to face with the very man they had been looking for, the Major. He was carrying in his arms a large bundle of dripping black velvet from which protruded two blue-white feet and a pale, whimpering face.

The Major stepped inside immediately, looking as surprised and disconcerted as the departing guests. Beyond him, in the dark drive illuminated here and there by the lamps of the waiting motor cars, a number of uniformed chauffeurs impassively watched this curious scene.

The Major hesitated for a moment or two, long enough for his dripping black bundle to form a small pool of water on the gleaming tiles, long enough for the departing guests to notice a dark snake of pond-weed dangling from one of the slender ankles.

'Ah, you're off then,' the Major at last murmured somewhat grimly. 'I do hope you've enjoyed your … ah!' His words ended with a grunt as the velvet bundle thrashed petulantly, causing the limp strand of water-weed to slither to the floor. The ladies in furs stared at it as if it were an adder.

Meanwhile the Major had turned and was striding swiftly up the stairs with his dripping cargo. He stopped abruptly, however, before he reached the landing and looked down.

'I'll say goodbye to you for Edward. I'm afraid he's indisposed.'

With that he vanished, leaving only that sinister coil of water-weed as testimony to his passing. The departing guests cautiously groped their way out into the night.

As for the Major, he was carrying Padraig swiftly along the corridor towards the linen room, the warmest and driest place he could think of. The boy was trembling, his pearly white teeth were chattering. And no wonder! The water in the swimming-pool must be icy at this time of year. Kicking open the linen-room door he dropped Padraig into the nest of pillows and said sternly: 'Now take that wet dress off immediately. I hope this will be a lesson to you, Padraig. If I ever find you dressing up as a girl again I'll throw you in the swimming-pool myself.'

Padraig said nothing, but his whimpering increased in volume. The Major stooped and struck a match to light the oil lamp on the floor. By its light he could see that clouds of steam had begun to rise from Padraig's wet clothes. Poor Padraig! Not only had the Auxiliaries coaxed him with honeyed words to a tryst by the swimming-pool, not only had they thrown him cruelly in, they would also have left him to drown if the Major had not come to the rescue. Poor Padraig! He remembered how Sarah had once said: 'With the twins everything has a habit of beginning amusingly and ending painfully.'

In the corridor the Major paused to listen. Had he just heard a cry of pain from somewhere close at hand, perhaps from one of the rooms that lay along this very corridor or the one above? But all the doors were closed; from the linen room alone a thin trickle of yellow light daubed the carpet. Elsewhere all was dark. The cry of a girl? 'One of the twins?' he thought anxiously. But he hurried on. He must get some brandy and hot water for Padraig lest the boy catch pneumonia. Perhaps, after all, it had only been the cry of a seagull swooping close to the house.

The number of guests collecting themselves in the foyer had increased, but they and the Major ignored each other. Outside, motor cars continued to arrive, illuminating the green lawns with their sweeping headlamps. A white-haired old gentleman seated on a sofa, palms resting with dignity on a silver-embossed cane, noticed the Major slipping by and wagged a stern reproving finger at him. But the Major paid no attention and hurried on. Hardly had he escaped from the foyer, however, when he came face to face with Miss Archer who said: 'Those wretched young men are causing trouble in the ballroom. They've been threatening to shoot the orchestra if

352

they don't go on playing. And they've been making the maids dance with them.'

'My God! You haven't seen Edward? We must find him. Would you mind getting a hot drink for Padraig? He's in the linen room on the first floor. They threw him in the swimming-pool. Thank heaven most of the bloody guests have gone!'

The orchestra stopped playing just as the Major reached the ballroom. The music had grown hysterical, haphazard, a discordant scraping of violins, an outraged groaning of cellos that bore witness to the exhaustion and alarm of the musicians. Then, abruptly, in the middle of the most frenzied passage it had stopped. Now there was utter silence.

A girl was standing in the doorway. She moved aside to allow the Major to pass. It was Sarah.

'What's going on?'

But Sarah ignored him, intent on what was taking place in the ballroom. The Major brushed past her and went inside.

Edward was standing on the orchestra dais, his face dark and congested with blood, his massive body vibrating with fury. He was glaring down at the young men frozen like statues here and there on the empty floor. Behind him the musicians were swiftly and silently packing their instruments into cases and collecting their music. Three or four maids who had been dancing with the Auxiliaries melted away from the floor and vanished.

Edward had begun to stride back and forth along the narrow platform with short, violent steps ... a wooden music-stand got in his way, he kicked it aside with a deafening crash, then silence returned except for the ominous creaking of the boards under his weight. As he prowled back and forth his furious eyes remained on the faces of the young men on the dance floor.

Then one of the young men laughed. And at the same time a cold gust of wind blew through the open windows, swirling the curtains and fluttering the tablecloths, making the regiments of candles splutter and grow dim, sending up a blizzard of

353

white petals from a wilted flower that lay beside a lady's forgotten handbag. And then they were all laughing, rocking, hooting with merriment as they strolled unconcernedly towards the French windows. Outside on the terrace they could still be heard laughing as they moved away into the darkness.

Edward stopped pacing. His shoulders sagged and he looked ill. A minute or two passed and then the Major strolled across the floor and looked out over the terrace to make sure they had gone. He only saw a brief glitter in the darkness as an empty wine-bottle flew up from the terrace below, hung for a moment and then plummeted towards the glass roof. It smashed through the roof in a diamond rain and exploded on the floor in a thousand fragments. Edward, Sarah and the Major waited motionless. Presently from the glass roof there came another deafening crash and shower of glass, but this time the bottle dropped unbroken into the empty cushions of a sofa. And that was the end. It was only now that the Major noticed there had been somebody else in the ballroom all the time: sitting on another sofa in the darkest and most obscure corner holding hands were the racing motorist and his lady. But nobody acknowledged their presence and in due course they disappeared without a word.

'Where have you been?' demanded the Major bitterly. 'And thanks for leaving me to cope with everything.'

'We'll talk about it tomorrow,' Edward said curtly. Turning to Sarah he added: 'I must take you home.' They left the Major standing resentfully amid the broken glass in the middle of the floor.

Unknown to the Major there still remained two Auxiliaries at the Majestic. After Charity's fall the two young men who had been escorting them, the somewhat dubious Matthews and the clean-limbed Mortimer, winked at each other and hastened to assist the girls up the stairs. Charity needed this assistance; she had become extraordinarily sleepy and lethargic all of a sudden; she could hardly keep her eyes open or put one foot in front of the other. Faith, on the other hand, raced up the stairs unaided and even tugged at Mortimer's sleeve (which made Matthews wonder whether his great experience of women, which had led him to choose the more intoxicated of the twins, had guided him to such a wise choice after all) whenever Mortimer, who had become strangely talkative, hung back to chat with his friend Matthews. The truth was that Mortimer, though determined to put the best possible face on it in front of Matthews (to whom he had once, in a moment of weakness, confided the description of one or two fictitious conquests), was distinctly alarmed by the turn events had taken and was secretly wondering just what he was in for ... that is to say, he already *knew* more or less what he was in for, having had (or almost had) a thoroughly nauseating experience in a brothel in France, one of those 'reserved for officers' (one shuddered to think what those reserved for the other ranks had been like). Even now, chatting garrulously on the stairs about Jack Hobbs hitting long-hops over the pavilion, he had only to close his eyes to see glittering-ringed fingers parting thick white curtains of fat to invite him into some appalling darkness.

Gay as a skylark and with more energy than she could find a use for, Faith had now begun to climb using only one leg, her crinoline ballooning prettily with each hop—but even so she found she was ascending more quickly than the others. Back she came to tug at Mortimer's sleeve again, telling him that he was a slowcoach and that he should forget his beastly cricket and come on up and ... 'My God! Just look at Catty! You'd think she was sleep-walking!'

Indeed, Charity was swaying helplessly, loose-limbed as a puppet, divinely relaxed. Her eyelids kept creeping down and it took all her strength to force them up a millimetre or two to see what was going on. Climbing unaided would have been out of the question but fortunately Matthews's shoulder was under her left armpit, his powerful arm was wrapped round her back and a hand like a steel hook gripped the bottom of her rib-cage as if it were the handle of a suitcase (this hurt, she knew, but for some reason she couldn't feel it) ... 'Jolly decent of him to help me, anyway,' she kept thinking.

'Hey! Are you all right, Catty?' Faith's grinning face was saying a few inches in front of her own, emerging out of a grey fog of sleep.

'Of course I am!' she said crossly—or would have said if she had not been so busy with the weight of her eyelids.

'Of course she is!' Matthews echoed her thoughts, though rather defensively. 'She's as right as rain.' But at the same time he was becoming increasingly anxious lest he had picked the wrong one. This one was *too* drunk—either that or not drunk enough. Fortunately, while his right hand, fingers dug deep into the soft, elastic flesh of her waist, was holding Charity up by the ribs, his left hand was gripping the neck of a bottle of chilled champagne that he had thoughtfully caught up out of an ice-bucket in case a further anaesthetic should be needed. But what was the matter with that ass Mortimer? Was he showing the white feather in spite of all his big talk? In which case ...

But meanwhile they had at last reached the second floor and Faith had picked out two adjoining rooms which she knew to be unoccupied. Having deposited one twin in each of them, the young men emerged for a hasty conference, Matthews suggesting that Mortimer might like to swap ... 'I think this one prefers you, anyway.'

But Mortimer considered his honour to be at stake and rather haughtily rejected the suggestion, though he knew (and knew that Matthews knew) that he would have been only too glad to accept if it had not been a question of honour.

'But you aren't going to be a cad, are you, Matthews? I mean, your one is dead to the world.'

'Matter of fact, you're wrong there. She's already getting interested ... '

Matthews and Mortimer separated on this disagreeable note,

the former with every intention of being a cad if he possibly could, the latter determined to put up a good show (or at least not to be sick like last time). Matthews, returning to the room where Charity lay fast asleep on a dusty counterpane, cast an expert eye over her inert form and saw at a glance that he would have to be quick.

It's not at all easy to undress someone who is unconscious — and Charity was wearing a great many layers of clothes. Fortunately Matthews was deft and experienced at removing ladies' garments, otherwise he might have been so discouraged as to give the whole thing up as a bad job, thereby losing a heaven-sent opportunity. Besides, he knew himself to be a good worker and was proud of his skill. This was something of a challenge, all the more so since the clothes Charity was wearing were unfamiliar: crinoline and petticoats and odd pantaloons with all sorts of hooks and ribbons and laces and safety-pins in places where one would not expect them. He lit the oil lamp, removed his jacket and made a rapid preliminary check to make sure that what ought to be there *was* there — and it was (for even divinely beautiful girls are constructed on the same general principles as their more homely sisters). Then he rubbed his chilly fingers and set to work, his eyes bright with concentration.

Charity was rolled on to her front, so that the eye-hooks that meandered up her spine could be unfastened one by one ... but then something became stuck in front, so she had to be rolled on to her back, then on to her front again so that half a dozen white laces in granny-knots could be untied. Next he had to work his forearm under her stomach in order to lift her off the bed an inch or two, with the other hand trying to work the clumsy hooped skirt upwards ... but he found this too difficult and had to stop and scratch his head in perplexity. It was clear that the only way was to roll her backwards and forwards working the skirt up a few inches at a time.

Each time he rolled her over Charity groaned, dreaming that she was crossing the Irish Sea to school in a black gale;

giant waves swept her up and down, up and down ... Of course she was never seasick ... it would be too shaming if she was sick ... but what if the boat began to sink? Up and down, up and down ... Ah, no wonder it hadn't been moving, Matthews was thinking, there were a million pins he hadn't even noticed, he must be losing his touch ... Now over she goes again, a firm shove on the hip and on the shoulder and ... 'No, no, straighten out your legs,' he muttered crossly. 'We'll get nowhere like that ... It'll take us all night.'

The temperature had been dropping steadily as the night wore on. By now it was freezing in the room. His fingers were stiff with the cold and lacked their usual dexterity, but he worked on without a pause. In a moment the first layer of clothing would be lying on the carpet. After that, things should go more smoothly.

Next door it was cold as well; at least Faith thought so. She was sitting in bed with her knees up to her chin, naked and shivering. The room was pitch-dark except for a faint orange glow that leaked under the communicating door from the oil lamp by which Matthews was working. Mortimer was striding up and down in the darkness. Although she could not see him she could tell more or less where he was by the sound of his voice and the creak of the floor-boards.

For some minutes he had been telling her about a master at school who had got drunk on Speech Day. Young, handsome, courteous, artistic, a wonderful athlete, the whole school had loved him from the loftiest prefect to the most insignificant fag until that day when he had gone weaving across the quad in gown and mortarboard shouting that the Matron was a flabby old bitch before the horrified eyes of a lot of chaps' parents ... But Faith's teeth were chattering and try as she might she was unable to see the relevance of this story to their present situation. Was Mortimer trying to say that he was drunk? No, it couldn't be that. But what was it, then? Having failed, together with Charity and Viola, to understand and identify on her own person a fair proportion of the technical terms used in the brown-paper-wrapped book that Matthews had lent them, she was vague about what exactly was supposed to happen to begin with; but instinct told her that this sort of preamble was not necessary. Perhaps she had got undressed too promptly? On the other hand, what else was there to do? If only there had been a light burning she might have been able to see his face and get some clue as to what he was thinking. Mortimer had refused even to permit a candle to be lit. He had become hysterical when she had struck a match to see where the bed was. After that she had had to grope her way towards it in the dark. The whole thing was turning out to be decidedly odd and a much bigger bore than she had anticipated. Discouraged, she dolefully rested her trembling chin on her knees and wondered whether it wouldn't be best to give it up and start slipping on a few clothes again.

Mortimer was now telling her in a rapid, high voice about a fellow in the army who had gone for a trip on a whaler before the war, all those mountains of blubber, cutting through the mountains of blubber with flensing-knives! Ah, he could have done with a flensing-knife himself ... The truth was that he was finding it increasingly difficult to avoid the curtains of white fat in which the room was draped. But now, striding about excitedly in the darkness, he had completely lost his sense of direction so that presently, ducking to avoid some limp tassels of lard that hung from the ceiling, he caught his foot in a rug and crashed forward into the bed, winding himself badly. Seizing her opportunity, Faith cast aside her sheet and pinioned him promptly against the mattress planting lean, dry kisses on his lips.

As he recovered his breath it slowly dawned on Mortimer that the sensation of touching a naked girl wasn't at all what he had expected ... Little by little the curtains of white fat began to liquefy about the edges. Soon they were sliding down the walls to the floor and melting into a colourless liquid that seeped rapidly away through the cracks in the floorboards. His hand touched one of Faith's shoulder-blades ... splendid, hard as a rock, nothing flabby about that! Next it alighted on her hip-bone and pelvis ... solid as an iron casserole, it would chime as clear as frost if one tapped it with a fork (no need to think now about the spongey tripes that might be cooking inside it). Then came the ribs, every one clean and hard as the iron bars of a railing, drag a stick along them and they'd chatter like a machine-gun, a jolly good show (provided one forgot about the two oozing octopuses that were busy squeezing slimily in and out behind the bars). 'Really,' he was thinking, 'girls seem to be perfectly splendid little creatures!' But at this moment his hand, which had been hovering in the darkness over her ribs, swooped down to land by misfortune on Faith's ample bosom – which fled silkily in all directions, quivering like a beef jelly. A vast dough of white grease (which Mortimer had somehow failed to notice suspended above the bed) at this moment detached itself from the ceiling and dropped, engulfing him.

Next door Matthews was crouched low over the bed working on a last stubborn knot in the region of Charity's lower vertebrae; his mouth was open as he worked, partly from concentration, partly because he suffered from catarrh. As he bent closer, anxiously trying to see the ins and outs of this knot, the vapour that sped like smoke from his lips stirred the tiny blonde hairs running up Charity's spine, causing her to groan and mutter. For a moment she even tried to lift her head. Matthews shifted his worried gaze to her face. She was going to wake up any minute! That would be just his luck! She was already half-conscious and every few moments she would thrash out blindly with her legs; once she had caught him a painful blow on the elbow. Now that he had only one miserable knot left to deal with she would be bound to wake up and call the whole thing off!

His eyes moved to the bottle of champagne on the floor by the bed. Better give her some more to drink before she became sober enough to refuse it. He left the knot and shifted his attention to the bottle, hastily working the wire harness away from the cork. He had just begun to dig out the cork itself when he heard footsteps. He paused. He held his breath.

It seemed to come from from the floor below (in fact, he had just heard the Major carrying Padraig to the linen room), but supposing someone came up here and saw the light under the door! It would take some explaining away—him up here with a half-naked filly! He'd have to say he had just found her like that. Maybe he'd better give it up ... But the sound had faded. All was silent once more.

He breathed again. In the room next door that idiot Mortimer had at last stopped pacing up and down and got down to business. Charity was lying peacefully again now. He judged that the champagne was no longer necessary. Putting the bottle down quietly on the floor by the bed he returned, rubbing his knuckles and blowing on his fingers, to deal with this last knot. It was definitely the last, he had assured himself of that ... Charity was already naked to the waist; all that now remained was a wretched knee-length camisole, tied firmly round the waist with (of all things) coarse brown string. Really, the things girls trussed themselves up with! As it happened it was Faith who had tied this knot for her sister— and as a joke (Charity had not been able to see what she was doing behind her back) she had tied it as tightly as she could, one knot on top of another, so that Charity would never never ever be able to get it undone. Matthews had stubby, thick fingers which were stiff with the cold although he had tried warming them over the lamp. To make things worse, he was in the habit of biting his nails with the result that he was now picking away at the knot as clumsily as if he had been wearing gloves. He could cut it with a penknife, of course. He paused, tempted. But no, that would be unsporting. This knot was a challenge and he wasn't the kind of man to duck a challenge. He'd already got so far, besides, he didn't like to think of all his patient work going to waste. Breathing through his dry mouth, tongue between his teeth with concentration, he applied himself to his task.

And then his parcel was untied at last! It had taken him another three or four minutes before his diligence was at last rewarded. All he had to do now was remove the final wrapping; he would just have to roll her over on to her front and on to her back a few more times to ease the camisole off and then ... he would have opened the small locked door leading into the garden of delight.

All this time Charity was being tossed savagely to and fro on stormy seas and by now she was feeling alarmingly sick. One moment she was rocking back and forth on the mail-boat with that dreadful lurching one feels as one first leaves the protection of the Howth peninsula and forges out into the open sea; the next she was shipwrecked and bobbing about helplessly in the water. It was icy cold and she had lost all her clothes—a huge wave had just come and turned her completely over, dragging away the last stitch she had on— and then somehow she was lying on her back on a rock and some appalling Creature (that resembled a black sea-lion with a white shirt and black bow-tie, rather like an illustration from *Alice in Wonderland*), an appalling Creature was trying to dislodge her from the rock and send her sliding back into the black water ... and now a moist pink tongue was licking her kneecaps and a scratchy moustache was tickling her thighs ... At this moment, as luck would have it, her roaming hand closed over a very cold, elongated stone and she swung it up and hit the Creature with it. With a soft moan the Creature vanished back into the water ... but Charity continued to feel sick until at last she vomited enormously, volcanically, over the side of the bed. Then the waves calmed down and she felt very much better.

The bottle of champagne had not broken, however, when she hit Matthews (who was now lying on the floor with a fractured skull); her fingers had released it and it lay like a block of ice between her thighs. The cork, meanwhile, had begun to travel imperceptibly away from the bottle as Charity floated peacefully onwards (and Faith in the next room groped around in the darkness trying to collect up as many of her garments as possible). Presently it gathered momentum and exploded. A long cry of pain broke from Charity's lips as the freezing liquid bubbled over the warm skin of her stomach.

Downstairs the Major paused and thought anxiously: 'One of the twins?'—but he had Padraig to think of and hurried on.

In the next room Faith paused in alarm at her sister's bloodcurdling cry and thought that perhaps, after all, it mightn't be such a bad thing that her own escapade had proved a failure—while beside her in the oily darkness Mortimer thought bitterly: 'What a cad the fellow is! Taking advantage of her like that ... '

Another person heard the scream. This was Murphy, who had been lurking in the shadowy corridor and seen the twins come up with their young men. When he heard it he chuckled; then his gaunt figure melted back into the darkness. As he went, the moonlight from an uncurtained window glinted momentarily on a long, curving blade, for he had brought a scythe up from the barn, to hone and grease it in the attic where he kept his belongings.

It seemed to the Major that the night had already lasted an eternity, but the clock on the mantelpiece of the residents' lounge (specially repaired and wound to mark off the blissful moments of Edward's ball) had scarcely conceded three o'clock. A few moments ago he had caught sight of himself in a mirror unexpectedly: two eyes round with worry in a pale face had stared at him unblinking as an owl, making him think of shell-shock cases in hospital, men who used to sit up in bed all night, wide-eyed, smoking one cigarette after another as they tried to probe the darkness around them.

'I hope this will be a lesson to you!'

All the lessons that were being learned that evening! But what good did they do? By the time one had learned them it was too late. He would move on, but life would not go with

363

him. Life would stay where Sarah was; all the great explosions of joy would take place in her vicinity.

'Drink it all up. Every drop. If it tastes bad you should have thought of that beforehand!'

The house was empty now and silent, except for an occasional faint scratching sound; the Major postulated a rat under the floor-boards. Edward had disappeared once more, leaving him to cope with everything as usual, but he was too tired to feel any resentment. Besides, in a moment he would go to bed.

The Major was standing beside the dying fire, resting one elbow on the mantelpiece, his hand sifting slowly through his untidy mass of hair. Next to him, huddled in dressing-gowns, sat the twins, looking pallid and chastened, each of them nursing an enormous glass of bicarbonate of soda mixed with water from which, wrinkling their noses in disgust, they sipped miserably.

'Anyway, you're sure you didn't do anything you shouldn't have done? It's far better to tell me now if you did ... '

'Oh no, Brendan!' murmured Charity hoarsely, avoiding the Major's eye.

'What sort of thing do you mean?' inquired Faith more strategically.

'Never you mind. Just drink up. Come on now, take a deep breath and drink it down all in one go. It's the only way.'

Half an hour earlier the Major had come upon a strange quartet proceeding slowly down the stairs. First had come Mortimer, grunting and dishevelled, wobbling dangerously under the weight of the limp and senseless Matthews (who had 'bumped his head in the dark'). A few stairs above the labouring Mortimer the two sisters were supporting each other, pale as ghosts, their clothing disarranged and somehow ... well, *different*, he could not help thinking (in their debilitated state they had left off some of the inner layers that had earlier exercised Matthews's skill to the utmost). With one dismayed glance at the twins the Major had leaped to assist Mortimer with his unfortunate friend; the 'bump' was a bad one, the poor chap was out cold, though breathing steadily enough.

Once Matthews had been deposited on a sofa in the foyer the Major telephoned the camp at Valebridge and asked for an ambulance. 'No, no, it was an accident,' he had explained several times. In due course the ambulance arrived; the men who came with it looked around suspiciously for a while ('No, nothing whatsoever to do with Sinn Feiners. He simply bumped his head!') and then left with poor Matthews who still had not regained consciousness. Indeed, it was several hours before he finally came round and even then was unable to remember just how he had come to bump his head in the dark, an uncertainty of memory that was to persist, together with bouts of double vision and absent-mindedness, for the rest of his life.

The twins had heaved a sigh of relief when they saw him go. Charity in particular experienced a surge of joy and for a moment almost forgot to appear more ill than she felt (she and Faith had had the presence of mind to powder their faces with chalk in order to incite sympathy and deflect punishment). She *did* feel ill, of course, *inside*, though luckily she had vomited the contents of her stomach. But her face in the mirror had looked all too shiningly healthy. It was boring of the Major to insist on them drinking this vile stuff, but it was comforting too in a way—after all, she had had a fright. Tonight, for once, she would remember to say her prayers!

At length, the twins in bed and brimming with bicarbonate of soda, the Major himself climbed the stairs, though not without checking once more in his mind that everything had been taken care of ... The twins? Yes. Padraig? Sent home in dry clothes. The wretched tutor? Deal with him tomorrow. The guests? Well, nothing could be done about the guests. Sarah? Forget about her. Mrs Rappaport? Disarmed and in bed, as far as he knew. And Sarah? Forget about her. But how could he? He must. And Sarah? Think about her tomorrow, perhaps. And Sarah?

His room was bitterly cold; the sheets on his bed were damp and icy to the touch. Tired and in despair, this lack of comfort was almost more than he could bear. If only he had had a hot-water bottle! He lay there, craving physical comfort as, earlier in the evening, he had craved sweetness. Of course a hot-water bottle was out of the question. 'All the same,' he thought, 'I shall never manage to fall asleep like this,' as worn out by the happiness, disappointment, unhappiness, bitterness and chaos that had succeeded each other throughout the day, he fell asleep nevertheless, forgetting to blow out the candles at his bedside.

They were still burning when he woke a little later; in fact, they had hardly burned down more than an inch or two. He called: 'Come in,' because someone was knocking at the door. He expected to see Edward appear; it was just like him to wake people up inconsiderately because he suddenly felt the need for reassurance. But no, it was the cook.

'Ye're t' come at once!' she exclaimed breathlessly. 'The divil's below!' And she gabbled a further torrent of words which the Major found quite incomprehensible. He stared at her in astonishment.

He had had very little to do with this woman since the time of Angela's illness when he had been in the habit of haunting the staircase at mealtimes. Indeed, he had made it his business to avoid her because she still showed signs of being uneasy in his presence. All the more surprising, therefore, that she should be now standing at his door, her plump figure swathed in what looked like an army greatcoat, unlaced men's boots on her feet, the grey hair that was normally tightly rolled into a bun on the back of her head frothing wildly over her shoulders.

'What's all this?' he demanded sternly. 'The devil? You must speak plainly and slowly. I don't understand you.'

But the cook plunged on faster than ever, repeating the same mysterious phrases again and again while the Major tried in vain to fit them into some coherent pattern. Could she be speaking Irish? Or was it merely her defective palate, abetted, he suspected, by the absence of teeth?

'Wait!' he said severely (this sort of thing must not be encouraged). 'I shall come and see for myself.' And he threw aside the bedclothes, causing the cook to back away apprehensively, her flow of speech suddenly arrested. He paid no attention to her but pulled on slippers and a dressing-gown, knotting it tightly round his waist. By this time the cook had vanished along the corridor, but as he hurried after her and turned a corner he saw a sputtering candle ahead of him, the flame dragged horizontal by her haste, the men's boots slapping clumsily on her bare feet. As they descended the staircase the candle shining through the banisters made clumsy, swollen cartwheels that accompanied them down into the foyer.

The house was in complete darkness. Everyone had retired for the night. But no ... a glimmer of light was still shining from under the door of the writing-room. The cook pointed at the door and stepped back.

The scene in the writing-room was a dismal one. It had proved impossible to clean all the rooms on the ground floor in time for the ball; rather than allow the guests to cover themselves in dust it had been thought best to seal off the most distressing places. One of the gas mantles was burning, but no answering gleams were reflected from the dust-laden furniture and woodwork; at best a stray gleam radiated from the glass fairy that Mrs Bates had given her life to place on top of the grandfather clock; the remainder of the Christmas decorations still hung from the corners of the ceiling, grey and sinister as the toils of a giant spider.

A small man was standing with his head directly interposed between the gaslight and the Major so that his face was in darkness. His elongated shadow stretched out gigantically over the open expanse of floor to engulf the Major—indeed, all the shadows seemed to stretch out from him and that single light behind his head, lending him the appearance of a black spider at the centre of another web. The Major failed to recognize the silhouette. But there was no mistaking the deferential yet agitated tones in which the man, advancing, began to speak. It was Mr Devlin and he regretted very much disturbing the Major at this unpardonable hour but he would surely be forgiven when the reason was known ... ('Is the wretched fellow incapable of speaking straight?' wondered the Major, grinding his teeth).

'Yes, yes. What is it?'

It was his daughter, Sarah ... she hadn't come home yet and though he knew she was in safe hands ... in short, he'd heard that the ball had terminated more early than was expected ... mind you, everyone had said what a great success it was ... and therefore, because there was such trouble in the country round about ...

'Sarah? What time is it now?' He had left his watch in the pocket of his waistcoat. He thought of the candles left burning in his room.

'Mr Spencer took her home ... perhaps an hour ago, perhaps more. More, I should think. Where *is* Mr Spencer?' He looked round for the cook, but of course she had disappeared.

Grasping Devlin by the arm, he dragged him deeper into the room, nearer the solitary gas jet so that he could see the man's face. From the darkness there came a faint, distressed mewing and a dislocation of shadows. The cats had returned. For a moment he had thought that the mewing was coming from Devlin himself.

But Devlin had also begun to speak, in a high, frenzied tone which grated unbearably on the Major's nerves. He'd known as much! He'd warned her against it ... But no, she wouldn't listen. No decent girl would show her face with those drunken devils on the loose. He'd warned her! They'd gone rampaging through Kilnalough not an hour ago and she hadn't come home ... She'd been so intent on dancing with the quality, well, that was where it had got her. He'd seen the damage they'd done ... they'd overturned the milk churns so that the main street was like a white river, Finnegan's window with a black, star-shaped hole in it ... and the butcher's shop-window lay piled under the sill like a snowdrift! And they'd been dressed up in their finery, in their claw-hammer suits like gentlemen. Ha, fine gentlemen! And he'd heard girls screaming ... But she'd not come home even then ... It was he, the Major, who was responsible. She had been left in his care. He was not a gentleman. Indeed, he was a swine and a cad to leave the girl on such a night ... Ah, a cripple and without protection ... And Mr Spencer who thought that he could buy him, Devlin, with his money and his hypocrite's talk, what sort of a man was that? D'ye hear me?

The Major shook Devlin so violently that his last words were uttered in gasps. He fell silent then.

'Sarah will be all right with Edward. Nobody will touch her.'

'Nobody, is it?' Devlin leered. 'And where is she at this minute? Tell me that. All right with him, d'you say? Sure he's likely worse than any of them!'

'You're speaking of a gentleman!' snapped the Major. 'Mr Spencer is a man of honour.'

Abashed, Devlin fell silent. The Major peered at his face, certain that he had been drinking. For once the bank manager looked dirty and dishevelled; his hair, oiled and combed, had swung forward over his forehead, curving ridiculously upwards like a pair of horns. His trousers were secured with bicycle clips. 'They're all the same,' mused the Major. 'Even when they hold responsible jobs they're liable to go to pieces at the first sign of trouble.'

'You see, you came here on a bicycle. Heaven only knows how long you took on the way. Your daughter is probably back at home by now.'

Devlin paid no attention, his eyes had strayed into the shadows and he was mumbling incoherently. 'He's been most good ... She was a cripple ... the best doctors, indeed I am, sir, more grateful than I can say ... Ah, it wasn't the sort of expense I'd be able to permit myself ... He did everything for her! Nothing was too much ... '

'You must go home, Devlin. Sarah will be all right. I'll answer for it.'

But abruptly Devlin burst out: 'He's been most good ... He's been a swine!'

This cry echoed emptily around the panelled walls, shrill as a girl's scream. It was followed by a few moments of utter silence.

'You must go home, Devlin. Come along, there's a good fellow. I'll see you to the door.' And the Major caught hold of the bank manager's elbow and dragged him round to face the door. As he did so he noticed a bluish light flare in Devlin's eyes. But it was only the reflected glint from the gas mantle. By the time they reached the foyer Devlin had recovered a little and was excusing himself in a low, monotonous voice for getting the Major up at this hour, he must be tired after the ball which had been, he had heard, a famous success, the Major must forgive him this liberty given the desperate circumstances, ... the last time they had met and had their most enjoyable chat the Major had given him to understand that a certain young lady's well-being was of importance to him, had he not? and with all the drunken shouting and singing and smashing of windows and accosting of respectable girls he had felt it his duty to take the grave decision of calling for assistance ...

'Shut up, for God's sake! Go home and have some sleep and we'll talk about it in the morning. It must be almost five. There! Now good night and go straight home!'

Devlin was standing uncertainly at the top of the steps. He seemed anxious to continue his apologies but the Major's patience was at an end. He slipped back inside the door and closed it. Then, without waiting to see whether Devlin was going to take himself off, he climbed the stairs to bed. 'And Sarah?' he thought as he was climbing between the sheets.

'Wake up, Brendan! Wake up!'

The Major was floating in soft black water in a disused quarry. The depth of the water was so great that when he dropped a white pebble into it he could still see it minutes afterwards, winking in the darkness as it sank. Then he was sinking beside it, down and down. 'Death is the only peace on earth,' he thought as he was sinking.

'Wake up!'

A hand touched him and he sat up with a start. The room was black and he could see nothing. But he knew that he was not still dreaming: a hand was grasping his wrist, warm breath fanning his cheek.

'Who is it?'

'Where are the matches? I can't see a thing.' It was one of the twins.

'What's the matter?'

'Brendan, are you awake?'

'Yes, what is it?'

'There's been a terrible fight downstairs. We think it must be the Sinn Feiners.'

A match flared, illuminating Charity. She held it up above her head, looking for the Major's candles. Presently the match was swamped by darkness; then another match was struck, this time on the other side of the bed, and Charity was lighting the candles.

'We were too frightened to go down.'

Unable for a moment to recall the events of the past few hours, the Major waited with instinctive dread for consciousness to start the first few rolling pebbles that would generate an avalanche of remembered disasters. Then, as one memory after another hurtled down on him, he heaved his drugged limbs over the side of the bed and massaged his face wearily. He stood up and for a while looked in vain for his dressing-gown. Then he realized that he was still wearing it.

'I'll go down and see. You'd better wait here and lock the door if you hear anyone coming. Get into my bed or you'll catch cold.'

It seemed to him that there would never be an end to this blundering through the darkened, empty corridors of the Majestic. What time was it? Surely it should be light by now! But the black windows he passed were lit only by the reflected flame of his candle.

After the darkness of the corridor the study seemed glaringly bright. Still holding the candle and oblivious of the drips of hot wax that spilled over his clenched fingers, the Major stood in the doorway and looked about with shocked eyes at the bizarre scene of destruction that greeted him. At his feet the floor was littered with broken glass and tarnished silver cups. A framed cartoon by Spy which had once hung over the desk lay on the floor, its glass cobwebbed; the desk itself had been swept clean except for an upturned ink-well which was still leaking a steady black drip on to the dusty carpet. Even the air showed traces of the room's chaos—hazy with white powder, turf-ash scattered half across the floor from the embers of the fire, in which, moreover, a man's shoe lay smouldering. Beyond the fireplace a Welsh dresser had tilted forward to unload a shelf of books and half a row of dusty upturned brandy glasses on to the floor. As he watched, another glass crept forward, slithered off the topmost shelf, turned slowly in the air and dissolved in a bright puff as it struck the edge of the dresser.

In the middle of all this confusion Sarah was sitting, alone. She said calmly: 'Go away, Brendan. Things are difficult enough already.' And then, as the Major neither moved nor spoke, she added impatiently: 'Edward is a fool, an absurd and pitiful creature. Mother of God! And as for my father ... He seemed to think that he was actually going to kill Edward ... Of course he couldn't even do that successfully.'

Sarah was sitting with her legs drawn up beneath her in a deep leather armchair. Around her shoulders she had swirled a vast khaki blanket which hung to the floor in an irregular cone. One naked arm clasped the blanket to her chin. The Major's eye, stung by the nakedness of this arm, travelled away and was promptly stung again, more severely: this time by a door beside the desk that stood open to an adjoining room. He had never seen this door open before. Within he could glimpse an iron bed and a tangle of dirty sheets.

'Was anyone hurt?'

'Hurt?' cried Sarah gaily. 'If they had managed to hurt each other perhaps they wouldn't have looked so ridiculous ... Why is everyone here so ridiculous? Yes, you're ridiculous too, goggling at me with your sheep's eyes ... Can you guess what happened? Did he cut Edward's throat? At least that would have made some sense ... but no, not even that! He kept shouting that his honour was besmirched ... as if he had any honour to begin with! He said that Edward had bought me with thirty pieces of silver ... Naturally Edward couldn't find a word to say to all this. Oh, they make me sick, both of them. "Now look here, Mr Devlin, can't we be sensible about this?" Ah, and my father was drunk, of course, or else it would never have occurred to him to assault one of the gentry, a member of the quality, mind you, a Protestant gentleman ... one of his own customers at the bank. My God! Can you imagine his daring? Oh yes, and Edward ... don't think that he was any better. He was worse ... he was ready to grovel too ... and I used to think he was a man with dignity, shows what a poor little fool I am. You should have seen them fighting, you'd have died laughing. They make me sick!'

Sarah's face had turned white and against this pallor her eyes seemed black and very large. As if to give substance to her words, she leaned forward, hanging her head over the arm of the chair as if she were, in fact, about to be sick. The Major took a step forward to comfort her, but stopped again. Lying folded on the arm of the sofa his eyes encountered an oblong of grey silk that might have been a woman's dress. He stood there, painfully absorbing every detail; when he turned his head away every tiniest thread was stitched into his memory. He was certain that Sarah was naked under her blanket. On her naked arm, near the shoulder, he noticed the blue mark of

373

a bruise and in his mind's eye he saw Bolton standing beside her chair at the ball, his finger and thumb whitening around her soft skin.

'Where are they now?'

Sarah lifted her white face and stared at him without comprehension. Eventually she said: 'Edward took him home when they'd finished fighting. I wouldn't go with them. What d'you think? They're probably the best of friends by now. Even before he left he was beginning to apologize. "You'll understand my position, Mr Spencer ... " and Edward was saying that he, my father, had every right, that he understood what it was to have daughters ... Edward was terrified of him ... I've never seen anyone look so shaken and guilty and wretched. It was disgusting!'

The Major stepped forward and knelt by the fire to pick the shoe out of the ashes; the leather sole was blackened and charred. He blew a blizzard of white ash off it and set it down indecisively in the hearth. A deluge of hot wax scalded his fingers, reminding him that he was still holding the candle. He threw it into the fire and picked the wax off his knuckles with a dull resentment, staring at his fingers. Sarah was weeping bitterly by now, but the Major continued to pick at his waxed knuckles. Then, when at last he had finished, he went to stand over Sarah's chair and took hold of her naked arm and tried to kiss her wet face. As she resisted he began to struggle with her, wrenching at the blanket that covered her: 'You dirty whore!' He was certain that she was naked beneath the blanket. She struck him heavily in the face. He stepped back surprised, and after a moment said: 'I'm terribly sorry, Sarah.'

But Sarah did not seem annoyed. She merely said with indifference: 'That's all right, Brendan. But now leave for heaven's sake. I couldn't stand another scene tonight.'

'Can't I take you home?'

'No. I telephoned a friend to come for me. He'll be here in a minute.'

His room was in darkness and he no longer had the candle he had taken downstairs. It was not until he had reached his bed and groped for the bedclothes that he remembered the twins.

'Are you awake?'

'Yes.'

'It was nothing serious. You can go back to bed now. A bookcase fell over in your father's study.'

'Can't we stay? It's almost morning and our beds will be freezing.'

'Certainly not.'

'Just for a little while?'

'No, of course not. Go back to your rooms.'

But the twins made no move and the Major was too weary to argue. For a while he stood in the darkness thinking of nothing, then he took off his dressing-gown and got into bed. 'Well, just for a little while.'

It was comforting, he had to admit, to have a warm body beside him. Presently he had two warm bodies beside him, for one of the twins had slipped out of bed, around it, and in at the other side. He formulated in his mind the words of rebuke that would send them both back to their cold beds but his vocal chords seemed to be paralysed by weariness and despair —and so it was in the middle of this chaste, warm, heavenly sandwich that the broken-hearted Major finally fell asleep. A faint smell of wine and perspiration presently began to perfume the air around this peacefully sleeping bed, for not only had the twins forgotten to say their prayers, they had also forgotten to wash themselves.

By now, at last, it was beginning to get light at the Majestic. The breeze from the sea which had chilled the few remaining guests during the early hours had dropped again and all was still. In a few minutes it would be daybreak: the rising sun would warm the weather-beaten stone that faced the sea.

Presently Mr O'Flaherty arrived in his trap with the three

375

lads who worked for him. He was the local caterer who had been commissioned to provide breakfast in the ballroom (the other firm of caterers having returned to Dublin after supper). He had retired early the previous evening in order to have his wits about him at breakfast-time and thus no news of the outcome of the ball had yet reached him. Certainly he was surprised to find everything so quiet— but that was hardly any of his business. By now the guests would have been sporting and dancing all night. Doubtless they were rather tired.

Laden with baskets of eggs and trays of bacon, the boys staggered after him as he made his dignified way round to the kitchens – which had been left in a shocking state (he clicked his tongue in disapproval). Mr O'Flaherty was a portly man, very red-faced, a Sinn Feiner by conviction but disapproving of violence (indeed, of any kind of excess). He disapproved of a good many things – at least, in general terms; in particular cases he was inclined to be tolerant. He disapproved of the Anglo–Irish 'quality', who seemed to him idle, luxurious, and very often slow-witted into the bargain. He disapproved of Hunt Balls and similar shenanigans. But he had nevertheless a job to do and he intended to do it.

'Look at the filth of it ... That's Dubliners for ye!'

While the lads were cleaning up the kitchens he went upstairs to fetch the silver. For it seemed that ordinary china was not good enough for these people: they must eat out of silver dishes and drink their coffee from silver pots. Edward had shown him where to find this glistening treasure and handed him the key to the cupboard where it lay. Mr O'Flaherty could not resist a momentary feeling of pride at being trusted in this manner, and perhaps this did a little to palliate the unpleasant thought that while Mr Spencer and his guests were eating off silver there were people in the West of Ireland with hardly a bite to eat of any sort.

The eggs were broken into cups ready for the pan, the rashers spread out in leaves beside the mounds of kidneys, the cauldrons of water brought to the boil for the silver pots of coffee or tea. When everything was ready Mr O'Flaherty took two of the lads upstairs with him, warm plates stacked up to their eyes, leaving the third to start the frying and toasting.

With a clean chef's hat set firmly on his head he advanced on the ballroom with short dignified steps. He was disturbed, however, by the unnatural quiet of the place. There was no sound in the corridor except, once, the distant scream of a cat. The walls gave back that special echo that one only seems to hear in deserted rooms. Still, rather than lose face in front of the lads by showing that he was perturbed, he made no comment. His face remained as grave and impassive as if everything had been perfectly normal. Besides, with these people one never knew how they would behave. Even if (and the possibility had occurred to him) he found them lying scattered all over the floor 'stiff with the drink' his job was not to pass comments but to serve breakfast to those who could revive themselves sufficiently to partake of it—and this was what he intended to do. But in the ballroom there wasn't a soul.

Mr. O'Flaherty advanced into the middle of the floor with measured steps, his face still studiously impassive. Behind him the eyes that peered over the stacks of plates were positively bulging with surprise and wonderment. Ah, but now he had to look down at his feet for he was crunching through a litter of broken glass; in fact, there was broken glass everywhere and wilted flowers and cigar ends and heaven only knew what else! 'What a rabble, did ye ever see the like?' he thought.

'Tell Christy to stop the frying till we see how much we'll be needing ... Then bring up the dishes, toast, tea and coffee, as much as he's done.'

He took a cautious look outside on the terrace, which was also littered with broken glass. 'What were they doing at all?' he wondered. 'Was it a battle they had, or what?' The sun had risen by now. It was going to be a lovely day. The smell of the countryside in the spring ... he took a deep, contented breath, but then remembered his duty and, shaking his head

377

regretfully, stepped inside once more to organize the boys at the buffet tables and tell them where to stand.

By seven o'clock there was still no sign of anyone wanting breakfast. The first dishes, though kept warm for a while with hot water, had had to be discarded and replenished, though it was a shame to waste good food.

'Stand up straight, Paddy, and stop your fidgeting or you'll get what's what.'

Of the three of them only he was permitted to move. But still, it was hard on them standing there with nothing to do.

Presently, however, a peahen came in through the French windows with nervous steps, looking for the long-tailed blue-green magnificence that had been her mate. She picked around for a while amid the broken glass, watched by the three silent men in white hats and aprons. At length Mr O'Flaherty tore off a corner of buttered toast and, bending with a sigh, offered it to her in the palm of his plump hand. She took it and ate it distractedly, a faint breeze ruffling the biscuit-coloured feathers of her breast. Then she hurried fretfully back to the terrace to continue her search. She was Mr O'Flaherty's only customer that morning.

It was almost noon when the Major awoke. The maid was opening the curtains to let in a cascade of golden sunshine and the twins were still in bed with him, giggling fit to burst. For an instant he and the maid stared at each other in silent horror; then he had rolled the girls out of bed in a flash and with as much bravado as he could manage sent them on their way with a ringing slap on their fat bottoms. A furtive glance at the maid, however, was enough to tell him that this play-fulness had, if anything, made the situation worse.

Edward was penitent. He had behaved foolishly and deserved the Major's contempt. He had been weak and knew it. He had slipped but, by a miracle, he hadn't fallen.

The Major supposed Edward to be referring to his physical

378

relationship with Sarah and for a moment was cheered. But no, Edward meant falling as Ripon had fallen: in other words. becoming like putty in the hands of a Catholic lady, becoming enslaved to Rome. This was a slippery path which ended in marriage, which ended in turn by having one's faith torn out by the roots.

'Don't be absurd, Edward,' sighed the Major, who would have asked for nothing better. 'This notion of the Roman Church is puerile and your marvellous faith, if you ask me, is nothing more than a vague superstition which makes you go to church on Sundays.'

'You don't know what living in Ireland is like.'

'Oh yes I do. You forget that I've been living here for some time now.'

Edward's face darkened but he was too harrowed to argue the point. 'It was I who gave her up, you know, Brendan. Not the other way round.' As the Major made no reply he added: 'Could you give Murphy a shout to bring more hot water?'

They were in the laundry, where Edward was taking a bath. The boiler, strained beyond its powers by all the washing that had gone on before the ball, had gone wrong, but Edward's craving for a bath had been too strong to be denied. Sunk in the bath, a great urge to confess had come over him, or, if not exactly to confess (for he really hadn't done anything so very dreadful), at least to share his troubles with someone who might understand. Hence the presence of the Major.

At first the Major believed that he had been summoned to hear and sympathize about Ripon, because Edward had started to describe the scene that had taken place the evening before when, after supper, he had sought out his son to give him a cheque ... how he had found Ripon skulking in the library, leafing through a book on urino-genital matters that he had idly removed the shelf. And what had he done with his wife? No doubt she was pining away in some ladies' retiring room. Ripon, in any case, was not showing much interest in her these days. On seeing his father he had started guiltily and replaced the book in the shelf. Then Edward advanced on him, flourishing the cheque. Ripon had taken it and read it (it was for a handsome sum) and had seemed puzzled ... What was all this for?

'I know you must be getting short. Sorry it's not more, but I scraped up what I could,' Edward had told him gruffly.

'But Dad,' Ripon had cried, stuffing the cheque back into his father's top pocket. 'You mustn't! I don't need it ... Just take a look at this.' And he had proceeded to pull thick rolls of banknotes from one pocket after another, dropping them on the carpet in front of him until his shoes were all but hidden by the mound of money.

'Look here, Dad, why don't you take some to help out with your expenses? No, I mean, go on and help yourself. There's plenty more where that came from.' Ripon, his eyes moist with generosity, had stood there inviting his stiff-necked old father to delve into the pile of currency. 'Take it all if you want to. Easy enough to get some more.'

Edward had stopped talking. The Major had glanced at him sympathetically but had deemed it best to say nothing, sensing that the worst was yet to come.

The laundry was a vast, desolate cellar, a continuation of the kitchens; ranks of Gothic arches fled into the dim, greenish distance, each arch made of thickly whitewashed stones. Tubs, basins, a gigantic mangle with rollers as fat as pillar-boxes, a few trays of shrivelled apples from some summer of long ago, pieces of greasy machinery carefully spread out on oilskin but long since abandoned (belonging perhaps to the defunct 'Do More' generator) — the Major looked around with melancholy interest.

Edward's head, the only part of him visible over the dark soapy water, was grey and wild-eyed. Most likely he had not slept at all. The business with Ripon had no doubt been humiliating enough — but it was the question of Sarah that was really causing him pain. It did not seem to occur to him that the Major might also still be sensitive on this subject; he was too occupied with his own distress. 'How selfish he is!'

Murphy now appeared carrying a jug of steaming water. As he passed he leered knowingly at the Major—that wretched maid must have spread the news below stairs! Edward waited for the elderly servant to pour the steaming contents of the jug between his knees, then went on with his rambling description of how he had nearly fallen into the papist trap. He had been lonely after Angela's death, intolerably lonely: the Major (his 'only close friend') in London with his moribund aunt, the twins not yet expelled from their school, Ripon away all the time and busy confecting his dishonourable marriage, the Majestic peopled as it was with its sparse platoon of guests from the last century, the melancholy Irish winter setting in ... Was it any wonder that a cast-iron depression, like a bear-trap, had closed its jaws on him?

Edward, slumped in the bath, had sunk lower by degrees so that now the water rimmed his chin and a second haggard face floated on its placid surface.

A young person whom he was, literally, putting back on her feet. It had given him an interest. ('I can imagine,' said the Major sarcastically.) And it had been Sarah, of course, Edward continued, not noticing the Major wince at the mention of her name, it had been Sarah, of course, who had made advances, who had led him on. Not that he was blaming her. He knew as well as anyone that it was the man's duty to be honourable, that women are weak; but all the same ...

Edward stopped speaking and there was a long silence. With the stillness of the water his body had become dimly visible: the hairy chest, the massive white limbs ... From the nether regions, that darker area that might have been a submerged water-lily, the Major averted his eyes with distaste. 'How could any young woman possibly be interested in *that*?' he wondered glumly.

At length the Major cleared his throat. He wanted to talk about the ball. Perhaps by talking about it one might make its memory less terrible. But so far Edward had not said a word on the subject. All morning the old ladies had been chattering like parakeets, discussing it with any sentient being who came within earshot, servant or fellow-guest, it made no difference. The presence of Edward alone had stilled their tongues. Though outwardly calm there was something in his face, a lurking pain or fury ... whatever it was, it had silenced the old ladies just as now it silenced his 'only close friend', the Major.

'It was I who gave her up,' Edward repeated. 'That's something to be thankful for.'

But the Major knew that he was not telling the truth. Besides, Edward's wounded pride seemed as nothing compared with his own absolute loss.

'You know, sometimes ... ' Edward began; his lips moving only a millimetre or two above the surface sent tiny waves out towards his knees.

'Sometimes what?'

Edward wearily rolled his eyes towards the Major and then dropped them again.

'Sometimes I even used to forget that she was a Catholic.' And he shook his head, perhaps at the narrowness of his escape.

And so at the Majestic everything returned to the way it had been before. The gleaming tiles became dulled. Sofas as sleek as prize cattle lost their glow. Rooms that had been cleaned needed cleaning again while those that had been locked up were reopened, and still nobody could find the heart or the energy to take down the Christmas decorations (besides, presently it would be Christmas again). Two or three litters of rapidly growing kittens had more than restored the population of cats, although, for the moment, there was no corresponding decrease in the number of rats sighted. Mrs Rappaport's marmalade kitten (fertilized by heaven knew what hideous monster on a moonless night) caused a surprise (everybody had assumed it to be a tom) by contributing no less than half a dozen of these kittens ... enchanting little fellows, though, that one simply couldn't help adoring as they wobbled blind and mewing across the carpet. But the cries of delight became muted when the kittens at last opened their eyes and six pairs of bitter green orbs were seen to be staring around with malice at the new world in which they suddenly found themselves.

The groaning tables of the night of the ball were now only a distressing memory as the food served in the dining-room returned to normal. One day at lunch, while the guests were sustaining themselves with an Irish stew ('A Chinese Irish stew,' muttered Miss Johnston in disgust), a supplementary dish was brought in by Murphy. On it rested a large sirloin steak. Pushing aside his plate, Edward proceeded to cut the steak into small cubes and place the dish on the carpet in front of Rover who by now was almost totally blind, surrounded day and night by lurking horrors. Rover licked the meat experimentally, masticated one or two pieces, then lost interest. With a sigh Edward returned his attention to the Irish stew on his plate. A moment later the new favourite, the Afghan hound with golden curls, came skipping up, bent his long nose to the meat and wolfed it down in a flash. The guests watched him in thoughtful silence.

In the last week of April the Major, returning from a melancholy stroll in the park, met Edward crossing the drive by the statue of Queen Victoria. He stopped. Edward's service revolver dangled from one hand. From the other, dark spots of blood were dripping on to the gravel. He stared in alarm at Edward's stricken face.

'What on earth happened?'

'I shot Rover ... He was getting old. I thought ... ' He peered at his dripping hand. 'I thought I ... ' But with that he turned and went into the house, leaving the Major to borrow a spade from Seán Murphy and wander off in search of the body.

The hole he dug at the foot of an oak tree near the lodge was constricted by large roots. He should really have begun another hole in a more suitable place, but sadness made him stubborn. The result was that, in order to receive the entire dog, his hole had to be narrow and deep. So it was that Rover was buried standing on his hind legs, his shattered skull only a few inches below the surface of soil.

The Major had filled in the grave and was hammering it down with the back of his spade when he spied a delegation of old ladies approaching, well furred against the restless spring breezes. Miss Johnston was the spokeswoman. They had heard what had happened and had come with a suggestion: Rover should be sent to Dublin and stuffed. They would make a collection to pay for the work and present him to Edward on his next birthday. The Major thanked them but explained that the heavy bullet had smashed the dog's skull beyond repair. It would be hopeless, the dog was unrecognizable (all of which was untrue, but the Major could not bear the thought of Rover stuffed and in some debonair attitude, front paw raised perhaps, gathering dust for the years that still remained to the Majestic ... It was bad enough to think of the poor dog begging below ground as the worms did their work.) Later the Major learned that Edward, cradling the dog's head in his free hand, had accidentally wounded himself with the same bullet. But luckily it was only a flesh wound.

At about this time in Dublin a number of statues were blown up at night; eminent British soldiers and statesmen had their feet blown off and their swords buckled. Reading about these 'atrocities' threw Edward into a violent rage. These were acts of cowardice. Let the Shinners fight openly if they must, man to man! This sort of cowardice must not be allowed to prevail ... skulking in ambush behind hedges, blowing up statues ... Had there been one, even one, honest-to-God battle during the whole course of the rebellion? Not a single trench had been dug, except perhaps for seed potatoes, in the whole of Ireland! Did the Sinn Feiners deserve the name of men?

'Of course, there *was* Easter 1916,' suggested the Major mildly.

'Stabbed us in the back!' Edward bellowed with a kind of pain, almost as if he had felt the knife enter between his own shoulder-blades. 'We were fighting to protect them and they stabbed us in the back.'

'Well, not if one looks at it from their point of view, of course ... Mind you,' he added soothingly as Edward's features stiffened, 'one has to consider both sides.'

A dispiriting silence fell on the room. The Major decided that it would be a sign of strength not to press the matter. Edward inspired more pity than anger these days. Privately, though, he retained his conviction that it was rather amiable of the Sinn Feiners to prefer attacking statues to living people – a proof, as it were, that they too belonged, or almost belonged, to the good-natured Irish people.

'You don't suppose they'll have a shot at Queen Victoria, do you? Perhaps we should think of getting her moved a bit farther away from the house ... ' But Edward merely curled his lip contemptuously at this further proof of the Major's lack of martial instincts.

The Golf Club these days was thronged with members whom the Major had not ever seen there before: fat, wary men with copious moustaches who cupped their ears whenever the 'troubles' were mentioned but said very little, contenting themselves with an occasional mild reminiscence of Chittagong or Cairo or some other place under foreign skies. They seem to be waiting uneasily for something; perhaps even they themselves did not know what it was. They would stand there, hands in pockets, staring moodily out of the club-house windows at the acres of blowing grass. Nowadays not so many players would venture out there; and all those who did, like Boy O'Neill, carried rifles in their golf-bags. Once or twice, indeed, distant shots had been heard over the hum of conversation in the bar, causing the drinkers to fear the worst: a massacre at the fourteenth hole, bodies spreadeagled on the velvety green or bleeding in bunkers. But no, presently a laughing, windblown group would come into sight on the fairway of the eighteenth and as they came up towards the club-house one or other of the party would be seen swinging a putter in one hand and a dead hare in the other. Not that they would have minded a 'scrap' — some of them were young and brave, others middle-aged and fierce, and none of them had been to the war in France.

For the most part, though, the members stayed in the bar drinking whiskey-and-sodas and waiting. There were still a few ragged, shivering caddies waiting to besiege any plus-foured gentlemen willing to risk themselves in the open spaces — but their numbers had decreased considerably over the winter. Now only the very young and the very elderly remained. And the others? Perhaps instead of hefting golf-bags on their shoulders they were roaming the hills with some flying squad carrying rifles for the I.R.A.

'Hello, Major.'

'Oh, hello, Boy ... Didn't see you there.' O'Neill was leaning on the bar, his shoulders two great bunches of muscle outlandishly swollen by the thick sweater he was wearing. More aggressive than ever, he had recently acquired the habit of grinning sarcastically after anything he said, whether it was supposed to be humorous or not. The Major found this habit upsetting.

'Seen old Devlin?'

'Can't say I have, Boy.'

'Giving us a wide berth these days. Too bad because I've a joke to tell him. Listen. It's about a girl called Mary from Kilnalough. Mary goes to England in rags and comes back a year later in fine clothes and throwing away money right and left. Meets Father O'Byrne who says: "Tell me, Mary. How did you get all that money?"

'Says Mary, shamefaced: "Oi became a prostitute, Father."

' "What's that you say?" cries Father O'Byrne in a fury.

' "Oi became a prostitute, Father," says Mary again.

' "Ah, sure that's all roight," says Father O'Byrne with a

sigh of relief. "Oi was after thinking you said you'd become a Protestant!" '

Laughter from one or two of the men at the bar near by. But these were the old hands. The Colonials (as the fat, wary men with moustaches had come to be called) looked blank, being more used to a division of people by race than by religion. This sort of thing was too subtle for them. After all, a white man is a white man when all is said and done.

'Very funny,' said the Major without enthusiasm. He had heard the story before.

Across the room, sitting in an armchair under a portrait in oils of the Founder, the Major noticed young Mortimer. He went over to ask him how Matthews was getting on. Mortimer stood up politely and offered the Major a chair, causing him to think: 'At least some of these young fellows have been properly brought up.' And really there was no denying it. Mortimer was a fine young fellow, been to a good school, nicely spoken, good at games ... really Charity (or was it Faith?) could do a lot worse. The only trouble was that although he obviously came from a decent family, this family just as obviously had no money or they would hardly have allowed one of their offspring to join the riff-raff in Ireland for the sake of earning a few shillings a day. Still, it was a shame. A nice young fellow, though rather more nervous than one realized at first sight.

Matthews, it seemed, was much better. Still a bit groggy, of course. That bump on the head had turned out to be rather a bad one. But Mortimer had another, much more sensational piece of news. Had the Major heard about Captain Bolton? He had left Kilnalough after a frightful row with his superiors. Dismissed for insubordination. In short, he had told them to go to hell! And he'd immediately gone off to Dublin with an Irish girl. Who would have thought it of Bolton ... having a love-affair on the quiet?

'The girl was at the ball at the Majestic. You may remember her?' The Major remembered her.

'You wouldn't have thought it of old Bolton, would you? I mean, he always seemed such a man's man. They say that if she so much as looks at another man he knocks her cold on the spot!'

'How d'you know about all this?'

'One of our chaps was up in Dublin the other day and saw them together in Jammet's. There was a scene with some fellow who was staring at her. Personally, I thought she looked a bitch, didn't you?'

At the end of April the last of the great spring storms blew in from the north-east and once more all the windows in the Majestic were rattling in torment, while the chimneys groaned and whined like unmilked cows, half threatening and half pleading, and draughts sighed gently under doors like love-lorn girls. At the same time curious cracking sounds were heard, difficult to identify; perhaps the sort of sound one might associate with the breaking of bones. Difficult, also, to say where they originated; they seemed to come dully through the walls or the ceiling, even up through the floor once or twice — or so it appeared; with the howling of the wind and the noise of the breakers outside it was impossible to be sure.

The Major was worried, of course, and sometimes went to investigate. Something had snapped, he could *feel* it, the special vibrations of something breaking somewhere; one can always tell when something breaks. But when he pulled himself out of his armchair and, puffing his pipe thoughtfully (so as not to alarm the ladies), sauntered into the next room or the one above, expecting to see diagonal cracks appearing in the walls ... well, there was never anything to be seen. All was silent. He must have imagined it. But one knows perfectly well (thought the Major) whether one is imagining something or not, and he *knew* this was real. Besides, other people heard it too. Crack! And one or two of the ladies would look up vaguely, not wanting to make a fuss and not really trusting their worn-out old ears. Then, since nothing had actually happened, they would drop their eyes to the fingers which nowadays seemed all joints, one joint on top of another, strung like fat beads, all this time patiently knitting in their laps (but no longer able to sew) ... and then a few minutes later: Crack! It would happen again. And this time even the Afghan hound on the hearth-rug would prick up his ears and go sniffing round the walls or doors before he was diverted by noticing someone asleep in a chair who needed to be licked awake, or one of the ladies trying to smuggle a peppermint from handbag to mouth without being nuzzled by his long greedy snout.

'Did you by any chance hear a cracking sound just then?' But Edward, concerned about the possibility of a tidal wave swamping his piglets, shook his head.

'Listen for a moment.'

But there would only be the sound of wind and rain, the groaning and the sighing, and Edward would become engrossed in his problems once more so that when it did come, he still did not hear it.

Remembering the bulges, real and imaginary, which he had discovered with Sarah, the Major moved aside the sofa in the lounge. The root throwing up the parquet blocks had swollen from a forearm into a thigh—thick, white, hairy and muscular. The Major thought it best to roll the sofa back promptly over this obscenity.

That night he lay awake listening to the wind and the waves, thinking that he might have been alone in a great ocean liner, drifting in the eye of a storm. Instead of decreasing with daybreak, the storm continued to mount throughout the following morning. By the afternoon Edward had become seriously concerned about the welfare of the piglets. They had not been fed since noon the day before. All this time they had cowered without physical or moral comfort in the roaring black squash court. Something must be done. But in this weather one could scarcely put one's nose outside, let alone walk a quarter of a mile, so he waited for a lull standing by one window or another with an unread newspaper trailing from his fingers.

'Almighty God! Did you see that?'

The Major had glimpsed a volley of slates climbing out into the driving sky from one of the roofs to windward, perhaps from one of the out-houses. He waited to hear them smash on the rain-scoured terrace beyond, but he heard nothing.

At four o'clock it grew dark. They decided to wait no longer. Wrapped in oilskins they battled across the drive and round the Prince Consort wing in order to get to windward of flying slates, Edward carrying half a sack of cakes and currant buns. Head lowered, one hand crammed on to his hat and eyes half shut against the lashing rain, the Major struggled in Edward's footsteps. The air was full of dead leaves, twigs and branches stripped from the creaking limes and maples beside the potato field. Cold rain seeped into his collar. So difficult was it to see where one was going that when Edward stopped a few paces ahead to gaze back at the hotel the Major blundered into him.

Edward's eyes were lifted to the black, rainswept hulk of the Majestic, his thick locks of grey hair writhing and flickering like snakes in the screaming wind. In that dim light his head appeared more massively sculpted than ever; beneath the heavy frontal bone his eye-sockets were pools of shadow and his cheekbones, glistening with rain, might have been carved by crude strokes of a chisel. With one hand he grasped the sodden sack of confectionery, with the other he pointed up at the building, shouting wordlessly at the Major. But the Major did not need to be told that there was something wrong; he could see for himself the gaping black hole in the roof of the servants' wing, he could see the slates blowing away into the swirling rain, free as petals ... a sudden strong gust and a flurry of them would lift to soar away end over end into the darkness. And the black hole grew steadily larger like a woollen sleeve unravelling. Presently white wooden beams became visible.

Edward tugged at his arm and plunged on into the rain. They reached the lee of the high wall that ran down to the sea from one terrace to the next. There was a narrow path here which the Major had never noticed before, and broken steps thick with weeds which clung wetly to his ankles. It seemed strangely quiet in the shelter of the wall and the going was easier. But as they made their way down towards the lowest terrace the rain increased to a deluge. The Major licked his lips and tasted salt from the clouds of spray whipped up by the wind to cascade on to the boiling mud around them. By the time they had turned and headed with the wind behind them at a reluctant gallop towards the invisible squash court, the water had seeped inside the Major's oilskin and he had lost his hat which had blown off his head and sailed ahead into the darkness.

'That's strange. They usually come to meet me. They must be frightened.'

With the outer door dragged shut it seemed, by comparison with the roaring wilderness outside, very still and quiet in the squash court, despite the drumming of the rain on the glass roof and the muffled thunder of the breakers, now only a few feet from where they were standing. Edward had taken a lantern from its nail on the wall and while he was lighting it the Major peered into the darkness in search of the piglets, listening for the rustle of straw. The ammonia smell was even more intolerable than on the Major's previous visit; with every breath it seized his nose and throat. He longed to be back outside in the gale of fresh air. Edward did not seem to notice it, however. He was emptying the contents of his sack into a filthy wooden trough and cooing gently to attract the attention of the piglets. The iced cakes, buns and barm-bracks had amalgamated inside the sodden sack into a glutinous mass and dropped into the trough with a carnal, sucking sound ... But even this failed to produce the piglets. The interior silence remained unbroken.

'Can they have got out?'

Frowning, Edward lifted the lantern and took a few steps forward on to the squelching straw. The Major, who had stayed where he was (the thought of treading in that mess revolted him), watched the rim of light creep up the far wall—on which, crudely smeared in scarlet, were the words: SPIES AND TRAITORS BEWARE! And he knew instantly what the scarlet was and where it had come from. Edward's eyes were on the ground, however, expecting to see sleepy piglets emerging to greet him, so he continued to advance until his lantern light stole over a friendly, pliable snout, on to illumine the sleepy eyes and drooping, pointed ears ... and then over emptiness (except for a dollop of intestines and a discarded corkscrew tail). Between the ears and the tail there was no longer any pig. The pig had gone.

A sharp intake of breath—a sound which the Major never forgot. And then Edward stumbled forward with his wildly swinging lantern, making the walls rock.

When Edward emerged and stood beside him once more (not yet having spoken a word) the Major glanced down and noticed that his shoes were bright scarlet, oozing, the lace-holes bubbling with scarlet liquid. On the threshold of the door he left one, two, three red footprints ... But then they dissolved under the lashing rain.

'If she looks at another man he knocks her cold!' Of all the Major's troubles (of which there was no shortage) this was the one which preoccupied him the most. It was also the one he could do least about. More precisely, it was the only one which he could do nothing at all about, except wonder and distress himself.

He knew that it was futile. After all, he was not a complete fool. He knew that now there was really no further hope on earth of a successful union with Sarah. Apart from everything else, he now bore her a considerable resentment. Even if they met, this resentment would prevent him (probably against his will) from being friendly. Doubtless one day it would fade into indifference and allow him to be friendly again; but it would only disappear *on one condition*: namely, that he was no longer in love with her. Thus, his only hope of success depended on his not wanting to succeed! An appalling but not uncommon situation in the game of which the Major was so painfully learning the rules.

Meanwhile, although he did his best to put her out of his mind by concentrating on the other manifold troubles at large under the roof of the Majestic, she continued to emerge in random but painful thoughts that sprang sharp-clawed out of the hidden lair in his mind to which they had been banished. 'What sort of gentleman would "knock a girl cold"?' he found himself wondering with amazement, even while he was examining a truly alarming crack which he had discovered in the wall of the writing-room behind the faded tapestry. But for all he knew this crack might have been there for years! And then, what sort of girl would allow herself to be repeatedly 'knocked cold'? It was all quite beyond him, both the man and the girl (and, come to that, the crack in the wall). He simply did not understand. He tried to imagine himself knocking a girl cold; but it was easier to imagine himself flying up into a tree and singing like a blackbird.

Then, later on, while he was standing, hands thrust gloomily into the pockets of his jacket, by the gatepost at the end of the drive and looking up at the notice posted by Edward: TRESPASSERS FOUND TAMPERING WITH THE STATUE OF QUEEN VICTORIA WILL BE SHOT ON SIGHT. BY ORDER and thinking: 'But he's gone clean out of his wits! He's trying to provoke them!'—while staring up at this defiant and reckless object, he found himself thinking instead: 'But how often does she 'look at other men'? How often is she 'knocked cold'? Is it likely to damage her brain?' And his thoughts would meander away, low in vitality, convalescent, as if he had really been sick (and perhaps he really was sick), round and round like tired animals in a circus ring ... to arrive at last at the exit (which looked strangely similar to the entrance), concluding that it certainly couldn't be very good for one to be continually knocked senseless.

But no, it wasn't that at all ... It was the intimacy which distressed him. Sarah felled in a restaurant for fluttering her eyelashes at a head-waiter; Sarah felled among the teacups at a Viceregal garden party for a lingering glance at some young officer; Sarah felled in Jury's Hotel for looking out of the window ... His mind, tired and dutiful, furnished him with any amount of these images. And they were always together, Bolton and Sarah, and he was always excluded (attempts to imagine himself stepping forward to correct Bolton with a classic uppercut proved hopeless). Bolton and Sarah ...

Late in the evening, while listening patiently to Miss Bagley complaining that a maid had taken up residence in the room next to hers and the cook in the room opposite, it occurred to him that now, at this very moment, it was quite likely that Sarah and Bolton were preparing to get into bed together. His vitality dropped a few points lower and the muscles of his face became numb with despair; the moustache on his upper lip felt as heavy as antlers. He explained carefully, nevertheless, to the indignant Miss Bagley that the servants' wing was uninhabitable: the roof had been taken off as cleanly as the top off a boiled egg.

On returning from the squash court his watery footprints had diverged from Edward's bloody ones and made their anxious way along dim corridors to 'below stairs' where they were baulked from proceeding any farther. A foaming cascade of water was pouring down these stairs, and farther on down where they continued into some cellars which he had never visited. Odd bits of bric-à-brac slipped gently down from one stair to the next: pieces of wood, a coloured picture of the Holy Virgin, scraps of newspaper, rags of cloth that might have been underclothes or antimacassars, a sodden Teddy bear.

Weeping and shivering, a young girl in maid's uniform, drenched to the skin, sat with her ankles in the torrent. The

Major, still wearing his oilskins, had picked her up since she refused to move by herself and carried her back and down the other stairs to the kitchen, which was fortunately still warm and dry, depositing her without explanation on the kitchen table before the astonished, wild-eyed cook (who had never entertained a high opinion of the Major's morals and sanity). Heaven only knew what she had thought!

He described the pertinent parts of this experience to Miss Bagley, and to Miss Johnston, Miss Devere (who had returned to the Majestic after a brief and unsatisfactory flirtation with the outside world) and Mrs Rice, who had come forward with similar grievances. And he listened carefully while they demanded with indignation whether it was a 'free-for-all', guests henceforth to 'fight it out' with the servants for the use of bathrooms and other amenities; and said that no, of course not, that he was sure they wouldn't want the poor servants to sleep out under the stars and catch pneumonia (even though, as the hastily arriving Miss Staveley had just pointed out, 'they were only servants') and that it was, again *of course*, only a temporary measure, while the roof of the servants' wing was rebuilt. But they knew, and he knew, that the roof would never, this side of paradise, be rebuilt—which weakened his argument to some extent.

And all the time, even while he listened to the reassuring tones of his own voice, he could feel the extraordinary sloth of the hurt muscles of his smile, unable now to prevent himself from thinking of Bolton and Sarah making love. But perhaps, finally, the searing quality of this thought had a good effect. It helped to cauterize his festering emotions. At first he imagined that Sarah, with brutally parted thighs, was being violated—but later, simply worn out with caring, he became hard-hearted with this weakness and said to himself harshly: 'Look, she wouldn't do it if she didn't enjoy it!'

True, Sarah was a woman. Therefore she was physically suited to accomodate men. There was no violation, except to the Major's feelings.

On his way to bed the Major, who had by now stayed in so many different rooms at the Majestic that he very often became confused, absent-mindedly presented himself at the door of a room he had been occupying a few days earlier. In the light of a candle he was astonished to see a young girl standing naked by the wash-basin. Without embarrassment she turned and smiled at the startled Major—who withdrew with a hasty apology. There must be a new guest in the hotel whom he had not yet come across! But surely that was impossible, for nowadays the servants came directly to him for their instructions. He found the incident most puzzling.

He had reached his room (the right one this time) before he realized who this new guest must be. It was simply one of the maids who had been obliged to move out of the servants' wing. And this was the very matter that he had spent the evening discussing with the old ladies.

Later, lying in bed, he mused: 'She could have been a lady for all the difference there was ... Of course, without clothes on everybody looks the same. They look just like we do.' And he remembered thinking on some occasion during the war how, with all the distinctions of class effaced, one dead body resembles another ... and ... and ...

These democratic notions must have soothed him, for he began to feel drowsy. Yet even as, hands in pockets, he strolled peacefully away into the tall waving grass of sleep, baleful yellow eyes were watching him, and then ... Ah! The thought of Sarah once more pounced and clawed his sensitive heart.

'You really sympathize with Sinn Fein in many ways, is that not so? No, no, don't bother to deny it, Major. With me ... och, I'm just a useless old man, you know, everyone says so ... with me you don't have to pretend. Well, you must leave now before it's too late. This wretched affair in Ireland is none of your doing. No doubt you haven't helped matters, but that's neither here nor there. Now, if you've a grain of sense, you'll leave while you still have a chance.'

'I can't leave with the way things are. The hotel's in a dreadful mess.'

The Major had called on old Dr Ryan to ask his advice on what should be done with Edward, about whom he was becoming progressively more concerned. Edward was seldom to be seen these days. He spent a great deal of time out of doors engrossed in some work he had undertaken in the grounds (not even Seán Murphy had been able to tell him just what this work was). Once, on his way up the drive, the Major had glimpsed Edward's massive silhouette standing on the topmost roof, outlined against a bank of white cumulus clouds over Wales. On another occasion, while feeding the dogs in the yard (Evans the tutor had left on the day after the ball without waiting to be sacked, taking with him all Mr Norton's silk shirts which had been drying on a line), he had heard harsh laughter echoing amid the slates and turrets overhead—but then there had been silence, and no reply when he had called Edward's name.

What could be done to improve Edward's state of mind? But Dr Ryan, who as usual appeared to be fast asleep, had shown himself disinclined to talk about Edward. Instead, he had kept on insisting that the Major should leave, which for the Major was quite out of the question.

'Very well. If you want to act like a young fool and get yourself in a scrape ... !'

Yes, yes, but about Edward? If, for example, he could be persuaded to take a holiday for a few weeks? But the old man was impatient with the Major's theories and laborious qualifications as to Edward's state of mind. Edward was a confounded nuisance and had been raving for years!

'But the holiday?'

'Yes, yes, take the old divil away and see he never comes oack!'

The Major ground his teeth with exasperation and thought that it was really high time the old buffer retired. He was becoming more senile every day.

397

Naturally, when the Major suggested to Edward that it might do the twins good if he took them away for a few days or even longer ('I could look after the hotel while you're away') Edward looked at him in amazement. Leave Ireland at a time like this! At the very moment when one must stand firm! Only yesterday his property had been abused; a warning notice he had placed on the gate-post had been removed. The guilty party must be found and punished!

The Major (who was himself the guilty party) sighed and stared at his finger-nails. Edward was clearly inaccessible to reason. But perhaps the whole thing would blow over, the 'troubles' would sort themselves out, Edward be restored to his senses. Although mild, the Major was a stubborn young man and determined, in any event, to salvage whatever he could. The twins should be sent to England to stay with their aunt, the one deemed 'fast' who was married to a clergy-man, it couldn't be helped. Besides, she was unlikely, in the Major's opinion, to prove 'faster' than the twins already were. Mrs Rappaport should also be dispatched. Perhaps the guests might be encouraged to leave as well ...

'Do whatever you think best, old man. I leave it in your hands,' Edward replied vaguely, with the air of someone who has more important things on his mind. And he stared into the distance, cracking his knuckles and looking insane.

When the day came for the twins to leave neither they nor Edward seemed in the least upset by their departure or by the prospect of separation. On the platform of Kilnalough station Edward grabbed a handful of blonde hair on each side of him and said: 'Will you behave yourselves in London?'

'Yes, yes!'

'Will you?'

'Ouch! Daddy, you're hurting!'

'D'you promise?'

'Yes, yes!'

And with that he bundled them into their compartment and rejoined the Major, who was the only member of the party to be moved by this leave-taking. Still, he was glad to see them out of danger. He only wished Mrs Rappaport had agreed to leave also, but he had only succeeded in arousing her obstinacy. She loathed Calcutta; always had. Refused to go there. The heat was appalling.

'Calcutta? But nobody wants you to go to Calcutta!' A long and debilitating argument had ensued. She agreed that she would be safe there. But safety wasn't everything. One had one's duty, after all. She would stay where she was. She remained quite deaf to the Major's protestations. Once, fleetingly, she seemed to grasp that the Major wanted her to go to England, not to Calcutta, for she exclaimed: 'I'm not pregnant, am I?'

'Good heavens! I certainly hope not!'

'Well, the climate here is perfectly suitable.' During this baffling conversation the huge cat that crouched on her lap like a furry bulldog stared piercingly into the Major's eyes. But at last the Major acknowledged defeat; sensing this, the cat relaxed and rubbed its head against the hard leather holster which Mrs Rappaport now habitually wore strapped round her waist (the calm and practical Mrs Roche had taken care to remove the cartridges, however). The cat yawned and licked its paw to wash its face. The audience was at an end.

One success (the twins) and two failures (Edward's holiday, Mrs Rappaport). Next the Major turned his attention to the Majestic itself, afraid that the collapse of the building might be imminent. The Major, of course, knew himself to be anxious by nature and inclined to get things out of proportion. Yet he still believed that he could hear the curious cracking sounds which he had first heard during the roar of the storm. Now that all was quiet and tranquil one should have been able to hear them quite clearly. But the fact was that, although he could *feel* them, he could not hear them at all. It was merely an abrupt sensation of strain, followed by an ominous relief—a sensation that might be represented as the snapping of rotten branches under water. No doubt it was pure imagination.

Nevertheless, in order to set his mind at rest he telephoned an architect in Dublin by the name of Delahunty and explained his fears, asking him if he would come down and look the place over.

Delahunty was a confident, jolly man of middle age who had been recommended to the Major by a mutual acquaintance. He laughed at the Major's anxiety; he knew the place well, he said. He had often stayed there with his parents as a child. Solid as a rock! One might just as well expect Dublin Castle to fall down. But if the Major really wanted reassurance he'd be delighted to come and have a look round. It would be good to see the old place again after all these years. If it was a nice day he might even bring his swimming-costume and take a dip in the swimming-pool ... Was it filled at the moment? well, yes ... though, strictly speaking ... that was to say, there was water in it ... Capital! The Major should expect him on Tuesday. And Delahunty, who was a busy man, had rung off before the Major had time to append any more of his laborious qualifications.

On Tuesday he duly made his appearance, a bald, tubby man with sparkling eyes who greeted the Major as if they were old friends. Splendid to see the old place again. Donkey's years since he'd been in this corner of Ireland. Needed a bit of spit and polish by the look of it but solid as a rock. After all, it wasn't the paint that counted but what was underneath. Look, now that he was here why shouldn't he stay for supper as well? They could put his name in the pot, couldn't they?

'By all means.'

Ah, they knew how to build in those days. They didn't just throw a house up with a couple of bricks and a lick of mortar the way they did nowadays. See, Major, listen to that — and he rapped the wall of the corridor with his chubby knuckles.

'It's quite a relief to hear you say it. I'd begun to imagine things.'

'You haven't a thing to worry about. Take my word for it.'

And Mr Delahunty, with a smile, indulged the Major by going with him, even so, to take a look at the crack behind the tapestry in the writing-room. Nothing structural, he declared, simply an 'easing of the brickwork'. Happened in all old places. But the upper storeys? The dry rot? The place the Major had put his foot through?

'You're bound to find that some of your woodwork doesn't come up to scratch. 'Tis the damp in the air that does it. Any old house in Wicklow or Wexford will be the same. But that's not to say they're going to fall down. Far from it. When you feel like it, Major, do a bit of re-timbering. Take your time. There's no hurry. The old Majestic will still be here long after you and I are dead and gone.'

'There's no need to take a look upstairs then?' Mr Delahunty laughed out loud at this. Taking the Major's arm he said: 'Look here, Major, you can say what you like against me but I know my buildings. Take it from me, this one will last another couple of hundred years if it lasts a month. There it is. Say what you like against me ... ' He hesitated, as if he half expected a denunciation from the Major. As none came, however, he added quickly: 'Now let's go and have some of that lovely tea you mentioned.'

The Major had gone to some pains to organize tea for himself and Mr Delahunty in the privacy of the writing-room, which he had taken the precaution of locking earlier in the afternoon.

Curiously, however, after his first cup of tea Mr Delahunty's conversation languished, his amiable barks of laughter became intermittent. He even failed to respond to one or two, admittedly rather dull, anecdotes the Major found himself recounting.

'Tea all right?'

'Oh, splendid. Absolutely top-hole.'

The Major attempted several topics, regretting that he knew so little about architecture. Finally he tried to interest Mr Delahunty in the situation in Ireland today, a subject on which he surely had a great deal to say. But although he smiled and murmured vague replies he seemed preoccupied. His eyes roved absently around the walls and the ceiling. He appeared to be listening for something. When the maid, coming for the tea-tray, slammed the door he jumped violently.

Presently he looked at his watch and held out his hand to the surprised Major.

'But I thought you were staying to supper?'

'Appointment I forgot about, old chap. Maybe another time.'

As they took leave of each other in the foyer Mr Delahunty's eyes continued to rove absently here and there.

'Well, I'm glad to hear there's nothing to worry about. You've taken a load off my mind.'

'Oh yes, you haven't a thing to worry about,' murmured Delahunty and once more before leaving, though rather cautiously, rapped the wall with his chubby knuckles.

Now that the Major's mind had been set at rest about the structure of the Majestic it seemed less important to him that the guests should be encouraged to leave. However, the collapse of the building itself was not the only factor involved. There was also the increasing violence in the countryside, where the Majestic stood in vulnerable isolation. There was the simple absurdity of continuing to run the place as a hotel when it had long since ceased to resemble one. Above all, there was the deterioration in Edward's state of mind (not to mention the suspicion that he'd gone clean out of his wits) since the slaughter of the piglets. Bacon off the menu for ever, so the cook had been instructed. Revolvers to be laid out with the knives and forks in case of emergency at mealtimes. Clearly the fewer strains on him the better. Sooner or later, in any case, the guests would have to be got rid of. The Major was still haunted by the the harsh laughter that had echoed over the rooftops.

But some of the ladies had been there for a very long time

indeed. They had lasted through the winter; they had a right to stay through the summer as well. Of course they had no real rights at all. They had simply been there for so long that they seemed to have acquired the right to stay for ever—that is to say, until they died, which they would presumably do eventually. But the process might still take a considerable time.

The Major went amongst them and intimated vaguely, nothing definite yet, of course, that one of these days it mightn't be such a bad idea if they gave a little thought to where they would be moving on to after ... well, after what? After Edward went completely off his head, perhaps ... After the I.R.A. established their headquarters at the Majestic (and good luck to them!) ... After the unforeseen, whatever it turned out to be, had happened ... What could the Major say that would not be unsuitable?

He was so vague that he succeeded only in alarming them. They listened unsympathetically. Gradually they became indignant. The Major fell to a lower point in their esteem than he had reached since the day he had put an end to their punitive shopping expeditions. First they found themselves having to 'fight it out' with the servants for the use of the bathrooms (the axiom that the servants 'never washed' and at home kept coal or potatoes in the bathtub seemed to have proved faulty). First that and now this. It was intolerable. They had a jolly good mind to leave! The Major, eyes on his shoes, nodded miserably and looked chastened, having forgotten for the moment that this was precisely what he wanted them to do anyway.

'All I really meant was that Mr Spencer has decided against taking in any new guests—with a view to closing the place down eventually.'

But the ladies were not soothed, particularly as Murphy chose this moment to shamble forward and announce that a party of young gentlemen had arrived.

'But that's impossible!' cried the Major, dismayed by the

speed with which he had been unmasked. 'Tell them they can't stay.'

'But the master does be saying they can,' countered Murphy with relish.

The Major hurried off to find Edward and remonstrate with him. But Edward had already welcomed the party, half a dozen young undergraduates from Oxford spending their vacation in Ireland in order to get to the bottom of the Irish question. He was full of enthusiasm. They were Oxford men! At last a chance for some intellectual discussion ... They had chosen to make a special study of Ireland and discuss matters with various strata of society, a real attempt to get to grips with the feelings of the Irish people, not just the Shinners! There was no gainsaying the fact, young people today took a more direct, more sensible and generally less hypocritical approach to politics than the older generation. They were imbued by a new sense of social justice ... 'No, no, Brendan, I can see you smiling but it's true. We can learn from the young if we keep our ears open. Besides, they're only here for a night or two.' And Edward went on to describe how, long before the war, he had eaten a splendid dinner in All Souls ... Ah, the quotations from Aristotle and St Thomas Aquinas! The shellfish, too, had been magnificent. And the port peerless.

There was nothing to be done about it. The Major was turning away when Edward added: 'By the way, a parcel didn't arrive for me from London, did it?'

'Not that I know of. Something from Fortnum's?'

'No, as a matter of fact. I wrote away for one of these things I saw advertised in the paper.' He fumbled in his pocket and at last located a newspaper clipping which he handed to the Major. With raised eyebrows he read that Messrs Wilkinson's Sword Company was offering bullet-proof waistcoats—steel within silk, weighing only five pounds. 'Send us the following particulars and we guarantee you a perfectly fitting garment. Waist and chest measurements, sloping or square shoulders, hollow or round back. Five guineas well spent would be the means of preventing a fatality.'

'Would you say I have a round back?'

'Oh, I shouldn't have thought so.'

'Ah, well, thanks ... D'you suppose they're any good?'

'Afraid I never met anyone who wore them.'

'Just thought I'd ask. It's not that I'm getting the wind up or anything like .that. It's foolish, though, to risk a fatality for a ha'porth of tar. That's the first thing they teach you in the army.'

Five of the undergraduates had been correctly identified by Murphy as young gentlemen, rather noisy and talkative ones. From a first-floor window the Major watched them dubiously as they sauntered out on to the lawn where Seán Murphy had been instructed to set up croquet hoops. The sixth, however, was an older man, taciturn and rather self-conscious. He sometimes laughed when the others laughed but not quite so spontaneously. If he cried: 'Good shot, Maitland!' or 'Your turn, Bunny!' or 'Bravo, Hall-Smith!' it was usually to echo one of the others who, for the most part, addressed him with distant politeness or ignored him altogether. Later, when they came in for a specially arranged tea with cucumber sandwiches (served in the gun room to inhibit the ladies) the Major learned that this older man's name was Captain Roberts and that, yes, he had been 'up' when the war broke out. And yes, it was a bit hard getting back to one's studies – at least, he added with an agonized smile, he'd found it so at first anyway. But now, of course ... And his sad, shocked eyes returned to the faces of his high-spirited companions.

Presently, the latter having drunk their tea and eaten their sandwiches as unconcernedly as if such things were an everyday occurrence in their lives (as no doubt they were), they returned to their game on the lawn and Captain Roberts trailed after them, a walking reminder of the follies of the older generation if his young companions had needed a reminder (which of course they did not).

The Major viewed dinner that evening with foreboding. There was a faint possibility that Edward, who seldom appeared for meals these days, might forget to attend. Before anyone else arrived, however, he was standing at his chair in the dining-room. On each side of his own seat three empty places had been reserved for the young men: the places of honour, a fact which did little to mollify the indignant old ladies.

The undergraduates arrived late and somewhat out of breath after ragging through the corridors while changing for dinner. There had been an attempted debagging of Maitland, who was the elected butt of the party. Then someone had pinched one of his socks and thrown it out of the window, so that when he followed the others into the dining-room he was wearing odd socks and looking so humorously aggrieved that the others could hardly suppress their laughter.

But Maitland was promptly forgotten when the impatient Edward showed them to their places. In fact they positively goggled with amazement. Laid out at each place beside the silver cutlery was a ... revolver! Amazing! Everything people said about Ireland was true! The Irish were completely mad! They hardly dared catch each other's eye.

Only Captain Roberts, gloomily eyeing the dim and distant contours of the room, seemed to have noticed nothing unusual. While they were waiting for soup to be served he absently picked up the revolver set at his place, spun the empty chamber, hefted it for a moment in his palm, then put it down again, picking up a silver fork instead. Having twirled it briefly between finger and thumb, he replaced it carefully, peering in a worried fashion across the table at the three bright and gleeful faces of his companions opposite. What on earth was the joke *this* time? Not for the first time since the vacation had begun he wondered uneasily whether he might not have lost his sense of humour.

'Pass the word along,' Bob Danby on his left whispered, groaning with pain, into his ear. 'What can the last course possibly *be*?'

So it was the revolvers set out with the cutlery that was arousing the mirth of his companions! As he passed Danby's joke on to Bunny Burdock on his right he reproved himself for not having noticed—though, as a matter of fact, he *had* noticed, assuming merely that the hotel had rats. In the mess dug-outs in France they had been in the habit of blazing away throughout the meal at any rats scampering by—otherwise the beggars would have eaten the food off your fork. He cleared his throat, on the point of describing all this to young Hall-Smith opposite, but then he thought better of it. These young chaps listened politely, of course, when he talked about the war. On one occasion, however, while he was describing some 'show' or other, Maitland had said: 'Oh, give the bloody war a rest will you, Roberts? It's been over for three years!' Of course Maitland had had a few beers and no doubt he had been egged on by his desire to please the others. Still, it was all past history now, all that; no reason why they should be interested.

Meanwhile an argument had started between the huge craggy-faced individual at the end of the table who must be the owner of the place (he was hardly obsequious enough to be the manager) and Bob Danby, who was their spokesman for political and intellectual matters (and was strongly fancied as the next President of the Union). And Danby seemed to be in particularly splendid form this evening.

'But what you're saying isn't the least bit logical,' he was now protesting. 'Although I agree that the Irish people may not be the most intelligent in the world I simply can't believe that they would *voluntarily* choose to elect bandits and murderers, as you call them, to handle their affairs ... Come now, that really *is* a bit steep, sir!'

'Tell me then what they've done except ambush unarmed men from behind hedges, shoot innocent people, drive cattle and plunder farms and generally bring the country to her knees, eh? Tell me!'

'You're missing the point,' groaned Danby, throwing up his

hands in mock despair while the others watched him with amusement (old Danby was off again!). 'The point is *democracy*, plain and simple. Only a few days ago Sinn Fein swept the country in the elections as they did in 1919. For every seat in the Southern Parliament except the four from Trinity they were elected without opposition. Look, sir, I'd even go as far as to say that if the majority of the people actually *want* to be governed by murderers (though I don't agree that they are for a minute) rather than by us British then they have a perfect right ... after all, it's their business. I mean, have you even read Rousseau's *Le Contrat social*? The fact is that in 1919 the Irish people elected the people they presumably wanted ... Why should they elect people they didn't want? The result was that Sinn Fein won seventy-three seats and the Unionists only won twenty-six ... Now if that isn't a clear expression of the will of the people frankly I don't know what *is*!'

'What did they do when they were elected?' demanded Edward, mastering himself with difficulty. 'They refused to take their seats in Westminster! Is that responsible behaviour? If they were anything but a worthless bunch of braggarts and corner-boys they'd have gone to do their duty by the people who elected them instead of running around with guns.'

Danby had listened to this outburst, nodding and smiling at his plate as if this was exactly what he had expected to hear.

'Very well, then. Why didn't they go to Westminster? It's a fair question. Why didn't they? The answer is because they knew it wouldn't do any good. What did Parnell ever accomplish? Nothing at all in practical terms. And Redmond? Even less. The point is that the Sinn Feiners knew very well that they could talk themselves blue in the face in the House of Commons without it doing them the least bit of good. They had to make a stand. Now I don't condone violence, of course, I'm a pacifist ... as I think we all are here ...' He looked round at the other undergraduates, who nodded their support. 'But it can be argued that the source of the violence was not on the Irish side at all. The original and *motive* violence comes from us British who have been violently repressing them since Cromwell and even before that … '

'Don't talk such utter bilge, boy!' snapped Edward, a purple flush rising to his cheeks. 'I know a murderer when I see one! If you'd lived in Ireland as long as I have you wouldn't talk such drivel. You talk as if they're patriots when they're just a stupid and vicious rabble, out for what they can get!'

'Well, I don't know that I can altogether agree with you there,' replied Danby with an irritating smile. 'Shall we think of a few examples? How about that Lord Mayor of Cork chappie?'

'I know who you mean,' piped Hall-Smith. 'The one with the gorgeous name. What was it? MacSwiney … '

'That's the fellow. Went on hunger-strike and starved himself to death for the cause he believed in. To say that he was out for what he could get is absolute tommy-rot, sir, if you'll excuse me saying so.'

'A fanatic! His head had been turned by the priests. Bleeding hearts and crucifixes!'

'That sounds suspiciously like bigotry to me, sir,' intervened Maitland, sweetening his impertinence with a dimpled smile.

'Bigotry be damned!' roared Edward in a voice that made the windows rattle. 'What's your name, you ill-mannered pup?'

'Maitland, sir.'

Tight-lipped in an effort to prevent themselves smiling, the undergraduates exchanged covert glances. With a trembling hand Edward reached out for a glass of water and gulped it noisily. Nobody said a word or looked in his direction. Presently he dropped his eyes and seemed surprised to find a plate of roast beef in front of him. Slowly he began to chew it. The meal proceeded in silence except for the chink of plates and cutlery. The blood had drained from Edward's cheeks. His rasping breath was clearly audible.

Little by little, however, casual conversation grew up over this violent outburst like a benevolent cloak of grass and weeds hiding some unsightly abandoned object. The weather was discussed. Miss Archer passed along a message from the far end of the table to inquire whether the young men had had good weather so far during their stay in Ireland. Yes, on the whole, reasonable enough, the answer came back. And soon the other ladies were passing their inquiries along, like so many lavender-scented handkerchieves for the poor undergraduates to wipe their bleeding lips on and return. And then, when this had taken some of the chill from the air and the line of communication had become clogged with too many questions and answers coming and going, they began to sing out their questions directly, person to person. Even some of the ladies at the other table (where the Major sat like a block of salt in front of his untouched plate) were unable to resist carolling a question or two across the intervening space—balm to the wounds of the nicely-spoken young men who had just suffered Edward's boorish outburst. In no time the cacophony had rendered even this method of communication uncertain. 'It sounds like the parrot-house at the zoo,' mused the Major grimly. And he glanced at Edward, who was staring straight ahead, features still set in a mask of rage from behind which, for the moment, the fire had consumed itself.

Besides, it was quite plain that the ladies had got the whole thing wrong—that far from being wounded the undergraduates were absolutely delighted with Edward's outburst and were thinking: 'What a perfectly splendid old Tory! What a rare find!' The whole thing was priceless: the old ladies, the revolvers (what a shame they weren't loaded!), the decrepit palace around them—and brooding in the middle of it, John Bull! Never-say-die in person! The evening would make a rare saga when retold over beer-mugs in the buttery next term. It might be entitled: 'How Maitland Put His Cherubic Head In The British Lion's Mouth ... And Got It Bitten Off!' Only Captain Roberts, who had lost his taste for battles of any description (even verbal), felt uncomfortable and heartily wished the meal were at an end.

Coffee, these days, was no longer served in a separate room but wheeled in tepid and acid to the tongue on a trolley by Murphy, who confected it himself out of heaven only knew what ingredients in some little alcove reserved for the purpose. The bright chatter of questions and answers had continued to ring undiminished throughout the dessert of apple fritters and Edward, brooding at the end of the table, was all but forgotten. But hardly had the first acid fumes of coffee from the approaching trolley reached the nostrils of the diners when he spoke again.

His words were lost in the hubbub to everyone except Danby, to whom they had been addressed. A chilled hush fell on the two long tables as Danby, smiling faintly, prepared to reply. At length, flicking aside the long lock of hair that drooped over one eye, he said: 'That all depends, sir, from which side you look at it. From the point of view of the Volunteers the Easter Week rebellion must seem incredibly heroic and patriotic. As for being stabbed in the back, I'm afraid I don't quite see how you can justify that as a description of the situation.'

'The British Army fought to defend Ireland against the Kaiser while the Catholics stayed at home safe and sound. Justify that if you can! And then ... and then ... and then they attacked the very lads who were giving their lives to save them! If that isn't treachery, I'm damned if I know what is!' And Edward sat back quivering with righteous indignation.

'But you don't even know your facts, sir ... You don't even know your facts!' cried Danby, raising his voice to the thrilling pitch that had so often brought him deserved applause from the Oxford Union. 'I say again, you don't even know your facts ... Do you realize that there were a hundred thousand, I repeat, a hundred thousand Catholic Irishmen fighting in the British Army? There was no question of treachery at all. The war against the Kaiser had nothing to do with the fight for Ireland's freedom.'

'Pacifists! It's all very well for you lily-livered youngsters who were hiding at home behind your mother's skirts. Think of the men who were risking their lives in France and risking them for *you*! Major, you were risking your life in France ... Perhaps you'd tell these young pacifists whether it was treachery or not!'

The Major sat dumbly at the end of his table. There was a long, an interminable silence. Even Murphy, carrying round the cups of coffee, froze in his tracks and arrested his laboured breathing. At length the Major heaved a sigh and said, softly but audibly: 'You're perfectly right, Edward. I think we all felt we'd been stabbed in the back.'

'There, you see,' cried Edward triumphantly.

'What did I tell you? Treachery!'

But Danby, his eyes twinkling with the pleasure of doing battle with this redoubtable old juggernaut, appeared not in the least abashed. He smiled impishly at his friends and then said: 'Really, sir, you can't classify us all as cowards quite as easily as that. My friend Captain Roberts here, for example, served most heroically in France and I believe he feels, as we all do, that the Easter Week affair was perfectly justified. How about it, Roberts?'

Once again there was a pause and a seemingly interminable silence while everyone held their breath. Captain Roberts blinked and licked his lips. His balding undergraduate head was a great mass of wavy wrinkles as he contemplated the toad which had been put on his plate. For a moment even Danby wondered whether he might not have been over-confident. But then at last Captain Roberts cleared his throat and murmured hoarsely: 'Perfectly justified ... We all thought so ... '

He had opened his mouth wide. He had swallowed the toad. 'Good old Roberts!' the undergraduates were thinking and, beside him, Bunny Burdock surreptitiously gave his arm an encouraging, comradely squeeze. But Captain Roberts was careful to avoid the Major's eye.

A thunderous crash cut short the undergraduates' jubilation.

It came from Edward's heavy oak chair, which had flown back ten feet and overturned. He was on his feet, his face white and working with fury, glaring at Roberts. But then, without a word he turned and strode out of the room.

The Major, who had glimpsed the expression on his face, hurried after him, napkin in hand—but when he reached the door he thought better of it. He listened to the diminishing echo of Edward's heavy footsteps on the tiles of the corridor and then, folding his napkin, returned to his place.

It was at this moment that Maitland, who had taken a sip of Murphy's bitter brew, took the lid off the sugar-bowl in front of him. Instead of lumps of sugar it contained a pile of dully glistening metal lozenges ... revolver bullets! Making a droll face he picked one up, dropped it into his coffee and began to stir it with the barrel of the revolver beside his plate.

This was altogether too much for the undergraduates. They had been close to bursting all evening. Now all they could do was throw back their heads and howl with laughter till their ribs ached.

This great gale of youthful laughter filled the dining-room and echoed away down dim, empty corridors, ringing faintly through all the familiar sitting-rooms, dusty, silent and forgotten; penetrating to the floors above with their disused bedrooms and dilapidated bathrooms and to the damp, sleeping cellars, quiet now for eternity, unvisited except by the rats. It was such healthy, goodnatured laughter that even the old ladies found themselves smiling or chuckling gently. Only Captain Roberts at one table and the Major at the other showed no sign of amusement. They sat on in silence, chin in hand, perhaps, or rubbing their eyes wearily, waiting in patient dejection for the laughter to come to an end.

The body might well have been left in the potting-shed where it had first been carried, or dragged rather, and laid out on a pile of old potato sacks. But the shed was a damp and draughty place, smelling strongly of earth and rotting vegetation.

413

Gardening implements hung from nails, some of them so rusty that they were now only skeletons of themselves: a spade with its broad face eaten away, a rake with its teeth flaked into threads as thin as needles, all thanks to some gardener who in happier times had been too idle or trusting to oil the metal. Not so long ago, perhaps only two or three years earlier, some lazy person had dumped a pile of grass under the work-bench, the mowing from one of the lawns. In the interim it had turned into a yellowish, putrid mass with a hard outer crust indented with the print of a boot.

Altogether the potting-shed had seemed to the Major too stark and comfortless a place to leave a young man's body, even for so short a time. So with the help of Seán Murphy he had carried it into the house and placed it on a side table in the gun room. Here at least one could be fairly sure that the sight of it would not disturb the ladies. All the same, once it had been laid out on the table and Seán Murphy had retired, his friendly face still registering shock at this sudden contact with mortality, the Major found himself wondering whether it might not have been better to have left it where it was. The ragged clothes of a labourer, the muddy boots laced with string, the threadbare jacket and patched trousers—all this seemed out of keeping with the gracious oak panelling and the antlers on the walls, even when stretched horizontal with death on a side table. It was almost as startling, mused the Major, as finding a chimney-sweep lounging on the sofa in one's drawing-room. Now that it was here in the gun room the body seemed to have been more at ease in the potting-shed.

He stood back, head on one side and finger to his mouth. Well, it would be absurd to have it carried back to the potting-shed now. He would have done better to leave it as it was, perhaps, but there was no point in worrying about that. His eye fell on another incongruity: above the body on a shelf there were a great many tarnished silver cups, for Edward had been a marksman in his day. Still was, apparently, in spite of his shaking hands. But the less one thought about that the better.

Shaking his head wearily he looked round for something to throw over the dead man. But there was nothing, so he left the room for a moment and returned with a clean tablecloth which he unfolded and threw over the body, taking another look as he did so at the young man's white face and bright red hair, at the bluish eyelids which he had closed himself. The mouth was hanging open, however, and this gave the face an imbecile appearance. Turning, the Major's eye at this moment encountered the resentful, open-mouthed pike in the glass case over the mantelpiece and he thought: 'That won't do at all. I must close the poor lad's mouth before it gets too stiff.'

Touching the face gave him an unpleasant shock. The skin was still soft and pliable to his fingertips. It so obviously *belonged to someone*! He shuddered as he gently squeezed the chin until the lips closed.

But when he took his hand away the mouth fell open once more. He tried again and the same thing happened. The position of the head was wrong, that was the trouble. On the shelf below the silver cups he found a copy of *Wisden's Almanac* for 1911 which he judged to have the right thickness. He blew the dust from it and slipped it under the boy's head. This time the mouth stayed closed. Taking a deep breath, the Major went to sit down in one of the armchairs by the empty grate.

He sat for five minutes without moving a muscle. Then there was a knock on the door and Edward came in, somewhat apologetically.

'Ah, there you are, Brendan. I was wondering where you'd got to.'

He looked round the room and gave a slight start when his eye fell on the bulging tablecloth. But he made no comment as he came to sit down opposite the Major. Nor did the Major speak.

Presently Edward, with his head tilted back and mouth open in a way that strangely resembled the corpse's attitude of a few minutes earlier, said: 'My nose has been bleeding ...

divil of a time trying to get it to stop. They say you should put a cold key down the back of your shirt, don't they, Brendan? Or is that collywobbles, I can never remember?'

The Major made no reply. Edward sighed faintly and his uptilted gaze wandered around the panelled walls at the various antlers, at the winter forest of stags, at the ibex and antelope and zebra watching the men with calmly accusing glass eyes. For an instant the dreadful thought occurred to the Major that Edward had now gone completely insane and was looking for a place on the wall to mount the Sinn Feiner. But no, Edward had tugged a bloodstained handkerchief from his pocket and was patting his nostrils gingerly. His face had assumed a faintly martyred expression.

'What you don't realize, Brendan, is that we're at war ... If people come and blow things up they must take the consequences! They must be taught a lesson!'

'Oh, Edward, these are our own people! They aren't the Germans or the Bolshevists ... This is their country as much as it is ours ... *more* than it is ours! Blowing up statues is nothing!'

Edward's face darkened and he said bitterly: 'I always knew you were on their side, Brendan. I'm only thankful that poor Angie didn't live to see it. A man of your background, I'd have thought you'd have been more loyal.'

'Oh for God's sake shut up, Edward.'

'I caught them at it red-handed. I don't shoot innocent people from behind hedges. It was perfectly fair.'

'For days you've been waiting for them to come!' Edward grunted but made no attempt to deny it. In any case it was now clear to the Major why he had been spending so much time up on the roof. For days Edward had been using the statue of Queen Victoria the way a big-game hunter uses a salt-lick in the jungle, knowing that sooner or later it would become too much for them to resist. And what was the difference, he wondered, between shooting someone from behind a hedge and shooting them from a roof?

'It was perfectly fair!' Edward repeated, cracking his knuckles.

True, the Major was thinking. Edward probably did not see Sinn Feiners as people at all. He saw them as a species of game that one could only shoot according to a very brief and complicated season (that is to say, when one caught them in the act of setting off bombs).

'It was perfectly fair!' Edward said for the third time and the Major thought: 'No, it wasn't that at all. It was an act of revenge. Revenge for his piglets. Revenge for Angela. Revenge for a meaningless life. Revenge for the accelerating collapse of Unionism. Revenge for the destruction of the sort of life he'd been brought up to. Revenge for the loss of Ireland.' He didn't see Sinn Feiners as human beings at all. And after all, would the Sinn Feiners be any more likely to see Edward as a human being and take pity on him?

Edward was frightened, the Major realized abruptly. The man was terrified! That bullet-proof waistcoat had not been an idle whim, it had been a desperate measure to shore up his crumbling nerve. Suddenly this was so clear to the Major that he wondered why he had not realized it before.

'You'd better go upstairs and go to bed,' the Major said, not unsympathetically. 'You're exhausted. I'll see to the doctor and the D.I. when they get here.'

But when Edward had left him alone with the presence bulging under the tablecloth all the horror returned. He saw Edward triumphantly dragging the dead Sinn Feiner across the gravel. He closed his eyes ... Edward comes nearer and nearer, one of the dead man's ankles gripped under each armpit like the shafts of a hand-cart. Behind him the heavily muscled shoulders and lolling head leave a long trail on the dew-laden gravel and the friction causes the arms to spread out wide into the attitude of crucifixion. Released from somewhere inside the house, the Afghan hound comes bounding up and whisks cheerfully around the body which Edward is dragging towards the potting-shed.

417

'Thank heaven I sent the twins away. Edward will go too now. Today or tomorrow. As soon as possible.'

The Major underwent a craving to light his pipe, but respect for the dead young man across the room prevented him. Thwarted, the craving for tobacco transformed itself into a craving for something else that was normal—anything: to go fishing, to watch a cricket match, to take tea with his aunt in Bayswater. He couldn't, of course. Everything had to be settled in Kilnalough. Besides, his aunt was dead also—for a moment he found himself thinking of her with great sadness and love. But then the bulging tablecloth restored him to that morning's tragedy.

He looked at his watch and was astonished to see that it was not yet eight o'clock, scarcely breakfast-time. Had his watch stopped? No. Which meant that little over an hour had elapsed since he had been woken by the explosion which had preceded the firing of a single shot.

At first, examining the body in the potting-shed, he had been unable to find any trace of a wound and had wildly hoped that he had been deceived, that there had been no shot from the roof, that the lad had been killed in some other way—by the blast from the explosion, perhaps. But then, looking more carefully at the lolling head he had seen the widened, blood-rimmed hole in the ear, which the bullet had exactly entered. Suddenly the head moved. Balanced on folded potato sacks, it had rolled a little to one side. Now, from that neatly circular but too large hole in the young man's ear, liquid began to well up—slow and thick, like dark oil from the neck of a bottle. The Major had watched it drip from the ear to the work-bench and from the work-bench to the putrid mown grass. Presently, however, it diminished and stopped.

'Who is it?'

A maid was standing timidly at the gun room door saying that the doctor and the man from the police ... But they had already edged past her and entered the room, the doctor struggling forward with his frail, white head on a level with his shoulders. It was intolerable, thought the Major, that an old man should be got out of bed at such an hour of the morning. His shoelaces were undone and a sparse frost of white beard showed on his cheeks. As he came forward he glanced once, briefly, at the Major with eyes that were alert and curiously full of sympathy, as if this body under the tablecloth were in some way related to the Major instead of a complete stranger.

'When you've finished here I shall go back with you into Kilnalough. I must speak to the boy's father ... '

'That would be absurd, Major.'

The Major passed a hand over his brow, which was damp with perspiration. 'Of course he must have been told by now. There's nothing I can say to console him, I realize that. All the same I must speak to him. He must be told that Edward acted only for himself. What he did was inhuman and intolerable ... I tried to get him to leave with the twins but he refused, yet perhaps I didn't try hard enough to persuade him. I should have realized what he was up to, but I never thought ... For the past few weeks he has been full of hatred and despair. I tried to get him to leave ... He's a little mad, I'm sure. Why should I be responsible for everything he does? The man is no concern of mine. This morning he accused me of being disloyal! It's intolerable ... and yet what can I do? People must be told that Edward is no longer able to control himself. I'll see that he goes away, of course, whether he wants to or not. Clearly he can't stay here. The boy's father mustn't be allowed to think of his son as a martyr of the British, that would be unjust. What hope is there for Ireland if people are allowed to behave in this way? That poor boy was the victim of a private hatred and despair ... I'm sure you understand me, Doctor. If you don't understand me, nobody will!'

The old man sighed and shook his head, raising a feeble hand to pat the Major's arm. But he had nothing to say.

Later, while waiting for the doctor, the Major stood beside the shattered statue of Queen Victoria and talked with the D.I., whose name was Murdoch, a curiously dry, pedantic man with a crooked smile which lit up one side of his face in wrinkles, leaving the other perfectly smooth. He had reacted to the death of the Sinn Feiner with equanimity, if not indifference. At most he had betrayed a mild, as it were, official satisfaction that a criminal had received punishment. The Major conceived a dislike for him and turned his attention to the statue.

It had been damaged but not completely destroyed. Although a gaping hole had appeared in the horse's flanks, the august cavalier had managed to remain in the saddle, leaning acutely sideways in the manner of a bareback rider in a circus ring. The blast had immodestly lifted her steel skirts a few inches, he noticed.

'Gelignite and a coffee tin,' explained Murdoch at his elbow. 'A temperamental explosive which kills the Shinners and British with perfect impartiality. In Irish they call the stuff "Bas gan Sagart" – "Death without the priest".' And while one half of Murdoch's face remained smooth and solemn, the other half lit up with wrinkled glee.

Later again the Major sat for a long time in the room of the priest, Father O'Byrne, sometimes talking, sometimes in silence. The room was very small, dark and cluttered with books. The Major was abominably tired. He frequently looked at his watch, but the hours of the morning refused to pass.

'Edward Spencer is a coward and a murderer, Major ... You're a poor sort of man that you'd take it on yourself to make excuses for him.'

The Major was abominably tired. Yet he was fascinated by the priest's threadbare cassock and by the hatred in his eyes. At length he lifted his eyes from the Major's face to the crucifix on the wall. To the Major the steadiness of this gaze on the crucifix seemed blind, inhuman, fanatical. The yellowish naked body, the straining ribs, the rolling eyes and parted lips, the languorously draped arms and long trailing fingers, the feet crossed to economize on nails, the cherry splash of blood from the side ...

'That boy got what he deserved,' he said harshly. 'I only hope it may serve as an example to some of the other young cut-throats who are laying Ireland to waste!'

And with that he turned and strode out of the house, slamming the door with a crash.

In the weeks which had elapsed since the night of the ball the health of Mr Norton had declined steadily. It was hard to say whether this was because the poor man had over-exerted himself on the dance-floor or whether it was merely a natural and inevitable decline of the faculties. In any event, he was now confined to bed, his mind wandering indiscriminately between mathematics and the boudoir, sometimes chuckling to himself, sometimes in tears, but constantly demanding company and attention.

Their sense of duty overcoming their distaste, the ladies would sometimes take their knitting and climb the stairs to the first floor to sit with him. And while they knitted he would gabble long, incomprehensible equations interlarded with scarcely more intelligible descriptions of his encounters with that sex to which, all his life, he had devotedly attempted to unite himself (only to finish his days, old and alone, between these chilly, rumpled sheets). The Major was sorry for him but glad, on the whole, that his reminiscences were so difficult to fathom ... The snatches that one *could* understand were extraordinarily indecent, even to the Major's hardened military ears.

One day, afraid lest Mr Norton's ramblings should offend the ladies (particularly those whose honour had remained unimpaired by marriage), the Major brought him an arithmetic textbook belonging to the twins which he had happened to come across in a waste-paper basket unemptied since the previous winter. Mr Norton seized it with delight and in the few days that remained to him (before his relations whisked him away to a more suitable institution) recited mathematical problems without pausing for breath, answering each one promptly before proceeding to the next. The Major sometimes paused to listen to this litany, and one of the problems, in particular, remained in his mind. It concerned a man who was unable to swim and found himself in a leaking rowing-boat so many hundreds of yards from land. He was faced with the alternative of baling rapidly with a tin cup (volume so many cubic inches; maximum rate of baling movement so many times per minute), the water entering at such-and-such a speed; or of ignoring the leak and rowing furiously (at so many miles per hour) for the nearest land ... or, of course, a combination of now one, now the other. How should this man best proceed?

'Can he make it?'

'Afraid not quite, old chap,' replied Mr Norton with unexpected clarity.

'Ah,' said the Major absently and wandered off puffing his pipe.

The Major was working hard these days, helped by Mrs Roche, Miss Archer and some of the other ladies. Edward's frame of mind had improved to some extent since he had killed a Sinn Feiner. An abscess had been lanced and a quantity of poison had been allowed to escape. Nevertheless the Major was aware that it would fill up again, given time.

Surprisingly docile at first, Edward had agreed to go to England and spend some time with the twins. He had even shown one or two faint traces of remorse. The Major had come upon him cleaning the congealed blood from the work-bench in the potting-shed. On seeing the Major, however, he had stopped and walked out into the light drizzle, a hatless and derelict figure. Latterly the Major had detected signs of renascent fear and bitterness. He was watching him more carefully now and it soon became clear that Edward was preparing plans for the defence of his estate. One evening when, in spite of the Major's absolute refusal to accommodate them, a frighteningly determined and aggressive young schoolmistress had succeeded in installing a brood of girl guides at the Majestic for the night, Edward, incoherent with whiskey and raddled with anger over the loss of Ireland, had discoursed to his tittering young guests and the gloomy, silent Major on fields of fire, enfilading machine-guns, flanking attacks and suchlike. It all boded ill. One must work quickly.

The explosion and the shooting had had at least one good effect: it had caused three of the less important ladies to leave immediately and had decided the others that they too must find a place to go. There was considerable distress, of course, in the residents' lounge, much weeping and sniffing of salts. But the Major was doing what he could to counter this despondency. He had written to the Distressed Gentlefolk's Aid Association and was considering other possibilities. There must be girls' boarding schools in Egypt, India and other places (remote, certainly, but where the natives were better behaved than the Irish) whose dusky little pupils would benefit from the dignity and moral rectitude of an elderly English lady, even an impoverished one. The trouble was that the ladies greeted this suggestion with further despondency and alarm, convinced that the Major was planning to send them off alone to some tropical knacker's yard.

Amid all this distress Mrs Roche was a great help and comfort. She encouraged the ladies, made practical suggestions, helped them to compose appealing yet dignified letters to more fortunate relations. She even took Edward in hand, telling him briskly that he shouldn't drink so much (which nobody else had dared do) and sewing a button on his jacket. The Major at this time entertained a faint hope that Mrs Roche might at last discover a romantic interest in Edward—after all, he was still, with his massive, handsome face and commanding presence, an imposing figure in his own way. But Mrs Roche had more sense and presently she left with her mother, Mrs Bates, for some happier destination. She left the Major wondering whether Edward could be relied on to look after Mrs Rappaport, since no institution was ever likely to accept both her and the hideous marmalade cat, not to mention her revolver.

Miss Staveley, who, having the money, could have left, surprised everyone by remaining stalwartly where she was. Indeed, once Mrs Roche had left she took on her role of comforter and adviser, becoming, in her rather muddled way, a tower of strength. In general, after the first despondency had worn off morale was excellent. The ladies, in adversity, were determined to show 'the stuff they were made of', which turned out to be a very tough weave indeed.

This was fortunate, because standards had yet again (and for the last time) begun to decline at the Majestic. By now most of the servants had vanished. From the day of the explosion they had gradually melted away, as native bearers on safaris are reputed to melt, one by one, into the jungle, taking with them anything of value that did not happen to be nailed down (not, however, that there was a great deal of value at the Majestic, nailed down or otherwise). Among the many objects whose disappearance for the most part went unnoticed the following items were seen to be missing: two of Edward's sporting rifles, his hunting pink, his velvet smoking-jacket, most of his fishing rods, a carved ivory chess-set from the residents' lounge, approximately half of the pile of stone hot-water jars on the first floor, a hundredweight of embossed cutlery and china (very popular), a portrait in oils of a former manager of the hotel clad in Napoleonic uniform, sheets, pillow-cases and blankets (also very popular), the unfortunate dog Foch (who had always been a great favourite with the kitchen staff) and the stuffed pike from the gun room.

One morning, returning up the drive from an early walk through the grounds, the Major was astonished to meet the cook, clad in a fur coat several sizes too big for her, with un-laced men's shoes on her feet, and pulling a hand-cart piled high with gilt chairs from the writing-room. At the sight of the Major she gave a shriek of fear and cried what sounded like: 'Jesus, Mary and Joseph!' But the Major averted his eyes and walked past her without even noticing, thereby proving to the cook the efficacy of prayer.

The cook was the last of the servants to go. Presently only Murphy remained, muttering to himself and haunting the staircases as he had always done. These days, of course, he was never asked to do anything, for his reason was quite clearly unhinged. He was merely *there*, a cadaverous relic of a happier time. Occasionally someone might glance at him curiously and wonder why he did not leave too. But he didn't. He remained to lurk in the company of the silent, prowling cats in the shadowy upper storeys. People were too busy to bother about him.

There was the cooking to be done, for instance. Miss Johnston had taken charge of the kitchens and established a hierarchy of helpers whose jobs diminished gradually in importance from her own to that of poor Mrs Rice who was considered only capable of washing the dishes. Strangely enough, the food was better in these last few days of the Majestic's existence than it had been for many years – indeed, since the hotel had reached its zenith in the 1880s.

The ladies tied aprons round their waists and put their diamond rings in a saucer on the sideboard while they kneaded the dough for apple pies or disembowelled chickens with trembling fingers. How exciting it was! If only the future had seemed less uncertain how they would have enjoyed this challenge to abilities which since girlhood, throughout all their long, dull and genteel lives, had lain dormant! Moved, the Major watched them at work, Miss Bagley's rheumy eyes blurred by incipient cataracts, Miss Devere's head permanently bent to one side, Miss Johnston unable to stand up for long because her ankles would swell, Mrs Rice stooped over the sink with the steam clouding her pince-nez, and all of them, without exception, forgetting things ('Now what was it I was going to do?') and losing things ('Now where on earth did I put ... ?') which very often turned out to be in front of their noses.

But then with a start, the Major would remember that he had letters to write, that he must telephone Dublin, that he

425

must put an advertisement in the *Irish Times* ... and many other things. In short, that he must continue to row furiously for the nearest land, for the boat continued to settle lower and lower in the water.

Unsavoury characters were noticed lurking among the trees (the Major remembered with nostalgia the 'unsavoury character' they had hunted chuckling through the park on the afternoon he had first arrived). Worse, the ceiling of the writing-room descended with an appalling crash, ridden to the floor by the grand piano from the sitting-room above. For hours afterwards a thick white fog of plaster hung in the corridors, through which the inhabitants of the Majestic flitted like ghosts, gasping feebly.

PREMIER'S BID FOR PEACE

Proposed Conference in London Following
The King's Appeal for Reconciliation
De Valera Invited by Lloyd George to London

Reuter's Paris Correspondent telegraphed yesterday: 'Commenting this morning on the letter addressed to Mr De Valera inviting him to attend a conference in London with Sir James Craig to explore to the utmost the possibility of a settlement of the Irish question, *Le Petit Parisien* lays special stress on the conciliatory and even friendly tone of the letter, which, in its opinion, marks a great and praiseworthy effort on the part of the British Government.'

❧

Every now and then, just for a moment, the Major would rest on his oars, lost in thought. It was early summer, a delightful season. The smell of grass and wood lingered delightfully under the mild sky. On his way to fix a FOR SALE notice to one of the gateposts he strolled through a grove of silver birches; it was hard to believe that there was any malice in Ireland. For a moment he felt almost at peace; but then it occurred to him that a few inches below where he was standing the rotting carcase of Rover sat up and begged, encased in earth.

A letter arrived from Faith with the news that Charity had fallen in love with Mimi's butler, Brown. But this was swiftly followed by a letter from Charity saying that it wasn't true. Besides, Brown was a Socialist and had ideas above his station and would the Major send her some money (it was hopeless asking Daddy) as she desperately needed some new clothes? She and Faithy were ashamed to be seen out of doors in their dreadful Irish rags and tweeds and all the men they met absolutely had fits when they saw what scarecrows they were. Also could the Major afford to buy them a motor car? In London a motor car was ABSOLUTELY NECESSARY! Just a small one would do as they didn't need anything big and it would only cost more. Mimi (Aunt Mildred) had crashed hers into a wall and the bally thing wouldn't work any more. A frightful bore! But the clothes were the most important because they simply couldn't wait and would he write back immediately sending a cheque.

The Major did write back immediately, sending a cheque for fifty pounds together with the news that Edward would be setting out for London in two days' time. He himself would follow when he had made final arrangements with an estate agent in Dublin. By now it was the end of June and almost everything had been settled. The dogs had been sent to a kennel while preparations were made for their new home. The ladies' trunks had been packed and delivered to the station, labelled for various destinations (those of Miss Bagley, Miss Porteous, Miss Archer, Mrs Rice and Miss Staveley all bore the address of a boarding-house on the Isle of Wight purchased expressly by Miss Staveley to give shelter to her friends, a most satisfactory conclusion). Old Mrs Rappaport had been dispatched to London, still armed to the teeth and the wonder of her fellow-passengers, carrying the marmalade cat in a wicker basket. She was accompanied on her journey by an indigent cousin of Edward's, specially hired for the purpose.

In the course of Edward's last afternoon at the Majestic he and the Major took sledge-hammers and rained blows on Queen Victoria and her horse in an attempt to restore her to a more vertical position. For half an hour they hammered away at her shoulders, her head, even her bosom, the sound of their blows ringing cheerfully over the countryside. As they worked, her delicate green metal became pocked with brown marks … but little else was achieved. She was still leaning drunkenly sideways. At most they had managed to correct her position a few inches by the time they retired, perspiring, to drink some tea (in plentiful supply now that the old ladies commanded the kitchen). After tea they returned to hammer down her ruffled skirts. That was all they could do for her.

'I shan't be leaving tomorrow, Edward. There are still a number of things I have to do here.' The Major had delayed informing Edward of his decision to stay for fear that Edward too might change his mind. This fear had been illusory, he decided, seeing the stricken, anxious expression that appeared on Edward's face.

'But you *must* leave! It's dangerous here.' Calmly, but feeling that he hated Edward, the Major said: 'I don't intend just to walk off and leave the place to the bloody Shinners.'

'But Brendan, you must face reality. You've read the newspapers. You know as well as I do that it's all over here. It's finished. Any day now that blighter Lloyd George is going to throw in the sponge and then there'll be hell to pay for people like you and me who've been loyal.'

'I'm damned if I'm going to take to my heels, Edward, just because there's a possibility of trouble. If I go at all I shall go in my own good time.'

'But good God, Brendan! Things are bad enough already. When they send the army home it'll be the law of the jungle.

Every Unionist in the South will have his throat cut. Go to Ulster if you want to stay in Ireland.'

'I've made up my mind that I'm staying, Edward. At least for a while.'

'But you can't stay *here*. The old place is falling to pieces. It's dangerous. You've been telling me for months how dangerous it is ... Think of the writing-room ceiling! That could happen anywhere at all in the building, anywhere.'

'I'll stay in the rooms that have the fewest cracks in them,' said the Major smiling.

'Without servants?'

'Oh well, there's always Murphy.'

'*Murphy!* Besides, just look at the size of the place, it's absurd. You can't live here all by yourself. And you just told me the place is up for sale.'

'I'll wait until it's sold, then. But I refuse to be hounded out of the place by a handful of labourers with guns in their hands.'

'Well, I shall stay with you, of course,' Edward murmured unhappily. 'But I must say I think it's most unwise.'

'There's absolutely no question of you staying, Edward. You have the twins to think of.'

Edward had dropped his sledge-hammer and was sitting on the stone steps facing the shattered statue, watching the jagged, freshly torn edges of metal glimmer in the sunshine. A faint breeze stirred the shaggy mass of grey hair above Edward's grim, defeated face. 'Absurd,' thought the Major, 'that we should go on competing when the thing that we were competing for has long since vanished.'

'I agree that it's maybe not wise,' the Major said gently. 'But my mind is made up. Besides, I'm getting to be too old a dog to learn new tricks. Now let's forget about it and talk about something more pleasant on our last afternoon.'

Edward was looking relieved. His eyes wandered away from the statue and came to rest some distance away on the bed of lavender planted by his wife 'before she died'. What was he thinking about? wondered the Major. Of his dead wife, perhaps ... of his eldest daughter, the dead one whom he had loved the most and even now continued to love more than he could ever love Ripon or the twins.

And presently, as if the Major had been able to divine his thoughts, Edward said: 'I remember the day we brought Angie home in the snow. She was only a baby. It hardly seems any time at all.'

The telephone was ringing in Edward's study. So still was the afternoon and so silent the house that the Major heard it ringing from outside in the park. District Inspector Murdoch was calling from Valebridge.

'Is anything wrong? Did they get on the train all right?'

Well, that was what he was calling about. The train hadn't yet left Valebridge because of some trouble on the line between there and Dublin. It wasn't yet clear what was wrong but it might mean a considerable delay.

'They're all elderly. They mustn't be put under any strain. If there's no chance of them reaching Dublin before nightfall you'd better send them back here and we'll try again tomorrow.'

'Very well, Major.' There was a pause. 'By the way, I'm sending one of my men over to have a look round the Majestic.'

'Why?' asked the Major. But Murdoch had hung up the receiver.

'How dead everything is!' thought the Major as he wandered aimlessly through the empty rooms and corridors. Utter silence. He could no longer even hear that strange underwater cracking sound. Strange to think that Edward and a few old ladies could make such a difference to the place.

The parting had been a painful one. Convinced that they would not live to see their dear friend the Major again on this earth, the ladies had allowed themselves to surrender to their emotions. He had been obliged to kiss one faded tear-stained cheek after another, clasped to one frail lavender-scented bosom after another—all this combined with the alarms and distractions usually attendant on old ladies travelling: forgotten purses, mislaid tickets, letters for the Major to post, tips that they had forgotten to administer (but who was there left to tip at the Majestic, unless the Major himself?), addresses and timetables that had to be remembered and consequently were swiftly forgotten, little parcels (containing handkerchiefs on which his name and rank had been elaborately embroidered) for him to open after they had gone, urgent visits to the lavatory that had to be made at the last minute when everyone was ready to leave. The Major endured all this with good humour and insisted on remaining cheerful, chaffing the ladies briskly lest they should incapacitate themselves completely with sobs and be obliged to lie down, missing the train.

But at last the ladies motoring to Dublin in the Daimler with Edward had moved away, followed by the hired char-à-banc taking the rest to the railway station at Valebridge. The Major had found himself standing alone in the drive. Of the ladies nothing remained except a faint odour of smelling-salts on the still air.

Not yet accustomed to the strangely silent and deserted house, he had decided to continue his interrupted stroll through the grounds. On his way he began to come across traces of Edward's activities that he had been too preoccupied to notice before; a small cache of ammunition wrapped in an oilskin package was the first thing he happened to see. All the time that he had been working frantically to close down the Majestic Edward had been outside in the park planning its defence. Now that he was looking for them he began to find oilskin packages of ammunition everywhere. But that was not all. There were foxholes too dug in the potato field and in the meadow beyond, and first-aid boxes lodged in hollow trees in the woods. Every rise in the ground had some cover, in some places metal shields cut from segments of old boilers and equipped with slits to fire from—all facing outwards towards the boundaries of the estate as if, just out of sight over the rise of the next hill, silent armies had been massed, waiting to attack a slightly mad old English gentleman who drank too much whiskey and raved about the loss of Ireland. Poor Edward! No wonder he had discoursed with such energy to the tittering girl guides at the dinner-table about fields of fire, flanking attacks and strategic emplacements! Sitting on the steps the other day for a moment, he must have had a vision of being left alone with the Major to man all these positions against the vast and ruthless armies of the Pope.

Standing at the highest point of the meadow, the Major scanned the bright, peaceful countryside looking for the menace. He thought of a competition he had seen in one of the newspapers. There was a photograph of some footballers frozen at a dramatic moment in the game, but with the image of the football itself removed from the picture. Readers were asked to make a cross on the photograph where they thought the ball must be. Somewhere before his eyes in the sleeping countryside there was a threat to his safety. He knew it was there somewhere. But to him it was invisible.

As he was walking back to the house he paused at the edge of the drive to wait for a young man on a bicycle who had just emerged from the trees and was pedalling towards him. He had a rifle slung across his back and was wearing a curious mixture of uniforms: his pedalling legs were clad in dark-green R.I.C. trousers; the upper part of his body, however, was clothed in khaki service uniform, while on his head was perched a flat civilian cap bearing the crowned-harp badge of the R.I.C. A long white hen's feather was stuck into this cap behind the badge. 'A fine expression of the muddled will of the great British people!'

This strangely clad individual had now halted his bicycle by dragging his boots along the ground and, not without suspicion, had spoken out in tones of pure Cockney, wanting to know if the Major was the Major.

'Yes I am. What can I do for you?'

He had been told to have a look round the Majestic in case

there was trouble. The whole countryside knew that the people living in the Majestic had moved away and there might be hooligans coming to loot the place. He patted the butt of his rifle, but without confidence, more as if he were superstitiously touching wood.

'By all means have a look round the out-houses. But be careful; a lot of the timber is rotten and you could easily break your neck. Another thing ... if you happen to see a mad old man with a wrinkled face, don't shoot him. He's one of the servants. When you've finished come inside and ring the bell on the reception desk. I'll give you a cup of tea.'

For an hour the Major tried to read an out-of-date copy of *Punch* in the gun room, but the silence made him uneasy and he found it hard to concentrate. Once more the telephone rang in Edward's study down the corridor, but it stopped before he had time to reach it. He waited for it to ring again, but it didn't, so he made his way down to the kitchens in order to brew some tea for himself and the young Black and Tan. On his way he smiled: he had caught himself glancing nervously into the open doorways he was passing. 'Really, I've become an old lady myself, I've spent so much time with them. When all this is over I really must find myself some younger members of the sex!'

By five o'clock the teapot had grown cold and there was still no sign of the Black and Tan, so the Major went out to look for him. First he wandered through the kitchen garden towards the stables—but they were empty, as were the garages and out-houses. The door of the barn was open, so he peered in. A pleasant scent of summer hay greeted his nostrils. There was no sign of the young man. With misgiving he approached the ladder up to the loft and set his foot on the worm-eaten bottom rung. It took his weight, so he began to climb. When his head and shoulders had emerged through the trap-door he looked around. It was lighter up here. One of the wooden leaves of the loading-gate was open, allowing a shaft of sunlight to fall on the floor.

Someone had been here recently. Dust hung in the air and, where the sun touched it, blazed like a furnace. On each side the towering banks of hay had a grey look, as if cut many years ago and abandoned. But there was no one here now. He cautiously backed down the ladder. 'I could look for him here for ever and not find him.'

He continued, however, to move through a succession of courtyards, past the well and the pump, towards the apple house, of which the door also stood open. It was here that the superfluity of the Majestic's huge apple crop was stored: windfalls and 'cookers' for the most part. At the time of the Major's first visit they had been piled on top of each other, bruised and rotting, to within a few feet of the roof; but in the interim the cook had made her daily visit to fill a coal-scuttle with apples for pies and desserts (and perhaps the old crones in black had also been filling their flour sacks). The result was that a hollow had been scooped out of this ocean of apples, a valley that built up from knee height to shadowy slopes reaching well above the Major's head. There was silence here too, and a pungent smell of rotting fruit. 'In a few weeks', the Major was thinking, 'this place will be so full of wasps that one won't be able to get near it ... But then, in a few weeks will it matter any longer?' And he took a few steps forward into the gloom. As he did so there was a convulsion of the shadows behind him and he pitched forward into the apples. Losing consciousness, he was aware that the apples had begun to roll; a great avalanche of apples thundered down on him and buried him in blackness. But he was not dead yet, so he had to be dragged out by the heels.

The Major was left lying on the ground for a few moments while his wrists were tied behind his back. When he was picked up again a pool of blood was left in the place where he had lain. All the way down the steps from one terrace to the next, past the black and silent swimming-pool with its skeletal diving-board, past the derelict tennis courts and the empty weather-beaten urns that lined the route like grim sentinels, blood continued to splash every few paces. Presently the lowest terrace was reached. Then the Major's limp body was conveyed lower still, on to the rocks, and from there with considerable difficulty was handed down to the beach.

Some distance away was the young Black and Tan whom the Major had been attempting to summon for tea. Bound, gagged and, like the Major, scarcely conscious, he had been buried up to his neck in the sand, ready for the incoming tide. His head was lolling to one side and he did not raise it as the sound of clinking pebbles drew nearer and came to a halt beside him. His eyes were closed, his young face had a peaceful expression, and his breathing was slow and steady.

Beside the Black and Tan a hole was begun for the Major; but before it was more than two feet deep the digging spade rang against rock and this hole had to be abandoned. The spit of sand was narrow, the shape of a blade pointing towards the sea. Since the Black and Tan already occupied the only suitable position another hole was dug a few yards farther back. This time there was no impediment.

When the new hole was deep enough the Major's limp body was lowered into it and the crook of a walking-stick was used to drag his bound ankles back into a kneeling position. A heavy rock was then laid on the back of his calves, packed down with smaller stones and covered with sand. By this time only his head remained visible.

His wound had stopped bleeding now but he was still unconscious. Gradually, as darkness fell, the tide crept up the beach towards him. It was a mild, windless evening and the sea was calm. As it grew darker lonely, heart-rending shrieks were heard from some distance away—but it was only the peacocks, whom nobody had remembered to feed that day, preparing to roost for the night in the branches of an oak on the highest terrace.

Meanwhile the flooding tide continued its advance. Soon

after the moon rose there was a snorting, gasping sound from further down the beach but presently silence and peace closed in once more.

When the whispering fringe of surf was still a few feet short of the Major's head, however, the tide reached its height and in due course began to ebb once more. By this time he was semi-conscious. Questions, impossible to seize and examine, loomed in the shadows. What was he doing buried in the sand? Had he been left to drown? And his mind wandered away, buoyant and aimless as a drifting balloon, to the trenches—to some 'show' or other in some godforsaken wood without a name.

At first light people came to dig him up and he became feebly conscious once more. They dug with care, as if aware of the danger of slashing his bound wrists with the spade. They used their hands to feel out the edges of the heavy rock that lay on his calves and gently lifted it away. Then, in turn, they lifted out the Major and laid him on the sand.

By now he was completely numb. He could feel nothing. But the involuntary movement of his limbs had awoken a terrible cramp, so that it seemed as if his body was doing its best to tear itself to pieces. Each muscle in his stomach, thighs and shoulders had contracted as hard as marble, vying with its opposite number to snap his bones and ligaments. Yet at the same time his mind was quite peaceful. It was as if, after all, this body did not belong to him. As he lay there quietly on the sand, a great feeling of serenity stole over him—the sort of feeling one might have for a few moments after a serious accident when one realizes that one is no longer one's own responsibility. Other people were taking care of him. He could hear their voices faintly from farther down the beach where they were probing the sand with the spade. Presently they began to dig another hole.

The Major was now thinking about Sarah ... and about love. And then, without being aware of any transition, he was thinking about Ovid, an author he had read without pleasure at school. Strange to think that some people should actually enjoy reading Ovid as much as, say, that story of T. C. Bridges which had been serialized in the *Weekly Irish Times* last year. What a charming story! There was one episode which had particularly taken his fancy: the young man confessing to his girl-friend that although in appearance a gentleman he is really a burglar, and that consequently it is inevitable that she must detest him ... But the girl (and what a splendid surprise this had been both to the young man of the story and to the Major) ... the girl sticks by him, stoutly says she loves him and doesn't believe him capable of stealing. (And true enough, there had been something rather rum about his theft. He had had a bump on the head or he'd been hypnotized and couldn't actually remember doing it.) Jolly decent of the girl, in any case, to stick by him. Sarah, of course, would undoubtedly do the same in that situation. And with this agreeable thought the Major's weary, salt-caked eyelids crawled down over his eyes and he slept, or became unconscious, it would have been difficult to say which.

When he next woke up he was again buried up to his neck in sand. The sun had risen and was blazing directly into his eyes, dancing on the surf not far away. This light blinded him, so that for some time he was aware of nothing but the pain of his retina. When he had become more accustomed to it, however, he realized that he was no longer alone. Scarcely more than a yard to the left there was another head poking out of the sand on the same level as his own. He recognized the fellow immediately: it was the young Cockney who had come up to him on a bicycle the day before ... He had invited the chap to tea.

'Why didn't you come to tea?'

But the man made no reply, merely continued to stare round at the Major in an insolent fashion with one cloudy blue eye opened very wide and the other one closed to a glinting slit. From his open mouth a wisp of something dark was trailing: it might have been seaweed. Presently a bluebottle came buzzing round and at last decided to settle on that wide blue eye. But the eye did not blink.

As the sun rose higher the Major's awareness improved and once again he did his best to rally the thoughts that sped here and there like small slippery fish, impossible to grasp. 'Death!' he thought. And: 'To drown.' But this seemed inadequate, so he made a further effort and achieved: 'To drown is awful ... '; but this, although also inadequate, exhausted him for a while. Soon, however, he was able to scale another flight of steps up to consciousness and said to himself: 'My side is deuced painful. Hurts like the devil.' Then thoughts of Sarah, Edward and the twins occupied his mind, but they were no help to him. He must think of something else.

The movements of his limbs had in the meantime worked a gap of three or four inches between his body and the sand which moulded it. This gap had filled with water oozing up through the sand. He now noticed that the water had a reddish tinge and knew that he must be bleeding. At the same time as his consciousness improved he was tortured by thirst, and the aching of his limbs became intolerable. Nevertheless he decided that, however painful it might be, he must move his head to see who else was on the beach beside himself and the insolent young Cockney. Millimetre by millimetre, a fraction of a degree at a time, he twisted his neck and moved his sluggish eyeballs, first in one direction, then in the other. On the beach there was not a soul to be seen. It was completely deserted.

The water took on a deeper shade of red. 'Soon Sarah will come and dig me out,' he thought with a mixture of love and agony as the swimming sunlight crept nearer and nearer. Then, once more, he lost consciousness.

Another three-quarters of an hour elapsed before some rescuers arrived to assist the buried Major. These rescuers were led, not by Sarah, but by Miss Johnston and Miss Staveley. Miss Bagley, though terrified and out of breath, was

438

not very far behind. Bringing up the rear was poor Mrs Rice, who could not see very well and who had been given the spade to carry. Puffing and exhausted, she kept calling out to the others to wait for her, she was afraid she might fall and break her hip and then ... heaven only knew what! Pneumonia, perhaps. When one gets on in years one must be careful.

In due course they set to work. Miss Staveley, who had seized the spade while Mrs Rice had a little rest, began to dig (and not a minute too soon). But she too was very tired (none of them had slept a wink, having returned from Valebridge to find the Major gone) and tiredness made her clumsier than ever, so that she seemed to be shovelling as much sand back into the hole round the Major as she was taking out of it. When at last the water was beginning to surge round her ankles, Miss Johnston, who had taken charge of the operation and was becoming apoplectic with impatience, seized the spade in her turn and, pneumonia or no pneumonia, began to dig with frenzy. But in the end it was only Miss Bagley (feebly assisted by Mrs Rice) — Miss Bagley whom the Major had never really liked as much as the others — who could muster the strength to lift out the heavy rock which pinned him in his watery grave. The young Cockney, however, was left for a second immersion.

From a window on the fourth floor of the Majestic a shadowy figure paused to watch the old ladies drag the Major's inert body back from the advancing sea.

'Dead!' Murphy's wrinkled old face convulsed with glee as he wandered on, crooning a song he had learned some fifty years earlier as a young man in Wicklow Town. 'Ní shéanfad do ghrá-sa ná do pháirt 'n fhaida mhairfe mé ...'

And as he shuffled from one silent, deserted room to another he watered the carpets with the liquid from the watering-can he was carrying; he sprinkled everything with it, the flowers on the curtains and the coronets on the faded red carpet in the corridor. He soaked the bedding with it and poured it into

439

empty drawers and cupboards, crooning gently all the time. When he came upon a pair of long-abandoned ladies' shoes in a dusty drawing-room, chuckling, he filled them till they were brimming. Several times he padded slowly down the creaking stairs to fill his watering-can from the tank in the garage. Then the sound of his wheezing breath would alert the cats to the fact that their friend Murphy was back amongst them once more and they would all come galloping up, postponing whatever they had been doing—their bloody territorial battles in the attics or their fierce and appalling carnal endeavours on the battlements.

'Pussies!' Murphy would mutter. 'Have a sup now, will ye?'

And he would sprinkle the seething quadrupeds until their fur became slick and oily (and the cats inside the fur became definitely displeased). Lick themselves though they might, there was nothing that would make their fur return to normal; howling with grief they slunk away, sticky and wretched.

'Dead!' said Murphy, standing in a patch of afternoon sunlight. 'Sure I'll drink to that ... ' And gripping the watering-can, he raised it to his blue lips and began to gulp, pausing every now and then to make a smacking sound, it tasted so good.

'Now then, where're me matches?'

Wearily he turned out his pockets. On to the floor he dropped, one after another, a penknife, a raw potato with a bite out of it, two silver teaspoons, a devotional communication from the Society of the Daughters of the Heart of Mary, a ball of twine, a lump of tobacco, and a dead thrush. But no matches! Murphy scowled and popped the tobacco into his mouth, chewing morosely until he remembered how he used to make fire without matches as a boy. Once more he descended the creaking stairs, this time to Edward's study where he had seen a magnifying glass. Then up to the sunlight on the fourth floor where he trained the blazing golden eye on a piece of paper. Just as it was beginning to smoke, however, the sun passed behind a cloud. Murphy took another drink and sat down to wait impatiently for it to reappear.

The Major was not yet dead, however, though by now not very far from it. He was about a mile and a half from the Majestic, lying on Dr Ryan's kitchen table. The old ladies would never have had the strength to transport him here by themselves. Fortunately they had come upon Seán Murphy who, although he had gone into hiding, had been unable to resist lurking in the vicinity of his familar potato diggings. At first he had seemed too frightened of the I.R.A. to help, but a brief conversation had convinced him that he was even more terrified of Miss Johnston. So the limp Major had been trundled up to the house in a wheelbarrow and then put in the Standard. The journey had reopened his wound, however, and now as he lay on the table he was once more bleeding copiously.

While the ladies were trying to staunch the flow of blood with towels the doctor, who was tired and upset by this sudden invasion, wandered away to look for a needle with which to stitch the wound. 'Ach, old women! What a fuss they make! Always making a fuss, always talking, gossiping, good for nothing except drinking tea and causing trouble.' It annoyed him to think that he had once actively sought the company of these creatures. What a young fool he must have been! he was thinking as he rummaged through the instruments scattered on his desk (now what was it he was looking for?). A young man is better off minding his studies. The musty, faded smell of old women drifted up out of his imagination as he slumped wearily in his armchair beside the empty grate. Women! Ah, his wife had been different of course, yes, but that had been many years ago. Years before the rise of the new Ireland. The new Ireland would get rid of all these old women. They wouldn't be allowed. His wife had smelled of skin, like a young girl, not of lavender water and peppermints. Ah, she was different, he was thinking sleepily; 'people are insubstantial. They never last. All this fuss, it's all fuss about nothing. We're here for a while and then we're gone. People are insubstantial. They never last at all.' As his ancient wrinkled eyes gently closed, he said to himself absently: 'Now wait, there was something I was going to do ... '

In the kitchen the Major's face was as grey as oatmeal and the blood was flowing faster than ever, so that the old ladies were beside themselves with desperation. The sight of the blood all over the place would have been enough to make anyone quail, let alone an old lady who was not used to that sort of thing. But they hung on grimly, determined that the Major should live, come what might. By now they were pale and trembling themselves. Mrs Rice had already fainted, revived, fainted again, and now she was drinking a cup of tea to give her strength and courage. Meanwhile, where was that dratted doctor?

In due course the doctor awoke, refreshed by his nap, and remembered that he had been looking for a needle and that he had to stitch that young fool the Major, who had got himself into a scrape. He had told the silly ass to go while the going was good! He had known that something would happen. Only young fools would get themselves into trouble for nothing. And really, he thought, more disgruntled than ever, it was all for nothing! What purpose did anything serve? It all ended in the graveyard. He ought to know. He'd been to enough funerals in his time. And he tottered peevishly back to the kitchen, muttering: 'People are insubstantial. They never last, they never last ... '

'Of course they don't!' snapped Miss Johnston. 'If you treat them all like this!'

'Old women!' snorted the doctor petulantly, looking more senile than ever. But the hands with which he set to work were surprisingly deft and steady for such an old man.

Presently the Major, stitched, bandaged, and given some beef tea, had been tucked into bed and his body had at long last been allowed to start on the business of repairing itself. The four ladies had all locked themselves into one of the upstairs bedrooms for fear of being molested by that dreadful old man. The doctor, for similar reasons, had locked himself into his study, and soon everyone was fast asleep. By this time the sun had set and it had grown quite dark. But about an hour later, while down on the beach the young Cockney was being immersed for the third time, yet another sunset lit up the sky, for Murphy had at last realized that the cloud behind which the sun had disappeared was, in fact, a hill to the west. And so he had resorted to matches instead, having come upon a box in an old silk dressing-gown of Edward's.

By the time the inhabitants of Kilnalough had noticed the glow in the sky and motored, ridden or walked out to the hotel, the Majestic was an inferno. Streams of fire the size of oak trees blossomed out of the windows of the upper storeys. Caterpillars of flame wriggled their way down the worn and threadbare carpets and sucked at the banisters and panelling until all the public rooms were ablaze. The heat grew so intense that the spectators were driven back with flushed faces, first to the edge of the gravel, then farther and farther back over the grass, which the heat quickly shrivelled to raffia—until at last they were standing right back among the trees, gazing with shaded eyes at the blinding magnificence of the burning Majestic. By now only the attics under the roof were recognizable, their windows still black and empty.

It was from these black windows that flaming, shrieking creatures suddenly began to leap—hundreds of them, seething out of the windows on to the gutters and leaping out into the darkness. Those not already ablaze exploded in mid-air or ignited like flares as they hurtled through the great heat towards the earth. Someone in the crowd remarked that it was like watching the fiery demons pouring out of the mouth and nose of a dying Protestant. But that was not all, for now a hideous, cadaverous figure was framed for an instant, poised on the roof, his clothes a cloak of fire, his hair ablaze: Satan himself! Then he vanished and was never seen again in

Kilnalough. But he was thought to have swooped down to eat a meal of children in the infernal regions.

For a few minutes more the Majestic became brighter and brighter until, like a miniature sun, it was impossible to look at for more than a moment with the naked eye. Then with a shuddering roar it caved in upon itself and an immense ladder of sparks climbed into the sky.

And that was the end of the Majestic. It continued to burn and smoke, however, for two more days and nights. Nobody considered burying the charred and scorched demons that littered the surrounding land. Soon they began to smell atrocious.

In July Dr Ryan received a visit from Mrs O'Neill and her daughter Viola. He had been asleep on the couch in his study and was displeased at having been woken. For some time it was not clear whether the visit was a social one or whether his professional services were required. Assuming the former, since both mother and daughter looked to be in good health, he showed them into his front room, a damp and depressing place which rarely encouraged visitors to prolong their stay more than was absolutely necessary. Having done this, he sank into a chair and closed his eyes. Mrs O'Neill chatted away sociably about this and that, while Viola smiled prettily, showing her dimples, occasionally directing a meaning glance at her mother ('Is he asleep?').

At last, after a long silence which the doctor had found agreeable but which his guests had found disturbing, Mrs O'Neill said: 'Viola would like you to recommend a diet for her, Doctor. She finds she's getting rather plump and needs to lose a bit of weight.'

With an effort the doctor got to his feet and shuffled off down the corridor to his study followed by Mrs O'Neill and Viola, both of whom wrinkled their noses when they saw the state the place was in. But still, one had to make allowances. He was elderly, and the only doctor in Kilnalough.

When Viola had partially undressed, the doctor looked

444

briefly at her breasts and at her stomach and then motioned her to get dressed again.

'Well, Doctor?'

'She doesn't need a diet.'

'But she's getting fat, Doctor!'

There was another long silence. The old man stood there wool-gathering, eyes half closed. Mrs O'Neill and Viola exchanged a significant glance. 'Impossible,' Mrs O'Neill was thinking, 'impossible for him to keep his mind on anything for more than two seconds!'

'A diet, Doctor,' she reminded him. But the doctor merely sighed and it looked as if they were not ever going to get any sense out of him. At last, however, his trembling, wrinkled lips parted and he said: 'Your daughter doesn't need a diet because she's pregnant, Mrs O'Neill.'

'Pregnant! But that's impossible. Viola is only a child. She doesn't even *know* any young men, do you, Viola?'

'No, Mummy.'

'There, you see ... It's absurd. And what a thing to say! Really, it's disgusting!'

'None the less, Mrs O'Neill, she's pregnant.'

'But how many times do I have to tell you ... ?' And again Mrs O'Neill patiently explained (nothing was achieved by losing one's temper) that what Viola wanted was a diet, nothing more complicated than that. But the old doctor persisted in being obstinate and senile. Gradually it became clear to Mrs O'Neill that it did no good to explain anything to him, however patiently. The old boy was beyond it. His mind was made up and there was no hope of making him see reason. Dr Ryan, who had served Kilnalough so well for so many years (and this was true, he *had* done a splendid job, one must give him his due), had at last reached the end of his career in medicine. In some ways it was rather sad. But it was no use complaining.

Dr Ryan shuffled as far as the gate with his visitors and watched them walk away towards the main street. Then with a sigh he made his slow and laborious way round the house to the back garden, where the Major was sitting in a deck-chair reading a newspaper.

On his last day in Kilnalough the Major paid a melancholy visit to the charred rubble which was now all that remained of the Majestic. He did not linger there, however, because he had a train to catch. Besides, there was very little to see except that great collection of wash-basins and lavatory bowls which had crashed from one burning floor to another until they reached the ground. He inspected the drips of molten glass which had collected like candle-grease beneath the windows. He noted the large number of delicate little skeletons (the charred and roasted demons had been picked clean by the rats). He stepped from one blackened compartment to another trying to orientate himself and saying: 'I'm standing in the residents' lounge, in the corridor, in the writing-room.' Now that these rooms were open to the mild Irish sky they all seemed much smaller – in fact, quite insignificant. As he was carefully stepping over a large pile of wood-ash (which he suspected must have once been the massive front door) he looked back and happened to notice something white, half concealed by rubble. It was the statue of Venus, strangely undamaged. It was much too heavy for him to lift by himself, but when he got back to Kilnalough he made arrangements for it to be packed and shipped to London.

As it turned out, this lady of white marble was the only bride the Major succeeded in bringing back with him from Ireland in that year of 1921. But he was still troubled by thoughts of Sarah. His love for her perched inside him, motionless, like a sick bird. For many weeks he continued to think about her painfully. And then one day, without warning, the bird left its perch inside him and flew away into the outer darkness and he was at peace. Yet even many years later he would sometimes think of her. And once or twice he thought he glimpsed her in the street.

All Orion/Phoenix titles are available at your local bookshop or from the following address:

Mail Order Department
Littlehampton Book Services
FREEPOST BR535
Worthing, West Sussex, BN13 3BR
telephone 01903 828503, *facsimile* 01903 828802
e-mail MailOrders@lbsltd.co.uk
(Please ensure that you include full postal address details)

Payment can be made either by credit/debit card (Visa, Mastercard, Access and Switch accepted) or by sending a £ Sterling cheque or postal order made payable to *Littlehampton Book Services*.
DO NOT SEND CASH OR CURRENCY.

Please add the following to cover postage and packing

UK and BFPO:
£1.50 for the first book, and 50p for each additional book to a maximum of £3.50

Overseas and Eire:
£2.50 for the first book plus £1.00 for the second book and 50p for each additional book ordered

---

BLOCK CAPITALS PLEASE

name of cardholder ....

address of cardholder ....

delivery address
(if different from cardholder)
....
....
....

postcode ....   *postcode* ....

☐ I enclose my remittance for £ ....

☐ please debit my Mastercard/Visa/Access/Switch (delete as appropriate)

card number ☐☐☐☐ ☐☐☐☐ ☐☐☐☐ ☐☐☐☐ ☐☐☐☐

expiry date ☐☐☐☐   Switch issue no. ☐☐

signature ....

prices and availability are subject to change without notice